Seeds of Destruction

By the same author:

Dorset in the Civil War
The Disaffected County

SEEDS OF DESTRUCTION

Tim Goodwin

Constable · London

First published in Great Britain 1998
by Constable & Company Limited
3 The Lanchesters, 162 Fulham Palace Road
London W6 9ER
Copyright © 1998 Tim Goodwin
The right of Tim Goodwin to be
identified as the author of this work
has been asserted by him in accordance
with the Copyright, Designs and Patents Act 1988
ISBN 0 09 478900 2
Set in Palatino 9.5 pt by
SetSystems Ltd, Saffron Walden, Essex
Printed and bound in Great Britain
by MPG Books Ltd, Bodmin, Cornwall

A CIP catalogue record for this book
is available from the British Library

1

LARSEN

The small red and white propeller-driven plane flew east, leaving the inner reaches of the dusty, greening fjord behind. As it crossed over the rim of the ice-cap, huge lakes of spring meltwater appeared below, some of them fifteen or twenty kilometres across, their floors of ice giving them the rich dense blue of flawless turquoise. Beyond came the cold desert that made up five-sixths of Greenland. Tomas Larsen didn't feel in the mood for reading, so he continued to look out of the plane windows, until the unrelieved featurelessness of the inland ice began to depress him. He turned his attention to his fellow passengers. Two withdrawn-looking Danish men were gazing morosely outside. A large Inuit family, clustered in the rear of the plane, chattered quietly while one of the women produced a steady supply of food – bread, cheese, strips of dried meat and fish, pastries, drinking yoghurt. Six or seven other single Greenlanders, all men, sat in silence, read, or dozed. Larsen leaned back and scratched his thick neck.

It had been a shock when Chief Thorold told him he was to go to Sermilik. Almost a quarter of a century had passed since he had last been there, and in all that time he had never felt any real desire to go back again. His mother and uncle were both long dead, and his cousins had left the town years before. Memories of his childhood lingered, of course, and he felt oddly nervous of confronting them, but there would be no people to make them solid. Almost certainly no one would even recognise him. And for that, at least, he felt thankful.

Lying back in his chair, and closing his eyes, he wondered if Sermilik had changed, and doubted it. Carefully he began to piece together a picture of the town as he had last seen it, perched precariously on steep hills between the deep-cut fjord and the mountains. His thoughts were broken by a loud, harsh voice.

A small, sharp-featured Greenlander was standing in the aisle, swaying a little. In one hand he held a large whisky bottle, almost empty.

'I'm not going back,' he shouted again. 'I'm not going back to that fucking place.'

The plane shook slightly, and he lurched forward, then caught himself. The stewardess, a short neat Inuit woman of about twenty, came up to him, smiling pleasantly.

'Please, if you wouldn't mind sitting down – ' she began.

He lashed out, and knocked her sprawling into an empty seat.

'We're not going to Sermilik,' he said hoarsely. 'I'll go and tell the pilot to take us somewhere else.'

He stumbled down the aisle. Larsen got up.

'You've had too much to drink, haven't you?' he said quietly.

'No, I haven't. I haven't had enough.'

'Sit down and we'll talk about it.'

Larsen reached towards him, and suddenly there was a skinning knife in the man's hand.

'Don't touch me,' he hissed. Then looked swiftly around. 'No one touch me. I'm going to talk to our fucking pilot. I'm going to tell him we're not going to Sermilik. You'll all thank me. No one ever wants to go to Sermilik. And us poor bastards who live there just want to get away.'

He glanced down at his wide knife blade. No one else moved. Faces set, swallowing hard, hands gripped uselessly at their chair arms, everyone stared at the little Greenlander. The only sound was the unchanging roar of the engines.

'It's all right,' said Larsen, soothingly. 'Go back to your seat and sit – '

'Sit down yourself,' snarled the Greenlander. The knife flashed before Larsen's eyes. 'Sit down or I'll slit your throat.'

'You're drunk. You don't – '

The knife jerked closer, its tip quivering eagerly.

'Sit down!'

Larsen sat down. The Greenlander raised the bottle in his other hand, emptied it down his throat, then tossed it irritably on to the floor.

'Shit,' he muttered.

'Shall I get you another bottle, Øle?' asked the stewardess.

Larsen tensed himself to spring, but the knife was still towards him. The Greenlander's eyes flitted restlessly around the plane. He ran his thumb along the knife blade, and a moment later a thin line of blood welled up from the ball of his thumb. He licked it off.

'Go on then,' he muttered.

The stewardess got to her feet and slipped past him, up to the front of the plane.

'Tell them we're not going to Sermilik,' shouted the Greenlander after her.

She vanished into the cabin, then reappeared a few moments later with a fresh bottle of whisky, leaving the door to the cabin swinging open behind her.

'Poisoned it, have you?' he growled.

She shook her head.

'Of course not.'

'And you told the pilot what I said?'

'Yes.'

'Then why haven't we changed course?' His knuckles were white on the knife hilt. 'I'm not going back.'

'He and the co-pilot thought that with the following wind, and the weather as it is, it would be best to continue on to Iceland.'

'Iceland? All right. Why not? Anywhere's better than Sermilik. After God pissed there, even He forgot about it. Open the bottle, good! Now give it to me.'

He snatched the whisky from her, tipped his head and began to drink. As he did the plane suddenly dropped, then banked steeply to one side. There was a chorus of screams from the passengers. The Greenlander slipped against a seat, and dropped his bottle. As he bent to pick it up, the engines shrieked and the plane swung savagely upwards, then switchbacked down again. Helplessly off balance, the Greenlander staggered across the aisle and fell on Larsen, who swiftly and efficiently ripped the knife from his hand, then pushed him down into the next seat.

'I feel sick,' mumbled the Greenlander.

He rubbed his forehead, then slumped back and closed his eyes. Within a minute he was asleep, breathing heavily through an open mouth. The stewardess got a cloth and began to mop up the spilt whisky.

A tall skinny man had appeared out of the cabin, and was walking down the aisle.

'Good afternoon,' he said calmly. 'I am the co-pilot. Is everyone OK?'

'What the hell was all that?' growled one of the passengers.

'Just a drunk. Nothing to worry about.'

He stopped by Larsen, and looked impassively at the sleeping Greenlander.

'What you did might have angered him even more,' said Larsen.

The co-pilot shook his head.

'He was too drunk to be really dangerous.'

'Have you got any sort of restraint we can use to strap him in with?'

'I doubt it's necessary. When he wakes up, he'll probably have such a head he won't be able to remember anything anyway.'

'Even so,' said Larsen.

'There's a child belt in the back,' said the stewardess. 'I'll get that.'

7

She hurried off.

'I was told we had a policeman on board,' remarked the co-pilot.

'Yes.'

'You don't need to make a big thing out of this.'

'What do you mean? It was an attempted hijacking – '

'No, it wasn't. Something very similar happened a couple of years ago, and the man was just put on probation for threatening behaviour while drunk.'

Larsen had a vague memory of the case, and of Chief Thorold just shrugging and saying, 'That's Greenland!' It was a phrase he used a lot.

'Something must be done about it.'

'You're right, of course,' said the co-pilot hastily. 'He should never have been allowed to get on the plane that drunk. I'll write a report about it. And of course he shouldn't have had that knife either. Security can get lax on internal flights, I suppose it's because we've never had any serious incidents.' He frowned. 'Perhaps we ought to give all the passengers another free drink.'

'Do you think that's wise?' asked Larsen.

The co-pilot shrugged and turned away. The stewardess had come back and was strapping a child's safety harness around the sleeping man.

'There,' she said at last, with a smile.

'How much longer before landing?' asked Larsen.

'We should be at Cap Gad in less than an hour.'

Larsen bent over his sleeping prisoner, and went through his pockets. All he found was an identity card in the name of Øle Olssen, a few small coins, the knife sheath, and a return plane ticket from Cap Gad to Godthab, dated two days ago. Larsen looked at the man's battered clothes, and wondered what he had been doing in the capital for such a short time. And where he'd got the money, for flights in Greenland didn't come cheap. Nor did whisky. But the foxy face, mouth gaping, eyes tight shut, revealed nothing.

Outside the grey ice-desert was finally past. They were slowly descending over a hard monochrome country of precipices, canyons, and ragged black mountains, without the slightest hint of vegetation anywhere. Pinnacles of bare, frost-shattered rock thrust themselves up through the white of glaciers and snowfields like broken teeth from bloodless gums. Suddenly the plane swept past a line of towering cliffs, and swung out over the sea. It was frozen hard, a cracked mosaic of abstract white patterns, where trapped icebergs stood out like great stranded castles.

Cap Gad was like most Greenland airstrips. But more so. On one side rose a precipitous snow-capped hillside which the plane skirted cautiously before dropping towards a stretch of beaten earth bordered by a few uninviting buildings. A couple of kilometres away lay a small settlement of perhaps fifty houses, crowded round a branch of the frozen sea.

The landing was bumpy, and as they came to a stop, to Larsen's astonishment, the passengers all clapped. A bearded man, obviously the pilot, appeared and raised his hand in acknowledgement, with a cheerful grin. The plane was soon empty, except for Larsen and his prisoner. After unstrapping the harness and trying ineffectually to wake the man, Larsen was forced to carry him through a wicked wind that whipped up dustings of snow from the stony ground. The stewardess came behind with his bags, and helped him to the bleak waiting-room, where he dumped the Greenlander on a bench. The man grunted and slept on.

An hour rolled slowly past, then a second. A few people spoke in low voices. Most stared patiently in front of them at the peeling paint. The sun sank towards the encircling mountains, though the sky remained perfectly light.

Abruptly the Greenlander half rolled over, just saved himself from falling off the bench, sat up and opened his eyes. For a moment he did not seem to see anything, then he groaned and put his hands to his head.

'Where are we?' he mumbled.

'Cap Gad,' said Larsen.

The Greenlander looked at him. His pale eyes were bloodshot.

'Who are you?'

'Sergeant Tomas Larsen. Who are you?'

'Olssen. I live here.'

He got slowly, carefully, to his feet, massaged his forehead for a moment, then stumbled towards the door.

'You pulled a knife on the plane, Olssen,' said Larsen sharply.

The Greenlander stopped. His eyes widened to empty pools.

'Did I?' He groped in his pockets, produced the empty sheath and contemplated it for a moment. 'Where is it then?'

'I've got it.'

'Keep it. It's useless.'

He dropped the sheath on to the muddy floor and went out. Larsen got up to go after him.

'Don't worry.' The stewardess had just emerged from a small side room where she and the pilots had been drinking coffee. 'Everyone knows Øle Olssen. You can always find him, either at his parents' house, or at the seed bank, where he works.'

'How do you know?'

'I used to live here, until I got this job and moved out.'

'Were you pleased to leave?' asked Larsen curiously.

She shrugged.

'I suppose so. Not much happens in Sermilik.'

Larsen went to the door and looked outside. Olssen was about a hundred metres away, bent forward, vomiting. After a minute or two he wiped his face and continued to trudge slowly down the track to the village.

'Didn't he have any luggage?' asked Larsen.

The stewardess shook her head.

'No. He got on to the plane empty-handed.'

Larsen could make no sense of it.

'Does he fly a lot?'

'I don't think he's ever done it before. Maybe it doesn't agree with him.' She smiled and vanished back into the side room.

Larsen watched Olssen until the swell of the ground hid him from sight, then took a deep breath and glanced at his watch. Allowing an hour's change for crossing a time zone, it was 9.30 p.m. It felt a lot later.

When the helicopter came it was small and old-fashioned, with skis for landing, and room for only eight passengers. Just as it had been in his childhood. Perhaps even the same machine. Larsen seized his bag and hurried outside well before it landed, to make sure he was on the first flight out. No one else seemed concerned. People joined him on the two frayed passenger benches almost, it seemed, by accident.

The helicopter flew low over the frozen sea as the sun glinted on aquamarine-tinted ice. A man with a dog sledge looked up then continued on his way. In South and West Greenland such a sight was almost unknown now, and Larsen found it vaguely disturbing, heightening the sense that he was an alien re-entering a land whose ways he had long forgotten – if he ever understood them. Most of his life stood between him and this place.

However the sight of Sermilik itself provided a reassuring return of familiarity. The same simple wooden houses, multi-coloured but predominantly dark red, detached from their neighbours, scattered haphazardly over the steep rocky hillsides. The small protected harbour showed open water, although the fjord was still frozen. Radio aerials, more numerous than Larsen remembered, reared high on the hill crest.

The helicopter pad was an unmarked square of beaten earth just above the fjord. As people dispersed up the kilometre-long track into town, the helicopter left to pick up the rest of the passengers from Cap

Gad. Abruptly Larsen realised that he had no idea where the police station was. When he had lived in Sermilik there had not been one. Two passengers he asked merely shook their heads and walked on. The third person he approached was a tall, blonde Danish woman in her mid-twenties.

She stopped.

'What did you say?'

'I asked the way to the police station.'

'There is no police station.'

Larsen's head spun.

'But – '

'There's a house with a room used to keep drunks in. Is that what you mean?'

'I hope so.'

'I'll show you the way.'

'Don't trouble. If you could just tell – '

'No trouble.' She smiled hurriedly. 'My name is Gudrun Eistrup.'

'I am Sergeant Tomas Larsen.'

'So you are a policeman?'

'Yes.'

She fell silent and led him up the sharply rising road. It was exactly as he remembered, though more exposed to the wind, colder. They passed the house that had belonged to his uncle Axelsen. Then it had always had sealskins outside, stretched to dry. There were none now, and Larsen had no idea who lived there. His own family house had been pulled down after his mother died, and replaced by a communal block for young people to live in when there was no longer room for them with their parents.

'Are you here as cover for Steffen?' asked Gudrun. 'I heard he is still in hospital.'

'It was a nasty break,' said Larsen. 'But the doctors think he should be back on duty in three or four weeks.'

'So until then you'll be working with Kalaasi.' For a second there seemed something close to a smile on her face, then it was gone. 'Where are you from?'

'Godthab.'

'Godthab? You may have to be careful here.'

'What do you mean?'

'You should call it Nûk as the Inuit do, not Godthab like us Danes.'

Larsen considered.

'Do you work here?' he asked.

'Are you interrogating me?' she countered, uneasily. 'No, you don't

11

have to answer that. I am a biologist. I am completing a postgraduate thesis about the impact of the human population of Sermilik upon the local flora of the Asiaq fjord complex. Does that answer your question?'

'I think so. Do you know a man named Øle Olssen?'

Again she seemed tense.

'Olssen. Of course. Why?'

'He tried to hijack the plane.'

She laughed.

'Little Olssen? You must be mistaken.' She pointed to a small red building near the large blue corrugated-iron hangar that was the KGH supermarket, complete with its white polar bear symbol. 'That's where you are going. Goodbye.'

Gudrun turned and walked back the way they had come. Larsen watched her go. Her long legs covered the ground in wide masculine strides, her hands swung easily to and fro. She was taller than most Greenlanders, including Larsen, with broad hips and a good curve on her body. Her blonde Scandinavian hair was a little darker than was common, and she wore it cut severely short, revealing an elegant neck. Larsen found her attractive, but also unsettling, for she reminded him of Ann-Marie. He wondered if she was alone out here, and if so how she coped with the Greenland men. Efficiently probably. Yet there had been some agitation in her manner.

The door of the police station was unlocked, but there was no one inside. The desk was grubby and bare, except for an old coffee mug, and some nondescript files. The door to the cell swung in the draught. Larsen found an oil heater and tried to turn it on, but there was no fuel. Behind the desk was a small room with a sink, a few shelves piled high with more files, two electric rings for cooking, and a radio. Tired, cold, and feeling suddenly lonely, Larsen turned on the radio.

'. . . this Thursday night, the headlines have been a fresh row over fishing quotas, and a widely welcomed settlement to the Greenlandair dispute, which is expected to be agreed by both sides tomorrow. Next, "Our People, Our Country" has an exclusive interview with top international sports journalist, Solomon Rosing.'

Larsen switched the radio abruptly off. His memories were not so easy to blank out, for the last time he had come back to Sermilik had been with Solomon Rosing. Eighteen years old, and close friends, they had just won scholarships to Copenhagen university, so they went home to tell everyone. That evening had been a chaos of clamouring, proud, happy faces, of laughing, cheering, and clapping. It had seemed that the whole of Sermilik was celebrating with them. Although there had been alcohol rationing then, it hadn't mattered. Everyone had given them a drink, and Solomon, typically, had passed out on the floor half-way through the evening

Larsen remembered Solomon's wild childish enthusiasms, his inability to concentrate on anything for more than two or three hours, his ceaseless talking. He remembered Solomon coming last in yet another race – Solomon always did come last – and rushing off to talk to the winner, hero-worship glowing in his eyes. He remembered his pointless competitiveness about things that couldn't possibly matter: who knew all the capitals of the American states, who read *Kristin Lavransdattir* first, who could get that girl in the café to give you a free drink. He remembered the faintly, only very faintly patronising Christmas cards he received every three or four years. And all the time he knew that Solomon was a nice guy, hard-working, clever, who deserved his success. The only Greenlander in the world who would be recognised by millions of people in Europe and America.

His mind was drawn back to that last visit to Sermilik. Solomon, of course, had been carried home and put to bed by his grinning brothers, but even then Larsen had been strong, with a good head for alcohol. And there had been good reasons to stay awake.

As the night had gone on, all the girls of the town had gathered round him, talking to him, touching him, gazing at him with yearning eyes as if he radiated something they needed. He remembered sitting there like an emperor, kissing one girl who was sitting on his lap, caressing a second, feeling the warm breath of others on his neck and his cheek. But he had ended up with just one of them.

Her name slid away from him, and all he could see was long dark hair falling round him like a curtain, eyes of black obsidian, and a quick, soft, hungry body. Hungry for him. Days and nights had come together and mingled in a haze of ever-replenished alcohol and sex. The passage of time marked only by the bass-beat of constant sweet pleasure, of uncontrolled love-making, thrusting deep into her willing body. He could have had any of the girls, all of them even, and he only wanted that one. Jenufa – that was her name. After that first night, he hadn't left her side for three weeks, until he left Sermilik. And then, with the arrogant insensitivity of his age, entranced by Copenhagen, he had barely thought of her again. Unless it was her memory that had kept him from ever coming back. He closed his eyes and dragged up from the far past a brief fantasy of her body covering him, enclosing him. It faded away. Now, like him, she would be past forty, and surely unrecognisable.

Larsen went upstairs, where he found a rickety bed and a few musty-smelling blankets. He huddled them round himself, put his anorak over the top, and lay down, trying to forget that he had not eaten since a snatched lunch on the way to the airport. The room smelt unclean. When he got up and turned the mattress, in an attempt to make himself more comfortable, he found it was stiff with old blood. Just period blood, he hoped.

2

SERMILIK

When Larsen woke early, shivering, his broken thin sleep had left him more tired than when he had gone to bed. It was bad to sleep alone, he thought, but then he had not slept well during his marriage either. He remembered many nights lying on his back, eyes wide open, staring into nothing, wondering if Ann-Marie desired him. He had never wondered if she loved him, only if she really wanted him. It had not been like that with Jenufa. Again he wondered if he would see her. And if he wanted to.

He got up, flapped his arms around his body a few times, then washed his hands and face in the sink. The water was bitterly cold, but he found it refreshing, stripping away his weariness. He looked up into a large, slightly cracked shaving mirror, and saw his reflection watching him. A broad fattish face, which smiled easily, set firmly on a powerful thick-set body; coarse black hair thick as tow and frosted with grey; long thoughtful eyes making cracks on his flat unlined skin. The European in his blood was only revealed by subtle clues – big unlobed ears, a long straight nose, and the spreading stubble. Perhaps he would grow a moustache, a gesture towards his Danish father. But that would just underline his status as another piece of litter left behind by the ebb-tide of European colonialism. The Danish men came, lived with Inuit women, bred children, then one day without warning they went back to Denmark and their 'real' family. And that was usually that. Larsen had been lucky. His father had cared enough to send some money which, together with scholarships, had paid for Larsen's education. He had even let Larsen stay with him and his young white wife and his young white children for a few months.

He remembered his father saying to him, 'You have such a calm temperament, Tomas. And you're self-sufficient, aren't you? You don't worry, you just accept things. I wish I could be like you.'

Other people said the same sort of things to him and, coward that he was, he always just smiled, self-deprecatingly.

A gap in the rime ice on the window showed him the frozen inlet of Asiaq fjord close by. Larsen's grandmother had told him it was named after a rain goddess married to a boy who wet his bed at night. What she wrung from his bedclothes fell as rain or snow. And the fjord

15

received a lot of both. Now he came to think of it, there was a lot more snow lying than he would have expected at the end of June, and the fjord was usually open from the beginning of the month. A late spring, he thought. Not that it had stopped the first mosquitoes from arriving. He could see one on the office wall, its slim striped body and angled legs moving gently as it warmed itself.

I'd better start work, he thought to himself.

Instead he kept staring out of the window at the only usable anchorage in East Greenland. At least that was how the Danes with their big ships had seen it, and that was why Sermilik had become the only town on three thousand kilometres of virtually uninhabited coastline. For seventy or eighty years after its discovery whaling and exploration ships from several nations had come every summer, when the pack ice retreated. But now only two or three ships a year visited Sermilik, and they were only to supply the town. Generally they left empty. The collapse of the international markets in whale oil and sealskins had hit Sermilik even harder than the rest of Greenland. Once the fishing had also been good, and spawning capelin were literally shovelled ashore in May and June, but the catch had been declining for many years. Larsen could see barely a dozen fishing boats in the harbour, and most of the fish-drying frames seemed to have vanished.

Even before he had left, there had been no jobs in Sermilik, except in the supermarket, bars and local administration. There was no worthwhile school for the older children, so the clever ones left, and never came back. Except that he had. Larsen had only been back in Sermilik for a few hours and already there was a taste in his mouth. The taste of staleness. Of a town that no longer had any point to it.

A thorough investigation of the house revealed some hard black bread and a piece of even harder cheese. Chewing doggedly, Larsen returned to the office and started to investigate the painstakingly recorded files. Someone seemed to write down everything, even details of the minister's Sunday sermons. Larsen flicked through a few folders, then went outside.

Clouds hid the encircling mountain peaks, but it wasn't cold. Along the channel of open water by the harbour small grey waves washed sullenly against rocks, pushing plastic bottles and cartons up on to the littered shoreline, together with stained shards of ice. Larsen walked down to the harbour. An old woman was scouring out a small open boat. She looked up as Larsen passed.

'Are you the new policeman?' she asked, her voice creaking like a badly oiled door.

'I am Sergeant Larsen. How did you know?'

16

The old woman smiled. More and more creases appeared on her seamed face.

'We do not have many visitors.' Her long bright eyes were scanning Larsen anxiously, hoping he was not leaving. 'There used to be a family called Larsen here.'

'It's a common name.'

'You have come about the killing of Jonis Hendrik?'

Larsen sat down, his legs hanging off the harbour wall, kicking his heels. Just as he had sat hundreds of times in his childhood. He felt unexpectedly young.

'What do you think about it?'

'The same as everyone else.'

'What do you mean?'

'Last Monday night Mitti is in the hotel bar with Otto Frederiksen – '

'Did you see them?'

'Oh yes. I was there too.' She grinned toothlessly. 'Of course.'

'Go on.'

'Jonis comes in, has some drinks, then hits her. He dare not hit Otto Frederiksen or he would be out of a job. On Tuesday afternoon Jonis is found dead. What is anyone to think? But that fool Kalaasi will not arrest her until she admits she killed Jonis, and she is too clever a bitch to do that.'

'You are talking about the dead man's wife?' asked Larsen cautiously.

'Wife, yes. Though why they married is anyone's guess. No one marries in Sermilik, they just change bedmates when they feel like it. It was not like this when I was a girl, but now scarcely a child knows its father – how could they when neither do their mothers? Still, Mitti and Jonis were married. Perhaps he wanted it because he was so much older than her, but I would say it was so she could think herself better than everyone else. She has always liked to do that.'

Larsen digested the information.

'And Otto Frederiksen. Who is he?'

'You do not know Otto Frederiksen?'

'No.'

'I thought everyone knew him. He is the richest man in Sermilik. He lives up there.'

She pointed with a clawed fleshless finger towards a new house, well placed, overlooking the harbour, and much larger, better built and better kept than any of its neighbours. Attached to the south side of it was a large conservatory. The old woman saw where he was looking and laughed.

'That is to make sure everyone recognises his house. He has a heater in there, sits and shows himself for a few days every year, and grows fresh lettuces, a few tomato plants, and some herbs so he can parade them to everyone. As for the rest, he owns the hotel, the shop up the hill, the three largest boats in the harbour and our cinema. It is said he does business in America. And he runs the seed bank. No one can understand why so rich a man came to this place a few years ago, nor why he stays when he does not have to.'

'Maybe he likes it,' suggested Larsen mildly.

'No one likes to live here. But I know some of the things he likes. Oh yes.'

She began to chuckle to herself, but the laughter rapidly turned into hacking coughs and the look of malevolent smugness was replaced by pain.

'You should go and see a doctor with that cough,' Larsen remarked.

'That Danski fool knows nothing,' she wheezed between coughs. 'I will not pay him good money for his little pills. As well suck a stone.'

Larsen got up. Gradually the woman was regaining her breath, though her old face had taken on a dingy greyish tinge. A boy of perhaps eleven or twelve, but small for his age, came racing up.

'Grandma, grandma,' he called excitedly. 'Look what I have – '

'Ssh, ssh,' interrupted the old woman.

'But look.'

He held up a large fish.

'Someone gave you that. How kind. Here is the new policeman, Kamik.'

'Oh!' The boy's hand flew to his mouth.

He had a mop of thick black hair cut in a straight line, his skin was very dark like the old woman's, and his mouth was broad and mischievous.

'Kamik?' said Larsen, surprised. 'That means a boot.'

'My real name is Timooq.'

'Everyone calls him Kamik,' said the old woman. 'When he was a little boy he would play with my kamik boots all the time, and the first word he learned was "kamik". He had a cousin who was also called Timooq, so to stop ourselves being muddled over which Timooq was which, we called this one Kamik. And we still do. He is my little boot.'

She laughed again, and again the laughter turned into hacking, coughing and choking, until she spat heavily into the oily water of the harbour.

A hand tapped Larsen on the shoulder. He turned and saw a lean Greenlander with a thin oval face, cropped hair and dark sun-glasses.

'Sergeant Larsen?'

Everyone seemed to know who he was.

'Yes,'

'I am Kalaasi.'

The only policeman left in Sermilik was not at all what Larsen had expected. It looked as if he watched a lot of Hollywood films that he didn't quite understand.

Back at the police station, Larsen collected a plastic chair from inside the cell and gave it to Kalaasi, but the young man merely put it down in front of him and remained standing, stiffly, formally. Larsen went over to him, and gently pushed him into the chair.

'That's better,' said Larsen, perching himself on the edge of the desk. 'Now, I'm afraid I've been told almost nothing about this case, so I'd be grateful if you could go through what you know.'

'The body was found by Robert Maataq, sir,' said Kalaasi.

'Don't call me sir. Tomas is fine. Go on.'

'On Tuesday afternoon he went out to Lake Tugdlik to hunt duck and ptarmigan. It was there he found Jonis's body, and he brought it back to town.'

'That's it?'

'Yes. Everyone says Jonis must have been killed by his wife, Mitti, because they quarrelled the night before, but she swears it was not her.'

'I see.' Larsen picked absently at his upper lip. 'Do you know a man named Øle Olssen?'

'Yes. He is from Cap Gad.'

'Does he have much money?'

'I don't think so. He is a watchman at the seed bank.'

'Can you think of any reason why he should go to Godthab – I mean Nûk – for a day or two?'

Kalaasi shook his head incuriously.

'No.'

'Neither can I. It doesn't matter. Let's go and visit the murdered man's wife.'

The narrow porch was unremarkable, crowded with petrol cans, the pieces of a dismantled outboard engine, a warped stretch-board for sealskins, fishing tackle, a broken gun, sledge parts, drying driftwood, and rusting iron. Beyond, Larsen and Kalaasi entered a large badly lit room that took up all of the ground floor, except for a cramped kitchen off to one side. It was as crowded as the porch, packed full with chairs, tables, a bed that served as a sofa, a huge colour television, cupboards and cabinets. The walls were covered with crude, acidly coloured religious pictures, curling ancient photographs, and shelves of small ornaments. Every flat surface too was swamped in things: a model umiak boat made of bone, wood and leather; stacks of magazines and newspapers; an old radio; cups and saucers stuck together by ancient coffee; packets of cigarettes, half-full ashtrays, matches; bits of unfinished carving; even toys, though Kalaasi told him there had been no children in the house for years. The ledges under the small double-glazed windows were thick with plants, geraniums and poinsettias which appeared to flourish in the hot, fetid air. A tape recorder on the main table was giving out a complex, rapid percussion beat.

Sitting in a tall chair, alone, was an old man.

'Jonis's father,' whispered Kalaasi.

Larsen was overcome by a fresh sense of familiarity. He was certain he had known this man, but that had been twenty-four years ago, when he had probably been one of the strong, hawk-faced hunters the little boys of Sermilik had looked up to in awe. It must be another old man he remembered. An old man long dead probably.

'Who is it?' The voice was gentle. Contemplative.

'It is Kalaasi,' said the policeman. 'I have brought Sergeant Larsen with me. He has come from the west coast.'

'Ah,' said the old man stolidly.

Kalaasi leant over to Larsen.

'He is almost blind,' he whispered.

'But not deaf,' said the old man. 'And I can still distinguish light and dark, though sometimes it is easier to see nothing at all. Would you like me to turn the music off?'

'If you do not mind, sir.'

The old man's hand hovered briefly over the tape recorder.

'It is an East Greenland drum dance,' he said. 'There is only one person left in the world who still knows how to play them properly. She lives in Ikateq, but she is older than me. Too old to teach now, even if there were anyone who wished to learn. This is a tape of her playing at Jonis's wedding. I think it will soon be the only memory of that music in the world.'

He switched off the tape recorder with a sudden decisive gesture.

'Ask your questions.'

'Is your daughter-in-law in the house?'

'Mitti is out. She went down to the KGH to buy fish.'

'Was she at home on Tuesday?'

'She did not kill my son,' said the old man. 'I would know if she had.'

'I am sorry about your son.'

'Thank you.'

Larsen looked around.

'That is a fine gun on the wall, sir. Is it yours?'

20

'Yes.' The ghost of a smile floated among the lines of the old man's severe face. 'It killed me many a seal.'

'Did your son use it?'

'Jonis? A little, but like most of the young men he was not a hunter. The fjords were no place for him. He preferred to teach himself English. He thought that if he learned English he could find a job elsewhere, maybe in America even. Always he wanted to leave Sermilik and yet, like his father, he will never leave.'

He sat rigidly upright, a statue in his dark world. There was no longer any trace of emotion on his face, but tears dribbled from his unseeing eyes. Kalaasi went over and patted his shoulder, then sat back down, suddenly self-conscious.

'I am sorry,' Larsen repeated.

'God's will,' said the old man. 'God's will. He takes many untimely, why not my son?'

The tears still fell, but never a sob escaped his lips. And Larsen had a sudden insight. A woman might have married Jonis because she wanted this dignified old man as her father.

The outside door opened and a woman called out.

'I'm back, father-in-law.'

'How was it?' asked the old man.

'They look at me all the time. Even the dogs growl, and those that are not chained skulk up to me looking for a fight . . .'

She came in, a bag in her hand. Then stopped in the doorway.

'Mitti.' The old man's voice was grey, level as a frozen tarn. 'The police are here.'

'So I see.'

The woman stayed where she was a moment longer, then made her way through the gloom to the kitchen, where she began to unpack her meagre shopping.

'Would you mind if I turned on the light?' asked Larsen.

No one answered. Larsen reached out and turned the switch. Harsh overhead light flooded the room, making it seem sordid. Dirty. Mitti was staring over her shoulder at him.

'You are Sergeant Tomas Larsen?' Her voice was husky, attractive.

'Yes.'

'So you came back after all.'

3

INTERVIEWS

Larsen looked at her in surprise.

She was in her early or mid-twenties and pretty. Very pretty. His gaze took her in carefully, the delicate face, fine-boned, with eyes that slanted exquisitely upwards, and a generous mouth. Thick, long hair fell in an unbrushed black wave down her back, and her skin was clear and pure and pale. She was perhaps a little short and broad for true beauty, but her lips were firm and her expressive hands ended in long fingers, uncalloused by work. She stared defiantly back at Larsen, and that defiance seemed buoyed by something else. Satisfaction. Even triumph.

'What do you mean?' he asked.

She did not reply.

'I've never seen you before in my life,' pressed Larsen.

'I have seen you,' she said. 'Many times.'

She was trying to confuse him. Her eyes, that looked at him with such knowlege, were lying. Must be lying.

'Let us talk about Jonis, your husband.'

'I didn't kill him. I have already told Kalaasi that. What else is there to say, that I miss him? It is true.'

And suddenly, completely unexpectedly, she began to keen. A tearing sound of intense grief that ran up and down the nerves like coarse sandpaper.

'I must speak to you,' rapped out Larsen.

She ignored him and the sound of her grief rasped on.

'I must speak to you,' he repeated.

'Mitti, will you not talk to him?' said the old man.

The keening went on and on. A single unbreaking tortured note.

'Better leave her,' said the old man after a minute. 'It has been a great shock.'

Larsen and Kalaasi left.

'Both Jonis's brothers are dead also,' said Kalaasi, as they walked down the muddy road. 'One in a boating accident. One from pneumonia.'

'It is an evil thing for a father to outlive his children,' said Larsen. He paused. 'I was told that there are a lot of murders here in Sermilik.'

Kalaasi looked surprised.

'I do not think so.'

'Sixteen in just over five years. Don't you think that's a lot?'

'There's nothing special about them,' replied Kalaasi. 'Husbands, wives, girlfriends, boyfriends, people who quarrel when they're drunk. Everyone always knows who did them. Usually the killers come and tell us themselves.'

'But not this time.'

'No,' agreed Kalaasi. 'That's why you've come, isn't it? Where do we go now?'

Dr Sven was a Dane, a huge man with a body like a soft barrel, fast-thinning fair hair, a thick beard and a booming voice. His pale eyes were close to the centre of his ruddy face, and his manner was jovial, breezy. The surgery was separate from his home, which Kalaasi pointed out among the bigger, better houses on the hill overlooking the harbour.

'Ah, the new policeman,' said the doctor pleasantly. 'Come in and have a drink. Both of you.'

'No drink, thank you,' said Larsen.

'Do you not drink then? Wise man. Very wise man. But I know Kalaasi will join me.' He poured out two large glasses of akvavit, and swallowed half of his in one mouthful. His eyes ran thoughtfully over Larsen.

'How old are you, Sergeant Larsen?' he asked.

'Forty-two. Why?'

'You look in very good shape. More like a hunter than a policeman.'

'Are they so different?' asked Larsen, good-naturedly.

'In Sermilik they are,' replied the doctor, without any trace of a smile. 'You know, if this was not Greenland, I would guess you regularly worked out with weights.'

'I do.'

The doctor swallowed the rest of his drink.

'Why?'

'I just like to. It's good to feel fit.'

'You're a wise man,' said the doctor. He gestured towards the far door. 'The body's through here.'

Larsen followed without enthusiasm. Kalaasi stayed where he was, nursing his drink.

Jonis was lying on his back, packed about with ice and naked except for a pair of pathetic black and white squared pants. The slack face said little about the victim's age or character, but seemed vulnerable, pitiable, a reproach to those whose hearts still sent blood coursing round their veins. The eyes were shut, and the thin mouth scarcely more than a scar. The empty skin was the colour of powdered milk. Dr Sven carefully rolled the body over to show the death wound, a deep broad cut in the back that had sliced cleanly into the flesh.

'Stabbed from behind as you can see,' rumbled the doctor. 'A single blow, not very powerful, angled slightly upwards from low down the back. It slipped neatly beneath the ribs – perhaps luck, perhaps judgement – but didn't kill him straight away. Might not have killed him at all if it had not been for the unusual width and sharpness of the knife. The direct cause of death was loss of blood, possibly exacerbated by exposure.'

'Do you have any idea what time he was killed?' asked Larsen.

'When the body was brought in, about seven on Tuesday evening, rigor mortis was well established. But cold can bring on the onset of rigor very fast, and may also exaggerate the length of time it continues. Under normal circumstances I would have said that the man had been dead for about six hours before I saw him, but out here one cannot be sure. It might have been an hour or so less, or a lot longer. This damned climate breaks all the medical rules and makes half my textbooks useless.'

'Is there anything else?'

Dr Sven sucked in his cheeks, then leaned forward. When he spoke his voice was untypically quiet.

'There are marks on his wrists and ankles.'

'Marks?'

'Yes. Chafing. The skin is bruised and broken in several places.'

'You mean his wrists had been tied?'

'I could not say for certain, but it seems likely.'

'It might have happened after death, when the body was dragged along perhaps?'

'No. Look, just here, the abrasions bled quite profusely. Also there is some bad bruising on the back of his head, see. It probably came from falling after he was stabbed, but he was certainly still alive when it happened.'

'Do you have the dead man's clothes and possessions?'

'Over here.'

Larsen glanced at the pile of belongings: a crumpled 100-crown note, a half-empty packet of cheap cigarettes, a roll of wire, a dirty rag, some matches. The flotsam of a finished life. He turned his attention to the clothes, then surprise broke through his countenance.

'You are sure these are the only clothes he was wearing?'

'Of course I am sure.' Clearly the doctor did not like to be doubted. Especially not by a Greenlander, Larsen suspected. 'I took them off myself.'

24

'How was the weather on Tuesday?'

'Fairly ordinary, cold, a bit of sleet in the air. There's been a lot of snow and sleet over the past week or two. Why?'

'You did not think Jonis's clothes strange?'

'A bit thin perhaps.'

'A bit thin! Dr Sven, this man was found several kilometres from the nearest habitation. No one would go out into the wilds dressed as lightly as this.'

The doctor looked bored.

'Well, he did. Anyway, the cause of death is straightforward. I'll make out a death certificate and then hand the body over for burial, unless there is anything else you want . . .'

'No. Thank you, doctor.'

Kalaasi did not appear to have moved, although his glass was now empty. The doctor saw them out briskly. His waiting-room, ruled over by a fine-featured young Greenlander man, was filling up.

Once outside, Kalaasi gave a vague smile and set off down towards the harbour.

'Where are you going?' called Larsen.

'Dinner-time,' said Kalaasi simply.

'Not yet. I want to meet the man who found the body.'

Robert Maataq lived a little apart at the western end of the town. Although the only visible boundary was an insignificant little creek, there had always been a dichotomy between West Sermilik and the rest of the town. It had its own small shop, its own bar, its own social life. When Larsen had been a child he had scarcely known any children from West Sermilik. They came to the school of course, but they rarely played with anyone except their own neighbours. And yet, hadn't Jenufa come from there? Or was that his imagination?

Robert Maataq's house was messier than the others around it, but it showed all the marks of a successful hunter – several very fine sealskins on frames; flesh drying on nearby rocks, watched over by a boy who was carving something with a knife; an assortment of ducks, auks and gulls strung up from a beam; and two magnificent narwhal tusks leaning against the door post. Maataq himself was feeding his dogs, tossing them chunks of raw seal meat. He was a squat man with thick coarse black hair. His cheekbones were high, his nose sharp, his chin firm and determined, and his skin deep mahogany. But his long eyes were a startling, piercing blue. He looked a formidable man, in spite of his small stature, hard and decisive, and it was plain Kalaasi was in awe of him.

The huskies howled and snarled and squabbled as Maataq deftly threw them their food, making sure each dog got its fair share. Two small children were playing tag close by, while a fat woman placidly sat and plucked a ptarmigan in the strengthening sun.

'You wish me to tell you how I found Jonis's body,' said Maataq, throwing out the last piece of meat and patting one of his children on the head. His East Greenland accent was very thick.

'Please.'

'There is little to say. It was about four in the afternoon. I was going up the ridge through Lake Tugdlik and I saw a shape on a small snowfield. I went closer and found Jonis, cold and growing stiff. There was much blood on the snow. I picked him up and brought him back on my sledge. It cost me several hours' hunting.'

'I am sorry,' said Larsen, who never minded apologising. He turned to ask Kalaasi if he knew the place. But Kalaasi was no longer there. Larsen turned back to Maataq. 'Did you see anyone?'

'No.'

'Were there marks around the body, footprints, that sort of thing?'

'Of course.' Maataq's voice was contemptuous. 'Jonis was no angel that he could walk to the middle of a snowfield without touching the ground. But the snow was scattered, kicked and broken up, as if someone wanted to hide the tracks.'

'Did you find any weapon nearby?'

Larsen seemed to detect a flicker of hesitation, but it was gone before he could be sure.

'No. But some would say it is not hard to look for the hand behind the knife.'

After Larsen left, the dark mood that had been upon him much of the morning grew heavier. Whenever he had investigated murders before, there had always been fascination. People asked questions, offered unsolicited snippets of information; following just behind his back would be a cloud of gossip and speculation. Here hardly anyone seemed interested. It was only another killing, and killings in Sermilik were a way of life. There was no surprise or worry or upset . . . or anything.

He sighed, pulled out a toothpick and began to chew it as he walked along. Two middle-aged women passed him, talking intently to each other, and he found himself scanning their faces, wondering if one of them could be Jenufa.

The wooden bridge over the rocks to the KGH supermarket was slippery and treacherous from melting frost. Larsen crossed it cautiously and went inside. It was a large shop, but many of the shelves were empty.

'People have been stockpiling,' explained an assistant, yawning. 'The shortages are expected to grow worse.'

'What shortages?'

'We have not had any sugar for months.'

'Neither have we on the west coast,' said Larsen sociably. 'I was told it was something to do with the American sugar beet crop. How much is rye bread?'

The girl shrugged.

'We have none.'

Larsen was astonished.

'None at all?'

'No.'

'When do you expect more stock in?'

'When the boat comes. But everything it brings will be very expensive. Last year a cucumber cost a day's wages.'

'That doesn't sound good shopkeeping.'

She shrugged again.

'I do not own the shop.'

When Larsen returned to the police station, Kalaasi was sitting by the window, carefully cleaning his nails with a biro top. He leapt to his feet, and knocked his sun-glasses on to the floor. Larsen picked them up.

'Where did you go?' he asked.

'It was dinner-time.'

Larsen handed back the sun-glasses, then sat down behind the desk, stretched out his legs and studied his feet.

'You'd better get Mitti Hendrik for me.'

'Now?'

'Yes. Now.'

'Now,' repeated Kalaasi. He paused to look at himself in the mirror, gave his hair a quick and unnecessary back-comb, then hurried out, nearly running. He was back with Mitti inside quarter of an hour.

The more Larsen looked at the widow, the less sign of her loss she showed. Her face had none of the hollow colourlessness that comes from lack of sleep. Her eyes were dry with no traces of red. There was a gold bracelet on her wrist, and she wore a pair of good fur-lined boots as well as a new and very impractical cherry-red suede jacket. He wondered where she had bought it. It was not the sort of thing available in the Sermilik KGH.

'Thank you for coming so promptly,' said Larsen politely, half rising then sitting down again. 'Please make yourself comfortable. I would like to ask a few questions. I hope you don't mind if my assistant takes notes.'

Chief Thorold was a precise man, and he liked to receive a transcription of all relevant interviews. But although Larsen had been asking for a cassette recorder for eighteen months, all he got was vague promises.

'Whatever you like,' said Mitti.

She pushed back her hair, closed her eyes for a moment, then exhaled noisily, relaxed, and unzipped her jacket. A faint fragrance of some expensive scent drifted through the room.

Importantly Kalaasi got out his notebook and biro, minus its top, and settled himself behind her. Larsen put his elbows on the desk, cupped his chin in his hands, and considered Mitti. She carried herself with a sort of careless pride, which might come from having killed her husband. Larsen had seen such reactions before, women whose self-esteem had soared because they had finally done something they had wanted to do for years, something people would remember. But in his experience such women confessed rapidly.

'When did you last see your husband, Mitti?'

'Tuesday morning. He set off to work at about six. He was on the early shift.'

'Where did he work?'

'At the seed bank.'

That was where Olssen worked too.

'What did you do, after he left for work?'

She opened her hands casually. Her manner was no longer defiant, as it had been earlier. In fact she seemed quite willing to help, but in the manner of an aristocrat helping a servant. A Dane helping a Greenlander.

'I have no work to go to, so I stayed in bed.'

'How long for?'

'I'm not sure. Until I woke up again.'

Larsen switched his questions. He preferred to approach matters from several different angles at once.

'You had a fight with your husband on Monday night.'

She crossed her legs then elaborately brought out a packet of cigarettes, selected one, and lit it with a small silver lighter. Larsen had the feeling that smoking was not natural to her. That she was doing it for him, not herself.

'I know. I was there.'

'What was the fight about?'

'Why ask me? Ask anyone who was in the hotel bar that night.'

'I am asking you because it concerned you.'

She blew out smoke.

'He accused me of going to bed with another man.'

'Who was the other man?'

'He did not say.'

'So he was wrong?'

'I do not see that it is important. He screwed that Danski girl whenever he had a free moment.'

So it was sex as usual, thought Larsen. The common, maybe inevitable, result of cultural confusion. Once, sociologists claimed, sexual jealousy had scarcely existed in Greenland, and the Inuit had been known as the happiest people in the world. Then the Europeans brought sexual disease, and a religion that preached monogamy. Now nearly all Greenlanders were practising Lutherans, but Protestant Danish morals conflicted with the old free and easy Inuit habits, and the contradictions of past and present ate away at the young nation's stability.

'What Danski girl?' asked Larsen.

'I cannot remember her name.'

'Gudrun Eistrup?' suggested Kalaasi ingenuously.

'Perhaps.'

Mitti was giving a pointless performance. Everyone in Sermilik must know the big Danish woman.

'And you do not know who Jonis thought you had been sleeping with?' went on Larsen.

'Ask other people.' Mitti's voice was suddenly thick with contempt. 'They will tell you quickly enough.'

'Tell us about the fight.'

'Jonis had been drinking. I was talking to someone, when he came over and grabbed me – '

'Who were you talking to?' Larsen interrupted.

'Otto Frederiksen,' she said, after a momentary pause.

'Go on.'

The story, as she told it, was like a hundred Larsen had heard before. A constantly repeated drunken ritual. But what interested him was that Mitti had been talking with Otto Frederiksen, the most important man in Sermilik.

As she finished, Larsen leant forward.

'You killed Jonis, didn't you?' he said gently.

'No, I didn't,' she replied, equally gently.

'It would be easiest to admit it. Easiest for everyone. And our judges are not severe on those who confess their crimes.'

'I did not do it.'

'What time did you say you got up after Jonis went off to work?'

The sudden switch caught her off guard.

'Ten maybe.'

'And what did you do?'

'I went out.'

'Where to?'

'Nowhere special.'

'For how long?'

'I'm not sure. I can't remember. I think I went to the supermarket.'

'Did you talk to anyone?'

'No.'

'Who did you see?'

She paused.

'Robert Maataq was feeding his dogs,' she said at last.

A pretty safe bet. Good hunters kept their dogs in top condition and, among other things, that meant feeding them at regular times.

'Did he see you?'

'Perhaps.'

'And you didn't murder your husband?'

'No.'

'Have you any idea who did?'

She shrugged in such a way as to say, 'That is your problem, not mine.'

'Thank you for your help. I will talk to you again soon.'

She got to her feet, zipped up her jacket, then bent towards him. Again there was that faint touch of scent. Like meadow flowers.

'What is it like to come home at last?' she asked.

So that was the source of her superiority. She knew he came from Sermilik. He wondered how. Larsen smiled non-committally, and she left slowly and self-consciously. Larsen turned to Kalaasi.

'I want you to find out everything you can about her.'

Kalassi nodded, then put down his biro and frowned.

'What sort of things should I try to find out?'

Not for the first time in their brief acquaintance Larsen wondered why on earth Kalaasi was a policeman. He was a skinny, lightly built man, with none of Larsen's raw physical strength, not nearly powerful enough to tear apart two fighting drunks. He seemed to have no initiative, no cunning, no strong sense of right and wrong, no desire to tell other people what to do, no curiosity. Just a wish to dress like a policeman in a third-rate TV series. Still, he was good-natured, enthusiastic, and willing to do what he was told.

'Find out if she has a boyfriend, or more than one. Find out if anyone saw her on Tuesday, and if so when. Find out if she ever goes near Lake Tugdlik. Find out where she got that jacket. Find out if she likes eating prawns . . .'

'Prawns?' repeated Kalaasi uncertainly.

'That was a joke,' explained Larsen. 'I just meant anything that might be useful. In other words see if you can find out if she did it. All right?'

The departure of that eager blank face, hiding behind sun-glasses, was something of a relief. Larsen picked up Kalaasi's notes and glanced over them. It seemed Kalaasi was trying to teach himself shorthand. He hadn't got very far. Larsen crumpled the piece of paper up and tossed it into the waste-paper basket.

There seemed no doubt that Mitti had killed her husband. Unfortunately her pretty round face spoke of stony stubbornness, and without a confession the case could yet take some time. Quite aside from the other job he had to do.

Larsen picked up the telephone and rang.

'Sermilik Seed Bank,' said a man's voice.

'This is Sergeant Tomas Larsen. Could you tell me if Jonis Hendrik came in to work on Tuesday morning?'

'Wait a moment. I'll look in the signing-in book. Yes, here it is. He did.'

Larsen would have bet several hundred crowns on the opposite answer.

'Are you sure?'

'Yes.'

'What time did he leave?'

'At three. At the end of his shift.'

'You are absolutely sure?'

'That's what it says here.'

'Thank you.'

There must be a mistake. The body had been found on the ridge by Lake Tugdlik. Larsen was not sure where the seed bank was – it had come to Sermilik since he left – but it must be at least five kilometres from Lake Tugdlik. Everything was. If Jonis had gone straight to the lake after work, he could not have got there until a quarter to four. Remembering Jonis's plump unmuscular body, Larsen guessed later. Yet the body had been found, 'cold and growing stiff' in Robert Maataq's words, at about four. There was no time for Jonis to have walked to the lake, been tied up and stabbed, bled to death, and then for the body to develop rigor mortis. It had to be a mistake.

Larsen made himself a coffee and drank it, missing sugar. A ray of sun lanced through the window and he closed his eyes and soaked it in for a few moments. Probably he was just looking for complications, it had always been one of his faults. However things broke down, it must all end up with Mitti. Finishing his drink, he got up, went outside, and leant against the wall.

31

The sun was shining brilliantly on the multi-coloured houses and the bare rocks. The air was pure and sharp. A redpoll sang from a nearby roof, and a few black and brown Lapland buntings chittered at each other as they flew up the hill towards the Sermilik Hotel that overlooked the entire town. A single delicate pale yellow Arctic poppy had opened close by, and the late spring sunshine was warm and soothing.

Below, on the grassless football pitch, the only flat space in the town except for the helicopter landing pad, some children were kicking a ball about. Among them, laughing and shouting, he recognised Kamik. And Larsen felt the sudden stab of memory, the memory of past happiness and youth. He had played on that pitch so often, running about in the snow and the mud, laughing and shouting just like Kamik, dreaming of playing midfield for Brondby, not caring for the future or the past or anything but the moment. And it was gone, long past catching. His eyes pricked and his breath came a little faster.

'Hello, sergeant.'

He started, then recovered himself. Gudrun, the biologist, looked apologetic.

'Did I startle you?'

'No, no, Miss Eistrup. I am glad to see you. In fact I was planning to visit you, to ask you a few things.'

'Me?' Was he imagining the faintest hint of fear? 'Policemen are never off duty, it seems.'

It was true, for Larsen at least. He smiled helplessly and realised afresh how tall she was, towering over him. She had on a heavy anorak, her hands deeply buried in the pockets, her broad shoulders hunched. The combination of pale unlined skin with eyebrows and eyelashes that were so fair as to be almost invisible, gave her an impassive look.

'Did you know Jonis Hendrik?'

'Sure. I spent time with his father only a few weeks ago. The old man has an almost eidetic memory for what Sermilik was like forty years ago, even extending to plants. It has been very useful for my research.'

'What was Jonis like?'

Gudrun shrugged.

'He was at least a dozen years older than Mitti, but he liked people to think he was still young. I found him quiet, friendly. I don't know. Ordinary.'

'Did you see him on Tuesday?'

'Of course.'

'Why of course?'

'I was working up at the seed bank. So was he. Of course I saw him.'

'And?'

'He seemed the same as any other day, and left at the end of his shift. That was that.'

Mitti had accused Gudrun of having an affair with Jonis. But Larsen could see no obvious signs of it.

'You don't seem very upset by what happened.'

'He was not the sort of person it was easy to feel sorry for, or who wanted you to. He was too wound up in himself.'

The answer felt unsatisfactory.

'What did you do after Jonis left the seed bank?'

'I stayed on. I had more work to do. Sergeant, I don't know what you are getting at, but I think you are going off in the wrong direction.'

Larsen stared at her, and remembered a time when he had been about twelve and he had taken a long summer walk along Asiaq fjord to a rarely visited part of the coast. On a sandy beach he disturbed a small shore-bird, a ringed plover, which had scuttled away in panic. As it ran it had desperately fluttered one of its wings against the ground, splaying it out at an impossible angle. The wing was clearly broken and Larsen followed, trying to catch the bird. Perhaps to put it out of its misery, for even then he had hated unnecessary suffering, perhaps to take it home in triumph. The plover piped shrilly and pathetically while darting over the sand just three or four metres in front of him, wildly flapping its loose, dangling wing. Larsen had pursued it down the beach for at least five minutes, when suddenly it stopped calling and flew calmly away. Only then did he realise how completely he had been fooled, and how expertly the bird had led him away from its nest. There was an unpredictable defensiveness about Gudrun that reminded Larsen of that bird.

'Shall I tell you the news now?' she asked.

'What is that?'

'The Greenlandair strike is to go ahead. On Tuesday night.'

'I thought they had come to an agreement.'

'It seems it fell through. And you know what the strike means, don't you?'

With that passing shot she strode off up the hill, swinging her hips.

Larsen did know what a strike would mean. With the sea still frozen hard, and the nearest open-sea port, Nanortalik, eight hundred kilometres away as the raven flew, and half as far again by land, across country that was hard even by Greenland standards, the strike meant total isolation for Sermilik. Without the airstrip, the town was cut off from the rest of the world.

The line to Chief Thorold in Godthab was poor and crackling.

'Hello, Larsen. Have you sorted the killing out already? Good, good. I knew it wouldn't take you long. But don't forget that – '

'No, chief. Not yet.'

'What? I can't hear you.'

'Not yet,' Larsen roared. 'I haven't cleared up the murder yet.'

'Why are you phoning then?'

'The strike, chief.'

'What?'

'The strike. The air strike.' Without warning, the interference ceased and Larsen found himself bellowing along a crystal-clear line.

'There's no need to shout. I can hear you perfectly well. The strike, yes. Annoying, but even if it does happen, there's still four days before it starts. Plenty of time to get everything sorted out.'

Thorold did not sound his usual self. Although he was a Dane, he liked Greenland, and he liked his job. He had a pretty young Greenlander wife and a spoilt little three-year-old daughter who occasionally came to the police station and played noisily with her dolls, while everyone petted her. Thorold was the sort of easy-going man who flourished in a quiet backwater. But today his voice was taut, unsettled, and Larsen could almost see him sitting behind his desk and scratching his thinning hair, his pale features crossed by a spider-web of concern.

'OK.'

'And Larsen, that includes the report as well. The interior department of the Landsstyre want it as soon as possible, but as I told you, the local people must not know such a report is being compiled.'

'Isn't it really a job for a sociologist, sir?'

It was rare for Larsen, even by implication, to query an order. But sensing the political pressure, he instinctively reacted against it.

'All policemen have a basic grasp of sociology,' said Thorold, mixing encouragement and dismissiveness. 'It's part of the job.'

And in my files it records that I studied sociology at university, thought Larsen.

'Goodbye, Larsen,' said Thorold briskly. 'Don't let me down.'

Larsen hung up, then put his hands behind his head and closed his eyes. Suddenly he heard a noise, and spun round, to find Kalaasi smiling at him.

'What do you want?' Larsen snapped.

'I've made you up a bed upstairs, sergeant, and bought some food. I'm leaving now. If that's all right.'

Larsen took a deep breath, then went upstairs. The bed was well and neatly made. It looked very comfortable. Larsen found the sight of it discouraging. Kalaasi should have been out working – or was that graceless? He ate a supper of tinned meat and biscuit, then undressed and tried to sleep. But his regular companion, insomnia, arrived promptly.

As usual he began to think of Ann-Marie. And as usual they were cold thoughts. Larsen still received occasional letters from his daughter, Vigdis, but nothing from her mother. Deep down Larsen accepted it was his fault. He could not really expect a sophisticated Danish woman with a degree to bury herself in Greenland. The astonishing thing was that after Larsen and she had moved to Godthab, the marriage lasted another four and a half years. Then, one late autumn day, she had announced that she and eight-year-old Vigdis were going to Denmark for Christmas.

'And we're not coming back,' she had added.

He hadn't said anything.

'You can come with us, Tomas,' she went on. 'I want you to. Vigdis needs a father, and what is there for you in the Greenland police?'

'What is there for me in Denmark?' he had answered. 'There are no openings for Inuit policemen in Denmark.'

'Why did you join the police?' she had snapped, suddenly angry. 'You were so clever, winning that scholarship, going to university, everything. Your tutor was sure you'd do postgraduate work, wasn't she? Why didn't you? A sergeant in the Greenland police. Jesus Christ! I thought you were going to make something of your life. Look at that friend of yours, Solomon. He's a name. People know about him. He travels, earns good money, does a job he enjoys. But you're trapped, Tomas. You're not going anywhere, unless you get out while you still can. Get out now and try again.'

But he hadn't. He couldn't leave Greenland, couldn't live without the great virgin ice fields, without the enwalling mountains, the flickering multi-coloured curtains of the aurora, the great blue-green bergs, the tiny spring flowers in rock crevices, even the shouts of the drunks as they staggered home by the light of the midnight sun. Western technology and religion might be destroying the last scraps of Greenland's culture, but at least the land itself was unspoilt. He had known many Greenlanders in Denmark, and it was the land they missed. Unable to find work except in the cities, their eyes showed how lost they were, adrift in an artificial world of concrete built by and for other people.

Larsen got up, collected some cheese from the kitchen and chewed it meditatively. Gradually his thoughts idled from his wife to Gudrun. He tried to push her out of his mind, but she was stubborn. Solomon had always preferred blonde European women, he called it Penetrating the Enemy, and now he was married to a very blonde, fast-rising

American actress of twenty-three, whose father was conveniently a top television executive.

At last the darkless night crept up on Larsen and he slept – and dreamt of Gudrun. A dream of surging sex that would not leave him until he woke in the small hours, hot and sticky with sweat, angry with himself. The objects of your dreams know nothing, regard you as they have always done, but you have a memory of love that you feel they should share. Larsen knew his vivid, clinging dream had had far more impact on his emotions than drunken sex after a party would have done. Even though nothing had really happened, he knew he would treat Gudrun differently when they next met. When he had been married he sometimes dreamt of bitter arguments with his wife, and then treated her coldly the rest of the day. He could not help himself.

Bitterness was strong within him that night. Bitterness that such a dream could confuse his emotions. Since his divorce, Larsen's sex life had been confined to brief meaningless grapplings, lubricated by alcohol and the simple desire for relief, regretted as soon as they were over, if not before. He suspected his father within him had infected him with a revulsion from sex that was altogether alien to Greenland. Some people might say guilt – if that was what it was – made the pleasure of sex greater, but he had never found so himself.

He yawned, and got out the book he was reading, a modern novel called *Failed Harvest*. A young Danish man discovered his wife was being unfaithful to him, left her, threw up his job and went to Canada, where he came across an old Chinese revolutionary, whose memories interweaved with the young man's story. Larsen had been struggling with it on and off for three weeks, but the young man's self-pity irritated him. Now, however, the book sent him back to sleep within a quarter of an hour.

Larsen was ripped awake by a hammering sound. He sprang unsteadily to his feet, the rags of sleep hanging around him, and staggered downstairs to the door. As he opened it, he was pushed roughly back into the office. Caught totally unawares, he slipped and fell. The door shut with a crash. A hunting rifle was pointed straight at the pit of his stomach.

4

RULER OF THE TOWN

Robert Maataq stood over him, holding his gun in the comfortable way of a man who knows his weapon well and uses it often. His dark, weathered face stared down, yet the piercing eyes seemed puzzled, as if he was surprised at what he was doing. Although the rifle muzzle was rock steady, Maataq himself swayed slightly and there was alcohol on his breath.

'What do you want?' asked Larsen.

Maataq did not reply. He continued to stare down for a minute, then unnervingly began to move the gun slowly up and down, first pointing it at Larsen's head, then his chest, his stomach, all the way down to his knees, then back up to his face again.

'What do you want?' Larsen repeated, struggling to hold his voice steady.

At last Maataq spoke. His words were slightly slurred, and spoken so slowly Larsen could hear his heart beat twice between each one.

'Kalaasi says I killed Jonis.'

'No.'

That angered him. He spoke more quickly and the gun barrel froze, levelled straight at Larsen's head.

'I have ears. I heard him. The slimy little piece of dogshit asked me about matters that were none of his business, and when I asked him why he wanted to know, he said you think I killed Jonis.'

'He is a fool.'

'You mean he is a fool because he told me what he should have kept hidden.'

'I mean he is a fool because he is a fool. May I get up?'

Maataq thought, then pointed to the chair. The gun slipped away a little, but remained in his hands, a constant threat.

'If he is a fool, why do you use him?'

'He is the policeman here, and I cannot do everything myself. It is not as if anyone else has offered to help me.'

'Why should anyone help you? There is no problem. There is no reason for Kalaasi to go around asking questions and causing trouble. Jonis was killed by his wife. Arrest her and take her away and we can forget the whole thing.'

Forgetting was what Sermilik seemed to want to do most.

'She says she did not do it.'

'She is a liar.' Maataq glared at Larsen. 'She has always been a liar, ever since she was a little girl, and stole pencils at school. That is how it is with children who do not have fathers.'

'Why are you so sure she killed Jonis?' asked Larsen carefully.

'I know her. Jonis beat her the night before he was killed, and she has often said that if a man hit her, she would kill him.'

'People say many things. Why did Jonis beat her?'

'Because of Otto Frederiksen, of course.' Maataq looked at him pityingly. 'Do you know nothing?'

Larsen shifted in the chair, taking care not to look at the gun. It was the moment for an instinctive stab in the dark.

'From what I have heard of Jonis, he was not a very jealous man.' That was not enough. He needed much more to shake Maataq. 'Someone told me you and Mitti were once bedmates, but no one was killed then.'

Maataq's face tautened so that the bones of his face stood out like mountain ridges. The gun swung up again, the barrels once more levelled on Larsen's eyes; for a timeless second, the policeman was sure that those black holes, filling with flame, were the last thing he would ever see. Then Maataq breathed heavily and sat down.

'If I had been ten years younger, you would be dead,' he said. 'But these days I have learned a little about control. Who told you that?'

Larsen said nothing.

Maataq leant back in the chair.

'I only slept with her a few times. She wanted things from me I could not give. I did not want to give.'

'And no one was hurt.'

'I suppose not.' He glanced down at the floor. 'But it is a woman's murder to knife a man in the back.'

Privately Larsen agreed. But that was not enough to convict Mitti.

'Was Jonis sleeping with another woman?'

'Probably. I do not know.'

'If you are going to drink, you should leave your gun at home,' said Larsen.

'I do not like to leave my gun. Last month a flock of fat white-front geese flew overhead, then landed well within range. I threw stones at them, but they flew away. Several would have stayed behind if I had had my gun.'

'Wild geese do not usually come near the town bars,' said Larsen. 'Leave your gun at home next time.'

'Perhaps.'

'May I ask you one more question?'

'What?'

'Were you feeding your dogs around midday on Tuesday?'

'Yes.'

'Did you see Mitti Hendrik while you were doing it?'

'That is two questions. I fed my dogs as I always feed my dogs. I did not see Mitti.'

There was a silence, impregnated with their breath.

'Thank you,' said Larsen at length.

'For what?'

'Would you really have killed me?'

'I did not think I was loading my gun for nothing.' Maataq got to his feet, then glanced over his shoulder at Larsen. 'People know why you do not arrest Mitti.'

'What do you mean?'

Maataq shrugged. He slouched out with his back bent, carrying the air of defeat like a heavy rucksack.

Although it was Saturday, Kalaasi came in the next morning.

'Why did you tell Robert Maataq that I think he is a murderer?' asked Larsen.

Kalaasi frowned. A frown did not sit comfortably on his smooth open face.

'I thought you did.'

Larsen sighed.

'Why did you think that?'

'I don't know, sergeant.'

'And why did you tell Maataq?'

'I don't know, sergeant.'

Larsen covered his mouth to hold back an untypical desire to swear.

'But I have news,' Kalaasi went on, the worried frown vanishing as if it had never been, to be replaced by his habitual smile. 'I have found someone who saw Mitti on Tuesday.'

'Who?'

Kalaasi opened the door, and an old man came in. His hair, parted raggedly in the middle, was thin for an Inuit and he had heavy eyebrows, a moustache and a straggling beard over a perfectly oval yellowish face. He was broad and very short, with deep lines reaching from the sides of his mouth up to his nose. Heavy wrinkled lids covered his dark eyes. He wore a thick shirt and trousers over seal-hide boots.

'Who are you?' asked Larsen.

'My name is Elias.' His voice was high and quick, almost feminine, though roughened by age. 'I come from Dove Sund.'

39

'It is a long way from Dove Sund. What are you doing in Sermilik?'

The old man gave a stern smile. A smile he did not permit to go too far.

'I came to see my daughter, who lives here with her family. I came to tell her to come back with me. This is a bad place and she must leave it.'

'What did she say?' asked Larsen curiously.

'She said nothing. The first time I came she laughed at me. The second time she grew angry. This time she said nothing. I told her that it is many years since she heard the whisper of the stars, and no Greenlander should forget that sound.' He looked up at Larsen with alert black eyes embedded in his tanned, wrinkled face. 'Have you ever heard the whisper of the stars?'

'What is it?'

'When your breath turns straight to ice, splinters and falls to the ground. Until you have heard that sound as the northern lights glow over the ice pack, you have never been an Inuit.'

Perhaps that is why I have never felt like a real Inuit, thought Larsen.

'Next spring I will come back again,' Elias went on. 'And next time, rather than face another year in this town, she and her husband and her children will agree to come back to Dove Sund.'

It struck Larsen that perhaps the old man's family should go with him this time. Dove Sund was well to the north, the only other populated area in East Greenland, except for a few isolated weather stations. Around it the land opened out and the mountains and ice-cap that hemmed in Sermilik retreated up to two hundred kilometres from the coastline. The area was excellent for hunting, probably the best in Greenland, with foxes, geese, ducks, hares, reindeer, musk oxen and polar bears. In the huge network of fjords, the largest in the world, seal and walrus were numerous. Only four or five hundred people lived scattered over the Dove Sund region, a third of the population of Sermilik, but because of the good hunting and the fur pelts they could sell to America, they lived well. People in Sermilik spoke of Dove Sund with the sneer of sophistication, but also an undercurrent of envy. Not that anyone wanted to live there. The climate was far more severe and there was no government aid. No social security, no modern council-built housing, no doctor on call, no television, no regular supplies of fruit, coffee, sugar, and the rest of the necessities of life. The people there retained the nomadic instincts of their ancestors and whole families set off in early spring, long before the ice-melt, and did not return to their homes for months. In comparison Sermilik was a packed, pressurised modern environment, where everyone lived in

40

each other's pockets, and men and women had lost the ability to be alone.

'You saw the woman, Mitti Hendrik, on Tuesday?'

'Yes.'

'How do you know it was her?'

'She is a cousin of my son-in-law. Once I told her to come to Dove Sund too, but when she laughed, I knew she meant it.'

'Did you speak to her when you saw her?'

'No.'

'Why not?'

'Because I had nothing to say to her.'

Larsen considered. Although Sermilik and Dove Sund were on the same coast, there was no direct air link between them. To get from one to the other it was necessary to fly over the inland ice to Søndre Strømfjord in the west, then back again.

'Did you know there is going to be an air strike?' he said. 'There is only one plane to Søndre Strømfjord before the strike, on Tuesday, and it may arrive too late for a connecting flight back to Dove Sund.'

Elias looked at the policeman as if he was a fool.

'I did not fly here.'

'What?'

'I did not fly,' Elias said again. 'I came in my kayak.'

Larsen stared at the little old man in disbelief. The journey must have been at least six hundred kilometres though largely frozen sea riddled with icebergs, past the sheer black cliffs of the Drachmann coast and the Kingigtorssuaq, one of the most terrifying and desolate places in the whole Arctic and still scarcely explored.

'You cannot have done.'

'It is a hard journey, but what is a month? She is my only surviving child.'

For a moment Larsen felt awed, as if he was in the presence of some mighty hero of ancient legend – Hercules, Arjuna, Siegfried, Kagssagssuk the wretched beaten orphan who came back to wreak revenge on his oppressors.

'What time did you see Mitti?' he asked at last.

'A little after midday.'

Exactly when Mitti said she was out walking.

'What did she do?'

'She went into one of the houses.'

'Which one?'

Elias shook his head.

'I do not know. All of them look the same.'

41

'That's what he said to me,' put in Kalaasi. 'I took him round the town, but he kept saying he could not feel it.'

This old man, who could bring his boat hundreds of kilometres through the most forbidding ocean in the world, could not find his way around a town of a few hundred houses. It was totally logical.

'Thank you, Elias,' said Larsen. 'When will you return north?'

'In half a month.'

'That soon?'

'I must be back before the wild geese have finished their moult.'

'I see. By the way, what is that medal around your neck?'

The old man's face grew proud.

'My father won it,' he said. 'He was in the Sledge Patrol and fought the Germans in the north, around Sabine Island. I wear it always.'

'I see,' Larsen said again. 'Thank you.'

The old man bowed his head and left.

'So Mitti did not do it after all,' said Kalaasi.

'We do not know that. Elias saw her after midday, but Jonis was not killed until sometime between three in the afternoon, when he left work, and four, when his body was found by Robert Maataq.'

'Oh.' Kalaasi's face fell.

'Did you find anything else?'

'I have a message for you, from Mr Otto Frederiksen.'

Larsen looked up.

'What does he want?'

'It was rather difficult to understand, sergeant.' Kalaasi gave a nervous smile, then hurried on. 'He said a very important American businessman would be arriving shortly, and that he wished to arrange police protection.'

'He said what!' exclaimed Larsen in disbelief. 'Does he think the Inuit Freedom Army are lurking in the hills, poised to assassinate all foreigners?'

'I have not heard of the Inuit Freedom Army, sergeant.'

'There is no Inuit Freedom Army.'

'I do not understand.'

'Neither do I. I had better visit Mr Frederiksen. As for you, I want you to talk to Jonis's workmates at the seed bank. Ask them when they saw him on Tuesday, how he seemed, if they saw him leave, if he left with someone else. All right? Do you have all that down?'

Kalaasi was writing furiously, the tip of his bright red tongue sticking out of the side of his mouth.

'. . . with someone else. Yes, sergeant.'

Larsen patiently made him repeat the instructions, corrected two mistakes, then sent him off with a parting appeal not to give anyone else the idea that they were under suspicion of murder.

On the point of leaving Kalaasi stopped.

'What now?' asked Larsen. He found it impossible to think with Kalaasi there.

'Who do you think did kill Jonis, sergeant?'

Larsen was warmed by this unexpected curiosity.

'Probably everyone is right. But I must have proof before making an arrest. Now, goodbye and good luck.'

Left to himself, Larsen put his feet on the desk and gazed up at the ceiling pensively. The last flight out of Cap Gad would be on Tuesday afternoon, then came the strike. It felt as if time was growing short.

Otto Frederiksen went over to the little bar in the corner of his large, thickly carpeted sitting-room.

'Beer?' he said. It was barely a question.

'Tea would be fine.'

There was a momentary flicker of surprise.

'Tea. Of course.' He raised his voice. 'Margrethe!'

A few moments later a Greenland girl of about eighteen came in. To Larsen's disbelief she was wearing a traditional French maid's uniform, complete with frilly apron.

'I like my servants to look smart,' said Frederiksen. 'Margrethe, tea. Quickly.'

The girl gave a bob and vanished. Frederiksen poured himself a large whisky. He was a long, formidable-looking man in his early fifties, with a massive chest, big face, and thick arms and legs. A luxuriant, carefully tended moustache almost concealed his small tight mouth, and he wore round, lightly tinted, gold-rimmed spectacles.

'Now, let me see, you're from Godthab, aren't you, Sergeant Larsen? I think I know your chief, Thorold.' He smiled with not-quite unconscious superiority, drank his whisky down and poured another. 'What do you think of Sermilik?'

'It is very isolated,' said Larsen cautiously.

'Yes, that's true.' Frederiksen sounded surprised, as if it was something he had never thought of before. He reached up a pale hand to brush back the straw-like hair that lay limply over his high, gleaming white skull.

The silence stretched out. Frederiksen took another large mouthful of whisky, then lay back in his chair. Larsen sat neatly on the edge of the soft sofa and waited.

43

Margrethe reappeared with an elegant wooden tray, a blue Chinese teapot and a single cup and saucer. She poured the tea out for Larsen, then left. Larsen picked up his cup and took a sip. It had an unusual musky flavour.

'Do you like it?' asked Frederiksen.

'It is very pleasant.'

'I have it specially sent to me from Tashkent. The best green tea in the world. You have come to Sermilik about the murder of Jonis Hendrik, I suppose. Did you know him?'

'No.'

'I'm not surprised. He was a total nonentity. But that was not what I wanted to discuss with you. Not at all.'

Again he stopped. Larsen was never surprised when people took a long time to come to the point, often they were simply not used to having to think quickly. But Otto Frederiksen had a reputation as a real, American-style businessman, and this reluctance seemed out of character.

Still Larsen waited. Calm. Polite. Immovable.

Frederiksen took off his spectacles and rubbed his eyes. He looked tired.

'What do you know of the Sermilik Seed Bank?' he asked, putting his spectacles back on.

'Very little.'

'I will explain,' said Frederiksen, adopting a lecturing manner. 'There are only three major seed banks in the world – one in Great Britain at the Royal Horticultural Gardens; one near Longyearbyen in Svalbard; and the last one here, in the old Sermilik platinum mine. Each of these banks holds something in the order of two per cent of all the world's major plant species. For the seeds to remain viable it is essential to keep them at an optimum temperature of $-19.8°$ at all times. This is, of course, an expensive undertaking, though less so in the Arctic. However, the collection and transport of seeds from all over the globe is expensive also.'

Larsen continued to sip his tea, which was refreshing but not strong enough.

'These banks are like zoos, a way of conserving species even if they are made extinct in the wild. Unfortunately, unlike zoos, there is no money to be made from letting visitors in. To cut a long story short, the country is seriously short of funds, the more so as Denmark plans to reduce its aid to Greenland by another forty per cent over the next five years, on top of the deep cuts it has already made. Obviously the government in Godthab is looking to make up as much of that shortfall as it can.

44

'Now East Greenland, specifically Sermilik, is the least viable part of what is, to be frank, an economically moribund nation. I have recently, as well as my other work, been acting as adviser to the Landsstyre for this region and I have made a series of proposals.' Frederiksen seemed to be inflating himself like a male ptarmigan in the breeding season. 'One of these concerns the seed bank, whose maintenance I have overseen for the last two and a half years. Recently it has become plain that the gathering rate of global plant extinction is reaching crisis levels. The result is that more and more agencies, governmental and private, are considering, or are in the process of, setting up seed banks of their own to preserve potentially valuable but threatened plants. As we have enormous expertise in this area, I have arranged that we should sell that expertise.'

'I see,' said Larsen, who did not.

'Most importantly I have made contacts with a well-known international agro-chemical combine and they are very interested,' resumed Frederiksen. 'Especially in the question of privatisation of the seed bank, and its consequent move from being a burden of expense on the Greenland government to a source of easily realisable profit.'

'How will you make a profit?'

'By selling some of the seeds. Agreements would be signed with the Danish and Greenland governments that would outline minimum requirements, while permitting the sale of surplus stock. Initially that surplus stock will probably appeal only to other, newly formed seed banks. Nevertheless we are confident that when plant species become extinct, assuming the seed bank to contain seeds of those extinct plants, it would be wise, and possibly highly profitable, to sell seeds so that extinct species can be brought back to life, as it were.'

'It sounds very worthwhile,' said Larsen, glancing round the comfortable, characterless, underfurnished room.

'It would be a most important conservation move, and absolutely crucial to the future of much of the world's flora.'

'I congratulate you. But I cannot see that your seed bank is a police matter.'

'I was coming to that,' said Frederiksen sharply. 'A leading director of the firm in question is coming to Sermilik to inspect the seed bank. Preparatory to signing the final agreement with the Greenland government.'

'Yes?'

'This distinguished guest will require police protection during their visit.'

'Why?'

Faint points of red appeared on Frederiksen's cheeks. Larsen had two feelings. One was that Otto Frederiksen and he did not like each other. The other was that he did not care.

'Because of this.' Frederiksen went over to a smart, walnut wood desk, pulled down the top, and shuffled around among a thick wad of papers, faxes and computer print-outs. 'Damn! It is very inconvenient Peter being away at the moment.'

'Peter?' queried Larsen.

'My secretary. He is in New York. Ah, this is what I was looking for.'

He produced an envelope, and brought it over to Larsen, carrying it with the very tips of his fingers.

'You don't need to be so careful,' said Larsen, taking it. 'We have no files on fingerprints from East Greenland, so even if there are prints on it, they would probably be useless.'

It was a cheap brown envelope with 'Otto Frederiksen. Personal' written on it in large clumsy letters. Larsen pulled out the letter, which was written in the same clumsy letters on cheap, blue-lined paper from the KGH stores. The message was straightforward. 'If your money grabber comes here we will kill him.'

For an irreverent moment Larsen thought of the Inuit Freedom Army. He imagined hard-looking Greenlanders in combat fatigues and headbands, armed with Kalashnikovs and grenade launchers, lurking in caves near the ice-cap, ambushing government search parties, distributing propaganda, sending out assassination squads.

'Where did you get this?' he asked.

'It was by the door when I got up this morning.'

'It's just a childish practical joke,' Larsen said dismissively.

'But I have told no one that this businessman was coming.'

'Are you certain about that? If you mention something to one or two people you utterly rely on, then they mention it to others they utterly rely on, it only takes a day or two before the whole town knows.'

'I told no one.'

'Well, there are other ways to find things out. A helicopter pilot, a booking clerk at Greenlandair, even a crossed telephone line. I assure you, Mr Frederiksen, this is nothing but a silly game.'

'No. It is real. I am sure it is. A rumour has gone round that if this agreement is signed, there will be redundancies.'

'A true rumour?'

'That would not be up to me.'

'You think someone is threatening your associate because they fear to lose their job?'

'Exactly.'

Larsen looked cynical.

'This is Sermilik,' Frederiksen snapped with scarcely concealed heat. 'There is little work here and what there is means a great deal – money, possessions, prestige, freedom. And do not forget that, to my certain knowledge, there are at least three murderers walking round the town quite freely. What if – '

Larsen interrupted impatiently.

'This is not a brawl over girlfriends, Mr Frederiksen, and I have never heard of anyone committing murder because they were about to be made unemployed. If you want my advice, just keep away from the town bars for a few weeks. Someone might get drunk enough to pick a fight with you, but that's all. Talking of which, there are a few questions I would like to ask you – '

The telephone rang. Frederiksen reached for it.

'Hello? Oh yes. Please wait a moment.' He put his hand over the receiver. 'I'm afraid this is a private call, sergeant. Would you mind waiting in the room opposite for a few minutes?'

Larsen went out. Across the corridor was a large, well-equipped office, with a colour photocopier, and three state-of-the-art Apple computers. Filing cabinets lined a wall. There were four telephones, and a single red light gleamed on the fax machine. Yet the whole room, with its expensive office chairs and bare magnolia-coloured walls, contained an aura of disuse, as if despite the gleaming well-dusted plastic, invisible dust lay over everything.

There was a rustle, then a steady grinding purr. A fax was coming through, the paper covered with column after column of figures. Larsen was an inquisitive man, but what interested him was people and their environment, not technology. He walked along the passage to the stairs, then climbed swiftly up them. At the top was another empty, thickly carpeted corridor, exactly like the one downstairs. He walked along it, cautiously opening doors and glancing in. A small bathroom; two guest bedrooms as uninformative as rooms in a middle-range hotel; a second bathroom, much larger and more luxurious, and arrayed with mirrors; Frederiksen's own bedroom, almost as drab as the guest bedrooms; and finally one last door.

It was the only room with a lock to it. Even the bathrooms did not have them. Cautiously Larsen tried the ornate brass handle, but the door did not open. After a moment Larsen tried peering through the keyhole, but saw nothing. It was none of his business of course, but Larsen was interested. Anything out of the ordinary interested him because it might explain untypical behaviour. He returned to the small bathroom, visited the toilet, flushed it, and went back down. Frederiksen was at the bottom of the stairs.

'There is a toilet down here,' he said, spacing his words carefully, and staring at the policeman.

'Sorry.' Larsen was unapologetic.

Frederiksen looked at him a little longer.

'I have this ridiculous thing that I don't like people in the room with me when I am on the telephone. Very stupid, I know, and often rather inconvenient. I believe you said you had a few questions to ask me. I hope they won't take too long as I have some urgent work to do.'

'I gather you knew Jonis Hendrik.'

'No.'

'No?'

'He worked for me, but I would not have recognised him.'

'I was under the impression that you were talking to his wife, Mitti Hendrik, the evening before his death, and that he came over and almost caused a fight.'

'I did talk to a woman in the hotel bar on Monday night, but I didn't know her name. We had a drink together.'

'Do you often drink with women you don't know?'

Frederiksen almost winked.

'Not as often as I'd like to.'

'What did you and this woman talk about?'

'What does one talk about with a woman in the bar?' Frederiksen threw Larsen another knowing smile, an all-men-together smirk.

Larsen ignored it.

'What do you talk about with a woman in the bar, Mr Frederiksen?'

'Anything. I do not remember. Anyway, this Eskimo . . .' He barely looked at Larsen this time, though both of them knew that Greenlanders hated to be called 'Eskimo', a contemptuous name given to the Inuit people by American Indians and adopted by white men. 'This Eskimo began shouting at the woman, then grabbed her and tried to drag her out of the bar.'

'What did you do while this was happening?'

'Other people's family life is none of my business. Is that all, sergeant?'

'For the moment, I think. Thank you, Mr Frederiksen.'

Larsen was shown out by the maid.

'When are you off work?' he asked quietly, as she held the front door for him.

'I do not know.'

'I want you to come down to the police station and see me.' Her dark, hunted eyes opened wider. 'There's nothing to fear,' he added. 'Just a few questions.'

She vanished wordlessly.

Larsen glanced up at the end of the house where the locked room was. The window was small and covered with a blind, and he had a sense that Otto Frederiksen was watching.

Back at the police station Larsen went into the bathroom and shaved. But he had left the stubble too long and patches of it resisted the electric razor. Giving up, he went back to the desk and sat down. No murder he had ever dealt with had taken more than a day or so to sort out. This felt different. Or perhaps that was just the tight, fervid atmosphere of Sermilik itself. He sighed and let his mind roam over his acquaintances of the day.

The doctor was an unlikely inhabitant. He gave no hint of the selflessness that might have brought some men to Sermilik, but with only seventy doctors in the whole of Greenland, Sven seemed too good at his job to have been driven here by incompetence. Unless he had a drink problem. Yet Larsen had an instinctive feeling that Sven was far too controlled for an alcoholic, and that underneath his convivial manner lay something else, a taut, gripping nature that gave nothing away. Then there was Robert Maataq, the fierce-eyed, hot-blooded man who had found a body that could not have been dead for more than twenty minutes, and claimed, impossibly, senselessly, that it was stiff and cold.

Perhaps he should visit the seed bank. It was the men at the seed bank who said Jonis had been there for his shift, even though this contradicted the evidence of Robert Maataq and Dr Sven. But the helicopter only flew to the seed bank twice a day. Larsen realised he had not done any proper groundwork, partly because the report he was supposed to be compiling hung in his thoughts, but mostly because he kept expecting Mitti to admit the crime. He had not even found out where she was between three and five in the afternoon, at the time of the murder. It was the sort of obvious thing he should have sorted out long ago.

Doubt ran through his mind on noiseless feet, like a scuttling beetle. Doubt that he might be seizing on the obvious and ignoring the truth. Shadows from the past flitted round him, cases he had never felt completely certain about. The thirteen-year-old boy who had admitted to killing his father. The good husband who had run away from his family to escape a charge of theft, and left his wife and new-born twins close to starvation. The fisherman's suicide in Fiskenaesset that had not felt like a suicide . . .

And suddenly Larsen's thoughts turned back to Gudrun. He wanted to go and see her, but even if she had been Jonis's lover, he had nothing to ask her.

He scratched his nose, then picked up the phone. His words flitted across the barren ice that was the heart, and nearly all the body, of Greenland.

'Hello? This is Sergeant Larsen. I'd like to know if you have files on any of these people . . .'

An hour later the phone rang back. Larsen picked it up eagerly.

'Yes. Yes, that's right. Which two? Otto Frederiksen, yes. And the other? Robert Maataq, yes. A murder charge. When was that . . . ?'

Larsen listened a little longer, then hung up. He had been given more to think about. But not yet enough. He was scribbling notes on a piece of rough paper when there was a soft tap. Larsen put down his biro, went to the door and opened it warily. Standing in the porch was Frederiksen's servant, Margrethe. Her plump, round face was shadowed by black hair cut in a low fringe. Long tight plaits hung down over her scruffy, well-worn anorak.

'I was sent out to buy some things,' she said nervously. 'I cannot stay long.'

'Thank you for coming. Please sit down.'

She flopped down, clasping her shopping basket to herself like a shield.

'Did you know Jonis Hendrik?'

A wary nod of the head.

'Did he ever visit Mr Frederiksen?'

Again that nervous bobbed nod.

Larsen leaned forward.

'Can you tell me when and where?'

'A few days ago,' she whispered. 'I was coming in to work early and I saw Jonis closing Mr Frederiksen's front door. Then he walked away very fast.'

'Have you any idea why he had visited Mr Frederiksen?'

'No. But Mr Frederiksen was very angry that morning.'

'Have you ever seen Jonis's wife, Mitti, at Otto Frederiksen's house?'

'Often.'

'Often?'

'Yes.'

'There is a locked room in Mr Frederiksen's house. Do you know anything about it?'

'It is where he and Mitti Hendrik go.'

'Have you seen inside it?'

'No. He always keeps the door locked.'

'Does Mr Frederiksen have other visitors?'

'Business people sometimes, yes. And girls too. But he is often away for weeks, even months. When that happens I am sent home and the house is closed up.'

50

'Do you know where Mr Frederiksen was on Tuesday?'

'He was at his home, working.'

'You are sure?'

'Yes.'

'All day?'

'Yes. I must go now, or he will want to know why I have been so long.'

'Thank you, Margrethe. You have been a great help.'

She bobbed her head again and slipped out.

Larsen was not really sure she had been a help. This haphazard accumulation of information made it hard to separate out what might really be useful. So Otto Frederiksen was almost certainly Mitti's lover, and a liar too. But it did not make him anything more than a liar. He had apparently seen Jonis early one morning, but what of that? Blackmail perhaps, but Larsen was not convinced. There seemed no good basis for sexual blackmail in a town where promiscuity was so common. Sex is never simple, and jealousy and lust and shame are not governed by logic or usage, nonetheless there was little to go on here. Little to go on anywhere.

Over several beers Solomon Rosing had once told him, in a loud pleased-with-himself voice, how he had got his first real journalistic breakthrough: by getting the first-string football reporter blind drunk at lunchtime, then doing the match report himself that afternoon. The story had annoyed Larsen because of Rosing's unashamed pride in his own duplicity. Now it rang differently. Larsen would get Mitti drunk instantly if he thought it would do any good, but he was certain it would not. She would just become silly and flirtatious, laugh a lot, and finally fall to the floor. Without letting slip a hint of what went on within her.

His university tutor had often told him he was too stubborn, too closed to new ideas, but Larsen had never lost his quiet insistence on sticking to his own line of argument. Just now he might be sure of Mitti's guilt, but he was also sure that without evidence he could not shift her denials. Surer in fact, for there was now a small doubt in the former belief. A hiss of interference that set his teeth on edge.

5

VANISHING SUSPECT

By Sunday evening, Larsen's hiss of doubt had grown louder, threatening to blot out all his preconceptions.

There was no question that Jonis had arrived at the seed bank at six on Tuesday morning and left at three that afternoon. He, Olssen, and Gudrun Eistrup had travelled in that morning on the helicopter, talking and joking with Bob, the American pilot. Gudrun had spoken to Jonis later that morning, and seen him again on the way out. So had the second-string pilot, a lean Greenlander named Evat, and Saqaq, the relief worker Evat had flown in.

Larsen had spoken on the telephone to Olssen, without mentioning the affair on the plane, and gathered that Olssen had been flown out at three that afternoon, and gone straight to Cap Gad to catch the flight to Godthab. Jonis had finished his shift at the same time, but he had not got the helicopter back to Sermilik, he had gone hunting. Olssen, Evat and Saqaq all agreed that while it was very unusual for Jonis to go hunting after work, it was not unknown. Lake Tugdlik, where one could find hare, ptarmigan and the occasional duck, was only about forty minutes from the seed bank. From there it was a little over two hours' walk to Sermilik.

Leaving the seed bank around 3 p.m. was the last time Jonis had been seen alive, except by his murderer. But Mitti had been seen by several people in the KGH supermarket that afternoon. The shift at the seed bank had given each other alibis, and Otto Frederiksen had worked at home all day. Which just left Robert Maataq.

When Larsen returned to Maataq's house, he was not there.

'He has gone hunting,' said his wife.

'Where?'

'I do not know.'

'How long will he be?'

'I do not know.'

'Tell me roughly. Three hours? Six hours? A day? What?'

'Sometimes he is away for four weeks.'

'Four weeks!'

'Or more.'

Maataq's wife, fat and contented-looking with a wriggling six-month-old baby in her arms, two small children clutching her legs, and a half-grown boy hovering nearby, waited patiently.

'Did your husband know Jonis Hendrik?' asked Larsen.

'I think so. Ssh, ssh, little one.' She rocked the thickly bundled-up baby to and fro.

'Did he know him well?'

She shrugged.

'Does your husband ... that is ...' There was no easy way to ask. 'Do you think your husband has girlfriends?'

'Men do.'

'You mean your husband does?'

'It is no business of mine.' A thin whining cut the crystal-cold air. 'Ssh, ssh, little one. Do not cry.'

'Was Mitti Hendrik one of his girlfriends?'

'I do not know.' Her face was impassive.

'Has he ever brought her here?'

'He does not bring women home. It can upset the children.'

'Six years ago he killed a man.'

'Yes.'

'What happened?'

'They had an argument over hunting. The man threw a stone at Robert and hit him in the face. Robert shot him.'

'Is your husband very hot-tempered?'

'He has always been kind to the children and to me. I have heard that some men beat their wives, but Robert would never do such a thing. He works hard and is a good husband. I am very lucky to have him.'

On his way through the town, Larsen met the doctor, who hailed him good-naturedly.

'Getting anywhere?'

'Perhaps,' replied Larsen. But his thoughts were elsewhere. 'Do you know of a girl, no, a woman about my age, who lives here, called Jenufa?'

'Jenufa? No. Sorry.'

That evening, outside the door of the hotel bar, two men were urinating against the wall. One of them swayed as he did so, and almost fell. From inside the hot, narrow room came the smells of stale beer, smoke, sweat. At least fifty people were crowded into the claustrophobic space, Danes and Greenlanders, men and women. And every person there was drunk. People sprawled against the bar, shouting at each other over the tables and chairs, building piles of cans, sleeping, being sick, or buying more drink. Girls, perched on men's laps, swallowed cans of beer with the same enthusiasm and speed as their male companions. In one smoky corner five old men were playing cards, but they threw their cards down randomly and paid no attention to what the other players did. Three or four couples were tightly entwined, unconscious of anyone around them. One teenager, flat and motionless on the floor, was repeatedly tripped over by people going to the bar. The television flickered and mumbled in a corner. Larsen tried to remember if things had been any better when there had been Dane-enforced drink rationing. He did not think so.

Familiar faces swam into reluctant focus through the yellow haze. Kalaasi sat alone, smiling as he drank. Kalaasi who had said he was going home to his family for the weekend. Saqaq, Jonis's workmate at the seed bank, was arguing hoarsely with another man. The old gossip Larsen had spoken to at the harbour was sitting and talking, her black button eyes darting round the bar, her bony hand gripping a can of beer, white-knuckled. But nobody was listening to her. The helicopter pilot Evat, wearing an embroidered purple waistcoat, green velvet trousers, and small round blue-tinted glasses, looked like a 1970s hippy, complete with carefully groomed mandarin moustache and pony tail. He was talking with the doctor, and the two of them swayed in perfect time, nodding seriously and making extravagant hand gestures which often hit their neighbours, though no one seemed to notice.

Larsen stood in the doorway for a few minutes, looking for Maataq. As he did so, a man staggered in past him. His foul breath stung Larsen's nostrils, his jeans were unzipped. His eyes saw nothing but the bar.

There was no tension inside, no brewing fights, and much laughter and good nature. But Larsen felt enclosed by an immovable mass of people who were unable to face others, or themselves. People without the initiative or energy to run away, people who could only take shelter under the shadow of alcohol, who sought only the blank peace of stupefaction, of temporary extinction.

As he walked away down the hill Larsen felt as if the universal drunkenness had infected his own mind. He was used to swiftly bringing things together, but now every piece of information he gathered only obscured his certainties. He knew he should call in help. A helicopter search would probably find Maataq within two days. But Larsen had not made the call.

Logic made a simple case of the whole affair, a meeting between Jonis and Maataq, probably accidental, followed by a quarrel. An argument over Mitti perhaps, or over who shot a particular ptarmigan or disturbed a duck the other was stalking. Then the death, so easy when Maataq possessed a hair-trigger temper and the instinctive lethal accuracy of a hunter.

Yet uncertainties buzzed in Larsen's head like summer blackfly. Why had Maataq said the body was cold and growing stiff? What were the marks on Jonis's wrists and ankles? Why had he been stabbed in the back? It came round to the simple fact that Larsen did not believe Maataq had murdered Jonis. When he had killed a man some years earlier, Maataq went straight to the commune Secretary and admitted what he had done. This time he denied the crime vehemently, even growing dangerous when accused. Also he had brought the body back to town, which felt like the action of an innocent man.

At the bottom of the hill the road split into two. One branch led to the helicopter pad, carved out of fjordside rock, the other swung up again into the heart of the town before darting back down to the harbour. Along the second came a group of Greenlanders. In the middle of them Larsen recognised old Elias.

'Where are you going?' Larsen asked. He smiled but his heart sank.

'We're taking grandpa for a drink,' said a girl of about twelve, who was holding Elias's hand.

'Or two,' said Elias. He too was smiling.

'Are your daughter and her family going back to Dove Sund with you?' asked Larsen.

Elias's smile did not change as he was pulled away by the girl. But the middle-aged woman behind laughed.

'God forbid we should go to live there,' she said. 'My father's coming to stay with us. He's getting old and it will be better like that.'

Brief summer twilight half hid the mountains, children ran by in gangs, sledge dogs lumbered around looking for scraps, or lay patiently on the rocks. The rest of Sermilik was in the bars. Unwilling to return to the cold hostile police station, Larsen turned off the road and scrambled over some lichen-stained rocks to a small house. When he knocked at the flimsy outer door, there was no answer. Larsen knocked again, harder.

There was a scuffling noise, then the door opened. Gudrun's pale face seemed even whiter than he remembered.

'What do you want?'

'May I come in?'

Gudrun stared at him.

'It is nearly eleven, Sergeant Larsen.'

'No one sleeps in the summer.'

'I do. I have to be at work at six tomorrow morning.'

'Just a few minutes.' Her very reluctance increased his determination. 'I need some help.'

55

'Tell me about it out here.'

'I'd rather come in.'

'I do not like people in my house late at night. Especially not Sunday night.'

'Because a single Danish girl is often considered an easy lay in Greenland,' Larsen broke in. Shame sent acid burning along his veins. 'Is that what you wished to say? A nice, clean, blond Danish boy would be OK, but Eskimos all get pissed, and then they want to go and screw someone. Isn't that it?'

Tears of rage rose in his throat. He fought to strangle them.

'That is not what I meant – ' began Gudrun.

But Larsen had found his voice afresh.

'You Danskis are all the same. You come and work here, you pride yourself on being fair and kind to us Eskimos . . .' He kept using the word deliberately, as a whip. 'But when it comes down to it, when a filthy Eskimo who pisses against walls and gets drunk and is good for nothing but studying, like a flea in formaldehyde, when such a filthy Eskimo comes and asks for help, Danskis all know there are only two things he wants. A drink or a fuck.'

'You are putting words in my mouth.'

'And words put into your mouth by an Eskimo taste of the cesspit.' Years of silent acceptance went up in flames as Larsen spoke. 'Yet you've put your words into our mouths for centuries. The history of our own country, taught in our schools, by our teachers, is the history of your people: the Vikings, the whalers, the explorers. What was it Shakespeare said, "If you prick us, do we not bleed?" But your people didn't even believe that. Eskimos were trolls, if you cut one, his flesh just turned white. Only when he was killed did the blood flow. And then in great spouts, like a stuck pig. Only when killed did Eskimos become a little human. You are so certain of your supremacy that you do not even realise it any more. Who was the first person to reach the North Pole?'

'Peary – '

'Yes. The all-American hero, Admiral Robert Peary. Everyone knows that. Yet six men reached the Pole together. As well as Peary, there was Matthew Henson, a black man, and four Eskimos – whose names no one remembers, not even their own people. Worse, Peary travelled half the way by sledge, he was dragged to the North Pole by the sweat of a black man and four Eskimos. And he is the one who is remembered!' Larsen laughed. 'There is a photograph of the Peary expedition at the Pole – '

'I know the photograph,' said Gudrun. 'As well as Henson there are four Inuits – Ootah, Seegloo, Egingwah and Ooqueah. They are holding little flags – the Navy League, Peary's college fraternity, the Daughters of the American Revolution. The picture is a caricature of polar exploration.'

Larsen blinked stupidly, as if hit in the face.

'Come in,' said Gudrun, with a sigh.

Like most Europeans Gudrun kept the temperature cooler than Greenland families did, but the room was busy and full. There were paintings and pencil sketches of plants on the walls, as well as a few postcards. Shelves were piled high with books, files and papers. There was a large desk covered with more books and papers, a laptop computer, and assorted pens, pencils and computer disks. A well-read copy of Böcher, Holmen and Jakobsen's *Flora of Greenland* lay open under the desk light.

'Why did you become a policeman?' she asked him, closing the door.

Larsen said nothing and sat down on an old armchair, which creaked and pulled him in deeper than was comfortable.

Gudrun went over to the kitchen area, collected two mugs and a large vacuum flask, and brought them back. Carefully, precisely, she pressed the top of the flask, and filled the mugs with strong black coffee.

'I'm very sorry,' said Larsen. 'I don't know why I said all that. I haven't even been drinking. I'd better go.'

'Have your coffee,' she replied, handing him a mug. She sat down on a hard chair, opposite him. 'Why come to me?'

Embarrassed, Larsen sipped the bitter coffee.

'You're the only person who doesn't live here.'

Her blue eyes stared into his brown ones for a moment, then slipped away.

'I'm from Sermilik,' Larsen went on. 'But I left to go to university in Copenhagen, and I haven't been back here for many years. Now I feel the whole town is united against me, that it has a secret I cannot be allowed to discover. Hostility blocks everything I do, clouds my mind and leaves me confused and doubting, as if the spirits of the place have turned against me.'

'You mean people will not answer your questions?'

'It is not that. Most are helpful, some even come and tell me things, but all the time I am sure they know something that I cannot unfathom.' Larsen tried to regain her gaze. 'I suppose you think I am just a stupid, superstitious Eskimo.'

'Stop using that word. Every time you say it you hurt yourself. No, I don't think you are superstitious. Nearly all East Greenlanders think that West Greenlanders despise them, and discriminate against them.

But there is something else as well, something about Sermilik that wishes to be left alone – to go to hell in its own way.'

'To hell in its own way,' echoed Larsen.

'I think it is that most people know they should leave, but few do. The young and clever, the strong and determined, go – and those who are left are more ashamed and cling closer to what they have. You got away and so that sense is directed in part at you.'

'But why should Sermilik be so different? The towns of the west coast, and even those of the north, Umanak or Upernavik, have their problems, but they are alive, growing, content to be what they are. This is a town with corruption at its very heart.'

Gudrun gazed out of the grimy window for several heartbeats before replying.

'Sermilik is not the real Greenland. It is lost, disconnected from the rest of the country. It has no belief in the future. No hope. And despair brings corruption.'

'What do you mean?'

'Five hundred years ago the last Norsemen in Greenland died. For many years they must have known their end was inevitable, but hemmed in between hostile Inuit tribes, and a frozen sea that thawed only to permit European pirates and slavers to attack them, there was no escape. Archaeology has shown that in those last years they became strange people with strange rites. I think Sermilik is a little like that.'

'That's ridiculous,' objected Larsen. 'We have no enemies, even the ice is retreating. A century ago there were less than a hundred people here. Now – '

'What do you know of the history of Sermilik?' she interrupted.

'There is no real history. It was just a port created by the Danes to use for whaling and exploration.'

'That is not all. A thousand years ago, before Erik the Red settled South-West Greenland, an Icelander named Snaebjorn Galti brought a ship here. They were blocked in by the winter ice, ran short of food, and were finally driven to cannibalism. The few survivors, who did not include Snaebjorn, struggled back to Iceland the next summer, to face vengeance from the relatives of those who had died.'

Gudrun was leaning forward. Her face was intent, concerned.

'We know nothing more until 1884 when a Danish whaling ship took shelter from a storm in Asiaq fjord, and found something very rare – a tribe of Inuit engaged in a blood feud. All the best hunters had been killed, and there was no food.'

Larsen thought of the empty shelves in the supermarket.

'Had the Danes not arrived when they did, there would probably have been no Inuit left in Sermilik. Or within five hundred kilometres.

And when another Danish ship visited a few years later, things were just as bad again,' ended Gudrun.

'What point are you making?'

'A century ago, the whole of the Asiaq fjord complex could barely support a hundred people. Seventy years ago the Danish authorities were so worried by the growth of population that they forcibly moved a third of the people north to Dove Sund. Now over twelve hundred live here. But the seals are going, and most of the fish. There is nothing except a harbour that is only open three months a year, and lost its point when whaling stopped. There are too many people in Sermilik. Many too many. It is that which brings fear to Sermilik. Fear of the inevitable moment when the government says this town is too expensive to keep.'

Only then did Larsen think of the report on Sermilik he had been told to compile. Surely the government wanted it to say just that.

'But what then?' he asked.

'Then they'll evacuate the whole area,' she said simply.

Gudrun pulled out a packet of cigarettes and offered one to Larsen, but he shook his head. She lit one herself and at the same moment Larsen was aware of something he had noticed when he first came in, but had not thought about. A musky smell in the air. A familiar smell.

'You have been smoking cannabis,' he said.

Gudrun said nothing.

'I can smell it,' Larsen persisted.

'Now you know why I didn't want you to come in,' she answered. Suddenly the life had drained out of her.

The sweet, heavy scent was a memory of Larsen's time in Denmark, of long nights, rock music, political discussions. It was being twenty and finding a new world of young people who went to museums and art galleries, watched French films, discussed racism, and thought the world could and must be changed. It was serious, gentle sex, and bursts of uncontrollable laughter. The fragrance raised up a glittering, sharp-edged recollection, and for a moment Larsen was back in Copenhagen, telling a rapt audience of long-haired men and ethnically dressed women what it meant to be an Inuit, and how it made him proud. Then the memory crumbled into dust.

'What are you going to do?' asked Gudrun.

'Give it to me.'

She hesitated.

'I was young once, you know,' he said.

'So was I,' she retorted. 'But it hasn't worn off me as much.'

'I suppose not. Where is the cannabis?'

She reached into the bookshelf and pulled out a small box, which she handed to him. Inside was a piece of black-brown substance a little smaller than the top joint of his thumb. He picked it up and pushed a fingernail into it, but it was hard and dry and old. Larsen smelt it, and back came that rich tapestry of memories, of listening to the blood circulating in his skull, hearing sounds pulse and echo, watching inanimate objects shimmering elegantly in and out of focus, crawling away before his eyes as their colours changed. The smell of youth.

'Is this all you have?' he asked.

'Yes. I brought it with me from Denmark. What are you going to do?'

Larsen's stomach was a void. His skin felt thin and stretched, as if the slightest touch would hurt. It had been on one of those cannabis-soaked nights in Copenhagen that he had met Ann-Marie and they had naïvely, ridiculously, discussed the possibility of revolution in Denmark and in Greenland. Youth is insane, but touching in its insanity. And at least it knows reasons for its own life. Now he was left with only regret for the loss of hope and potential, replaced by emptiness.

He got to his feet, went over to the sink and dropped the lump of cannabis down the plughole, ran the water for a moment, then returned to his chair. Gudrun was kneeling on the rug, watching him. The cigarette trailed smoke through her fingers.

'A woman called Jenufa used to live here,' he said. 'Do you know her?'

'Should I?'

'I don't know.'

Gudrun shrugged, stubbed out the cigarette on a piece of hollowed soapstone, then picked up a tupilak, the carving of a hunter made from a sperm whale's tooth, and stared at it.

'Do you really think there is no future for Sermilik?' said Larsen. 'What about global warming? If the world is heating up, people may be able to graze sheep and ponies here, like around Narssaq in the south.'

'No. Warmer weather will drive away most of the seals, but there is scarcely any soil, and the vegetation cover is so delicate a small herd of sheep would destroy it in five years.'

Her certainty irritated him afresh.

'I suppose, as a biologist, you think Sermilik would be a much better place if it was left to lichens and dwarf willow.'

'I never said that,' objected Gudrun, though without heat.

'But you believe it. Those who wish to conserve nature always consider local people and their hunting as totally destructive. In fact it would be easiest if we Inuit were filed away in a museum, like the seed bank, then we could be referred to when necessary, but would do no harm to mother nature.'

'All I believe is that hunting should be sensible hunting. Harpooning seals was sensible, now people shoot them and three out of four sink to the bottom, and are killed for nothing.'

'Exactly. You want to trap us in a time warp. If we went back to harpoons we would all starve or drown inside a month.'

'Of course. But things can be changed gradually. In parts of the Canadian Arctic the Inuit are returning to a more hunting-based culture, helped by tourism of course, and things are going well. But whatever happens, Sermilik cannot sustain the hunting pressure of twelve hundred people. Even two hundred might be too many until the environment has a chance to recover.'

'So you do think the whole population should be forcibly transported over to the west coast?'

'It is a pretty wretched life for most people here.'

'What has Denmark got that is so wonderful then?' Larsen growled.

'It's the seagulls I miss most,' she said, almost dreamily. 'When I first came here, I thought there would be gulls, not much else, but certainly gulls. There are always gulls by the sea. But not in Sermilik. The distant glimpse of a white wing now and then. That's all.'

'Gulls are good eating.'

'They are good listening,' she said. 'The triumph call of the herring gull, that great long repetitive cry like a wild laugh, is as much the sound of the sea as the crash of waves. When I was a little girl in Roskilde, I used to love that call, it meant summer and swimming, going out in little boats on the fjord, catching crabs and building sand castles. It was the sound of happiness. But you do not hear it here. Not ever.' She glanced at him. 'You've been to Denmark, haven't you? Was it strange for you to see so many birds?'

He smiled, unsure whether he meant it or not.

'It was birds that first made me realise just how rich Denmark is,' he said. 'Not the great buildings of Copenhagen, not the crowds of people in their expensive new clothes, not even the cars everywhere. It was the pigeons. Everyone complains about them, and no one eats them. Hundreds of thousands of meals, but it's far easier to get frozen chicken from a supermarket, and let the pigeons grow fat on the scraps.'

'I don't like pigeons,' she said. 'They're proud and stupid.'

'Do you think Sermilik should be abandoned?' he pressed.

'Proud and stupid,' she repeated. 'And complacent. Like that statue of Frederick V on his horse at Amalienborg. How I hate Frederick V.'

Larsen went over to sit beside her, where she knelt.

'I do not think you hear me.'

'I hear you. I do not listen to you,' she answered.

Larsen hesitated.

'Why are you sad?' he asked at last.

She hid her eyes and turned away. Larsen hesitated, then put his arms round her. She buried herself in his chest and began to cry. He held her for several minutes, feeling her body against his, murmuring soft things, stroking her fine hair, sensing himself soothe her. At last the floodwaters began to subside. Without any particular meaning, he kissed the top of her head.

To his astonishment she raised up her face, red-eyed, blotched from crying, like a child's, with tear stains glistening snail trails on her cheeks. Her mouth was open and she kissed him hungrily, fiercely, breathlessly. Gradually they slipped to the carpet together, entwined, tearing at each other's clothes in silence. The feeling of her soft bare skin, her breasts, her thighs, drove Larsen still harder, and sex was a sharp, rapid wrestling match, writhing, thrusting, disorganised, with first one, then the other on top. It was Larsen's dream of two nights before, enacted in the flesh.

After it was over they lay without talking for a few minutes before taking off the clothes that remained, and making love again, more slowly, more thoroughly, more pleasurably, without that first driving desperation. Enjoying it rather than needing it. And after a steady surging controlled climax, still neither said a word.

Lying on top of her, thinking of nothing, half asleep but also aware of a growing coldness along his back, Larsen heard a rattle at the door. Gudrun swore and pushed him out of her, but it was already too late. Evat, the helicopter pilot, had come in. Then stopped dead.

'You should have locked the door,' he said.

Gudrun was snatching at her clothes, and pulling them on as fast as she could. Larsen followed her example.

'I suppose you were making a few enquiries, sergeant,' said Evat, leaning back against the door, his hands in his pockets. He was about thirty, tall for a Greenlander, thin with high cheekbones and pale skin. His clothes implied that he had more money than other Greenlanders, and his voice was laconic, patronising. 'It is good to know that our policemen are never off duty. It makes me feel so safe. So . . . cared for.'

Gudrun was pulling on a sweater.

'Shut up, Evat,' she snapped. 'It is none of your business.'

'Oh, but it is. Every good citizen needs to be sure that our police are doing their job, and that they are gathering evidence in a legal and proper way.' He paused, then added with sudden iron in his tone. 'And that they are not using their position for their own profit and pleasure.'

Larsen scowled.

'The personal life of police officers is their own.'

'I wonder if that's true when it involves potential witnesses to a serious crime.' Evat's smile was rich with satisfaction. 'Shall we ring up your boss and see what he thinks?'

'Shut up,' said Gudrun again. She turned to Larsen, her voice cold as the mountains. 'Evat is right. You should not be here. You had better go.'

'But – ' he began.

'You used me,' she went on. 'For a few minutes I was glad that you were here. I let you comfort me, and you took advantage of it. It was not fair.'

The words were a savage blow to the stomach, winding him. Furious at how he had been misjudged, Larsen had a sudden desire to arrest her for drug offences. He held himself back, but could not resist a parting shot.

'First remind me where you were last Tuesday, between three and five in the afternoon.'

To his surprise she winced as if he had threatened to hit her.

'She's already told you,' broke in Evat.

'I want her to tell me again.'

'I was at the seed bank,' said Gudrun.

'It was not your shift.'

'I am allowed to use some of their facilities for my own work, so I often stay on when my shift is over.'

'When did you last see Jonis Hendrik?'

'I am not sure.'

Her discomfort was almost tangible, and Larsen had the policeman's instinct to attack any sign of weakness.

'Not sure?'

'This really is an exciting new technique of interrogation,' said Evat sarcastically. 'First fuck the witness, then question them. It requires especially dedicated policemen of course, but – '

'When did you last see Jonis Hendrik, Gudrun?' growled Larsen.

'Sometime before three, I suppose,' she said reluctantly. 'I was analysing data on a transect study of purple saxifrage and I think he came in, but I was working. I do not watch the clock when I am working.'

'How long did you go on working that afternoon? Did you see anyone else? Did you spend the night there?'

Throwing several questions at once was often useful. If nothing else the one people chose to answer could be revealing. But not this time.

'It's all in my statement,' muttered Gudrun. 'Now leave me alone.'

Evat went over to her and put a comforting arm around her shoulders.

'Yes. Go away,' he said.

As Larsen opened the door, he turned back and momentarily caught Gudrun's eye, then left.

'Goodnight,' called Evat after him.

Outside the midnight sun was still behind the mountains, leaving Sermilik in shadow. Heaped on what had happened, Larsen was tormented by the feeling he had been on the edge of an important discovery, and had missed his chance. And he also thought of Gudrun's last glance at him, which had not seemed anything like as hostile as her words.

6

TO THE LAKE

Looking for a short-cut back to the police station, Larsen scrambled over a rock outcrop. He found himself close by another house, and at the same moment a large black-faced husky burst from its kennel, snarling and rattling its chain. Larsen sprang back just in time, and the dog's teeth missed his leg by a hair, ripping open his trousers. As the husky barked wildly and wrenched at its chain, Larsen lost his balance and fell backwards. The dog's owner emerged from his house, took in the situation at a glance and burst out laughing, deep, satisfied, uproarious laughs, as he alternately beat his thighs and clutched his belly.

At last he recovered enough to shout: 'Quiet, Snoopy!'

The dog fell instantly silent and retreated into its kennel.

Larsen picked himself up. The dog's owner gave him a broad smile and retired back inside, still chuckling. Larsen made his way to the road, then looked down ruefully at his ruined trousers.

'Snoopy!' he muttered and shook his head. 'Thank God he was chained.'

Once or twice every year came reports of huskies pulling down and killing children, even unwary adults. Remembering the animal's massive jaws and powerful shoulders, Larsen shuddered.

As he stood in the road, recovering himself, the door of Gudrun's house opened, and Evat emerged.

'Were you waiting for me, sergeant?' he called lightly. 'A few questions perhaps? Should we go back to my place?'

'Do you think I behaved badly?' asked Larsen, falling into step with him.

Evat looked surprised.

I don't think I know the answer to that,' he said bluntly 'It is for you to decide.'

'I didn't plan it. It just happened.'

Evat stopped, turned to Larsen and put his hand on the policeman's shoulder. His face was quick and intelligent.

'If you think you need forgiveness, it's not up to me to give it to you,' he said. 'Not even up to Gudrun. Only you can do it. No one else can help you, sergeant.'

'That is what everyone seems to be saying to me,' replied Larsen.

'Perhaps because we're right. But don't worry too much, what's past help should be past grief. Or to put it another way, since there's no help, come let us kiss and part.'

Larsen stared at him. But Evat laughed.

'It's a quote,' he explained. 'Michael Drayton, an old English poet. Goodnight, sergeant.'

He gave an easy smile, and walked away towards the harbour.

Although it was into the small hours, Larsen did not feel tired. After listening to the howls of a few dogs and occasional shouts from outside the closed bars, he turned and walked up the hill to Otto Frederiksen's house. The front door was locked. That would have been remarkable in most of Greenland, but Larsen had already discovered that petty theft was endemic in Sermilik. Those who did not lock their doors probably had nothing they cared about losing, or else were too drunk to remember.

Glancing behind him, he saw two figures approaching the house, and hurriedly retreated into the shadows. The maid, Margrethe, was arm in arm with a man. As they came to the door, they stopped and kissed. At last she pushed him away.

'No more,' she whispered. 'Go home.'

'But – '

'Go home or Mr Frederiksen will hear us.'

'Just one more goodnight kiss, my little fox.'

'No.'

Reluctantly the man slouched away. Margrethe pulled out some keys then, as she opened the door, Larsen darted round the corner.

'Ssh,' he said, before she had time to protest. 'It's me, Sergeant Larsen. Is Frederiksen home?'

'Do you wish to see him?'

'I don't wish him to see me.'

She seemed unsurprised.

'I will go and look.'

Larsen closed the front door and waited for her in the dark hall. At last she came back.

'He is upstairs,' she breathed. 'In his locked room.'

'Alone?'

'He is never alone in that room. I am going to bed.'

Margrethe slid away into the gloom. Larsen felt oddly deserted, as if he had been relying on her and she had let him down.

The stairs were well made of pine and did not creak as he padded softly up them. At the top he looked right and saw a knife-slash of light under the mysterious door. He crept over and listened, but only

66

heard a soft murmur of conversation broken by occasional laughter.
After a moment he went into a bathroom, where grey pre-dawn light
through the frosted window showed him what he was looking for.
Having removed a toothbrush, he took the glass back to the door and
put his ear to it.

The voices became more distinct.

'No, not there. Higher. Yes, higher. That's better. That's much better.'
A muffled voice, perhaps a woman's, perhaps not.

There was a sigh. Then another. Then silence. Larsen scowled. It was
disappointing to discover the obvious, that the locked room was where
Otto Frederiksen performed his sex acts.

'It's me. Me now.' That was surely Frederiksen, though his voice
was breathy, staccato, distorted.

'You can wait,' said the first voice lazily.

'No. No. I will not. I cannot.'

'Oh dear. Cannot.' There was a giggle.

'Please.'

'What do I get if I agree?'

'We have agreed.'

'That was then. This is now.'

'But – '

'What if I just go home?'

'You would not dare.'

'Are you sure?'

At that moment something touched Larsen's leg.

He had been concentrating totally on what he was listening to, and
the shock of feeling something alive nestle up against him was stupen-
dous. He started back, almost fell, and dropped the glass. It hit the
door handle, then smashed on the floor, but he was already darting
away, leaping down the stairs and out of the front door. As he fled
light flooded the house behind him and he heard raised voices.

Running down the road, Larsen realised what had wrecked his
spying mission. A cat. A cat that had wound itself between his ankles,
purring. He felt aggrieved. Who would have guessed that anyone in
Sermilik was insane enough to keep a cat? Quite aside from the eight
months of deep snow, if even a whisker appeared outside the door,
the animal would surely be torn to pieces by Sermilik's ubiquitous
huskies. Yet it had certainly been a cat.

When Larsen got back to the police station he sat on the bed for a
long time, his head in his hands, feeling shame at his behaviour that
night. Eventually he painstakingly darned his trousers – he only had
two pairs with him and this was the better one – then went to bed.
When he fell asleep he dreamt of familiar faces calling out, 'Tomas,

Tomas!' in booming tones and laughing as they chased him over sliding ice floes. He woke with relief.

A shifting white skycloth of mist had closed in about the town, hanging from the mountains, and pressing Sermilik down on its barren brown rock. Larsen put on his warmest clothes and slipped some food into his pockets. At the door he met Kalaasi. Smiling as usual.

'Any news?' asked Larsen.

'About what?'

'About anything. The air strike. The seed bank. I don't know.'

Again Kalaasi smiled, but this smile had a different emphasis, helplessness rather than recognition.

'No,' he said.

'Does anyone know where Robert Maataq has gone hunting?'

'No.'

'I had a strange feeling that he might have run away,' continued Larsen. 'Or even that he might be dead.'

Kalaasi shook his head.

'Robert Maataq is the best hunter in Sermilik.'

Larsen scratched his chin. The patchy stubble was thickening again.

'I'd like to visit the place where Jonis's body was found. Could you take me there?'

'Yes, sir.' The 'sir' seemed thrown in as an accidental afterthought. Kalaasi began to lead the way along the road. 'It is quite a common place to go searching for ptarmigan.'

'I thought you said Maataq is the best hunter in Sermilik.'

'He is.'

'Then why should he go hunting in a place everyone knows?'

'It is not like that,' said Kalaasi. The smile had gone, and he spoke with more life and intensity than Larsen had yet heard in him. 'A man who is not a real hunter may go to a lake and he will sit there all day, as still as he can, and he will see maybe a karsak swimming deep in the water and one or two kordlutok, and he will think he has done well. But the good hunter will see much more. Perhaps agdlek duck are nesting on a scrubby hummock some way from the lake, or a harlequin is diving in a meltwater stream watched by a hidden fox. A little safarsuk sandpiper may run along the shore in a flash, a phalarope spin round picking mosquitoes off a tiny pool. Hunting is knowing when to go and when not to go, it is feeling the weather in your bones and skin, knowing whether the birds or the hares or the foxes will come out on that day, at that time, in that place. It is sensing the movement of reindeer and following them with your inner eye when they are twenty kilometres away. A hunter must touch the soul

68

of nature, and read what is written there, then he will know what to do, where to go, how long to stay, which way to look.'

Kalaasi stopped as suddenly as he had started. But Larsen looked at him with different eyes, realising that the young man came from a community of true hunters. And that to him hunting was the greatest thing a man could do. In much of Greenland hunters were regarded as men who were too old-fashioned to make a living some other, easier way. They came into town and spent their tiny profits on drink because they were fools, willing to suffer the beatings of the weather, to risk their lives constantly, for a pittance. Yet the values of Europe and America has not yet obliterated a sense deep in the Arctic psyche, that a hunter was a man who demanded admiration. So, even on the main streets of the capital, the broad-faced, frost-scarred old men with battered rifles slung on their backs were treated cautiously, and people were contemptuous about them only behind their backs and in quiet voices. In Sermilik the wilderness was closer, and hunters still carried the faded glory of the past.

'So Maataq could go to a place where other men had been, and he would find things no one else had?'

'Of course. It does not matter if the right place is a week's journey away, or outside his door, the good hunter will know. Two autumns ago Maataq shot a young natsek seal in Sermilik harbour as he stood and talked. None of the other men so much as glimpsed the seal, but he killed it with one shot.'

Past the lower edge of the town, Larsen and Kalaasi came to the cemetery. A bouquet of plastic flowers, a simple wooden cross, and a mound of earth and snow close by a small stream marked the freshly dug grave of Jonis Hendrik. Permafrost meant the grave was scarcely deep enough to cover the coffin. The winter had taken its accustomed toll, and there were other new graves nearby. Beyond the cemetery they continued along the west side of the fjord.

Kalaasi walked with an easy, loping stride that covered the rough ground with little energy, never missing a step among the sudden rises and falls, the frost and snowfields, the hidden patches of thawing bog. In contrast Larsen had to pick his way forward with caution. He slipped several times and his thick woollen trousers were soon spattered with snow and mud.

Although the mist had lifted a little, it took them the best part of an hour to reach the head of that branch of the fjord. Ahead snow-cloaked mountains loomed high and forbidding, their tops still hidden. Closer, blocking the way, was a river. Where the river met the frozen fjord there was a large area of open water, grey with mud, sand and debris brought down from the mountains, fringed by cracked and rotten ice. The ground close by was snow-free, swelling out in a rolling shallow slope, splashed with the colours of life, green, red, yellow. As they got closer, Larsen saw it was a field of rich-coloured lichens, deep and spongy, with open water lurking beneath the matted surface.

Higher up, on drier ground, stood a faded orange tent.

'Whose is that?' Larsen enquired.

'Visitors,' said Kalaasi, who usually seemed to know the answer, although he rarely volunteered information. 'English, I think. There are two of them. A man and a girl.'

'It is a very small tent. What are they here for?'

'A few people come every year. For the climbing perhaps, or just to see the country.'

Larsen went over to the tent, but it was zipped shut and obviously empty. Larsen wondered how the campers could be sure their possessions would not be stolen. Kalaasi was already striding along by the river, which was flowing in full spate, carrying ice floes with it. Larsen hurried after him.

Gradually the ground became more and more snowy. Occasional streams came down to join the main river, but there were also many small lakes and ponds still frozen hard and frosted with a cover of snow over the ice. On the far side of the river the ground reared up steeply to hidden peaks. Behind them the fjord had vanished, hidden by rolling ground and shreds of mist. Ahead also the mountains were rising.

'Did you know Jonis?' asked Larsen.

'We drank together now and then.'

'Did he drink a lot?'

'No more than others.'

'What was his temper like?'

'He grew angry sometimes.'

Larsen felt as if he was pushing against a door, and when it opened he went through and found himself outside again.

'Why do you think he was murdered?'

'Perhaps he was not murdered,' said Kalaasi vaguely.

'Men do not get stabbed in the back by accident.'

'My grandfather went out in a kayak one day. Next day they found the kayak upside down, with my grandfather underneath, frozen hard and still gripping the paddle, held in by the sealskin apron. Everything was still perfectly stored – the three harpoons, the bladder buoy, the ice chisel. Everything except his rifle, which was not there. There was a hole in the kayak, and a deep wound in my grandfather's right leg. It looked like a killing, but in fact his rifle must have gone off by

70

accident, holing the kayak and wounding him in the leg, then falling into the sea. My grandfather tried to paddle back to the shore, but did not make it. That was an accident.'

It occurred to Larsen that it might have looked exactly the same if someone really had shot Kalaasi's grandfather.

'This could not have been an accident,' he said impatiently. 'Jonis had been stabbed in the back, the knife had disappeared, and there were marks on his hands and legs and mouth as if he had been tied and gagged.'

'Stabbing in the back is a woman's crime,' said Kalaasi.

'It would also be a good way to make people think a woman had done it. And there is something else, no one can remember seeing Jonis with a gun that day, and no gun was found by his body.'

'Someone must have stolen it.'

'I was told Jonis did not have a gun of his own, and used his father's.'

'Yes.'

'But that is still in their house. So it seems Jonis went hunting without a gun and wearing very thin clothes.'

'He should not have gone hunting.'

'Or he did not go hunting.'

Kalaasi's expression broke up for a moment and he almost frowned.

'He told people he was going hunting.'

'Because he did not want anyone to know what he was really doing.' Larsen paused and looked at Kalaasi, whose suddenly intent face seemed like an expression of Larsen's own doubts. 'You are thinking that there is nothing to do, nowhere to go on foot from the seed bank, except hunting, or back to Sermilik.'

'I was not thinking that,' said Kalaasi.

'What were you thinking?'

'There is a ptarmigan up there, on the scree. And I too forgot my gun.'

Larsen stared, but saw only grey stones and white snow. Kalaasi was already creeping round the edge of the hillside, cautiously, noise-lessly, making his way upwards. The stolid smiling young man had transformed himself, his body seemed to have become leaner, longer, predatory. He moved smoothly, gracefully, rippling over loose stones without dislodging one, picking his way delicately but quickly, cat-like. Gradually he ducked down lower and lower until he was almost bent double, yet still making rapid progress. At last he slowed down, approaching his prey. Again Larsen scanned the area of hillside Kalaasi was homing in on, and still saw nothing.

Kalaasi's head and body were scarcely moving, only his legs slipped

71

back and forth and his arms hung down, loose, poised, ready to strike. Abruptly a fat greyish bird with pure white wings exploded away from the ground just in front of Kalaasi, and flew off over the curve of the slope, round wings beating rapidly then curving to glide, its large body and small head silhouetted against a snowfield. Kalaasi slipped over to where the bird had risen, looked around, then came trotting easily back down the hillside.

'A careless bird,' he said. 'Someone will kill it soon. It is always the same, come out without a rifle and the game will ignore you.'

'Have you ever caught a bird like that?' asked Larsen. 'With your hands?'

'Once. And many times I have found nests, but that was a male.'

Further up the valley the river took a sharp turn to the north and burst through a steep ridge, the terminal moraine of some huge ancient glacier, in a thundering waterfall. Amidst the water that crashed down the cataract fell ice floes, shattering at the bottom or gathering, bumping and jostling, in a shallow open pool cut by back-currents.

Kalaasi climbed the ridge, and Larsen followed, panting.

The view that met his eyes was impressive. Great mountainsides swelled up north, east and west. Down their precipitous slopes crawled the long white tongues of glaciers, most withering into leaping streams before they reached the valley floor. Confined by mountains and the ridge they had just climbed, lay an oval valley, perhaps three kilometres wide and two or three times that long. It was filled by a string of gently curving, linked lakes, interspersed with rocky bluffs and outcrops from the mountains. Although the lakes were still largely frozen, a line of open water marked the main flow of the river, which burst down shallow rapids between the lakes.

Kalaasi was already striding down the far side of the ridge, past a sheltered sandy beach and a low thicket of scrub Arctic willows close to the waterside.

Their way lay by the shores of the first lake, then along a wide rugged ridge that rose up like the backbone of the valley. After three-quarters of an hour's stiff walking, they approached the end of the now-tapering ridge. At its final headland, on a south-facing slope, some birches had, over the slow decades, clawed their way up to over a metre high, though the tallest parts of the bushes looked dead. The last and by far the biggest of the lakes swung round in a great horseshoe, almost surrounding the high promontory they stood on. On its far shore, near a tall waterfall that came arching in a free fall after a hectic tumble down the mountainside, there was a col between two mountains, a narrow saddle only a couple of hundred metres above the floor of the lake, and below the ceiling of mist.

'Is that where we're going?' Larsen demanded suspiciously.

'If you like.'

Larsen did not want to cross the lake ice. In winter it would have been easy, but now in late spring it was surely dangerous, especially considering the amount of open water he could see.

'Why didn't we go round the far side?' he asked.

'You wanted to come here,' said Kalaasi. He pointed to a small shadowed snowfield in a depression. 'That is where Jonis's body was found.'

The snow was tumbled and broken, with a few faint brownish stains that could have been made by anything. In places the underlying ground jutted out. Larsen scrambled down, looked around, then climbed back out.

'Have you been here before?'

'It is a good place for watching the north end of Lake Tugdlik.'

'Would you say it was a good place to commit murder?'

Kalaasi looked uncomfortable.

'I do not know. I suppose not. Hunters come here quite often.'

'That makes it a bad place to leave a body, but the hollow is very well hidden. Whoever killed Jonis went to great lengths to make sure they were not seen and could not be caught. But they did not bother to hide the only piece of evidence which proved there had been a murder at all: the body. It would have been easy to weigh the body down, then roll it into the lake, where it probably wouldn't have been found for weeks, if at all. So why wasn't it done? Or if the killing was an accident, why not admit it?'

'I don't know.'

'Exactly.' Larsen sighed. 'Where is the seed bank?'

'Through there,' said Kalaasi, pointing ahead to the saddle.

'How far?'

'If we cross the lake, less than an hour. If we go back and round the side of the valley, then twice that. Perhaps more with the glacier streams in spate.'

'I suppose we had better cross the lake,' said Larsen reluctantly. 'Is it safe?'

Kalaasi shrugged.

'All right,' said Larsen. 'I know. One can never be certain.'

He turned away and took a few steps down the hillside, then stopped as a spout of snow burst up a few metres from him. Larsen looked at it in surprise. He could not think what had caused it. A lemming burrowing? A bird? Or was it some strange phenomenon of the thaw? There was a small hole where the snow fountain had come from.

Larsen turned to ask Kalaasi what was happening, but his companion had disappeared. The same moment a piece of rock close to his left leg cracked and splintered, and there was an unpleasant whining sound.

Only then did Larsen realise he was being shot at.

7

RIFLE SHOTS

Larsen threw himself to the ground behind a rock and waited for the next shot. Seconds became minutes and nothing broke the silence.

'Kalaasi,' he hissed at last. Then louder. 'Kalaasi.'

There was no answer.

'Kalaasi!'

Larsen hesitated then peered over the edge of the rock in front of him. He could not see anyone. Surely Kalaasi could not have been killed in complete silence? But then where was he? And where was the gunman? Creeping closer? Running away? Waiting? He was not even sure from what direction the shot had come. Again he peered out from his shelter, scanning across the lake then round behind, and finally along the ridge.

Treacherous peace lay over the valley.

At last Larsen resolved to run for the hollow where Jonis's body had been found. In the middle of his fear, another question flashed through the policeman's mind. How did he know Jonis had been found there? The only evidence came from Robert Maataq, who had disappeared.

The thought passed and was stored away. Someone out there was armed with a high-powered rifle, and knew almost exactly where he was. For the first time Larsen found himself cursing the fact that he did not much like guns, and had left his own back in Sermilik, among his clean clothes. He took a deep breath, sprang up and ran as fast as he could to the hollow. No shot broke the silence. The hollow itself was empty.

After recovering his breath, Larsen put his head up to have another look. Nothing. Perhaps he should try to get away across the lake. If Kalaasi had been telling the truth, it was not very far to the seed bank. On the other hand he would have to cross the lake ice which was probably unsafe, and would make him an easy target from almost any distance, neatly silhouetted against the gleaming white. And he could not wait for night, there was none. Furthermore crossing the lake ice, or staying where he was, gave him no realistic chance of finding out who was trying to murder him, or what had happened to Kalaasi.

The decision was made. He would work his way slowly back the way they had come, even though the gunman was probably on the ridge too, so he would be walking straight towards his enemy.

Darting quickly from one spot of shelter to another, keeping low, dodging unpredictably from side to side, trying to run as a snipe flies, he set off to retrace his steps. It was hard work, for his body was built for endurance not speed, but he heard no more shots, saw nothing moving except a black-winged raven flapping unhurriedly on its lonely way.

It is difficult to keep up a sense of urgency when no threat appears. Larsen's darting runs between cover grew longer and slower, his dodging less sudden and less frequent. Soon he was scarcely more than trotting, wondering if he could have imagined the whole thing. He was now two-thirds of the way along the ridge, and close beside him a rocky tor rose above the surface of the lake. Breathing heavily, Larsen clambered up to the vantage point. His eyes began to water as he screwed them up and scanned one section of the valley, then another, then another. At last he glimpsed a flash of movement on the far side of the ridge, where it sank and narrowed towards the edge of the second lake. Gradually Larsen realised he was looking at Kalaasi.

The young policeman was crouched, crawling, not unlike the way he had stalked the ptarmigan, smoothly flowing from one rock to another. Larsen realised Kalaasi must have ducked down the moment the first shot had been fired, then immediately set off back along the ridge, taking in a second the decision he himself had spent ten minutes over, and keeping under cover all the way. Kalaasi's quick reactions had probably saved Larsen's life also, stopping the gunman from firing until he – or could it be a she? – could see both victims at once.

Looking ahead, by a tall rock with some tangled willow scrub at its foot, Larsen suddenly glimpsed a darkness. A shadow where no shadow should be. And it was towards the shadow that Kalaasi was advancing. Larsen wondered if he should do something, but the shadow was less than two hundred metres away, a fairly easy shot with a good hunting rifle. And Kalaasi might already know exactly where the gunman was. Larsen ducked back into cover. Uncertainty flailed his mind. If he did nothing, then the gunman would not move, which might be what Kalaasi wanted. After all, he was the hunter, and stalking was his skill. Warily Larsen peered through a crack in the rock.

The shadow still lay under the rock, with scrub on the left and a small drop on to the lake ice to the right. There must be a perfect view over the whole eastern half of the valley, though the slope of the ridge probably interrupted vision of the far side of the valley, and of a small strip along the shore – the very place where Kalaasi was edging forward. Ahead of Larsen's tor lay a low curving area of small broken rocks, snowdrifts, frozen pools and gravel banks, with no cover worth the name. A perfect killing ground.

Kalaasi had reached the very brink of the lake. Several deep gullies and a ragged outline of scars and overhangs provided good cover, but made his progress slow and dangerous, constantly threatening a fatal slip or stumble. And the dark shadow remained where it was, motionless, waiting, a spider confident in its web.

Agonisingly Kalaasi crept closer, slithering over obstacles like a snake, vanishing into hidden recesses to emerge unexpectedly a few metres further on. Larsen found something hypnotic about his advance, relentless yet breathless, taut with danger. It was not just that Larsen's own life surely rested upon him, it was the underlying certainty that Kalaasi could not succeed. That he could not surprise the killer, and was about to slip to his death.

Suddenly, clearly audible even to Larsen, there came a rattle of stones. Kalaasi instantly ducked out of sight. But when Larsen looked back, a cold shudder ran down his spine. For the shadow under the rock seemed also to have gone. A moment later two quick-fired shots lashed the air. The first whined away into emptiness, the second burst ear-splittingly on the rock close by Larsen's head, and simultaneously he felt sharp pain just below his left eye. He wrenched himself back into shelter and put his hand to his cheek. It came away smeared with fresh blood. Further investigation showed he had been lucky, it was little more than a deep scratch, though it stung savagely in the cold air. Larsen bit his lip and wiped away some of the blood, then crawled to another, safer, viewpoint.

There was nothing to be seen. No gunman. No Kalaasi. Just the desolate landscape roofed by mist, thick with menace. Again and again Larsen thought he caught glimpses of movement out of the corner of his eye, but when he looked there was nothing there. Somewhere the gunman must be searching the rough, tumbled ground in which Kalaasi had fallen. But there was still nothing he could do to help, for any attempt to cross those bare lethal metres in front of him would be suicide.

Gradually Larsen crawled along the rocky height until he came to an open slope. It was steep and in plain view, but if he could cross it safely there was cover lower down. Larsen poised himself, counted to five, then sprang from his hiding-place and half leapt, half ran into the open. Two more shots rang out, quiet like all the shots had been, but clear as screams in the still air. How close they came Larsen neither knew nor cared. He sped down the dusty incline, dived into shelter, and quickly began making his way towards the lake shore.

His heartbeat echoed in his head, his breath was raspingly loud, but he was beginning to feel encouraged. The gunman had had several shots at him and had not made one count. Furthermore, with Larsen now on one side of him and Kalaasi on the other, the gunman must be beginning to feel nervous, outnumbered and continually wasting chances. The tight, all-embracing fear, constantly near the edge of panic, that dominates the hunted creature began to leave Larsen. And for a moment he sensed, like a fleeting fragrance, the hungry, focused adrenalin of the hunter.

He scrambled down to the shore and ran along the narrow strip of grey and yellow-streaked sand until he found a damp, black overhang. Catching his breath, he crept on under the overhang. The sand petered out and he was forced on to the lake ice, but here by the shore it was solid enough and a sprinkling of driven snow made it easy to find a foothold. As the overhang faded away Larsen pressed himself as close as he could to the bluff that replaced it. Ahead lay another long beach of glacial sand with no cover at all.

The silence was broken again by the piercing whip-crack of a rifle shot, but this was much louder, much closer. Within a few metres. It was repeated twice more in rapid succession. Then came a crunch of boots on gravel.

'At last,' came a muffled voice.

Splayed against the rock face, Larsen dared not move, dared not breathe. If the gunman took just a few steps and looked over the edge, he would see Larsen, out of reach but within the sort of range that offered no possibility of missing. Larsen closed his eyes and waited. Was that the gunman's breath, or his own? Still he could not move, then came the crunch of boots again, close above his head. But they were gradually moving away. Larsen opened his eyes. His head was whirling.

A thin cold wind had blown up and was pushing rags of cloud and mist before it. Gazing out over the lake, Larsen noticed the light worsening as the curtain of mist dipped lower and lower.

Mist is never an unmixed blessing. It provides cover for the prey, but also for the predator. And if Larsen knew that the best way to escape without getting lost was to follow the river, so did the gunman. Fog would give Larsen a chance to cross the open beach ahead, but it was at least two hours back to Sermilik, more in the poor light. Even if his enemy was not waiting somewhere in ambush, Larsen had a hell-born vision of himself stumbling blindly through the fog, lost, driven on only by the knowledge that somewhere close behind him an armed killer was on his trail. The lake offered a clearer possibility of escape. If he could cross it without being seen, then he would be clean away.

Better still, if Larsen got to the seed bank quickly enough, he might be able to come back with reinforcements and catch the killer. Carefully he drew an arrow in the snow with his foot, showing which way he must go to cross the lake.

Fog rolled ponderously down the hillsides like a great tidal wave, and suddenly the valley sank into a damp featureless world of muffled grey. Larsen glanced at his arrow, then set off with the distant roar of the waterfall on his right.

The lake was hard-frozen around its edges and he walked quietly over the ice, stopping every few yards to try to ensure that the track of his footprints in the powder snow was straight, then doing his best to brush away the prints. In good light Larsen's trail would have been unmistakable, but if the gunman did see it, the confusions of mist might prevent him realising what it was.

After perhaps a hundred metres the powder snow ceased. At first Larsen was pleased for it meant he could move faster and leave no tracks. But the lack of snow meant the ice was beginning to thaw, and gradually Larsen's footsteps began to creak and he could feel movement. More alarming still, he could hear the sound of running water.

Advancing cautiously, testing each step before he took it, he became aware that the wind was blowing more strongly and the light had improved. Ahead of him, the stifling greyness was gone and the valley opened out again. Larsen saw he was well past the middle of the lake, but ahead of him the river, swinging left, had cut a swathe twenty metres wide through the ice. From the shore he had not thought it half as broad. All around him were cracks in the ice with water glistening through them.

As he hesitated there came the ever-more familiar sound of a shot. He spun round. The mist had lifted behind as well as in front, and he was clearly visible from the ridge. A second shot and the whine of a bullet. A third. Larsen began to run, trying to jump so that he straddled the cracks and landed only where the ice was still thick and opaque. It worked until he had almost reached the open water. Then, with a splitting crack, the sheet of ice he landed on detached itself, and was swept away by the river. Larsen fell to his knees as the ice swayed and tipped, revolved and rolled from side to side. Two more shots rang out and ice splintered within a metre of him. Larsen crouched down flat and covered his head.

Rotating faster and faster, the ice floe was carried down the river at gathering pace. After a few moments Larsen looked up. The gunman was a dense black shape, striding purposefully along the beach. A momentary wash of relief told Larsen his enemy was giving up, then the relief died. The lake was narrowing and the river was sweeping

Larsen towards its far end. If the gunman reached the outflow first, as he clearly would, then he could lie in wait for Larsen and squeeze off a volley of shots at point-blank range. And even if by some freak he missed, beyond the outflow lay the waterfall.

Fifty metres up the mist rolled as thickly as ever, circling and twisting and floating down towards the ground in unpredictable pillars and veils. But Larsen dared not bet his life on it descending again. And there was only one alternative.

As he plunged into the river and kicked out for the opposite shore, there was a moment when he thought it would be easy. Then the cold struck. The air exploded from his lungs in a scream of shock and he disappeared underwater. Desperately he lashed his numbing legs, shot back to the surface, knocking aside some brash ice, then hurled himself towards the far shore. The river was flowing fast, fighting to carry him away or suck him under the ice that encompassed it, but by expending every rag of his strength Larsen managed to flounder to the ice that fringed the far edge of the open water. As he grabbed at it, the ice broke in his bloodless hands and he began to drift downstream again. Towards the waiting gun.

Wildly, panicking, Larsen clutched out again and again, and every time the ice cracked and broke. His torn cheek was sending shafts of white stinging pain through him, and he could no longer feel his arms or legs as his sodden clothes dragged him down. He snatched at the ice again, trying to kick himself up on to it as a seal does, but again it cracked and his face dipped underwater, his mouth filling up with supercooled water. The life was being frozen from his body, but this time the creaking, shuddering ice did not split clean away, and he was able to throw himself further up on to it. Every second he was certain it would break beneath him, but gradually, sliding on his stomach, he wriggled himself clear of the water.

Distantly, as if through a long tunnel or a distorted loudspeaker, Larsen heard repeated sounds. He could not think what they were, though he knew that he should recognise them, that they were important. Overwhelming tiredness lay over him. Oddly he did not feel cold any more, although he was dimly aware of his clothes hanging wet and heavy around him, and his violently shivering body. In fact warmth seemed to be seeping into him from outside, from the ice on which he lay.

Deep in Larsen's brain a faint alarm was ringing furiously. A small voice cried out that he was in danger, that he must get up and get away. He sat apart from the voice, listening calmly to it and ignoring it, but he knew he must either silence it by letting go completely and drifting into the comforting blackness that invited him, or else obey it. For a timeless moment he did neither, enjoying the sensation of being perfectly balanced between two desires.

What brought him out of inertia he did not know. One minute Larsen lay contentedly on the ice, the next a shaft of despair stabbed through him, carrying with it a cold terror that was pain in itself. He wrenched himself up on to his knees and looked about, but saw nothing. He was shivering in a black world. Suddenly convinced he had gone blind, Larsen staggered to his feet and clawed at his face with hands that felt like dead meat, hanging uselessly at the end of long stupid arms. The blackness faded to greyness. Larsen could see, but there was nothing to see.

Lurching forward, he slipped and fell jarringly on to the swaying ice. It was a hard fall that left him half stunned, sprawling, as glittering lights rotated in his skull, occasionally exploding with soundless bursts of pain. As he recovered himself, memory crept back into his befuddled mind. He realised that the sound he had heard earlier had been the gunman shooting at him, and that he was no longer under fire because the mist had returned. The moment that thought completed its passage, another came. If the mist had come down to save his life, it might just as easily lift and betray him again.

Larsen got back to his feet and began to hurry towards the far shore. The fog swirled around him, thinning a little, then rolling in thicker than ever. Gradually the ice grew more solid. He tried to walk faster, but slipped and fell several times. Just as a black doubt grew that he had lost his bearings, and was circling back over the lake, he saw the welcome sight of rocks and a steep shore. He scrambled up on to the solid land and sat down, gasping for breath.

Within a minute he was standing again. Stillness brought with it unendurable cold. His wet clothes hung around him like great body-crushing chains, sapping his energy, driving nails of cold into his shrinking body as they stiffened and threatened to turn to ice.

In desperation Larsen began to run. As he ran he could sense blood begin to pump back into the outlying parts of his body. His feet ceased to feel like unconnected weights, even his hands came back to life. For a few hundred metres the sensation of running was a joy, a return to life. But the ground was hard, broken, sloping steeply and spattered with slippery snow. Larsen's body complained at the punishment being laid upon it, overbearing even his will, and soon he found himself driven to walking again. As he walked as fast as he could, along the shore, fresh worries flung themselves at him: if the mist remained thick it would be impossible to see the col in the hills through which Kalaasi had said the seed bank lay. And where was Kalaasi? Murdered? The growing certainty drove fresh fear down Larsen's throat.

Walking briskly was not unpleasant, for a while. He was travelling fast enough to keep most of his body warm – though not as warm as when he had been running – and he seemed to be covering the ground quickly as he tracked the side of the lake. Yet gradually the cold wind, like a creeping disease, started to insert its long claws back into him. So he ran again, running on and on, until air was screaming in his raw throat and his legs were staggering. At last he stopped to recover his breath, but the onset of the cold soon forced him to continue.

So it went on. But the times when Larsen could walk grew shorter and shorter, and he was driven to run more and more – just to keep warm. It was not until, gasping and tottering, he had to rest for a few minutes despite the ever-deepening cold, that he remembered an old Inuit saying: 'The man who falls in the sea then runs home is a dead man.' Running may warm you, but it causes sweat so your clothes do not dry, and the sweat grows cold on your skin and weakens you. Every time you stop running, you grow cold more quickly than the last time. So you must run more and more, and you must run faster and faster. You are caught in a spiral of destruction until exhaustion pulls you down and you never rise again. If it had not been summer the sweat would probably already have frozen on his body and he would have collapsed into exposure. Nonetheless he could sense his energy trickling away.

As this nightmare of having to run or die grew upon Larsen, so phantoms gathered in the all-enveloping mist. Somewhere out there was the gunman, searching. Searching with only one intention – to kill. As he must have killed Kalaasi. Kalaasi's shape too seemed to hide behind the mist, occasionally half appearing before Larsen or drifting accusingly on the edge of sight.

A second wind came to Larsen and for a little he ran faster and further, then it faded and his body drooped and shivered. A third wind took him only a little way before it too ran dry and left him tottering towards prostration as he circled the hostile lake shore, where every rock seemed an enemy, every stream a man-trap. At last the ground began to rise and Larsen climbed while below him cliffs plummeted ever steeper.

A sound had broken the silence, a sound he must have been hearing for some time before he became aware of it above the gasping of his breath and the thudding of his tortured heart. A dull steady roar. The sound of a waterfall. Despair took control of his mind. He must have run right round the valley and come back to the falls where the river issued from the lakes. And the waterfall would be guarded by the man with a gun. Only gradually did he realise that he had not been going for anything like long enough to travel that great circumference, and there was a waterfall at the north end of the lake also. The waterfall which marked where he was to leave the valley.

He scrambled on with a return of hope, moving so much faster he almost stumbled headlong into the deep-cut ravine that held a fierce white-water stream, leaping and foaming towards the cascade. Recovering himself he turned right, away from the lake. The mist was thicker than ever as Larsen climbed, and he was forced to go slowly among the crags and crevasses, while cold battled in from his extremities.

Not daring to cross the stream, Larsen made his way up the lofty hanging valley as best he could. It was hard going, and in many places he was driven to crawl on his hands and knees. Somewhere he had lost his gloves, and as he climbed the precipitous, frost-cracked scarp, he clung with his numb fingers, even his nails. Larsen knew it was dangerous to follow a river through mountains, for water will always find the quickest way down, and that means the steepest. But in mist and unknown country, too cold and exhausted to retrace his steps should he go wrong, he had no choice.

At last the roar of the waterfall faded, the rapids and cataracts grew less, and the ground flattened out. Larsen was at the end of his tether. He fell in some snow and was barely able to drag his weakening body up and force it onward. His run was no faster than an old man's walk, his walk a reeling stagger, his pauses for breath poised fractions short of falling. He dared not even sit in case exhaustion dragged him down into the sleep he craved. Great parts of his body had disappeared from his control and feeling, but somehow he drove his legs on, one step, two steps, three steps, each one hurt, each one seemed certain to be the last, but Larsen doggedly counted a hundred before letting himself briefly rest. One hundred paces walking. Stand, head down for a count of ten. One hundred paces running. Stand for a count of twenty. He no longer noticed where he was any more, scarcely even cared where he was going, did not think how he would find the seed bank.

The ground was flat and wet, covered in shallow streams and puddles through which he splashed. Thin ice splintered under him. The stream ran beside his feet as he raised his head dully to look ahead towards a small tarn, backed by more cliffs. Larsen's head fell and he looked down at the ground during his rest, seeing each stone, each snow patch, each glistening puddle, each microscopic patch of vegetation – yellow lichen, reindeer moss, or a tiny cushion of moss campion studded with dark pink buds.

Not until Larsen's next rest did it occur to him that he had seen what lay ahead. That he had not been surrounded by fog. He looked up again and found himself in a U-shaped valley with sheer sides but a broad flat base, down which the river ran sluggishly. Mist still hung in wispy, coiling curtains, masking the mountains above, but it had lifted from the valley floor. A few hundred metres away was an area of ground that had been raised up and flattened out. Larsen looked at it without understanding, then memory came like summer lightning from a clear sky. It was a helicopter landing pad.

Larsen staggered forward to the pad and collapsed on to it. Looking around at the valley, the river, the rocky sides of the valley wall, he sensed rather than saw the mist rippling down again. The world vanished from view as greyness returned.

Panic drove Larsen to shout, but the words were lost in his terror and all he did was let out a wild, hysterical scream. Something moved in the mist. A man with a gun. It was too much to bear. Larsen gave up. He closed his eyes and slumped back, unconscious within seconds.

8

SEED BANK

When Larsen woke he was lying on a narrow iron bed under a pile of blankets. The room was hot and he pushed away the blankets and sat up. He was wearing pants and a vest which were not his own. Draped over a chair beside him were more clothes he did not recognise, good quality overalls, a thick jersey, woollen trousers, socks and boots. Larsen picked them up and dressed. His cheek had a plaster on it, his body ached from head to foot, and three of his toes had an unpleasant bluish-black tinge that spoke of frost-bite.

There was a fur-lined parka on the back of the door, and Larsen picked it up and went out. He found himself in a passage lit from a window at the far end. He glanced along it, then felt giddy and had to lean against the wall.

'Hello,' he called out. 'Is anyone here?'

Another door opened and the helicopter pilot, Evat, appeared.

He looked down at Larsen from his tall, thin height. He too was wearing overalls, and his shoulder-length black hair was free rather than tied in a neat pony tail as Larsen had seen it previously. Two ear-rings gleamed in his left ear.

'How do you feel?' he asked, in his soft voice.

'A little dizzy. Is this the seed bank?'

'Yes. You were brought in hours ago, suffering from exposure. You have been asleep ever since.'

'Was it you who found me?'

'No, I was not at work then.' Evat smiled, and his black mandarin moustache gave him a faintly sinister air. 'Olssen found you.'

'Olssen?'

'Yes. It seems you were lucky, another hour or so and it might have been too late. What had you been doing?'

'It is a long story.' Larsen's memory was rapidly coming back. Most of all he remembered Kalaasi. 'Was anyone else found out there?'

'Who?'

'Anyone.'

'No.'

'Is there a radio here?'

'Of course.'

'May I use it?'

Evat led Larsen along the passage to a small room, piled high with old-fashioned-looking radio equipment.

'The transmitter came from one of the American early warning stations after they shut it down a few years ago,' remarked Evat, a mixture of apology and contempt running over his fine features. 'Governments always prefer to save $5000 now, even if it means they will have to spend much more later.'

He bent down and began to fiddle with the tuning mechanism while hisses and crackles burst out of the speaker above his head.

'Hello, hello,' he called. 'SB1 for SER, SB1 for SER, come in, please. Come in, please, SER.'

The only reply was more crackles and whines, punctuated with occasional explosions of white noise. At last Evat turned it off.

'It's getting less reliable all the time. Three days ago I was calling up Cap Gad and I got a Russian fish factory ship south of Spitzbergen. Clear as crystal.'

'Is there any chance of my contacting police headquarters in Godthab?' asked Larsen.

'Where?' said Evat coldly.

'Godthab.'

'I do not know that place.'

'For God's sake,' muttered Larsen, raising his hands and making a face. 'The capital of Greenland. Godthab.'

'The capital of Kalaallit Nunaat is Nûk,' said Evat, separating out each word, as if they were stones.

'Nûk. Yes. Of course. Sorry. Is there any chance I could contact police headquarters in Nûk?'

'No.'

Evat turned to go. Larsen followed him.

'When will I be able to leave?' he asked.

'Considering how hard it seems to have been for you to get here, I would have thought you'd want to stay a while.'

Larsen waited patiently for an answer.

'The helicopter should arrive shortly,' added Evat after a moment.

Larsen glanced out of a small double-glazed window and saw they were in a large building under the lee of a mountain. Out to the south-west the sun shone, and Larsen could see part of the valley he dimly recalled from the last part of his journey the day before.

'This is a strange place,' he remarked.

'It was a mine,' explained Evat. He walked into a small office full of dials and with several flickering screens. 'Nine years ago platinum was found here. Everyone was very excited. It was going to transform the oconomy of Sermilik, platinum, white gold. Worth three times as much as ordinary gold, and much more useful too. A vital component of catalytic converters. Everything was wonderful.'

Larsen thought back to a visit he had once made to the deafening chaos of the lead and zinc mine at Marmorilik.

'What happened?' he asked.

'The mine was deserted after less than five years.' Evat sat down, yawned and stared out of the window. 'The world price of platinum slumped because everyone started mining it wherever they could find it. And no one wants to mine up here anyway, it is too expensive. Even the uranium at Kvanefjeldet isn't really worth getting out.'

'So the platinum mine has become the seed bank.'

'Yes. Several organisations and countries were looking for a good site, and someone had the idea of using this mine.'

'You mean the seeds do not belong to Greenland?'

'Some do, and the Danish government handed over a lot more in exchange for some sort of joint deal. Others don't. It doesn't make a lot of difference. Instead of making work for more than a hundred people, as the mine did, the place employs ten, and five of those only part-time.'

Larsen's thoughts had gone elsewhere.

'Where is Olssen?' he asked.

'You wish to thank your noble rescuer?' said Evat facetiously.

'Something like that.'

'Well, you can't. His shift is over and he's gone out hunting.'

Evat yawned again, then absently picked up a pencil and began to sketch birds on a piece of rough paper. He drew them well and swiftly, a puffin, a flying snow bunting, and an elaborately detailed long-tailed duck.

'If I had exposure and frost-bite when I came in, why wasn't I sent back to Sermilik to see the doctor?' asked Larsen, after a few minutes.

'Because there hasn't been a helicopter in or out for over a day.'

'Over a day?'

'The mist has lain very thick. It's not uncommon. I've been stuck here for ten days during a spring blizzard. We always keep plenty of supplies.'

He was drawing in the duck's wing feathers, giving them a complicated, abstract patterning. Larsen looked at the drawing, and nodded in appreciation.

'I thought you said you weren't here when I was brought in. How can that be if there has been no helicopter in or out?'

Evat stopped drawing, and glanced up at Larsen with a half-smile.

'Policemen always ask questions,' he remarked.

'That is our job.'

'One of them. Not the most important. I walked here.'

'I thought you were a pilot.'

'Only the reserve one. There isn't enough work for two of us full-time, so usually Bob does the flying. The last week I've been covering Jonis's shifts.'

'That must be worth quite a lot of money to you.'

Evat laughed, and returned to his sketching.

'You don't know Otto Frederiksen. He pays very badly, and with such high unemployment in the town, he can afford to.'

'And you walked here from Sermilik? In the mist?'

'I know this area pretty well, and for much of the time the mist was above ground level.'

'Do you often walk here?'

'Occasionally. It gives me time to think.'

'What about?'

Evat had left the long-tailed duck unfinished, and was now drawing a swimming seal with deft strokes.

'Drawing. Poetry. Travel. Anything I want to think about. Now it's my turn to ask you something. Why all these questions?'

'Did you see anyone else on your way here?'

'That's not fair. You should answer my question first.'

'Did you see anyone else on your way here?'

Evat sighed, and put down his pencil. He looked at his drawings for a moment, then crumpled up the piece of paper and lobbed it accurately into a green metal waste-paper basket.

'I walked a little way with Dr Sven, then he went back to town and I came on here.'

'When did the two of you part?'

'About four yesterday afternoon, I suppose. I didn't notice.'

'And when did you get here?'

'Maybe two hours later. Sometime after they brought you in. Why are you asking all these things?'

'Because I think my partner, policeman Kalaasi, was murdered yesterday afternoon.'

Evat frowned.

'Where? What happened?'

'It was on the ridge down the middle of the Tugdlik valley.'

'That's where Jonis died.'

'Did you come that way?'

'No. There's a shorter route to the west, through the hills above the town.'

'And you saw no one?'

'Who should I see?'

'A man with a gun perhaps.'

'Any man more than a kilometre from town is generally a man with a gun,' commented Evat. 'I always carry my gun when I walk here. The KGH store is not well stocked, especially just now, and something fresh makes a lot of difference.'

The door opened and Gudrun came in. She smiled at Larsen, but her eyes did not meet his.

'You are looking better.'

She was not. Her face was drawn and pale, her hair was chaotic and unbrushed, and she was smoking a cigarette with quick nervous puffs.

'What are you doing here?' asked Larsen.

'I told you, I work here. I have done for months.'

Evat was tapping one of the dials and yawning again.

'You told me you were doing a thesis,' objected Larsen.

'It is because I'm doing a thesis that I need a job. Do you know how much I owe the Danish government for my education? $36,000. Every crown I can save is one less on my debt. Also I have permission to use the computers here. But my research is virtually finished, I'll be leaving within a few weeks.'

'Lucky woman!' commented Evat drily.

'And Larsen here is a lucky man.' Gudrun sat down on the last free chair. 'When Olssen dragged you in, you were barely conscious. We had to put you in a warm bath, and watch you all the time in case you collapsed and drowned yourself – '

'Sergeant Larsen says that his companion, Kalaasi, may be dead,' interrupted Evat.

'It is a dangerous time to cross sea or lake ice,' said Gudrun, grinding her cigarette into the ashtray. 'Especially after so late a spring . . .'

She stopped as all three of them became aware of a throbbing sound growing swiftly louder and closer. A small man came bursting in. It was Olssen.

'They are here,' he announced dramatically, then saw Larsen. 'Hello. I brought you in yesterday. You were lucky.'

'There was something I wanted . . .' began Larsen.

But Olssen had vanished again.

'I thought you said he was hunting,' Larsen said to Evat.

'It looks as if he must have come back,' replied Evat, going towards the door.

Outside dust and snow were blowing wildly about. Noise swelled up to a climax as the helicopter descended, the roar of its engines bouncing off the sheer valley sides. It landed smoothly and the rotor blades began to slow. A door opened and a man jumped out, followed more slowly by four more people.

Larsen and Gudrun had not moved. Unsaid things filled the wide space between them.

'Who are the new arrivals?' asked Larsen, after a moment.

'There is Bob, the pilot, and Karl and Saqaq, our relief. Also Otto Frederiksen.' Her face was scarred with disgust.

'You don't like him?'

'Does anyone? He'd sell his parents for a few dollars.'

Larsen got up to go outside, but a wave of weakness came over him. Swirling yellow ate up the world until all he could see was the helicopter, far away as though at the wrong end of a telescope. His legs wavered, his muscles turned to liquid, and the yellow haze blotted out everything. The next thing he knew, he was sitting on the ground while Gudrun forced his head between his legs. For a moment he thought he was going to be sick, then the feeling passed.

'It's all right,' he said. 'I'm all right now.'

'You had better sit down again.'

She supported him into a large sunny room equipped with a huge colour television, video recorder, CD/cassette player, games console, and a scattering of books and magazines, as well as a couple of large sofas and several comfortable chairs.

'Lie down,' she said. 'I'll get you some coffee.'

Larsen closed his eyes. He felt tired and cold. Before she came back he was asleep. Gudrun regarded him for a moment, then picked up a blanket and covered him.

Larsen was woken a few minutes later by loud voices outside.

'What do you mean, we've got to go? We only just got here.' The words were in English, the voice of a confident, determined American woman from one of the Midwestern states.

Larsen's English was adequate and he listened curiously.

'I'm sorry, but the pilot says the weather is closing in again and – '

'So it's closing in again. This deal is going noplace, Otto, noplace at all, unless I make a thorough inspection. You got that?'

'Of course. Of course. I could not expect anything else, Mrs Krinsky.'

'I'm glad to hear it. Incidentally, I don't like being called Mrs Krinsky. It makes me sound like some kind of third-grade teacher. My name is Marian.'

'Of course.'

'OK. Let's get on.'

'Mr Frederiksen,' broke in a third voice, also American but deep, lazy, male, and from well south of the Mason-Dixon line, 'I cannot guarantee flying you out of here unless we leave in the next quarter of an hour. The mist is thickening real fast and – '

'Otto,' broke in the woman, 'this guy's sitting on my nerves.'

'Yes, Mrs . . . I mean Marian. But he is trying to make a serious point about the weather.'

'I'm trying to make a serious point too. Half a million dollars' worth of serious points. It was plenty of trouble to get to this God-forsaken place. Worse even than when my brother – who wants to be a lone eagle but only makes it as a chickadee – invited us to Thanksgiving. He lives in Dull Center, Wyoming, and someone knew something when they named that town. Anyway, I'm not about to go back where I came from without sorting a few things out.'

Larsen sat up as the door opened and a lanky, grey-haired American in his late forties came in. He wore a baseball cap and a faded red sweatshirt with a savage-looking pig and the words 'Arkansas Razorback' on it. A cigarette hung from his lips. He sat down moodily.

'Great,' he muttered. 'That's really swell. We'll be lucky if we're away this time tomorrow.' Then he noticed Larsen. 'Hi. I'm Bob.'

'I'm Tomas Larsen.'

'Sure. The policeman.' The pilot casually flicked ash and tipped his cap further back. 'These East Greenland fogs are too much.'

'Have you lived here long, then?'

'Sure. I'd always wanted to see icebergs and stuff, and when I got called up for Vietnam I thought, fuck this, and took off. I knew no one'd find me up here – and no one did.'

'But that must have been over twenty-five years ago.'

'Sure.'

'You must like living here.'

'I don't know really.' He stubbed out his cigarette and stared up at the white ceiling. 'My first years in Greenland I shifted around a lot, but I've been here in Sermilik for a long time now. Sometimes I get sick to death of the place. A few times I've even fixed up a job someplace else, then the weather's turned sour, or I've thrown a big party, had a few beers and kind of ended up staying. Sermilik just isn't so easy to get away from. You picked up a touch of exposure yesterday, right?'

'How did you know?'

'They called in about you a while back.'

'I thought the radio was out of order.'

'No way. It's a good transmitter, not new but good. Old US military stock. Except for electrical storms or the aurora there's scarcely been a day's problem with the stuff.'

'Could I use it now?'

'Sure. I'll set it up for you.'

When Larsen came back, Bob, Olssen and the relief worker, Karl, a dark reticent man with an air of brooding aggression, were watching an old repeat of *Roseanne*, with Danish sub-titles.

'Where's everyone else?' asked Larsen.

Olssen looked up.

'Mr Frederiksen is showing the American lady round the seed store. Evat is finishing his shift in the control room, and as Gudrun does her own work there, she's probably with him.'

'Doesn't Frederiksen mind her using the seed bank computers?'

Olssen smiled a nervous, gap-toothed smile.

'I think he makes her pay.'

'I haven't thanked you for rescuing me,' said Larsen.

'That's OK.'

'You were here last Tuesday, weren't you?'

'Yes. I told Kalaasi, I left on the helicopter.'

'And took the flight to Nûk?'

Olssen nodded. His body seemed taut, scarcely restrained.

'Did you go there for any special reason?'

'No. It was just to have some fun for a couple of days.' A smile slid over his face almost too fast. His narrow eyes were flickering around the room, and his fingers beat a light tattoo on his knee. 'One of my cousins moved there a few years ago. I hadn't seen him since he left, so I went and stayed with him. He lives off Rinksvej, not far from the stadium. Do you want his address?'

'The flight must have been expensive.'

'I won some money playing cards, so I thought, why not.'

Larsen continued to look at him.

'I've been told about what happened on the plane back,' blurted out Olssen suddenly. 'I don't remember anything about it. I was drunk. I'm sorry.' He sounded like a little boy before his headmaster. 'But we're quits now, aren't we? You let me off that, and I rescued you.'

'That's right. You did.' Larsen turned on the helicopter pilot. 'Were you flying the helicopter last Tuesday?'

'Sure,' said Bob, his eyes not moving from the screen. 'I carried Evat and Olssen back to Sermilik, Jonis took off on his own. I told Kalaasi all this stuff. Let me watch the show, will you?'

Kalaasi. Larsen fell silent. After a moment he picked up his anorak, and went out.

In the control room Evat, wearing a personal stereo, was casually glancing across a bank of meters, on all of which the needles stood steady in the green-marked area of the dial, between −21° and −18°.

Gudrun was sitting at a desk, her fingers flickering over a keyboard as spreadsheets, graphs and statistics scuttered past on the computer screen. She looked up briefly then returned to her work with only the faintest nod. Evat stretched and closed his eyes. Larsen realised he was not wanted. Occasionally he felt a strong desire to be where he was not wanted, and he stayed in the doorway, listening to the rattle of computer keys and the itchy hint of music creeping from Evat's personal stereo. It seemed to him that Gudrun was trying to look as if she was doing something, and Evat was forcing himself to keep his eyes and mouth shut. At last Larsen left. There had been secrets in that room, but he could not decipher them. Yet.

Larsen wandered further, past a dormitory with half a dozen beds in it, another room with only two beds, a large clean well-equipped kitchen, a bathroom, a toilet, a room that housed the purring generator. At the end of the corridor was a door that led under the mountain. It opened into a small room with a large thick door on the far side, and a big cupboard. By the far door was a large board. At the top was the red and white Greenland flag with its colour-reversed circle inside. Underneath rules were printed out in English, Danish and Inuit.

WARNING. IMPORTANT. You are now entering the Sermilik Seed Store.

This seed store is the property of the Government of Kalaallit Nunaat. Unauthorised access is forbidden. The following rules must be followed at all times:

1. It is of crucial importance that the temperature in the seed store should remain at −19.85° Centigrade, or as close to that figure as is practicable.

2. No one must enter the seed store without wearing the correct clothing, see rules 10, 11, and 12, below.

3. No one may enter the seed store without written and confirmed permission from the relevant departments of the Government of Kalaallit Nunaat.

4. All seed stocks are the exclusive property of the Government of Kalaallit Nunaat, except where the contrary is stated, both on the label and in the official records.

5. No seed stocks are to be handled, except by authorised personnel, who will at all times wear officially provided gloves to prevent any warming of the seed stocks.

6. All additions to or withdrawals from seed stocks are to be recorded both on computer disk and in the written records – in accordance with shipping description and the training and catalogue manual number 4K/219, revised 1996 edition . . .

Larsen did not read any more; instead he glanced into the wall cupboard. Inside were several low temperature suits, together with detailed instructions about upkeep and putting them on.

The suits, some of which hung on named hangers, were made of some rustling man-made material which gleamed faintly silver. They came in one piece from feet to an attached hood like a balaclava with a sort of filter over the mouth. There were also boots, goggles and gloves – some thin for handling things, the others thick over-mittens. Two hangers were empty. Clearly Otto Frederiksen and Mrs Marian Krinsky were inside.

Larsen picked up a pair of mittens and went over to the far door. It was governed by a double handle, and opened into a sort of airlock with another equally thick door opposite. Larsen closed the first door behind him, then tried to open the second, but nothing happened. Only at the third time of asking did the inner door open, and he realised there must be an in-built delay to prevent warm air getting in.

He found himself in a large round space from which issued three tunnels. Bare long-life bulbs hanging from the ceiling cast a dim yellowish glow. Larsen put on his anorak and gloves, then closed the airlock door behind him. His breath smoked in the still cold air. Directly in front was a large well-lit notice-board that repeated all the rules he had already seen outside, and also provided a detailed plan of the seed store which he studied carefully.

The tunnels burrowed deep into the mountain and each was colour-coded and subdivided into smaller sections and separate chambers, like the stacks of a huge library. Tunnel One covered the Holarctic, the northern hemisphere. Tunnel Two, the longest, was Neotropical and Ethiopian – South America and sub-Saharan Africa. Tunnel Three dealt with the Oriental, Australasian and Oceanic regions. As Larsen wondered where Frederiksen and his American guest had gone, a murmur of approaching conversation drifted out of Tunnel Two.

Larsen looked around quickly, then went down Tunnel Three. The cold air stung his face, and he pulled up his anorak hood. Large cabinets marked with numbers and letters lined the walls. Coming to a side turning headed 'Sri Lankan Flowering Plants', Larsen went in and found himself inside a small chamber hacked out of the rock and full of more steel cabinets. By the entrance hung a thermometer, showing −19.8°, and a collection of numbered keys. Larsen took one down at random, searched out the file with the corresponding number and opened it. It was half full of tiny boxes, each also numbered and with Latin names written on them. Attached to each of the hundreds of boxes was a card with dates, descriptions and other details as well as a computer bar code. It occurred to Larsen that almost anything

94

could be hidden in these cabinets. Clumsily he picked up a box and opened it. Inside were perhaps sixty glossy brown oval seeds. He closed the box, put it back in its place, slid the file shut, and relocked it, then returned to the entrance of the chamber. The voices were coming closer.

'Well, it all looks very impressive. Very kosher. How many do you employ?' That must be Marian Krinsky.

'Ten, but half of them are part-time.'

'If my company took over we'd be looking to increase that.' Larsen's eyes narrowed. So Frederiksen had been lying about redundancies. 'What about qualified biologists?'

'Initially, during the set-up procedures, we had six on the staff.'

'And now?'

'Qualified people do not wish to stay here, so the Danish girl is the only one,' said Frederiksen. 'The rest of the staff are just Eskimos who know nothing about anything. And the girl is leaving very soon.'

'That sounds crazy.'

'Not at all. The procedures required to keep the store operational are very simple and require no expert knowledge. When deliveries are made they are always accompanied by at least one government-approved biologist or botanist who has been trained in the cataloguing systems. They double-check the seeds and make sure they are inserted in the correct place.'

'And having no on-site scientists of course slashes your wages bill in a big way.'

'It's not just that.' Frederiksen lowered his voice, but they were getting closer to Larsen. The policeman pressed himself back among the files. 'As the people who work here are unsupervised much of the time, I make absolutely certain that they do not realise the value of some of our seeds.'

'You're talking about crop varieties?'

'Exactly. And as another precaution, I have divided all crop varieties into two. A small proportion are in the correct place in their respective regional files.'

'Now we're getting to the beef.' Even the muffling effect of the hood and filter she wore could not disguise the eagerness in Marian Krinsky's voice. 'And the rest?'

'A section not marked on any of the plans. I'll show you.'

'You're sure no one else knows about this?'

'I am sure.'

The voices were fading away again. Larsen emerged just in time to see the glint of their silver suits vanishing into the Australasian section. He crept after them, past passages and rooms all full of line upon line of exactly similar storage cabinets. Frederiksen and Krinsky had gone into a chamber labelled 'Tasmania'. With deliberate caution Larsen followed them. The chamber was empty, and there was no door out except the one he had come in by. He stared in astonishment, then listened again. Voices ran on round the rock walls.

Noticing one of the cabinets was not flush to the wall, Larsen went over to it and tried to move it. Abruptly the whole side came away, revealing a passage that turned a sharp corner out of sight. Larsen crouched down beside the disguised door as the talk became suddenly clearer, like a retuned radio.

'. . . wild varieties of all the big thirty.'

'The big thirty?'

'That is what I call them,' explained Frederiksen. 'Virtually every scrap of human protein all over the world comes, directly or indirectly, from just thirty crops, wheat, barley, rice, oats, rye, maize, potatoes, soya beans, and so on – '

'Sure, sure. But you said wild varieties. Don't you keep the domesticated strains and cultivars here?'

'We have most of those in the seed store naturally, but they are too well known. What really matter are the wild varieties, they are what I have been encouraging our field operatives to collect. Of course others are doing it now, but we were the first to specialise. In here is the most complete collection of wild varieties of food crops in the world.'

'That's very interesting, but I told you that my company is primarily interested in the domesticated strains. They're what I thought you were offering.'

A strange creaking sound issued from inside the hidden chamber. It was Frederiksen laughing.

'Oh no, Mrs Krinsky. It is the wild varieties in this room that you want. And they will cost you, quite apart from any deal you may agree with our government, an extra $30 million.'

'$30 million!' Krinsky's voice was almost a scream. 'You must be out of your skull.'

'On the contrary. I am being very generous. These seed stocks are literally beyond price.'

'That's ridiculous.'

'Not at all. You know about the US sugar beet crop?'

'How could I not? The last two years almost the whole harvest has gone down with a new strain of rhizomania and raw sugar prices have quadrupled. The cane countries are laughing all the way to the bank. So?'

'In that cabinet is the solution.'

'Do me a favour, Otto. Every major agro-chemical company in the world has been working on the problem, and getting precisely nowhere.'

'Because they do not have the right tools to work with. In this cabinet are huge numbers of seeds from various wild beets. One of them is certain to be resistant to rhizomania.'

'Sure.' The American woman's voice was heavy with sarcasm. 'And I'm going to be the next pope.'

'I am sorry? What did you say, Marian?'

'Nothing. Except I'd like to know why you think we're stupid enough to hand over $30 million for a few crazy assumptions?'

'Because you are not stupid. Some truly resistant stock would be worth a fortune to you. And it is only one chance to recoup the cost out of thousands. How much is your firm spending on the genetic engineering of food plants?'

'About as much as our competitors, I suppose,' said Krinsky with cautious reticence.

'Millions every year, no doubt. And that's without the cost of taking out worldwide patents. But you've got to have something to work with, haven't you – and these seeds will give you a huge, and unique, new database.'

'Come on, Otto. Speak sense . . .'

'I am speaking sense. To take just one example, virtually every genetically engineered brassica has already been patented – and not by your firm. But my seeds include tens of thousands of wild brassicas which can't be touched by the patents and which you could do what you like with. Breed up into any number of new strains.' He swept over her attempted interruption. 'And what about the growing danger posed by lack of diversity? Genetically engineered plants all come from a very small number of originals. That means that, however they have been doctored, they are all fundamentally similar, and that large shared gene pool means they have similar weaknesses. The chances of a new resistant virus attacking the entire crop keep increasing every year.

'There are other problems too. It's all very well redesigning cereal crops so that instead of growing to a metre or more, they are less than a quarter of that size. It means there is less waste, they ripen quicker, and are less likely to be flattened by wind. But nature never gives anything for free. In a wet summer smaller plants are far more likely to rot on the stalk than larger ones. And the accelerating rate of climate change could make that crucial. With these seeds, you've got far more security, because you have so many alternatives. Remember the epidemic of stripe rust that destroyed half the Canadian wheat harvest a few years ago? Do you know what stopped that? A wild wheat from

Turkey that no one had ever thought about until it was almost too late. How about grassy stunt virus in rice? A single small colony of wild rice in central India provided resistance to that. And then – '

'OK. I take the point. But what about the other seed banks? They've got the same stuff in them.'

'No. For one thing they are under very tight government controls, for another this bank has specialised in crops since long before it was moved out here. You know how many species of plant are being wiped out every day? Between eighty and a hundred. Ten per cent of the entire flora on this planet will probably be extinct in ten years. And it's not just food crops, is it? What about drugs – a quarter of all drugs are directly derived from plants, but only a fraction of the planet's plants have been tested for their drug properties. Imagine the riches that must lurk in these cabinets – seeds which no longer exist anywhere else in the universe, seeds that are impossible to evaluate. Seeds that could hold the answers to any question you cared to ask. When they were looking for the resistant strain for stripe rust, scientists discovered that over ninety-five per cent of all wild and ancient wheats in the Balkans have become extinct in the last forty years. But some of them are here – all ready to be cross-bred to improve the stock. Of course, if you are not willing to gamble a measly $30 million, your company's profits for one month, on the prospects of a fortune, then that is your choice. I will not find it hard to get another company interested . . .'

'Nice advertising speech, Mr Frederiksen. But we both know that if the privatisation does go through, the rules under which we'll run this seed bank will be very carefully drawn up and – '

'That is why everything in this room is untraceable. You can remove the boxes whenever you like and no one will be the wiser. Most of the important ones could be taken out in a single helicopter trip. It is one of the good things about seeds, their lack of bulk.'

'OK. I think maybe we'll talk about this somewhere else, when I'm not dressed up like some kind of tacky spaceman. But first let's have a look in some of these files.'

After a brief pause, Marian Krinsky's voice came, cold and clear.

'There's nothing in here.'

'What?'

'I said there's nothing in this drawer. Or this one. Or this one. Or this one.'

'I don't understand.' Frederiksen's voice was high-pitched. Hysterical. 'It's not possible.'

'Wrong, Otto. It's absolutely possible. There isn't a single seed packet in any of these files. I'll be willing to bet there isn't one in this whole room. If you want $30 million for a few storage cabinets you can try elsewhere. Now, shall we go? I'm getting cold.'

Larsen started away back into the main tunnel, but in the direction of the exit was a long straight passage with nowhere to hide. He doubled back into another part of the Australasian section.

'I can't understand what's happened,' came Frederiksen's voice.

'I can. You tried to do my company out of a lot of money. You may talk pretty good, Otto, but you're a lousy con-man. You should have thought of salting the mine. If some of the seeds had been the real McCoy, our scientists might not have had time to check up everything before the deal was signed, and you might have got away with it. But to have no seeds at all, that was just dumb.'

'No. No. There were seeds there. Tens of thousands of varieties. A treasure trove. They have been stolen.'

Their voices began to fade away as they walked towards the exit.

'Uh huh. In a pig's eye.'

'I'm not lying. The seeds have been stolen. I knew I should have locked the connecting doors. But I'll find the thief . . .'

'What're you going to do? Get a gun and go hunting round the tunnels?'

'Of course not. But . . .'

Their voices cut off abruptly. Larsen waited a few minutes but there was no further sound. Cautiously he kneeled down and peered out along the tunnel, his head only a few inches above the ground. As far as he could see in the murk it was empty, but he did not intend to take the slightest risk of being seen. Only the realisation that he was shivering convulsively finally got him to move.

At the end of the Australasian section, dividing it from the Oriental, was a massive door, like the doors in the airlock. It had been wide open, but now it was shut. Larsen pulled the handle.

Nothing happened.

9

TRAPPED

Larsen tried to open the door again, then again, but it stayed stubbornly closed. Only then did he remember what Frederiksen had said about locking the connecting doors. Fear swelled inside him as he wrenched at the door, pushing and pulling everything he could, then in desperation hammering and shouting.

There was no point. The door was twenty centimetres of insulated steel, designed to resist a major rockfall and immovable except by earthquake or nuclear explosion. He returned to scrabbling with the locks and handles but none worked. And the longer he tried, the more the cold ate into him.

There must be a way to unlock the door. Rubbing his arms and chest to keep warm, Larsen looked around and saw another list of rules on the wall. He ran over to read it, wading through the small print, feverishly searching for some description of emergency procedure or of operating the doors when they were locked or jammed. All he found was rule number 26.

26. Staff must remember at all times that they must not spend more than 2 hours [TWO HOURS] in the seed store. Protective suits cease to be fully effective after 2 hours [TWO HOURS] and become steadily less so. In the event of a member of staff spending more than the specified maximum time in the seed store area, procedures should be the same as for outdoor exposure (see First Aid Manual, pages 17 to 23).

Larsen's teeth were chattering and his whole body shook as twenty degrees of frost closed around him. Surely someone would come back. Surely when people realised Larsen was missing they would guess where he was. But an apathetic voice at the back of Larsen's mind reminded him that because he had not used a protective suit there was no empty hanger to be noticed. No way anyone could guess he was in there. He seemed to hear Frederiksen's thin, self-satisfied voice adopting a caricature of sadness.

'Sergeant Larsen dead? Trapped in the seed bank? What a dreadful accident. I will report it immediately. But why on earth did he go in there? And without telling anyone where he was going, or wearing a suit either? There are notices everywhere warning people about the dangers of entering the restricted area, and they are there for their own safety. We take every precaution we can reasonably be expected to. If people still ignore all the safety regulations, then . . .'

Larsen hurried back along the passages of the Australasian sector, seeking another exit. He checked one tunnel after another, even visited the secret chamber where he had overheard Krinsky and Frederiksen and looked into the empty cabinets. But there was no way out. Every tunnel seemed to end in a blank rock wall. And all the time the cold blossomed within him. It seemed ridiculous that having narrowly escaped death by exposure only a day ago, he should face it again in such different circumstances, but the irony did not make Larsen smile.

Eventually he returned to the great door. Its heavy shiny immobility pressed down upon his mind and body alike. It was as if the door itself was his murderer. The voice of surrender whispered in his mind, telling Larsen to give up, to lie down, to shiver a little more then fall into the peaceful sleep of death. Already he could feel the false promise of warmth luring him.

But Larsen was stubborn by nature. His mind was a fighting dog, once it had bitten it would not let go. And Larsen had bitten into Jonis's murder. Even as he squatted on the floor by the door, with no future before him but the death of a trapped lemming or snared auk, still his mind ticked on, weaving suspicions, explanations, theories, then turning to Frederiksen and his blatant attempt to swindle Krinsky's company. To have left the cabinets empty was, as Krinsky had said, just dumb. And Larsen did not think Frederiksen was dumb. When clever men behaved like fools, there was generally a simple explanation. But he could not see that either.

The cold was tightening its grip. At last Larsen staggered back to his feet. On the wall beside him was another thermometer, set on −9.8°. He remembered the dials in the control room had all been set on or around that temperature too. It seemed it would be the number of his death.

A blankness swept over his mind and body. Larsen slumped back against the thermometer, then wondered hazily if the heat leaking out of his body would make it rise. After a minute or two he looked at it again. It had moved marginally, up to −19.7°. And only then did he realise his way out.

Larsen pulled off his mittens and clutched the thermometer in his naked hands. Savage cold ripped through his fingers like poisoned thorns, but he held on. After a minute he looked again. Yes, yes, it had crawled up to −18.9°. Larsen leaned forward and breathed on the thermometer as he gripped it in his bare hands. Breathe. Breathe. The cold dead air of the seed bank stung in his throat, a cloud of steaming smoke gathered around him, his face and hands were numb. Ice was forming on his lips and nose. But he would not let go. Would not stop blowing on the thermometer.

The next time he dared to look the thermometer was into the red at −15.7° and climbing visibly. Where were they? Where were they? In his head was the vision of Evat with his eyes shut, tapping his hand idly to the music of his personal stereo, or hard at work on a drawing, noticing nothing.

When the door swung heavily open Larsen was stuck to the thermometer by chains of ice. But the two faceless, silver-suited figures prized him gently free and carried him out of the seed store as fast as they could. As they left the airlock and re-entered the warm world of men, Larsen could hear the alarm bell ringing. The bell that had saved his life.

This time there was no difficulty about the radio not working. However, it was not a good connection, and Police Chief Thorold did not sound pleased.

'Larsen, what is happening out there?'

'It's complicated, sir.'

'Complicated! I'll say it is. As well as doing the best you can to kill yourself, you seem to have utterly failed to find the murderer. You have also angered the two most important men in Sermilik, Mr Otto Frederiksen and the commune Secretary – '

'I haven't even spoken to the Secretary yet, sir.'

'Perhaps that is why he is irritated. Politeness is important, Larsen. And I must tell you no one seems to believe this claim of yours that policeman Kalaasi has been murdered. A search party sent out by the commune to look for the body found no trace.'

'Sir, I am sure . . .'

'Well, if you are right, then a police-killer is roaming Sermilik. Someone who tried to kill you and did kill your partner. But you have no idea who it is, or why he is doing this. Is that right?'

'Yes, sir.'

'I like you, Tomas. You usually do a good job in a quiet way, and we have even been considering you for promotion. But . . .' A burst of timely static covered his next words.

'I need help, sir,' said Larsen.

'I think so too. But you can't have any.'

'Sir – '

'You have probably forgotten the Greenlandair strike. The last plane out of Cap Gad left half an hour ago. Until the strike is over, I cannot get anyone across to help you.'

'We have our own police helicopters – '

'Everyone is on strike, Larsen. There is no one on the airstrips to see them in and out, no air traffic controllers, no one.'

'The helicopter in and out of the Sermilik Seed Bank is still flying . . .'

'That is a very local service, which has nothing to do with Greenlandair. And they are entitled to take their own risks, which do not involve crossing the inland ice. I'll send you assistance the moment it's possible, but right now you're stuck.'

'What about Kalaasi, sir? I think – '

'Sorry. I can't hear. The static is blowing up again. I must go now, Tomas. Good luck. Give me a call when you can, and sort this out fast and without stepping on too many toes. All right? Signing off.'

Larsen sat alone in the radio room for several minutes. He was going to have to start being a lot cleverer than he had been so far. He also needed someone he could trust to watch his back.

Otto Frederiksen was walking up and down the corridor outside, a scowl on his pale face.

'I want to talk to you,' he said, leading the way into one of the bedrooms, then shutting the door and glaring at the policeman. 'What were you doing in the seed store?'

Larsen said nothing. His hand wandered over his cracked and chapped cheeks.

'You were trying to spy on Mrs Krinsky and me, weren't you? Trying to eavesdrop on a confidential business conversation. I thought someone must be sneaking around when I saw that door open. I will be making a very serious complaint, I can promise you. And I know who to complain to.'

Frederiksen stopped and breathed hoarsely.

'Well? Why don't you say something?' he snapped.

'Actually I was wondering why you told me that you did not know Jonis Hendrik, when he visited you at your house a few days before he died.'

Frederiksen said nothing for a few moments, twitching his head slightly, then made a pushing gesture with his hand, as if to throw away what they were talking about.

'I did not know his name. He came and shouted some nonsense to me about his wife. He was very rude and aggressive, so I told him he was to work out two weeks' notice, then go. He threatened me, told me I would be sorry. That is all. What I want to know is what you were doing in the seed store just now?'

'Someone mentioned $30 million,' said Larsen.

'So you heard about those seeds?' Frederiksen's manner was rapidly changing. 'They are very important, whatever that fool Marian Krinsky thinks, and someone has stolen them.'

Larsen sat down on a bare bed and put his hands in his pockets.

'They're worth a fortune,' went on the businessman. 'A fortune. If you were able to find them again, we could come to a very good agreement . . .'

Larsen's voice was non-committal.

'Theft. Bribery. The attempted murder of a police officer.'

An eye is usually expressionless, blank, the emotions reflected only in the skin around it, but in times of stress eyes can tell much. Larsen looked Frederiksen straight in the eye, and the businessman's pupils were wide black pits of terror, eclipsing the milky blue of his irises. They were the eyes of a man groping fearfully in the dark, a man in the grip of drugs he could not control, a man in mortal terror.

'Murder?'

'You have just admitted that you guessed someone was listening to you in the seed store. Why did you lock that door if not to try to kill me?'

'No. I did not really think anyone was there. The connecting doors are always supposed to be shut.'

'Shut and locked?'

'Yes. No. I did it without thinking. I swear it on my mother.'

'We will see what the public prosecutor thinks.'

'You don't mean that.'

'Oh yes,' said Larsen softly. 'Yes, I do.'

'What about the stolen seeds?'

It was a subject that also interested Larsen, but he was careful not to show it. 'We are talking about you.'

'But the seeds are the key. Whoever took them . . .'

Frederiksen stopped, then started again.

'You have seen how easy it is to get into the tunnels. But knowing which seeds were important, finding my hiding-place, that is different.' He leant forward, reached out his hands towards Larsen as if to take him by the shoulders, then thought better of it. 'Don't you realise? Those seeds are the most valuable things in the whole of Greenland.'

Totally unexpectedly the reality of the temptation struck home. Millions of dollars. Anything he wanted. The good life he had briefly promised to win for himself, and threw away by joining the police and then returning to Greenland. He thought of the drudgery of most of his day-to-day work, the petty controls inflicted by his superiors, the empty house he came home to, the smell of urine outside where drunks pissed against the wall, the tasteless tinned and dried food that was all he ever seemed to eat. He remembered that look of mingled hopelessness and contempt in his wife's eyes during the last two years of their marriage. The smug superiority of Solomon Rosing's Christmas cards. The patronising air of almost every European he met. All those things could be destroyed by money. Money bought everything. It was a cliché, but true like most clichés. Enough money would provide him independence, comfort, respect.

'If you find those seeds,' whispered Frederiksen. 'It would be worth millions. More than enough for both of us.'

'When are you going back to Sermilik?' asked Larsen quietly.

Frederiksen sat back, mystification on his face.

'The weather is clearing. We hope to leave within an hour.'

'I will come with you.'

'Fine.' Frederiksen got up. 'And what we have spoken of . . .?'

'You are not to leave Sermilik without my express permission.'

The helicopter flight was a short one.

'I'll be on my way tomorrow,' remarked Marian Krinsky, running a veined hand over her severely tied-back hair, then adjusting one of her plain gold ear-rings. Her shrewd eyes cast a disdainful glance at Frederiksen, who was huddled up in an expensive black leather trench coat, his hands on his knees, staring out of the window. 'This trip's been one massive waste of time.'

'Perhaps. But you're not going anywhere, Marian,' said the business-man dully.

Krinsky glared at him. She was about fifty, but the mixture of surprise and anger made her seem older.

'What are you saying to me?' she demanded.

'The strike. No planes in or out.'

'Jesus wept. Isn't that just my luck, bloody unions! The moment things start to get better, they screw you. When will the strike be over? One day? Two days? I've got things to do.'

'Do you remember how long the last Greenlandair strike went on, sergeant?' said Frederiksen.

'Four months,' said Larsen.

'Four months!' Her voice was a whisper of disbelief.

'That's right.' Frederiksen laughed. 'You'll be a real Greenlander by the time you finish here, Marian.'

'My company can send a private plane for me . . .' she said, recovering her poise.

'Not if nobody is manning the airstrip at Cap Gad.' Frederiksen was obviously enjoying himself. 'And even if they could get there, which they can't, the only way from Sermilik to Cap Gad will be by open boat, which is very dangerous during the spring thaw. You're not in Manhattan or Frankfurt, or even Tashkent or Lagos now, Marian. You're in the middle of nowhere. And stuck.'

Dr Sven removed the plaster on Larsen's cheek with a quick flick of his hand, then looked at the torn skin.

'How did you get that?'

'I fell over.'

'Hm. Well, it's nothing to worry about. Leave it open to the air, and it'll be gone in a few days. Now, let's see about the rest of you. Take off your clothes.'

Larsen began to strip.

'Come on, come on,' boomed the doctor impatiently. 'All your clothes. And your pants too. Good.'

Larsen submitted to a careful inspection.

'All right. You can get dressed again.'

'Why did I have to take off my clothes?'

'Checking the groin. Penile frost-bite is not uncommon, especially after a man has fallen in water which then refreezes. Some men are too embarrassed to tell me about it, so in all cases of frost-bite I make patients strip down. You've been lucky, it's very painful.'

Larsen began to pull on his trousers, wondering sourly if Dr Sven was telling the truth, or just indulging a private pleasure.

'How am I then?' he asked.

'Not bad. Your right hand has suffered mild frost-bite, and you'll get a certain degree of hardening of the fingertips as a result, as well as those blisters. You've also got a nice dose of desquamation of the cheeks – '

'Of what?' asked Larsen.

'Skin peeling off.'

Sven held up a mirror, and Larsen saw that as well as the livid scar along his left cheekbone, both his cheeks were flaking away in scales of dead skin. He grimaced.

'Does it matter?'

'Depends how you feel about it. It's not serious, if that's what you mean, though you'll be too sensitive to shave for a few weeks. It's quite interesting really, Greenlanders very rarely suffer from it, but you've got a fine case.'

'My father was Danish,' said Larsen.

'Hm. Statistics point to a growth in desquamation, and the general view is that it's due to mixed blood. My own opinion is that the real cause, like the massive increase in caries, has more to do with the change in diet, and the disappearance of the enormous quantities of blubber Eskimos used to eat – '

'Please don't call us Eskimos, doctor,' Larsen said wearily.

'I'm sorry.' Sven looked surprised. Doctors are not used to being corrected. 'Still, what's in a name?'

'Quite a lot,' said Larsen. 'Not that I mind much, but others feel differently. What about my foot?'

'Not quite so good. Bad blistering, but you shouldn't lose any toes. What it needs is rest and regular sterile dressings. I'll put one on now, and you'll have to have it replaced every day for a week or so. You should also stay in bed as much as possible.' The doctor knelt down, a dressing in his hands. 'Can you feel these toes at all?'

'Yes. They seem very hot.'

'As I expected. A dose of paraesthesia.'

'What does that mean?' asked Larsen, trying not to be irritated.

'Paraesthesia is a state where the affected area is pervaded by a variety of different sensations. Usually, as in this case, an abnormal sense of heat or cold. Your frost-bite was fairly severe, so it may persist, to a varying level, for several weeks, and could bring on some degree of formication.'

Larsen decided not to give him the satisfaction of explaining what formication was.

'So this burning sensation will continue for weeks?'

'Possibly, though most probably it will be residual, just coming and going occasionally. In addition you may lose one or more toenails, though they will grow back. You will notice they have been blackened as if bruised. All in all you were fairly fortunate. How long were you in the water?'

'I don't know. It seemed for ever. Five or ten minutes, I suppose.'

'Could have been worse. Survival time in water temperatures of around freezing is theoretically twenty to twenty-five minutes, though I'd give most people a worse than even chance of surviving much over a quarter of an hour. Incidentally, you've also got a touch of frost-bite on the tip of your nose, but it should heal without much of a scar. Now, please rest as much as possible, and make absolutely sure you don't get your toes frost-bitten again, or you'll lose at least one, and probably more.'

As he tied up the dressing, Larsen leant back in his chair and looked at the white ceiling.

'Do you know Otto Frederiksen well, doctor?' he asked.

'Fairly well.' Larsen could hear the caution creep into his voice. 'Why?'

'Would you say he was a trustworthy man?'

'Probably as much as anyone.'

'And rich?'

'So they say.'

'Is he a good shot with the rifle?'

'No.' Sven smiled. 'Not at all. I went hunting with him a few months ago and he missed everything he aimed at. He does not enjoy doing things he is bad at, so he goes out very rarely. Perhaps not at all now.'

'How about you?'

'A couple of fine fat ptarmigan.' He looked pleased with himself. 'Otto made me feel like Robert Maataq in comparison. A couple more years and I may be able to call myself adequate.'

'How was your hunting yesterday?' asked Larsen.

'Yesterday?' The doctor had finished the dressing, but he still knelt in front of the policeman, looking up. 'I didn't go hunting yesterday.'

'I understood you went hunting yesterday afternoon, north of the town.'

'Who told you that?'

'Is it true?'

'No. I mean I did set off to go hunting, but then came back. I didn't feel in the mood.'

'Did you see anyone while you were out of town?'

'No.'

'No one?'

'No. Except for Evat Jonsson, that is. He came some of the way with me. He quite often walks to the seed bank when the weather is good.'

'But the weather was not good yesterday.'

'It depends what you're comparing it with. What are all these questions about?' Sven got up. 'Has something happened?'

'Policeman Kalaasi was killed at Lake Tugdlik yesterday afternoon. A search party has gone out to look for his body.'

'Good God!' The doctor paused. 'Killed?'

'Murdered.'

'How can you be sure he was murdered if you cannot find his body?'

'I was there. I heard it.'

'Heard it?' The doctor looked at Larsen with surprise. 'How do you hear a murder?'

'The way that I did.' Larsen got up to leave.

Dr Sven shrugged.

'Don't forget what I said about resting as much as you can. And come back tomorrow morning for a fresh dressing.'

'But not undressing, I hope.'

The doctor laughed louder than the weak joke deserved.

That night Larsen went back to his solitary room with a sense of frustration. It seemed almost no one could have killed Jonis. On the other hand Larsen was rapidly building up a list of people who had been within an hour or two's walk of the lake on Monday afternoon when Kalaasi was killed. Olssen, Evat and Gudrun had been at or near the seed bank; the doctor could have been involved; then there was the vanished Robert Maataq – if he was still alive, which Larsen was beginning to doubt. Even Otto Frederiksen had no alibi for the time in question. And where did millions of dollars' worth of rare seeds fit in? Seeds that had vanished, or might have vanished. If they had existed at all.

As Larsen sat at the desk, and struggled to bring order to his thoughts by filling in endless sheets of rough paper with ideas and lists, the Secretary of the Sermilik commune came in without knocking. Theoretically Secretary Bronlund was only the spokesman of the elected council that ran the commune of Sermilik, but in practice he was the town boss. An amalgam of Inuit and Dane, with no clear lines where one ended and the other began, he was smoking a small cigar, and he was not in a good mood.

'The search party's just got back from Lake Tugdlik,' he growled, putting his stubby-fingered hands down on Larsen's desk and staring at him. 'They didn't find anything. Not a thing.'

'I'll go out with them tomorrow,' said Larsen, shuffling his pieces of paper out of sight. 'Perhaps they weren't looking in the right place.'

'There is no way the town is sending out another search party tomorrow,' replied Bronlund pugnaciously. He paused, waiting for a response, then swept on when one did not come. His small intelligent eyes roamed as he spoke.

'The commune is presently trying to make sure a supply ship visits us within a fortnight, in case the strike continues that long. That is important. So are the shortages in the shops. The disappearance of that idiot Kalaasi is not. Almost certainly he has simply wandered off and got lost. The boy has about as much common sense as a lemming, and he's gone walkabout before. So unless you can persuade me that he really is dead, I am going to take no more action. People have better things to do than look for him.'

Larsen wondered exactly what better things they had to do when over half the adult population was unemployed. It also struck him as strange that an idiot should be one of the few men in Sermilik to have a secure, full-time job.

'He was murdered,' he replied quietly.

'I don't think so,' parried the Secretary. 'I know this town better than anyone else, and I know Kalaasi. He's not the sort to get murdered. Forget him. Just do your job and arrest Mitti for the murder of her husband.'

'I can't do that yet. I have no proof.'

Bronlund considered for a moment. When he spoke again, his voice was different, softer, but more dangerous.

'I know the real reason you are here, Sergeant Tomas Larsen.'

'To solve the murder of Jonis Hendrik.'

Bronlund shook his head.

'I have many friends and acquaintances in Nûk, and they told me about your visit, and about the planned report.'

Larsen said nothing.

'Of course the excuse is our high death rate,' went on Bronlund. 'But things are just as bad all over Greenland.'

'No, they are not,' said Larsen, deciding to be frank. 'Sermilik is unusual, and not only because of the number of murders. The rates of unemployment and illegitimate births are also much worse than in the rest of Greenland. People in Sermilik virtually never marry, they have their illegitimate children young, do little if any work, then die young. The suicide rate is very high too, especially among those aged fourteen to twenty-two. There were ten in just ten months last year. That is why I have been asked to write a report on the town.'

'There's a group of politicians and civil servants who want to get rid of this town,' said Bronlund. 'To clear all the people out of it and let it rot. You're being used to do their dirty work.'

He turned to go.

'I gather it was you who first suggested to the government that the seed bank should be privatised,' remarked Larsen pleasantly.

Bronlund stopped.

'What of it?'

'Are you still sure it is a good idea?'

'Of course.'

'It could be very profitable, the sell-off.'

'Exactly.' The Secretary flicked his half-smoked cigar out of the door. 'Very good for the town.'

'For some members of the town at least. Did Otto Frederiksen suggest the idea to you?'

Bronlund shrugged.

'Finish your business and leave as soon as you can, Sergeant Larsen. We do not need you.'

He was gone. Larsen watched the door for a few minutes, then smiled to himself.

'I wonder who does need me here,' he remarked to the empty room.

10

ROOM OF MIRRORS

Larsen's foot exploded into pain that evening, first icy cold, then feeling as if it was burning up. When it finally settled enough to allow him sleep, he slid into a nightmare of faceless silver shapes hunting him. Hiding from them in a bare concrete room, he looked down and realised the ground was alive with ants. A crawling, scuttling, glossy black carpet. Running over his naked feet, in and out of his toes, up his ankles. He bent down to knock them away, but more and more poured on to him in a wave of hard, biting, stinging little bodies. He turned to run, but his legs defied him and he fell. And as he fell he knew they would cover him completely. That he would never rise again. He opened his mouth to scream, and his mouth too was full of ants, burrowing deep into his body, choking him.

Catapulted awake, sweating and terrified, Larsen tore back the blankets. He could still feel the patter of thousands of tiny creatures on the red stretched skin of his feet and ankles, but there was nothing there. Frantically he hunted through his bed, found nothing, then got up, filled a saucepan with cold water, and put his feet in it. The sensation slowly vanished, leaving him aching and shivering.

The doctor arrived in his usual robust good humour. When Larsen told him about the crawling feeling, Sven's mood improved even further.

'Ah yes,' he said, undoing the dressing. 'Excellent. Do you know, when I left Denmark I could scarcely recognise frost-bite, now I flatter myself I am becoming something of an expert on the condition.'

'Congratulations,' said Larsen.

Irony passed Dr Sven by.

'Yes, yes. It is always gratifying when a condition develops exactly as one has predicted. I did actually warn you of the sensation you have just described. It is known as formication, and is a fairly frequent variant of paraesthesia. Not only that, but I see you have lost a toenail during the night. Well, I'm afraid there is nothing much I can do, except put on another dressing, and again recommend complete rest.'

He left, radiating self-satisfaction.

With shafts of pain slashing through his feet whenever he moved, Larsen spent the day resting, listening to the radio, and dozing. In the

111

late afternoon he woke suddenly to a familiar voice coming from the chattering radio.

'... and of course Brian Laudrup, on his day, can turn any match with a single flash of genius.'

'So then, summing up, what would you say of Denmark's chances in next week's crucial World Cup qualifier?'

'Well, as I said, we have some very fine players, but because they play their club football in several different countries the manager has a big job to weld them together into a real team. I'm optimistic, but we'll just have to wait and see how it turns out.'

'Mr Rosing, thank you. And now *Sports Hour* continues with cycling...'

Larsen wondered sourly if Solomon Rosing was ever off the radio. It seemed he had achieved that elusive point at which celebrity becomes self-generating. Or at least he had reached it in Greenland. It would be interesting to know how much he had been paid for those few obvious clichés, which anyone with the faintest interest in football already knew.

Bored with lying in bed, he got up and made his way downstairs. At the bottom he heard a faint rustling outside the front door, and stopped. The noise stopped also. Larsen waited a few moments, then padded silently over to the door and stood there for a little longer.

Abruptly, without warning, he threw the door open and lunged outside.

There was a shriek of surprise, and Larsen found himself holding the arm of a small boy.

'Let me go, let me go,' squealed the boy, wriggling. 'I wasn't doing anything.'

'Kamik, isn't it?' said Larsen, remembering him from the harbour. 'Why were you outside my door?'

'I was just passing, sergeant. That's all.'

Larsen pulled the boy inside, shut the door, then looked him over thoroughly.

'Did someone tell you to hang around here?'

'No. No. I promise, I was just passing by. I was going to see a friend. I – '

'You wanted to know what I was doing, didn't you? You thought maybe you'd do a little spying. Well, did you find anything out?'

Suddenly, completely unexpectedly, the boy grinned.

'I know you are watching Mr Frederiksen. You were creeping around his house on Sunday night. Margrethe let you in, and then a little later you came running out so as not to be caught.'

Larsen was interested. He sat down and gingerly put his foot up on another chair.

'Did Margrethe tell you that?'

'No. I saw you. I think Margrethe wishes she never let you in.'

'Why?'

Kamik's eyes gleamed, and words came tumbling out of him.

'She often gives me some cake or bread and cheese at lunchtime. On Monday she only waved me away through the window, and I haven't seen her since. But what I did see was that she had a black eye and a swollen face.'

'Perhaps she had had an accident,' said Larsen mildly.

'No,' said Kamik again, and his voice was rich with contempt. 'Mr Frederiksen beat her, of course. He has done it before, though not as bad as this time. And I know something about Mr Frederiksen too. Something you don't know.'

'What?'

The boy paused impressively. Then the flashing grin reappeared.

'I have no money for sweets.'

Larsen warmed to him.

'Is that so? Well, listen to me, Kamik. You will get more than a few sweets if you help me. If I catch the man . . . the person I am looking for, there will be a reward.'

'What sort of reward?' Kamik countered, head cocked to one side.

'You will have to see. But it will be a good one.'

'How good?'

'Very good.'

Kamik was alive with excitement.

'OK,' he said breathlessly.

'What is it you know about Frederiksen?'

'The Yankee woman spent last night with him.'

Larsen stared in astonishment.

'She's staying in the hotel. You're talking nonsense.'

'I am not,' said Kamik, annoyed. 'Yesterday evening I was playing football and I saw her and Mr Frederiksen walking to his house. I did not see her come back, so she must have been with him until after midnight – '

'You go to bed very late,' put in Larsen.

'My grandmother goes to sleep early, so she does not know when I come home.'

'Where are your parents?'

'My father went to the west coast to look for work. Then my mother followed him, leaving me with my grandmother.'

'Why didn't they send for you when they found work?'

'Because they did not find each other. We have not heard from my father for years. My mother has a new man and he does not want me to live with his children. So I stay here.'

'I see.'

And Larsen did see. The effective orphaning of this child had sharpened his awareness of adult weaknesses, and opened his eyes to things most children of his age would not have seen. Which might mean that fortune had presented Larsen with a pearl. But then he grew unsure. Although Inuit children were generally doted upon and indulged, Larsen had doubts if it was still true in Sermilik.

Kamik had been watching while these thoughts ran through Larsen's mind.

'I will help you,' he said, before adding with a fine show of bravado, 'I don't care if it's dangerous. Anyway, they won't notice me. Nobody notices me.'

Seduced by Kamik's confidence, Larsen gave way.

'You are not to do anything silly, or ask people things that might make them suspicious. Just behave as you always do, but keep your eyes open, and answer my questions as truthfully as you can. That's all. OK?'

'OK.'

'I mean it. Or there will be bad trouble, for both of us.'

'I said OK. I understand.'

And Larsen convinced himself that he did.

'Good. Don't forget it. Now tell me about Mitti Hendrik.'

'She and Otto Frederiksen are lovers. Everyone knows that. But I did not see her last night.'

'Do you think she murdered Jonis?'

'Most people do. They say the only reason you have not arrested her is because . . .'

'Because what?'

'Because you know each other,' ended Kamik lamely.

'I have never met her before in my life. I haven't arrested her because she could not have done it. Mitti was in town at the time Jonis was killed.'

'Times are often wrong.'

'So you think she did it?'

'I suppose so.'

'Why?'

'Because husbands and wives do kill each other. It happens often.'

'Often,' repeated Larsen bleakly. He took a deep breath. 'Is that the only reason?'

Kamik thought for a moment, scratching his short, bristly hair. His smooth young forehead was corrugated with small wrinkles.

'A year ago there was a killing down the coast in Ikateq. I knew the woman who did it. She was like Mitti. She had a fierce temper like Mitti. And she also wanted to be rich, rich enough to leave. This woman married a man she thought had a lot of money, though he was not a good man. Then she found out he was not rich at all. She grew angry with him, so he hit her, so she shot him with his own gun.'

Smiling faces, singing and laughter in the bar, and underneath a hidden river of hatred and repression. An eleven-year-old boy assumed one of the things which marked a marriage was that husbands and wives beat and killed each other. Larsen felt sick.

'What about Gudrun Eistrup?'

'The Danski woman has seemed scared lately,' said Kamik. 'What could she be scared of, a big woman like that? I thought everyone liked her. Or wanted her to like them.'

'Including Evat?'

Kamik considered, moving his head from side to side.

'People say he is her boyfriend, but I do not think so.'

'Why not?'

'He often looks unhappy or angry. If I was going to bed with the woman every man in the town wanted, I would look pleased with myself. Wouldn't you?'

Larsen's laugh had little humour in it. Kamik glanced sharply at him.

'Go on,' said Larsen.

'Evat Jonsson is always talking. About being a true Inuit, about going back to the old days and saving our culture, about anything. But no Inuit dresses like him, or knows about the sort of things he knows about. When he is drunk he argues a lot, especially with the doctor. I keep away from the doctor, my nan says he is a poisoner, and Evat and he talk about things I cannot understand. Besides the doctor I do not think many people like Evat. And I think he wishes to leave Sermilik as soon as he can.'

'Doesn't everyone?'

Kamik looked surprised.

'Is there anyone else you are interested in?' he asked, after a moment.

'The Secretary of the commune perhaps.'

'You are watching many people. I will have to be like an oyster and have a hundred eyes.'

'I am not asking you to follow these people, just to notice if you happen to see them.'

'Of course. Well, Mr Bronlund is very clever. Everyone knows he makes money from his job, but no one knows how. Not that they care. He looks after the town, and gets things for it that other people could not get, so it is only fair he takes part for himself.'

Larsen nodded.

'Thank you. That is enough for now. Come to see me tomorrow. And here are ten crowns for some sweets.'

'I will not get many sweets for that,' Kamik remarked, neatly catching the coins Larsen had tossed him.

'If you want more, come back tomorrow, but do not try to be clever or you'll get nothing.'

Kamik winked at him and slipped lithely out of the door.

'Wait,' called Larsen.

The boy darted back inside, elated and mischievous.

'You want to give me more money? OK.'

'I want to know if Øle Olssen plays cards.'

'No. He prefers girls. Only old men play cards.'

'So he does not gamble?'

'Where would he get the money? He spends all he has on beer.'

'Thank you.'

'No trouble.'

The boy disappeared, leaving Larsen smiling, his spirits lifted by Kamik's quick wits and his love of life.

The harsh ring of the telephone flung Larsen into wakefulness. Glancing at his watch, he saw it was just after four in the morning. He dragged himself up, tried to ignore the pain in his foot, and went over to the phone.

'Is that the police?' It was Marian Krinsky, her voice high-pitched, shrilling on the edge of hysteria.

'This is Sergeant Larsen. How may I help you?'

'You must come quickly. Please, oh my God, it's horrible . . .!'

'Where am I to come to?'

'Otto Frederiksen's house. Quickly, for Christ's sake! Please. He's dead. Otto's dead. He's . . .' She was sobbing.

'I will come immediately. Do not touch anything, just phone Dr Sven, the number is 424, then stay where you are and wait for me.'

Larsen grabbed his jacket, pulled on his boots – which was painful, but not as bad as he had feared – and set off. It was a hard walk up the hill and Larsen's feet objected at every pace, but his mind was elsewhere.

Death was following him, a shadow which made itself visible only by its actions. The one man Larsen had had some power over, whom he might have been able to extract valuable information from, was dead. Larsen cursed himself for not squeezing Frederiksen while he had the chance. And now it was too late.

Outside the house, as if aware something had happened, several wolf-like huskies had gathered in a pack, running round and round, snarling, snapping at each other's flanks. As Larsen came to the front door, it was flung open.

'Thank God you've come,' gasped Marian Krinsky.

Close behind her was Margrethe, her black eye caught by the low rays of the sun.

'Is the doctor here yet?' asked Larsen.

'No, no. There's no answer at his number.'

'Where's Frederiksen?'

'Upstairs. In . . . in the room at the end of the corridor.' Larsen had somehow expected it. 'Shall I show you?' she asked reluctantly.

'No. Keep trying to ring the doctor.'

Larsen ran upstairs. A lake of contrasting emotions surged back and forth inside him, foreboding, curiosity, anger, confusion. The door was half open, a key in the inside lock.

The room was warm, thickly carpeted, lit by subdued wall lights. In the middle was a large bed, with red satin sheets rumpled and creased. A white fur rug lay on the ground. There was a large mirror on the ceiling above the bed, and other mirrors on the walls, reflecting away into eternity. The walls were decorated with large, expensively framed, erotic photographs, except for one which was taken up by a long cupboard with sliding doors.

On the bed was Otto Frederiksen. Naked. Leather straps held his hands and legs, so that he was spreadeagled. His face was distorted and discoloured, there was a bandage over his eyes, and another over his mouth. Larsen untied the blindfold. Empty eyes stared up past him, at the mirror.

Frederiksen's forehead was still warm, but there was no trace of breath or heartbeat. Larsen untied the gag and straps, thumped Frederiksen on the chest as hard as he could, then gave him artificial respiration. But even as he tried, the unequivocal cold of death came stealing over Frederiksen's body. Feeling eyes on his back, Larsen suddenly looked over his shoulder. Margrethe was in the doorway, staring inside with expressionless eyes.

'Go downstairs and wait there,' Larsen said roughly.

She showed no sign of moving, so he pulled her out into the corridor and pointed down the stairs. She went slowly. Larsen returned to the room. He pulled out the key, locked the room up, then followed Margrethe downstairs.

Marian Krinsky had poured herself a very large whisky and was holding the glass tightly, breathing fast. Her eyes did not see what was in front of them, only a sight imprinted on the retina. Margrethe sat close by, her hands on her knees, her body relaxed, a puzzled expression on her face.

'Who found the body?' asked Larsen, fingering the key in his pocket.

'I did.' Krinsky looked up jaggedly.

'Have you contacted the doctor yet?'

'No. The phone just rings and rings.'

'Margrethe,' said Larsen. 'Ring the doctor and tell him to come over here immediately. Mrs Krinsky, come with me, please.'

The American woman got up, then stopped.

'But . . .'

'I must ask you some questions.'

She was dressed in a thin, pale dressing-gown that floated around her whenever she moved, much as she tried to keep it clutched in. Underneath she wore a white nightdress down to her knees. Her feet were bare. Her loose hair was revealed as honey-brown with a slight curl in it, reaching just below her shoulders. Her eyes, without make-up, were gentler, softer than might have been expected, and she turned her head towards sound in the way of someone who does not trust what they see.

'What the hell is going on here?' she muttered. 'It's a nightmare. A fucking nightmare.'

Larsen put his hand on her arm. For a moment she must have thought he was about to take her up to the room of death, for she whimpered and froze. Then, seeing him going into the downstairs office, she followed meekly and sat down on a white plastic chair. Larsen stayed standing.

'Tell me what happened.'

'I was asleep in my room,' she began, with a visible effort to regain control. 'I was woken by . . . noises.'

'What noises?'' asked Larsen, speaking English as carefully and clearly as he could.

'Noises. Noises like . . . like people having sex. I tried to take no notice, but it isn't easy. You find yourself listening. There was some talking going on too. but I couldn't understand. Then it went quiet.'

She was shaking, clutching her whisky glass tight enough to crack it.

'Go on.'

'There's not much to tell. I didn't hear anything for five minutes. Maybe ten. Then a door suddenly opened, shut, then opened again and I heard people on the stairs. Going up and down. I don't know. I looked at my watch, it was coming up four o'clock. Even without interruptions I don't sloop as well as I need. I got up, put my dressing-gown on, and went over to . . . that room. The door was ajar, so I went in. I wear contact lenses, but I didn't have them on – I still don't – so I couldn't see much. I stood at the door and said, "Mr Frederiksen, could you please stop running in and out, slamming the door," or something like that. He didn't answer, so I went closer and I saw that . . .'

She collapsed into tears. Larsen let her cry for a little, then resumed his questions, as she wiped her nose with the back of her hand.

'Could you recognise the voices?'

'God, no! I couldn't even say if it was men or women talking – '

Larsen interrupted, putting hardness into his tone.

'How did you know Mr Frederiksen was dead?'

She looked up.

'What? What did you say?'

'I asked how you knew Mr Frederiksen was dead?'

'I just did.'

'When I went into that room I wasn't sure he was dead. How did you know?'

'Christ in hell! I knew.' She was almost shouting. 'I just knew he was dead. Anyone could fucking see it. The way his neck was every which way, his eyes looking nowhere . . .'

'His eyes were covered by a blindfold. You could not have seen them.'

'I thought I did, for Christ's sake, I don't know. But he was dead, right?'

The eyes could have just been her imagination. Or not.

'You didn't see anyone else?'

'No. I told you I didn't.' Suddenly she remembered her whisky and drained the glass. 'There were just these steps going down the stairs, running down the stairs. That's why I went out when I did. I thought they'd finished, so I could say something without interrupting . . . without . . .'

She turned away and hid her face.

Larsen led her back to the sitting-room. Margrethe was exactly where she had been when they left, except for the black cat curled up on her lap which she was stroking absently.

'Did you telephone the doctor?' Larsen asked.

'There was no answer.'

Larsen looked at the cat.

'Why hasn't that creature been eaten by huskies long ago?' he said, half to himself.

'The dogs are frightened of it,' said Margrethe.

Somehow it seemed typical of Sermilik. A world upside down.

Marian Krinsky was refilling her glass. Larsen glanced at her, then took Margrethe to the office. The cat followed, tail held high, purring.

'What happened?' Larsen asked.

Margrethe sat placidly in the office chair. She looked completely calm, yet there was a strange limpness about her. She was wearing nothing but a wrap over her solid, thick-set nakedness. Her low, widely spaced breasts with their dark nipples were very visible, swaying as she moved. Her legs were bare, so were her arms. Her hair hung long and dark, half-way down her back.

'I was woken by a scream, so I got up to see what was happening. It was Mrs Krinsky. She came running downstairs shouting something about Mr Frederiksen. I could not understand her. Then she shouted, "Police, police," at me. I picked up the telephone and rang, but she snatched it from my hand and spoke to you. Then we stayed here until you came.'

'That's all?'

'Yes.'

'You didn't see anyone else?'

'No.'

'You didn't hear anyone running down the stairs, or out of the front door, before Mrs Krinsky came down?'

'I was asleep. But I did see the front door was open.'

At that moment there was a piercing scream from the sitting-room.

11

AFTER THE DEATH

The American woman was standing by the door.

'A sound,' she mumbled hysterically. 'I heard someone moving. The murderer is still in the house.'

Larsen stood still and listened.

'There, for Christ's sake.' She pointed along the corridor. 'I heard it there.'

Larsen began to walk slowly down the corridor. As he did so he felt the weight of his gun on his hip, and could not remember putting it on. The kitchen door was open, but next to it was another door, tight shut. The door that must lead into Margrethe's room. As Larsen hesitated, there was a clearly audible rustling from inside. Carefully he unbuttoned the gun from its holster and pushed back the safety-catch.

'Come out of there,' he barked.

Instantly all movement in the room ceased.

'Come out,' he repeated. 'Police.'

Nothing. Larsen waited thirty seconds, counting them by the beating of his heart, then hurled the door open with one hand, while keeping well back against the wall. His knuckles were white around the gun, his finger trembling on the trigger. Larsen had never fired his gun in anger.

There was no need. The man who came out was stark naked. His flesh hung in small, limp rolls.

'It's me,' he quavered, as the gun pointed at his chest. 'Don't shoot. It's only me. Olssen.'

'I nearly killed you,' Larsen breathed, putting away the gun. His foot ached viciously. 'Get dressed.'

Olssen shivered. His sharp-featured foxy face glowered at the policeman impotently. He picked up his clothes, which were scattered over Margrethe's tiny room, and began to put them on.

'What are you doing here?' demanded Larsen.

With his trousers back on, Olssen regained some confidence.

'What do you think?' he said, with a leer.

'Have you been out of this room in the last hour?'

'No.' Olssen pulled on a filthy vest. 'I was asleep, then suddenly I

121

was woken by a scream. Margrethe went out to see what was happening. I stayed here. What is happening?'

'Have you slept with Margrethe before?'

'Now and then. Who screamed? Why were you waving your gun around?'

'Mr Frederiksen has been murdered.'

'It wasn't me,' Olssen said immediately. 'I haven't been out of this room. Ask Margrethe.'

'She said the scream woke her. So she cannot know where you were while she was asleep, which was when the murder happened.'

The panic was back in Olssen's face.

'I told you, I was asleep. And I don't wake quickly. When I opened my eyes, Margrethe was at the door.'

'You mean she could have done it? She could have just come in?'

'I don't know.'

'Where did you get the money for your trip to Nûk?'

'I told you. I won it in a game of cards.'

'You don't play cards, Olssen. You don't gamble either. Who gave you the money? And why?'

Olssen said nothing. Grim-faced, Larsen took him to the sitting-room to join Krinsky, then returned to the office. Margrethe was still sitting where he had left her, the cat once again on her lap.

'Why didn't you tell me about Olssen?' he demanded.

'I did not think it was important.'

'Are you a deep sleeper?'

She seemed unsurprised by the change of tack.

'I don't often wake up.'

'But this time you were woken by a scream?'

'Yes.'

'Where was Olssen?'

'Next to me, I suppose. I did not notice. I went out to see what was happening.'

'So Olssen might have killed Mr Frederiksen, then crept back into your room, and you would know nothing about it?'

Her eyes opened wide.

'Why should Olssen kill Mr Frederiksen?'

'Last week Olssen spent two days in Nûk. Do you know where he got the money?'

'I did not know he had been to Nûk.'

'How did you get your black eye?'

'Mr Frederiksen hit me. After I let you into the house.' She said it without a trace of accusation.

'Why did he hit you?'

122

'He found a broken glass outside his room.'

'Did you tell him about me?'

'No.'

'Why not?'

'He did not ask me.'

After Margrethe left, Larsen sat down and massaged his burning foot. To kill a helpless man was a coward's crime, and Olssen was surely that. Larsen's instinct was also to suspect anyone as keen as Olssen to incriminate someone else. But perhaps Margrethe was lying, just being more clever about it. There was another aspect, neither Olssen nor Margrethe seemed to have heard anyone running away. So Marian Krinsky could easily have murdered Frederiksen, slipped downstairs to leave the front door open, and only then raised the alarm.

He might even be face to face with that familiar Hollywood figure, the serial killer. The insane psychotic who murdered merely because he, or she, enjoyed murder. Briefly Larsen wished he had the sort of help policemen in Denmark routinely called upon – fingerprint and forensic experts who could probably work out exactly who had been in the room and what had gone on. But in Sermilik Larsen was now the only policeman, and the only forensic department he had was his own head.

Reluctantly he returned upstairs, unlocked the door, and felt his gorge rise at what he saw. This was no simple stabbing or shooting, this was a monstrous, sordid evil that did not belong under the gaze of the pure snowy mountains ringing Sermilik. Yet somehow it also seemed typical of the whole town: as the dead man's lust had long lost any point, becoming a gangrene that would destroy him, so it seemed to Larsen that Sermilik itself rotted slowly, uncleanly, away.

He sat on the edge of the soft, aphrodisiac bed, unconsciously rubbing his hands together, and stared at the corpse. The straps had left marks on Frederiksen's wrists and ankles. Marks not dissimilar to, though much fainter than, those on Jonis's body. But there were other marks as well.

After a few moments Larsen got up. There was a pile of discarded clothes in one corner of the room, a shiny black catsuit, long spike-heeled boots, gauntlets, a mask. He turned away in disgust and went over to the sliding doors in the far wall. Inside was a small changing room, equipped with lights, make-up table, and a full-length mirror. There was also a wardrobe and a chest of drawers, both full of a bizarre variety of clothes and accessories. Shameful things he did not want to look at. Larsen relocked the door and returned downstairs.

Margrethe, Marian Krinsky and Olssen were sitting in absolute silence. Larsen went across to the telephone and rang Dr Sven, who answered almost immediately.

'Doctor, it's Sergeant Larsen. Could you come over to Otto Frederiksen's house?'

'What time is it?' The doctor sounded sleepy.

'Five thirty. Please come at once. There's been another murder.'

Larsen heard a sharp intake of breath.

'I'll be right over.'

Larsen hung up. He glanced across the sitting-room, then felt a sudden overwhelming desire for fresh air, and went outside. A thin wind whispered up from the fjord. He leant against a rock and waited until Dr Sven drove up in his car.

'Where's the body?'

Larsen led him upstairs and unlocked the door. As the doctor stepped inside, he whistled.

'I knew Frederiksen had a reputation, but this looks like a Copenhagen brothel.' He knelt down by the body and began to examine it with the brisk, almost facetious practicality all doctors are taught. 'Died of strangulation, about two hours ago I would say. No serious bruises, he doesn't seemed to have struggled.'

'He couldn't.' Larsen pointed to the straps on the bed.

'That explains it. Stupid man.'

'I suppose there's no way it could have been an accident?'

'Not if he was strapped down. This was strangling not suffocation, see the bruising round the neck. He had the life throttled out of him all right, probably by someone who didn't approve of his décor.'

Larsen did not smile.

'Could you say if the killing was done by a woman or a man?'

The doctor looked surprised, then shrugged.

'A weak woman might have had some trouble, but if he was trussed up like a chicken she had all the time she needed. A strong man might perhaps have caused more damage round the throat and neck. But I didn't think there was any question that Frederiksen always chose women.'

'Someone as obsessed with sex as the man who made this room might try anything.'

'I suspect you misunderstand the room's purpose. Usually, though not always, people add unnecessary extras to sex because their sex drive is low and they need or want something to increase it. Of course we all demonstrate a little fetishism, if only in finding some clothes sexier than others, but very few either want, or can afford, to take it much further. Among those who do, what always surprises me is how repetitive things are, same domination games, same clothes and dis-

124

guises. When I worked in Denmark I had to deal with a fair number of sexual problems, and on occasion I recommended alternative forms of sex or sexual accessories, but here in Greenland that part of my practice has vanished. I'd thought the only sexual problems here are unwanted babies, and a steady round of venereal disease . . .'

'So you don't think Otto Frederiksen was murdered by a man?'

'It seems unlikely. This has all the marks of a sexual killing, and Frederiksen was not a homosexual.'

'You sound very certain.'

The doctor opened his large, white hands.

'All right,' he said at last. 'Although I prefer my patients not to know, I admit that I am gay. I have only had a handful of sexual encounters in the three years I've been in Sermilik, but I would certainly have guessed if Frederiksen had had leanings that way. You will not tell anyone?'

'Why should I? One more question, where were you between three thirty and five thirty this morning?'

Dr Sven laughed.

'In my bed, of course.'

'And where is your telephone?'

'I have two. One in my living-room, the other by my bed. Ah, I see. You were trying to phone me earlier and there was no answer.'

'Yes.'

'It would not be the first time someone has called me and the phone did not ring. Not the twentieth time either. All Sermilik phones are congenitally unreliable. I often complain, but nothing happens.'

So it was just an out-of-order telephone. The doctor had appeared unsurprised by the murder room, but that was not evidence. More and more it seemed nothing was evidence.

'While I'm here I might as well change the dressing on your frost-bite,' said the doctor. 'All this running around won't have done it any good – see, the blisters are as bad as ever.'

'There's nothing I can do about that.'

'I suppose not. And of course I'm speaking as a doctor, not a law-abiding citizen who wants to see a murderer caught. Grit your teeth, this may hurt.'

It did, and even after the foot was bound up, it went on hurting.

'I'll have another look tomorrow. I presume you want an autopsy on Frederiksen? I've brought a bag, so if you could just help me get the body into it, and carry it to my car . . .'

A few minutes later Larsen returned to his three not-quite-witnesses, told Margrethe and Olssen they could go, then turned back to Marian Krinsky.

'A few more questions, I'm afraid,' he said apologetically.

The last hour had seen her recover herself well. But the whisky bottle on the sideboard was empty, and there was still a tremor in her voice and restlessness about her hands.

'Why did you stay here with Frederiksen?' Larsen asked, sitting down in one of the deep armchairs.

'Because he invited me,' she answered simply.

'I would have thought a woman like you would prefer to stay in the hotel.'

'What do you mean, a woman like me?'

Larsen exhaled softly and studied his fingers. They were rough and still a little numb from the frost-bite. When he looked up, his impassive face did not show even a flicker of the sudden pity he felt for the hard, rich, self-assertive American facing him.

'I suppose I mean a woman who has made her way in business. A woman who must spend a lot of her time travelling and meeting powerful men. The sort of middle-aged woman who feels comfortable in taxis and airplanes and hotels because they are what she is used to. They are part of a game she knows how to play.'

'The sort of woman you know a lot about in Greenland,' she said scornfully.

'People here are no different to anywhere else.'

'No?'

'Do you think they are, then?'

'You're like no policeman I've ever met.'

'Have you met a lot of policemen?'

Her laugh was a snort.

'Yes. But they were men who had climbed high up the ladder. The ladder here must be very short.'

'And I am not even far up that short ladder, is that what you mean?' Larsen regarded her carefully. 'I cannot see why you should wish to run me down.'

'So what do you want me to say?'

'I want you to tell me why you came to stay here.' Larsen put his foot out in front of him to rest it. 'Especially after what happened in the seed bank.'

Her expression changed. The superficial superiority began to crumble away. Her grey eyes were watchful, intelligent, but shot through with sparkles of fear.

'You heard all that, then? It's not so rare to meet a con-man. In a strange way, when you catch someone trying to play you for a sucker, you can kind of like them. You feel you've seen through them, so they can't hurt you. It may not be true, but it's a thought. I felt it when we got back to town yesterday. I mean, the whole thing was such a stupid effort.'

'Go on.'

'OK. I don't like this, but you've got to know, I suppose. And maybe if I think of you as an analyst, telling it will help me to deal with it. I suppose policemen do have to be part-time psychoanalysts, like whores.'

She glanced over at the whisky bottle, then went on.

'There's another thing about guys you've spotted on the rip-off. You know you won't see them again, and I find that attractive. My therapist tells me it's fear of fresh involvement after my divorce, but I think he just says that to stop me worrying. I think it goes deeper than that. Anyway, knowing why something happens doesn't make it any less real when it does happen. Not for me anyway.'

Larsen did not move.

'After we got back from the seed bank Otto took me to the hotel, and we had a few drinks, then the bar started filling up. It's not that it got rowdy, in fact it was pretty quiet. But everyone only seemed to be there to get drunk as fast as they could. Maybe like our Indians you Eskimos can't hold alcohol . . .'

'The Danes were not getting drunk also?' asked Larsen, then wished he had held his tongue.

She looked up at him.

'Yeah,' she said at last. 'I guess it had to be like that here too. Actually I didn't notice. Anyway we talked about things, men and women and the differences, and we agreed there weren't so many it mattered. I invited him up to my room for a few more drinks. I was enjoying the talk, it wasn't late, I didn't have any plans, and he seemed like a good listener, which isn't so common. I told him about my work, and he was interested. He said it must be hard being a woman in top management, and I said not for me. I told him that my therapist reckoned I always needed to be in control, of everything, which is maybe why me and my son don't get along any more.' She paused. 'You got children?'

'Yes, a daughter,' said Larsen carefully.

'How old?'

'Fourteen. But she's with her mother.'

'How do you feel about that?'

The upfront bluntness of the questions, from a woman he did not know, a woman he was interrogating, caught him unawares.

'I don't know.'

'You mean you don't want to tell me. That means you care.' She interlaced her fingers and stretched her arms. 'Children are weird. You

127

just can't guess what's going on in their heads. I thought my little boy, Mike, was just perfect, hard-working, clever, neat, obedient. I spent a fortune on his education, best schools, Suzuki violin, swimming clubs, riding, summer camps, everything he wanted, and he went with it all. We got on so good, he wasn't just a kid, he was my friend. Then when he was seventeen he upped and left me. Went to live in Seattle. I see him once a year now, at Thanksgiving, and we've nothing to say each other. He likes his dad though, spends a lot of time with him even though that man walked out on us when Mike was only seven. Children always go on about things being fair – but they're not fair themselves.'

'Could we continue?' asked Larsen stiffly.

'If we must.'

'Well?'

'Well, I was saying that needing to be in control made me a good executive, but a lousy wife. So Otto said control was interesting, because he had to be in control of his work, but that meant sometimes he liked to be completely helpless, that it was a sort of necessary relaxation for him. I said I wouldn't like that a bit, and he said no, he'd figured that. And then he didn't say anything else. Well, that riled me, so I asked him what he meant, and he said I didn't really want to know, and I said I did. So he said he could show me back at his place.

'Now ninety-nine times out of a hundred I would have ignored his offer straight off, especially after that kind of obvious lead-in. But he was such a little skinny wimp of a guy that I didn't find him at all frightening. A little sad maybe, but not spooky. Anyway, I'd had a bit to drink and I was stuck in this dump, and I just didn't believe that the sort of things that go on in New York or Miami go on here . . . but I was wrong. Wasn't I?'

She closed her eyes.

'I suppose people in Greenland aren't any different. They're sick too. God, but I'm tired! Do you reckon he's got any more whisky around? No, you're right, I've had enough. More than enough. What's the time?'

'Half-past six.'

'Is that all? You don't have a clue when it's light all the time. It screws up my mind.' She leant back in her chair. 'In a way there isn't much else to say. I came back here with him, and we had a couple more drinks, and talked about sex in a sort of disguised way. I suppose I should have told him I'd slip into something more comfortable – my coat. But I didn't. In fact I started feeling pretty horny and then he showed me that room upstairs . . . Look, you don't want the details, do you?'

Larsen did not, but he said nothing. What she said and did not say were all revealing.

'Well, I was mellow, but not out of it. I was . . . . right for it, actually. So we played around, dressing up a bit and stuff, then I did just what I wanted with him, got him to do what I like, and pow! It was a big pow too, believe me. One of the biggest.'

And she breathed deeply. Remembering.

'But after the pow,' she went on, 'well, I'd done most of the work, and I was played out. One doesn't have the old staying power after about thirty-five. All I wanted was to crawl into a nice warm bed and crash out. As for the stuff I had on, things that had looked sexy and wicked just seemed limp and childish. I wanted them off. Fast. He wanted more, but I told him no way, got out of the super-hero costume, and went off to bed. I told him he could come and share with me if he wanted, but no more fancy games. He wasn't interested in that – not many men are, it seems.'

She lapsed into silence laced with regret and shame. Larsen leant forward.

'Go on,' he said softly.

She didn't answer.

'Why did you stay the next night if the previous one hadn't really been a success?' he asked.

That fired her up.

'What do you mean, hadn't been a success? OK, I felt a fool for a little, but the sex had been great, and I'd slept really good after it. Anyway, for Christ's sake, the air strike means there's no way out of here. I need something to keep me from going crazy from boredom, and if that means playing Catwoman in exchange for a good fuck, OK.

'Anyway, next night we went into the same routine. But it didn't feel so way out any more, didn't have the same edge. I felt a bit self-conscious, stupid even . . .' She shrugged and laughed forlornly. 'I suppose I hadn't had enough to drink. Not even the buzz was the same. Then I suddenly remembered how he'd tried to double-cross me. If it had worked, it would've cost me my job. So I lost my temper and got rough. Finally I chucked the stuff and just left him lying there. That was it.'

She looked Larsen straight in the face.

'That was it,' she repeated.

'You didn't kill him?'

'Christ, no! I mean, I behaved badly.' Again her fingers entwined then separated, stretching out as if to push away the memory. 'Like I never had before. Like I didn't know I could. I suppose the gear I had on sort of encouraged it, all that dominatrix stuff, but it wasn't really so big a deal. He was maybe a little hurt, but nothing much. He even seemed to half like it, which pissed me off even more.'

'And afterwards?'

'I got kind of scared afterwards, I didn't know what he might do back to me. So I went to my room and put a chair up against the door. I would've gone back to the hotel, but it was late and I didn't fancy going out with the drunks, and those wolves that pretend to be dogs, everywhere. Then a little later I heard someone join him.'

Larsen wondered if the whole story was an involved sex fantasy, sparked off by finding Frederiksen's body.

'What time was this?' he asked.

'Maybe two thirty. I'd been listening hard, in case he came to get me, and I heard someone walking up the stairs. They went into the room and I didn't hear any more. Sometime later, I don't know how long, I sort of was asleep and sort of wasn't, I heard someone leave. So I went in. I couldn't resist it. I had to know, maybe I wanted him to do something to me to make up for what I'd done to him. To get it over with. And there he was . . . like that.'

The adrenalin of telling her story had run out. She was drained and frightened and disgusted. Lines cut up her face and shadows pulled at her eyes.

'You must think I'm sick,' she said.

'I think you should go back to your hotel room and get some sleep,' he said. 'We'll talk again some other time.'

'OK,' she said.

It occurred to Larsen that her therapist back in America was on the edge of a nice fat windfall.

After she had gone, he closed his eyes and tried to sort out his thoughts. Even if every word of Marian Krinsky's story was true, it didn't really help. In fact the only person it ruled out of the list of suspects was Marian Krinsky. On the other hand there was no question who was the likeliest person to have been the late night visitor. The woman known throughout Sermilik as Frederiksen's mistress, the leading suspect for Jonis's death. Mitti Hendrik.

Larsen phoned Dr Sven.

'What can I do for you?' asked the doctor jovially.

'Just a couple of questions.'

'I've never known such a man for questions. Well?'

'Have you started the autopsy yet?'

'In the middle of it. I'd stopped for a cup of coffee just as you rang. Frederiksen was strangled all right.'

'Have you found any bruising on the body?'

'Some, yes, mostly around the ribs. Probably the blows were delivered about six hours ago, kicks perhaps. And there're one or two other marks that I'd guess, only guess mind you, could have been inflicted by stiletto heels.' He laughed knowingly. 'Painful at the time probably, but nothing serious.'

'Was there any sign of sexual activity?'

The doctor laughed again.

'You mean apart from where he was found?'

'I meant medical signs.'

'Yes, yes, I know you did. Well, there were also a variety of cuts and abrasions that could have been linked to sex. But the only thing I could say for certain was that he'd had vaginal sex with a woman who was menstruating.'

'You're certain about that?'

'Quite certain. Check the sheets, I'm sure there'll be traces. And one more thing I meant to tell you, I found an ear-ring mixed up in those clothes we wrapped him in.'

'An ear-ring?'

'Yes. That could be useful, couldn't it?'

'It could. Thank you again.'

'Always glad to help,' said the doctor.

12

MITTI

Before leaving Frederiksen's house, Larsen walked round the outside. One of the windows at the back was half open. He went over to it, and found himself peering into the spotlessly clean kitchen. There was no sign of any footprints or other marks, inside or out.

The second discovery was more confusing. In Otto Frederiksen's garage, tucked away behind his large, new, metallic purple Volvo, was a powerful quad-bike. Anyone who knew it was there could have used it to get to Lake Tugdlik in only about half an hour, rather than the two hours or more it took on foot. And that meant several alibis for Jonis's murder looked far less secure, even though it was hard to imagine that the bike would not have been noticed by someone.

Tobias Bronlund's house was small and unpretentious, near the north edge of Sermilik, where some of the poorer houses were huddled around three council-built blocks of flats. The Secretary came to the door himself.

'Ah, Sergeant Larsen. Good morning. Please come in.' He held out a large, cool hand. 'I presume you have come to tell me about Otto Frederiksen. Terrible news. Terrible.'

'You know already?'

'Oh yes. Dr Sven told me.'

Larsen had come expecting the Secretary to be the same irritable, aggressive man, barking out threats and refusals, he had been the last time they met. But Bronlund seemed to have undergone a remarkable transformation into a slow, short, fat man of about fifty-five, with a smiling, good-natured face and thick, greying hair cut very short to expose a knobbly skull. The sort of efficient, friendly person who got things done, and could expect to hold local office as long as he wanted it.

'I'm sure the commune will do everything necessary to help solve this hideous crime,' he went on, waving Larsen to a battered armchair. 'But you must remember this is a working town, and it's important that people are not alarmed. Also, of course, we must draw a sharp distinction between matters which are the responsibility of the police, and those that concern the local community.'

He shook his head and gave as sad a look as his heavy-jowled face could accommodate.

'Certainly these are hard times. The late spring, the strike, shortages in the shops. Seals are few. And now these unfortunate deaths. That of Mr Frederiksen is especially alarming, as he was the chief private employer in the town. Hard times indeed. Still, I am hopeful things are about to improve. In two weeks' time we celebrate Sermilik Day, the anniversary of the day that Lieutenant Gustav Berg became the first man to make contact with the indigenous population of Sermilik. The commune is planning a big festival this year – I think it will help the town put things behind us and strike out for the future. But of course any assistance I can give you . . .'

Larsen liked this new Bronlund rather less than the previous incarnation, and it struck him that the Secretary was not just a chameleon, able to change character in a flash, but that he was never off duty, and always had an eye on his own purposes.

'That's very kind of you, but to be frank, I don't think there is much help you can provide concerning the death of Mr Frederiksen. Not yet anyway.' The Secretary's obvious relief was immediately broken as Larsen pressed on. 'However, I still consider it most important that the utmost efforts are made to find the body of policeman Kalaasi . . .'

There was a momentary sting in Bronlund's reply.

'I thought we had covered this question.'

'I do not think so.'

Bronlund's button eyes were fixed on Larsen's face. Slowly he relaxed and patted his large, round stomach affectionately.

'Every year men are lost and their bodies never found. That is the Greenland way. We are an intrepid people, a people who, like no other in today's world, face nature in all her moods, work with her, yet must defy her simply to gain our food. Because of that we suffer the inevitable losses, the tragic accidents that every season bring new crosses to the cemetery – '

'Secretary Bronlund, last time we spoke, you said Kalaasi had just gone walkabout.'

'I still think, and hope, that is what has happened. But whatever the truth, these are hard times, so it is essential that people do not begin to brood and suspect each other. Such things are destructive of community spirit, Sergeant Larsen. Even such strong community spirit as we have here in Sermilik. The damage can take decades, literally decades, to repair. And my first thoughts must be of the people of Sermilik. That is what I have been elected for, as Secretary of the commune, as well as the local representative to the Landsting in Nûk. To watch over the people of Sermilik as a father.'

'I understand your concern, Secretary Bronlund, but this is a major

133

crime we are talking about. A policeman has been cold-bloodedly murdered.'

The Secretary hesitated, or seemed to hesitate. As he did so Larsen's eyes roamed around the little room. His gaze briefly stopped at the expensive CD player, the shelf of computer games, the videos, the laptop. The house was not as poor as it seemed.

'Very well,' said Bronlund at last. 'I will do what I can...'

'Tomorrow,' said Larsen firmly. 'I want another search made tomorrow. Thank you for your time.'

On his way back to the police station, he saw Olssen emerging from the supermarket. Larsen joined him.

'You still haven't told me where you got that money,' he said.

Olssen looked at him warily.

'Someone gave it to me,' he said at last.

'Who?'

Olssen sucked in his cheeks.

'Good morning, sergeant.' Larsen swung round, to find Evat behind him, smiling. 'Have you seen Mitti Hendrik anywhere? I dropped in on her last night to get back a book she borrowed from me, but she was out...'

'What book was that?' asked Larsen.

'Miller's *Off the Beaten Path in Alaska*.' Evat laughed. 'I wondered what she wanted with it, to be truthful. Anyway, I just wondered if you'd seen her recently. Don't worry.'

He strolled away, adjusting his sun-glasses. Larsen turned back to Olssen, but the little man had gone.

At the police station the telephone was ringing.

'This is not good news about Otto Frederiksen.' Chief Thorold sounded worried. 'He was an important man. He had contacts all over the place, in Denmark, America – '

'And with a certain multinational agro-chemical company,' interjected Larsen.

'No doubt. No doubt. Anyway, the first chance I get I'm going to send out someone to work with you.'

'Who?' asked Larsen.

'Lindegren probably...'

Aage Lindegren. Confident, reliable, blinkered, ambitious. The idea was not appealing. If the case was solved, Larsen did not doubt who would get most of the credit. Equally, if things could not be sorted out, Lindegren was a past master at shifting blame. Thorold was still talking.

'... I'll contact you when I can sort matters out. Until then, keep me informed of everything, and be careful. This case is costing the department money and notoriety, Larsen. We need results. And don't forget that report either.'

He was gone, back to his warm, comfortable office and his mothering secretary. Larsen scratched at the itchy scab along the line of his cheekbone, then closed his eyes and put his feet up, but all he saw in the darkness behind his lids was that body in the mirrored room, sprawled undignified and helpless, doll-like, reflected away into infinity. On Tuesday negotiating for $30 million, and two days later imprisoned in a cheap coffin in that humped, shallowly dug graveyard, with only a short-lived plywood cross to remind anyone who cared.

His face twisted in pity, Larsen fell asleep. When he woke, the sun in the north-west told him it was early evening. Larsen stretched, feeling the drug of sleep still circulating in his thick blood. He wondered what had woken him, then heard a steady tap-tapping at the door. He went downstairs, opened it, and was almost sent flying as Kamik streaked in, treading full on Larsen's frost-bitten foot. Pain lanced up the policeman's leg and he barely bit back a cry.

'What do you want?' he snapped.

'Money.' Kamik looked him expressively. 'Pay for information.'

'Information first,' said Larsen, sitting down and massaging his foot ruefully. 'And don't tell me about Frederiksen, because I know all about it.'

'All about it?' said Kamik, impressed.

'More than I want to anyway, though less than I need. What's your news?'

'Robert Maataq is back.'

So Larsen had been wrong. The finder of Jonis's body, the great hunter with the hair-trigger temper, was not dead. Larsen limped over to his desk and scribbled a note.

'Here,' he said, handing it to Kamik. 'Take this to Maataq.'

The boy stayed where he was.

'There's another thing.'

'Yes?'

'Mitti and her father-in-law were talking this afternoon, and the window was open, so I stopped and listened. She said ... wait a moment.' He burrowed in his pocket, produced a small notebook, and opened it with a flourish. 'Here it is. She said, "If I receive presents, am I to throw them away?" "Presents?" he answered. "Do not think that because I am blind I do not hear what people say." So she said, "People tell lies, but I hoped for enough money to take you to

135

Copenhagen and have your eyes operated on." "I am an old man," he said. "I am used to darkness. It is better like this. It is not worth the price you would have to pay." Then I heard someone coming and I ran away.'

Larsen gave the boy a 100-crown note.

'Don't forget what I told you. Nothing stupid.'

'No, sergeant.' Kamik stood stiffly upright and saluted. 'I'll take your note straight to Robert Maataq.'

He was gone in a blur. Larsen's smile faded and he wondered what the boy would do with the money. There was little to spend it on in Sermilik, except poor quality food, and very good quality guns.

The doctor arrived a few minutes later. He replaced Larsen's dressing with his usual brisk good humour.

'Anything new?' asked Larsen.

'Not much. Except that the woman with whom Frederiksen had intercourse was blood group A, which is very common in this town.'

'You said you found an ear-ring among Frederiksen's clothes.'

'Did I?' said the doctor vaguely.

'Yes. Do you have it?'

'I don't know. I think I may have lost it. Sorry.'

Somehow Larsen was not surprised.

'What did it look like, this ear-ring?'

'I can't really remember. Nothing out of the ordinary, just a small gold hoop. Do you think it was important?'

'It might have been. Would you mind trying to find it, please?'

'I'll do what I can.' The doctor's tone changed abruptly. 'Your foot is not in good shape. You are not resting it enough. I do have a small operating theatre here, but I would rather not have to amputate some of your toes.'

'Please find that ear-ring,' said Larsen.

Shortly after the doctor left, Robert Maataq arrived, hawk-like as ever.

'The doctor has been seeing you,' he remarked as he came in.

'I have some frost-bite in my toes.'

Maataq smiled.

'The only doctor for frost-bite is a good rub with snow or ice-water.'

'What if that is not enough?'

Maataq held up his left hand. The middle finger was missing.

'I am sometimes called the Man Who Can Only Count to Fifteen,' he said.

'Why?'

'Only six toes and nine fingers left,' explained Maataq. 'But I still have my thumbs and big toes, which are all that matter. Why did you want to talk to me?'

'You are the best hunter and tracker in the town?'

'God has made me so, yes. The old men say that in their youth there was not a man in Sermilik or Ikateq who could not track and sledge and hunt better than I. But old men will say anything to make you think they lived better than us.'

'Perhaps they did.'

'They wish to believe it. I do not argue.'

'How was your hunting?' asked Larsen.

'Not good. Seals, fish and birds alike grow fewer and more wary. Once thousands of auks would pass through the fjord in May and June, now I am lucky to see a hundred. Every year I have to take my boat further and further from the town. With the right weather and time, I used to be sure of catching an adult seal within a day's journey from my home. Now I sometimes travel six days to catch a half-grown thong seal. I did see narwhals this week, but I could not approach them because of the ice conditions, and they were gone inside an hour.'

'Is it just a few bad years, as the Secretary seems to think?'

'What does Bronlund know? Not one family in a hundred could survive if the government forgot us and the helicopters and boats ceased to come.'

'Why not move then?' asked Larsen. 'North to Dove Sund perhaps, or over to the west coast. There are many good hunting grounds, I am told, from Disko Bay north to Upernavik and beyond.'

Maataq shook his head.

'None as good as they were, I'd swear. Anyway, I am not one of those hunters who could wander from one place to another, and be equally at home in any. I have spent the thirty years since I was a boy learning the land within a month's journey of Asiaq fjord, and that is my knowledge. I must stay here. But I do not know where my children will find their hunting grounds. Perhaps Sermilik will be deserted, and then the seal and fish will return.'

'Do you really think the town will be deserted?'

'What is there of use here?'

Larsen was tempted to say millions of dollars' worth of seeds, but Maataq would not understand. He was younger than Larsen, but he came from an older generation, a generation that was almost gone. Not just in Sermilik, but throughout Greenland. Even the polar hunters of Thule, last upholders of ancient Inuit values, now made most of their living from artefacts and sealskins they sold to the rich Americans at their huge airbase nearby. People sat at home watching television, or went out and got drunk, and the old skills withered into forgetfulness. Larsen scratched his stubble, and decided to trust Maataq. A little way at least. If the hunter had the skills of another age, there was no real reason to believe he had the morals of that past age also. But he might have.

'I think my partner, Kalaasi, has been killed. I want you to find the body.'

Maataq's lean bony face showed no sign of surprise.

'Where am I to look?'

'You should start about half-way along the tongue of land that runs up the centre of Lake Tugdlik, on the eastern side – '

'Have you paper and a pencil?' interrupted Maataq.

Larsen got them, then watched in fascination as fluently, hardly pausing for thought, Maataq drew a map of the Tugdlik valley. A map of astonishing detail, every tiny promontory, islet and height marked out on it with uncanny accuracy. Larsen had no trouble picking out where Kalaasi had tried to stalk the gunman.

'Good,' said Maataq. 'I will search if you pay me.'

'Of course. I also want to know if you find anything else, traces, footprints, whatever.'

'Very well. I do not say I will find anything, but I will find what is there to be found.'

He left before Larsen could thank him.

Still Larsen could see no picture. Possibilities and alternatives twined and twisted among each other, while first one face, then another, would peer out at him from the undergrowth. In Sermilik a murder was too easy to provide a motive for, and too easy to hide.

Trying to detach himself from the depression that overwhelmed him, Larsen hobbled outside. It was grey and chilly, a few snowflakes flickered down on the dull rock, and the tops of the mountains were hidden.

Mitti was in the cramped kitchen, washing up. An American thriller was on her television, and she looked away from it reluctantly.

'Where is your father-in-law?' Larsen asked.

'Visiting a friend. They sit and talk together of the old days.'

'May I talk to you?'

'If you must.'

Larsen switched off the television, then turned to her.

'Where were you last night?'

'Here.'

'All night?'

'Yes.'

Larsen felt somehow disappointed at her lie. Her small, round, pert face was downcast and she would not meet his eyes. But he could not remember her looking him straight in the face the last time they had spoken. She always seemed to look at men sidelong, or from under lowered lashes. As for women, he was not sure she looked at them at all. He noticed that her ears were pierced, and she was wearing blue and white bead ear-rings.

'You have heard what happened to Otto Frederiksen?'

She nodded.

'When did you last see him?'

'Yesterday. We passed in the street.'

'Did you speak to him?'

'Perhaps. Is that against the law?'

Her swift, sharp answers prevented him using the silences he preferred. It was almost as if she sensed how he wished to question her and forestalled it.

'Listen, Mitti,' he said, making an effort. 'If you want my help, you must answer my questions truthfully.'

'Why should you want to help me? You never have.'

'Were you going to bed with Otto Frederiksen?'

She stopped her washing-up and gazed out of the window in front of her for a moment, before her eyes fell back to the sink.

'Why is that important?'

'Because I think it is.'

'I went to bed with him, yes. Like half the women in the town.'

'Did he buy you that jacket?' Larsen pointed at her suede jacket, which was lying on a chair nearby.

'Yes.'

'I doubt he bought expensive jackets for half the women in Sermilik.'

'Then he must have liked me more than the others.'

'Did you go back to his house with him?'

'A few times.'

'And you went to the room of mirrors, didn't you? When did you go there last, Mitti?'

Her growing alarm was almost solid.

'I don't know.'

'You had better try to know.' He put a hard, bullying edge into his words. 'In the last nine days two men you shared a bed with have been murdered. That does not look good. When did you last see Frederiksen?'

'I told you. Yesterday in the street.'

'And when did you last go with him into the room of mirrors?'

139

'It must have been two nights before Jonis was killed. That is why Jonis was so angry. That little bitch, Margrethe, told him, so he got drunk and came for me in the bar.'

She turned away and hid her face, with a sob. Larsen took a step forward and she shied away, but did not resist when he pulled back her hands. There were no tear tracks on her cheeks. Her eyes were dry.

'Listen to me,' he said intensely. 'Everyone says I should arrest you for the murder of Jonis. Because I haven't done it yet, doesn't mean I will not.'

She slipped away from him.

'I'll make some coffee.'

Larsen went out into the sitting-room, and sank into one of the chairs. After a few moments she brought in two cups of thick black coffee. She gave Larsen one, then sat down opposite him, and crossed her legs in a way she must have learnt from television, for it rang false on her broad frame.

'How is your foot?' she asked. Her voice seemed to have changed, to have become younger, scarcely more than a child's. She had too many faces, sullen, arrogant, non-committal, and what now? Larsen knew he must be wary.

'It is getting better. Slowly.'

'Good. I clean for Dr Sven once a week. What do you think of him?'

'He seems very competent.'

She rubbed the back of her hand over her long wide mouth, then leant forward.

'I was given back Jonis's clothes and belongings today. On the day Jonis was killed there was a lot of money in his pockets. I have been given only a few crowns. I want to know what happened to the rest of the money.'

'How much are you talking about?' he asked.

'A lot.'

'How much?'

'At least 10,000 crowns.'

Larsen was startled. Nearly $2000!

'What was he doing with so much money on him?'

She stiffened, and he caught a glimpse of the falcon that has struck and missed its prey.

'That is not the question. I want to know where the money is. It is my money now, and I want it.'

'Why should Jonis carry 10,000 crowns to work with him?' insisted Larsen.

'He was going to get it on his way to work.'

'From who? Why?'

'Trom Otto Frederikoon. It wae his wages.'

'Frederiksen had sacked him,' said Larsen.

'Yes. He was being paid off.' The answer was too glib.

'I can easily check how much Jonis was owed.'

Her resistance crumbled. Or some of it did. Larsen had the feeling that she had only retreated to build another wall to keep him from the truth.

'Perhaps it was not his wages, then.'

'What was it for?'

'I want my money,' said Mitti sullenly. 'And I think Dr Sven took it. He had Jonis's clothes, he could have taken anything he liked out of the pockets.'

'Don't be ridiculous.'

'I am not being ridiculous. Why do you think the doctor came to this God-forsaken place? Not because he likes it. In Denmark he married a rich woman, but after divorcing him she discovered he had spent all her money. She chased him through the courts, until at last he changed his name and came out here to get away from her and her lawyers. He knows they will find him one day, so he always wants money. He stole what was in Jonis's pockets.'

'There is no way I can prove that,' said Larsen dismissively. 'Do you know anything about a threatening letter sent to Frederiksen?'

'The Danish woman sent it to him.'

'Are you sure?'

She shrugged, leant back and closed her eyes. In the dim light she seemed like a carven jade statue.

All unbidden came Larsen's thought that if he were to make love to Mitti, he could find out if she were menstruating. He smiled to himself at the thought that he would then, as soon as possible, have to seduce Gudrun again, Marian Krinsky, and Margrethe as well, to check on them too. And maybe others.

'What are you grinning at?' demanded Mitti.

'Just a thought.'

But it was not, for the thought had unleashed something in Larsen. As he looked at Mitti, she seemed encased in a golden glow of eroticism. Blood pumped around inside him and his breath came faster. His head felt light from the raw power of the lust that had swept through him.

'Can I use your toilet?' he said.

'Out there.'

Larsen went through the kitchen into the tiny cold toilet and tried to urinate. It was a trick to calm himself down, but it did not work. As he flushed the toilet, he noticed a half-full bin in one corner. He bent down and looked inside. There was a used towel near the top. Quickly he picked it up, wrapped it in toilet paper, and stuffed it into his trouser pocket. His heart was thudding as he went out, and still he could not escape the desire that threatened to make a puppet of him.

'Did you ever tell anyone about you and Otto Frederiksen?' he asked, returning to the main room.

'Everyone knew.'

'Everyone did not know the details. But you told Jonis, didn't you?'

'It was after he beat me. I was frightened he would beat me again, so I told him.'

'And Jonis reckoned Mr Frederiksen had presented him with a nice easy way of making money. Did you tell anyone else?'

'Yes.' The word slipped out as if she had meant to say the opposite.

'Who?'

'It is not important. He is not that sort of man, not interested in women and sex. I had a few drinks and told him. I told him to make him laugh. But he did not.'

'Who was it?'

She did not answer. Larsen scratched his neck thoughtfully, still struggling to concentrate, to dominate his rebellious body. After a moment he decided not to press her just yet. He looked at his unsweetened coffee without enthusiasm.

'Do you have any beer?' he asked.

She went out and came back a few moments later with several cans. She gave Larsen one, then opened another for herself, drank it straight down, like a child with orange juice, and opened a second. Before Larsen was half-way through his first can, she was already on to her third. Larsen looked at her. His whole body seemed to be fizzing, his skin quivering gently, pleasurably.

Mitti shook her thick black hair out of her eyes and tipped back her head to finish the third can. Her throat was long and white and fine-skinned. Her breasts swelled under a white woollen jumper. She was utterly unselfconscious. From the moment she had had the beer in her hands, she drank with a determination and steadiness that entirely took her over.

Mitti reached out for the fourth can of beer from the table, but Larsen moved faster than her, and swept away both the remaining cans. She laughed.

'That's not fair. It's all we have left in the house.'

'You have to pay the cost of the drink.'

'How much is that?'

'A kiss.'

She laughed louder, showing good white teeth.

142

'A kiss for a can of lager. That is cheap, I will pay.'

She got up and came over, then bent down. Her lips brushed his, hot and dry, with a faint lingering taste of beer.

'There. Now the beer.'

Larsen reached out and gripped her by the waist.

'The price of lager is going up,' he said hoarsely.

He pulled her on to his lap and kissed her on the lips again. He could feel her large, firm buttocks and her breasts were soft sensations against his chest. Neatly she extracted one of the beer cans, opened it and drank. As she finished he put his arm round her neck, dragged her down and opened his mouth on hers.

She wrenched herself away with such force that his chair almost fell over.

'Oh no,' she said breathlessly, springing to her feet. 'No, no, no.'

Larsen scowled.

'Why not?' he demanded.

'Don't you know who I am?'

He stared at her, reading nothing in her long slanting eyes.

'What are you talking about?'

'I'm your daughter.'

13

MARIAN KRINSKY

Larsen's head was spinning.

'I don't understand.'

'It is not difficult to grasp. I am your daughter. You are my father. I thought you knew. Everyone else does.'

'But how?'

'You need me to tell you that?'

'You know what I mean.'

'You do not remember a girl called Jenufa, then?'

Larsen felt as if something had caught him by the throat.

'Yes. Yes, of course. I . . . I tried to find her.'

Mitti looked at him coldly.

'When?'

'A few days ago. I asked Gudrun Eistrup if she knew her, and the doctor . . .'

'You were ten years too late. She is dead.'

'And she . . .'

'She was my mother. And you are my father.'

Larsen wanted to ask if she was sure, how she could be sure, but he did not dare.

'How old are you now?' he said.

Mitti saw through him easily.

'You know how old I am. I am nine months less than the years since you left Sermilik. I am twenty-three.'

'Why didn't Jenufa tell me?'

Mitti's face was scarred with cynicism.

'What would have been the point?'

'I . . .'

'Taking on the responsibilities of a child at eighteen may be what half the population of Sermilik does, but you were special, weren't you? Would you really have given up your scholarship at Copenhagen, and come running back home to help look after your baby daughter?'

She was right. Larsen knew she was right. He might have felt guilty, or curious, or angry, but he would never have gone back.

'I'm sorry,' he said.

'What for?'

'For deserting you. For not knowing. For your mother.'

She laughed. Hard, choking laughs, like slaps.

'Those things were not your fault. But you haven't apologised for what is your fault.'

'What is that?'

'Failure.' She spat the word at him as if it were tipped with acid. 'You and Solomon Rosing set off to Copenhagen with the cheers of Greenland in your ears. He made money, fame, respect for himself and his people. His family left Sermilik years ago, and now they live in a smart house in Copenhagen, with a swimming pool. It's not just the money either. What other Greenlanders have made their way like him, become known and respected all over the world?'

'He's only a journalist,' objected Larsen, weakly. 'He just describes football matches – '

Mitti took no notice. The rancour of years was flooding from her.

'If I had been Solomon Rosing's child, if you had been him, I could have held myself proudly. My mother would not have been too poor to buy enough food, would not have died exhausted when she was just thirty. If you had been him, then my mother would have written to you, and you would have brought us over to Denmark to live with you. We would have been happy and rich. But what did all that intelligence, all that education, get you? Nothing. You wasted every scrap of what you had been and became a little policeman, running around after anyone who breaks the window of a liquor store. Now you come here, have a drink and try to fuck me like any other drunken Eskimo. The polar bear cub grows into a mangy Arctic fox. A father to be proud of. I knew you would come back eventually, but you should not have. Go away from here, Tomas Larsen. Go away now, for good.'

She turned from him.

He opened his mouth, but nothing came out. His tongue was thick and unruly, his mind a crashed computer. Shivering, he stumbled out of the door.

A few metres down the road he stopped, and began to weep. Somewhere at the back of his head was a wish, an impossible hope, that Mitti would come out and hug him, comfort him. But the door of the house remained shut. Several people went past, ignoring him. At last he recovered himself, and walked back down the hill.

Outside the police station a greying, middle-aged couple were waiting for him. They looked diffident, tired, their expressions and physiques interchangeable.

'You are the parents of Kalaasi,' said Larsen dully. It was not a question.

The man nodded.

145

'We have come from Ikateq. We hear he has disappeared.'

'I am very sorry.'

'You mean he is dead?' asked the woman.

Larsen nodded.

'I think so.'

'His brother says he is not. He says he knows. They are twins, you see.'

'I am sorry,' said Larsen again.

The two shuffled off towards the harbour, the woman's arm around the man. Overhead the white Arctic sun shone palely. Larsen took a deep breath, rubbed his forehead, and went inside.

That night the thought constantly recurred that Mitti had lied to him more than once. That she was lying about being his daughter. He tried to remember Jenufa's appearance, but all he could conjure up was coal-black eyes, panting breath, and the softness and sweat of her body. Yet in his guts he did not doubt Mitti had spoken the truth, and as the brief night scuttled by, he confronted the knowledge that he had another child. And that she was here. Yet he found no joy in him, only fear. He did not even try to sleep, but sat fully clothed on the bed, his head in his hands, and rocked imperceptibly to and fro as he gathered up all he knew of his daughters, and placed them alongside each other.

He had not seen Vigdis for three years, not since he had paid a Christmas visit to Copenhagen and been astonished at his eleven-year-old child, but she sat as firmly in his mind as if he saw her every week. Physically, except for her thick black hair and broad face, she was entirely Ann-Marie's daughter, pale and thin, with none of Larsen's stamina or his stocky strength. Mentally too her quick, nervous nature favoured her mother, though she shared Larsen's unfocused tendency to solitary introversion, and his love of the outside. The contrast with Mitti was enormous, and suddenly he realised that it was Mitti who looked like him, was built exactly like him. He had not seen it before because of her remarkable overlay of beauty, the perfect skin, long oval eyes, and high-boned face, which came together like a veil to make her into someone completely different.

The common ground between Vigdis and Mitti seemed minute. Yet Vigdis had been an emotionally jealous child – it was the reason they had not had another baby – and he guessed Mitti might have been the same. And both of the girls shared a remarkable ability, that he had never met anywhere else, of foreseeing what he would say. Or was that just his imagination? His wishful thinking?

At last, finding himself going through the same thoughts for the second or third time, Larsen went to the window. The sun was edging shyly above the mountain peaks, and he looked at it without enthusiasm, trying to remember how long it was since he had seen the stars. Several weeks at least. He rubbed his sore cheeks, and thought of the old man, Elias, and his whisper of the stars. There was a man. A true Inuit, who would not desert his children, or get desquamation of the cheeks. A man like Robert Maataq, who never doubted that his task in life was to be a hunter, as his father had been, and his grandfather, and every ancestor he had. Larsen's father had been a Danish civil servant with a briefcase, suit and degree. Perhaps he should have become a civil servant too. Ann-Marie had used to ask him, for God's sake why a policeman? And he had infuriated her by not replying.

The reason he had given himself was that he wanted to protect others from the brutality, the savage state of nature, that he always sensed looming just beyond the fringes of civilisation. It seemed plausible, and also nonsense. The truth was he did not know, other than that it had been a way to get back to Greenland. To get home. And as he walked in the tame, aseptic cities and towns of Denmark, that had been what he wanted more than anything else.

The thought struck him, as if blindingly new and seductive, that he could walk out of his job that day. Telephone Chief Thorold, tell him that he was giving up, and join Mitti and her father-in-law. But what then? Persuade the old man, Elias, to take them to Dove Sund? Listen to the whisper of the stars? Learn to hunt? Cast the skin of Westernisation and become a true Inuit at last? Mitti would have nothing to do with such nostalgic sentimentality. She was not a trusting little girl, she was a practical, hard-headed adult, whom he scarcely knew, and who wanted no part of him. And she was under suspicion of murder. His dream curled up and died on the touch of reality, like a snail sprayed with salt.

Outside there was no trace of mist or cloud. The ice on the fjord was finally beginning to melt, and the growing leads of open water glittered like gems. Flowers of wild azalea, diapensia and cassiope made tiny explosions of pink and white in the newly snow-free rock crevices. A middle-aged woman was prowling the stony waste near the police station, gathering the green stems and white flowers of the first scurvy-grass of the year. Spring had come at last.

The doctor was out. Larsen sat and read a three-week-old copy of the *Greenland News*, which he had already read at home. There was an article he could not remember seeing before about a possible international shortage of rye because a new fungicide-resistant strain of ergot had appeared in Denmark and Germany.

The waiting-room filled up. Two old women, two mothers with children around their feet and small babies in their arms, and a youngish man with his wrist in a sling. No one spoke to anyone else, no one read except Larsen, only the children tore around the room, chasing each other, hiding behind their mothers' legs, tussling on the floor like fox cubs, or falling over and crying until picked up and comforted. One boy made his fingers into a gun and pointed it at Larsen.

'Bang. Bang. You're dead, policeman!'

Larsen ducked.

'Missed,' he said, and seized the boy's arm. 'I've been looking for you for months, and now I've got you. You're under arrest, my lad.'

The boy squealed with delight, wriggled free and darted away across the room. As he did so Dr Sven arrived, and almost tripped over him on his way in. The boy squealed again and took shelter with his mother.

A few moments later the receptionist nodded, and Larsen went into the consulting-room.

'We must stop meeting like this,' said the doctor bluffly. 'People will talk.'

As his dressing was replaced, Larsen looked down on the doctor's fair, balding head.

'I have learnt something interesting.'

'Mm?'

'Do you know what the most valuable things in Sermilik are?'

Dr Sven shrugged.

'The larger fishing boats, I would imagine.'

'It is the seeds in the seed bank.'

'Really?' The doctor sounded entirely uninterested.

'Apparently certain sorts are worth a fortune.'

'I cannot imagine who to. But then there are always people who will pay a fortune for unusual objects of no intrinsic value, stamps, coins, paintings, whatever. There, that should last you through today. I'm glad to say things are looking a little better. Have you been resting?'

'A little.'

'Try more today. How have the cold and hot sensations been?'

'Better.'

'Excellent. I'm sure we will keep making progress if you rest. Come back tomorrow morning.'

'There are a couple of other things, doctor.'

'Make them quick. This is a busy morning for me.'

Larsen produced the sanitary towel wrapped up in tissue paper.

'I want you to test this and see if it coincides with the traces of the woman on Otto Frederiksen.'

'You give me the pleasantest jobs. How did you get this? No, forget I even asked. What else?'

'Have you found that ear-ring?'

'I'm afraid I haven't had time to look yet. Is that it?'

'Not quite. There is some question of money missing from the belongings of Jonis Hendrik.'

'What has that to do with me?'

'You were in possession of the dead man's clothes . . .'

The doctor smiled wryly.

'If Jonis was carrying money when he was murdered, then it seems to me – not that I am a detective, you understand – but it seems possible that the murderer took the money. Wouldn't you say so? See you tomorrow, Sergeant Larsen.'

The tall blonde figure of Gudrun Eistrup was just leaving the supermarket, with a couple of bags in her hand. Dismissing a fresh sense of foreboding, Larsen hurried to catch her up.

'Good morning.'

She started.

'Oh. Good morning.'

'I have not seen you around lately.'

'I've spent the last two days at the seed bank. I'm leaving Sermilik soon and there's a lot I must finish before then.'

'Has anyone mentioned some missing seeds?'

Gudrun darted him a look.

'What?'

'Three days ago Otto Frederiksen said some seeds had vanished.'

'Otto Frederiksen!' Her voice was contemptuous. 'He hopes all the seeds will vanish, sold off to that blood-sucking American woman. I went to the Secretary of the commune and told him the seed bank was invaluable, and that Frederiksen must be stopped from selling it off.'

'What did he say?'

'What he usually says – nothing worth listening to. He and Frederiksen are hand-in-glove.'

Larsen settled down to walk beside her up the hill.

'Will freezing seeds really preserve them indefinitely?'

Gudrun shrugged.

'Seeds have been found in glaciers that were still viable after many centuries, and wheat seeds in Egyptian tombs have sprouted after four thousand years. If they are kept at the correct temperature, virtually all seeds are expected to remain viable for a minimum of between one hundred and three hundred years. Whether there will be any clean earth left on which to grow them is another question.'

Larsen launched another of his characteristic sudden changes of tack.

'Did you see Evat Jonsson the night before last?'

'Probably. I am often on the computer while he is working his shift.'

'Is he your boyfriend?'

She gave him a cold look.

'You mean like you are my boyfriend?' she retorted.

That stopped him. His emotions flung themselves into a chaos where Jenufa, Gudrun and Mitti merged, clawing at his tangled mind. After a moment he thrust them back.

'I am sorry to pry,' he said stiffly.

'I know, it is your job.' Larsen could not tell if she was speaking sarcastically or with understanding. 'Evat and I see a lot of each other and he has helped me with my thesis. I like and respect him. Our friendship is not based on physical attraction, which is a little thing, but trust and shared beliefs. That is very important to both of us.'

'Do you know anything about a message someone sent to Otto Frederiksen? A threatening message.'

'In this town threats are not uncommon. Especially to outsiders. If I were you, I would take care.'

'Is that a threat, or a warning, Miss Eistrup?'

'It is friendly advice.'

Her expression seemed sincere.

'The message to Otto Frederiksen was maybe more than that,' said Larsen. 'He was murdered in the early hours of yesterday morning.'

Her face went ash-white and she gaped.

'I didn't ... when ... who ...? Are you trying to trap me? Is this true?'

'I'm sure you can find someone to tell you.'

She glared at him, then hurried off. To Larsen there appeared something disturbing in her sharp swings and changes of mood, from self-possessed, even patronising, confidence to what looked like blind panic. He sat down on a lichen-stained rock for his foot was hurting.

'I am a man in a maze,' he said quietly to himself. 'Every stride forward offers more and more alternatives. But in a maze, the closer you are to the heart, the more difficult it seems.'

The deaths were so different. Jonis tied up, stabbed in the back, and left to die. Kalaasi shot down by someone who was trying to kill Larsen, or wanted Larsen to think that. Otto Frederiksen strangled in his own bed. There was no pattern. No consistency except the brooding menace that lay over all Sermilik.

A menace interlaced with sex. But not sex as love, or even pleasure. Sex in Sermilik was a dark destructive force, a weapon between man and woman, used to taunt, to demonstrate power, to anger or disguise or mislead, to drive to crime or make money. He wondered why Gudrun had made love with him. And whether she had ever entered the corrupt, distorted world of Frederiksen's room of mirrors. Only

150

then did Larsen remember that his daughter had been in that room. Not once, but many times. Nausea was born in the pit of his stomach. It was something he dare not think of.

A heavy-shouldered husky trotted deliberately past him. Down the hill, near the deserted helicopter pad, a man was feeding his dogs, who bared their teeth and fought for their meal. An old woman came slowly up the hill, Kamik's grandmother. But as she came closer, she looked different. The malicious gossip in her had vanished and she had grown older. Broken.

'I have been looking for you,' she said, stopping and breathing rapidly.

'Yes?'

'Kamik is gone.'

'Gone?'

'He did not come home last night.'

A fresh shaft pierced Larsen.

The small cold sun cast cruel shadows into her wrinkled face and Larsen realised she had been crying, hard and long.

'I gave him his dinner yesterday, and since then I have not seen him. Nor has anyone else I have asked.'

'I will find him,' said Larsen.

She bowed her head, concealing fearful, pleading eyes. As he walked away, he heard her coughing.

The large, chestnut-blotched husky that lived by the door to the hotel got up sullenly and moved a few feet out of his way. She had been in a dangerous mood for the last week, since her puppies had been taken from her and sold. Larsen watched her warily until he was safe inside.

One of the smooth-skinned young men who served in the hotel was lounging in a chair, idly flicking through a dog-eared Batman comic. Larsen went up to him.

'I am looking for Mrs Krinsky.'

'Room number four. Up there.'

He turned back to his comic.

It was the best room in the hotel, facing east, so the view over the snow-whitened mountains and icy sea was unhindered by the radio masts. On the plain magnolia walls were two photographs of the town, sepia-tinted, although Larsen saw they were only a few years old, for his parents' house was not in them.

Marian Krinsky was sitting on a chair, reading Lovelock's *Gaia*. She gave him a swift, efficient smile, carefully marked her place in the book, and placed it cover-down on the bedside table.

'Sergeant Larsen. Can I help you?'

'I hope so, Mrs Krinsky.'

'Call me Marian, please.'

'A boy called Kamik has disappeared.'

'I'm sorry to hear that.'

'He is about ten or eleven, small, with very short hair. I wondered if you might have seen him.'

She opened her hands.

'I'd like to help you, sergeant. But there are any number of kids round this town, I wouldn't know one from another if they kicked me. Anyway, I've scarcely been outside since yesterday morning.' She gave a strained smile. 'I haven't felt up to it.'

Larsen had a fresh sense of pity for her. He did not think that Marian Krinsky had any idea of how to come to terms with the events of Wednesday night.

'Is there anything else?' she asked after a moment.

'I would like to go over some things with you again.'

Her face was drawn.

'Must you?'

'I am sorry.'

'OK. Get on with it.'

'You are here on behalf of the International Agro-Chemicals Federation to look into the prospects of taking over the Sermilik Seed Bank.'

'You know that, for Christ's sake.'

'Was that the only reason you came here?'

'Do you think there's any other reason?' She was getting unnerved faster than he had expected. 'Christ! I spend half the year in Florida. Have you any idea what it's like to come here from Florida?'

Larsen rubbed the patchy beard on his chin. Krinsky picked up her book and flicked through the pages with an unconscious gesture.

'Well?'

'It seems surprising that your firm should send such a senior executive all this way for a comparatively minor assignment. Especially as you are, you admit, no expert on seeds.'

'We've got top-notch biologists coming out of our ears back in the States. It's not them that make the decisions in IACF. Anyway, this isn't minor. We plan to sink a lot of capital into this seed bank. It could be an important investment for us . . .'

'And seeds can be very valuable items?'

'Sure.'

'Tell me about the seeds Otto Frederiksen was trying to sell you.'

'You know as much as me. He had nothing. It was all a con.'

'But would those seeds have really been worth the money Frederiksen wanted?'

'Possibly.' She was calming down, dealing with things she knew about, questions she expected. Which was what Larsen wanted. 'There's no way you can tell until you start the tests. It's a long business, two to three years usually, but no question any strong resistance to rhizomania in sugar beet would be worth good money. Very good money. Only, Tomas, there's no way he had those seeds. If he did, where the hell are they?'

'They might be anywhere,' said Larsen.

'They might be.' Krinsky leant towards him, her lean face intent. 'Only they were never anyplace except in his head. He was spinning me a line.'

'What if he was telling the truth and they had been stolen? He said he'd checked them only a few days ago, and the air strike means no one could have taken them out of Sermilik.'

'So you want to play let's pretend. OK. Well, depending how many there are, seeds don't need much room. Two large cupboards would probably do it.'

'I thought that even in specially designed containers, one couldn't be sure of keeping the seeds at the correct temperature for more than seventy-two hours. And any significant variation of temperature can destroy the seeds' viability. Isn't that right?'

'What you say is true, but most people wouldn't know it. Anyway, there's plenty of ice round here. Someone could just drill a hole in a glacier, say, and leave them there until they wanted them.'

'Yes, but couldn't they easily end up with a lot of worthless husks? Glacier ice here in spring won't be as low as $-19°$, and even up on the ice-cap, it's not consistent. There's a lot of temperature variation inside a large mass of ice.'

Krinsky was growing impatient.

'So you've done your homework, sergeant. Great. Well done. But it's all bull! The seeds haven't been flown out of here, and they can't be stored, and no one's seen them, so they never existed. OK. Believe me. Sure there must be important seeds in the seed bank, but who's got the time and expertise to have been through all those sections and picked them out?'

'Otto Frederiksen said he had separated out wild varieties of the most commercially significant crops.'

'I heard him. It's OK in theory. But – '

There was a knock on the door.

'Who is it?' called Krinsky.

'The manager, Mrs Krinsky. May I come in for a moment?'

'Sure.'

The stiff, tall, sallow-skinned hotel manager came in. His eyes darted over Larsen, then moved to his guest.

153

'You asked me to tell you the moment there was any news of the strike, Mrs Krinsky.'

'That's right.'

'The strike has been settled.'

'For real?'

'Yes. The news came in just five minutes ago.'

Krinsky hit the palm of her hand with her fist.

'Great! When's the first chopper out of here?'

'Hopefully in three hours' time, or rather . . .' He glanced fastidiously at his large gold-rimmed watch. Larsen wondered where he had made the money to buy such a thing. '. . . two hours and fifty minutes. The plane from Cap Gad is flying to Søndre Strømfjord. It will be necessary to spend the night there, but next morning there is a flight to New York.'

'That's what I wanted to hear.'

'If I may give you some advice, Mrs Krinsky. There will be a queue down at the helicopter pad when the news gets out.'

'But I've got a first-class priority ticket . . .'

'There is no priority on local flights, Mrs Krinsky.'

'Great! So I was conned again.'

'The plane is not large and because of flight cancellations caused by the strike many people will certainly have to be left behind.'

'OK. OK. I'm hurrying, for Christ's sake. Get me the check, will you, I'll be down in quarter of an hour.'

As the manager left, she began opening drawers and throwing things haphazardly into a smart leather suitcase.

'Sorry, sergeant, but I'm out of here. After that stuff I was given about the strike going on for months, I'm not taking any risks. I've had enough of this place. Believe me.'

It occurred to Larsen that she had scarcely looked at him once since telling him of her affair with Frederiksen. He was an embarrassment. Someone who knew too much about her. At the time she had had to unload it, but now she would be happiest if she never saw him again, for he carried knowledge about her that split her carefully manicured executive image clean apart. Once she was away from Greenland, she could forget what had happened, seal it away, or share it only with her therapist, who would understand and provide forgiveness.

'Now, if you will excuse me, sergeant, I must get myself together.' She gave an unexpectedly girlish laugh. 'I'm useless at packing, you know.'

'You will leave me an address where I may contact you?'

'Sure.' She pulled out a large, bulging wallet, leafed through a wad of cards, and finally gave him one. 'Here. If I'm not at this number, contact the company headquarters in Miami. They'll know where I am.'

'I did,' said Larsen. 'And they didn't.'

She froze, her arms full of clothes.

'What?'

'I telephoned IACF in Miami. They told me Marian Krinsky was on holiday.'

He paused. Still she had not moved.

'On a motor-cruiser somewhere in the Caribbean,' he went on. 'Off Saint Vincent or the Grenadines they thought. I asked if they could contact her for me, but apparently for three weeks every year Mrs Krinsky likes to completely cut herself off, and only her PA knows where to find her. Her PA is a man named Walter L. Wakefield. I spoke to him. He was very pleasant, but he absolutely refused to give me a telephone number where I could speak to Mrs Krinsky. Nevertheless, he agreed that she is on holiday in the Caribbean, and assured me she will be back in the office in five days.'

Outside a black-breasted Lapland bunting sat on a bare rock and burst into twittering song. Krinsky swung round and tossed the clothes she held into her suitcase.

'So what do you want me to say?'

'What is your real name?'

'Marian Krinsky. Being smart doesn't mean you're not wasting your time. I told you my company regards this business very seriously. A major seed bank has never before become available, and another may not appear on the market for decades. We learnt about it before there was any public announcement about the sale – '

'Through Otto Frederiksen. For which, no doubt, he was well paid.'

'People should be well paid for important work. Maybe you guys in Greenland have a problem with that, but it's the way the world works. Anyway, I came out here in secret, so none of our rivals would figure what was going on. There, now you know. And now I'm on my way.'

'Not quite. I asked Mr Wakefield to give me a physical description of Marian Krinsky. He was very reluctant, but I did eventually get one. It was not particularly useful, he is not an observant man, but there were interesting aspects. Especially that Marian Krinsky has steel-grey hair. And perfect sight.'

'For Christ's sake. I dyed my hair a couple of weeks ago, and why should Walter know about my contact lenses?'

'I would never have guessed it had been dyed.'

'Well, that's good. I paid serious money for it so people wouldn't notice.'

'Why did you dye your hair before coming to Sermilik?'

155

'Because I wanted to, is that a crime? Now get out of here while I pack.'

Larsen left, closing the door on a scene of frantic activity. There was no doubting her desire to leave Sermilik, but could he legally stop her?

Chief Thorold gave him the answer straight out.

'Are you out of your mind, Larsen?' crackled his voice down the hotel phone line. 'You can't lock up a big-wheel US businesswoman.'

'She's a witness. And I'm not sure she's really who she says she is.'

'Can you prove it?'

'I've told you I can't. At least not for several days.'

'Then you'll have to let her go.'

'Chief, she may have murdered Otto Frederiksen.'

'If you can't charge her, you can't hold her. You know that, Larsen. And if you've got this wrong, can you imagine what will happen? Squads of top American lawyers descending on us. US companies withdrawing from Greenland. Furious notes from the State Department. As Denmark gradually distances itself, we are becoming more and more dependent on US businesses. Trouble with them would be a complete disaster. Get something better, much much better, or you'll have to let her go.'

'But I've only got just over two hours.'

Larsen could almost hear the shrug.

'She has to come through Søndre Strømfjord, so in fact you have until tomorrow morning. But without cast-iron evidence, we're letting her go.'

Larsen hung up.

'Thank you,' he said bitterly to the telephone.

After picking his way back past the growling female husky, Larsen set off down the hill. The Greenlandair office in the centre of town was full, and the receptionist was struggling valiantly to keep up with five simultaneous conversations in three languages.

'It is possible there will be two helicopter flights to Cap Gad.' This was in English to a scruffily dressed man and woman in their twenties who Larsen guessed were the campers who had put up their tent on the way to Lake Tugdlik. 'I cannot say for certain. It depends how many seats are already taken. The plane will be filled on a first-come, first-served basis . . .'

'The helicopter will leave in an hour and three-quarters.' This was in Danish to a serious man in heavy boots with an enormous beard. 'Yes, there is a maximum limit on baggage weight and – ' The telephone rang. She picked it up.

'Yes. One minute please.'

'No.' This in Greenlandic. 'There will be no one arriving until the next plane arrives the day after tomorrow. The plane that is coming today is not a scheduled flight. It was caught by the strike in Mesters Vig and is flying down here on its way back to Søndre Strømfjord. It already has people in it, that is why there may be not be enough room for everyone – '

'I am sorry,' in Danish again. 'There is nothing I can do about that. You must either leave part of your baggage behind, or else wait for the next plane – '

'Hello, yes. The flights are running again ... Yes. All Greenlandair tickets dating from Tuesday have been extended ...'

Larsen untypically elbowed his way to the front, and spoke in Greenlandic.

'I am Sergeant Larsen of the Royal Greenland Police – '

Yes, sergeant,' said the harassed girl. 'I know. If you will all just wait a minute, please. Thank you. What can I do for you?'

'It is about the baggage on the plane today, and all other planes over the next two weeks. Nothing containing seeds, vacuum containers, plants, or anything similar, is to leave Sermilik. This is most important.'

'But, sergeant – '

'All baggage must be checked thoroughly,' said Larsen firmly. 'Any case that cannot be opened, or which the owner will not allow to be opened, is not to be taken on board. Anything that might reasonably resemble seeds or storage cases for seeds must be brought straight to me. Do you understand?'

'It will cause further delays,' said the girl.

'I cannot help that.' Larsen knew the searches would not be thorough, but they might serve as deterrents. If Frederiksen's seeds existed at all. 'Have these instructions telephoned through to Cap Gad immediately, in case any baggage has already been sent there. Two more things. An American woman, Mrs Krinsky, will be trying to catch the first flight. I do not want her to leave.'

'You mean you wish us to hold her up until you come?'

'No. I would just prefer she is not on the first flight.'

'I can't do that, sergeant. The rules are very precise, the first people – '

'I also wish to know when Gudrun Eistrup is leaving Sermilik.'

The girl hastily consulted several sheets.

'I do not seem to have her name booked on any flight out of Sermilik ...'

So apparently Gudrun was not leaving Sermilik yet. Unless there were alternatives.

'Are any private flights expected into Cap Gad in the next few days?'

157

'We have just been informed that one from Keflavik is expected tomorrow, at five in the morning.'

'That is very early.'

'They are probably tourists, who wish to spend as much of the day as possible in Greenland.'

'Tell me straight away if you hear of any more flights coming in. And don't forget the baggage searches.'

As Larsen left, two more people pushed past him, the phone rang again, and the hubbub in the office swelled up afresh.

14

THE KNIFE AND THE SEAL

A radio was playing quietly in the corner. Tracy Chapman's deep, sad, russet voice was singing: 'Finally the tables are starting to turn, I'm talking about a revolution. They're wasting time, standing in welfare lines . . .'

Dr Sven raised the dressing and nodded.

'Much better. How has your foot felt today?'

'I've hardly noticed it.'

'Good. Two or three days' more rest should do the trick.'

'Have you tested what I gave you?'

'I have. Yes.' The doctor looked up with amused eyes. 'You're a lucky man.'

'What do you mean?'

'If it had been wrong then, as a dedicated policeman, I suppose you would have had to check every dustbin, bathroom, toilet, and maybe bedroom, in Sermilik.'

'The traces match then?'

'They seem to. The woman has the same blood group as the one who had intercourse with Otto Frederiksen, and appears to be at the same point in her menstrual cycle. More detailed analysis, using equipment I do not possess, could prove beyond doubt if it is the same person, but I'd guess your suspicions have been confirmed. Am I allowed to know who it was?'

Larsen said nothing.

'I didn't really expect you to tell me,' sighed the doctor, fastening up the new dressing. 'People who aren't curious have no idea of the agony we inquisitive types go through. Ah well. I hope I've helped.'

'You have. Thank you.'

As Larsen left, he felt a pang from deep within. It was his own daughter he was on the brink of accusing of murder. Part of Larsen had begun to detach himself from the thought. But the detachment was fragile, and he knew that when she was there, when he found himself staring into his own eyes, it would crumble.

Back at the police station, a call came through that Lindegren and another policeman would be on the first plane into Sermilik.

'When will that be?' asked Larsen.

159

'Tuesday evening.'

Larsen felt a mixture of relief and irritation.

'But that's over four days away, and the strike is over.'

'I'm sorry, sergeant. It's the first scheduled flight, and if there's a bigger than expected problem clearing the backlog of people with valid tickets, you may have to wait until Thursday.'

After hanging up, Larsen's mind flickered uneasily from Mitti to Kamik. Although the old woman's tear-weakened face sat in his head, accusing him, he comforted himself with the thought that it was only one night. Kamik was undisciplined, a wanderer, there were plenty of places he might be.

Without warning, the door opened and Robert Maataq came in.

'Have you seen Kamik?' asked Larsen urgently.

Maataq looked at him.

'Not since yesterday afternoon when he brought your message.'

'Oh. What do you want then?'

'You asked me to go to Lake Tugdlik to look for Kalaasi. Had you forgotten?'

'I'm sorry. Things are not going well.'

'I went this morning, in the early hours. There was no trace of a body.'

'It sounds as if the lake will have to be dragged.'

'You cannot do that until the ice is gone, and even then it will be hard. The depths are filled up with fine silt from the glaciers. Well weighted with stone, a body might sink straight through.'

'Everything is good news today,' said Larsen wearily. 'Did you find anything at all?'

'There were too many tracks to separate them out. At least five or six people have been shooting there in the last two weeks or so, though one of them was certainly Dr Sven. His gun is the only one of its kind in the town. Also I went back to where I found Jonis's body, and discovered this.'

The lean-faced hunter produced a knife.

Larsen took it. It was not very long, but broad, and when he ran his finger along the blade, he could feel it had been whetted to razor sharpness. The handle was well worn, of bone, with a distinctive white fur trimming.

'It was Jonis Hendrik's,' said Maataq. 'He was very proud of it. But when he carried it, he usually hid it in his waistband, where it could not be seen.'

'Did people know that?'

'He was not a talkative man, Jonis.'

'So how did you know?'

'Mitti told me.'

Larsen pursed his lips.

'Why did he take such care to hide the knife?'

'He was frightened people would try to steal it. It is a knife with history.'

'What do you mean?'

'That is white wolf fur, the handle is solid narwhal tusk, and the knife is old. The story goes that during a hunt a great bear, queen of all the bears, was badly wounded and near death. When the man who made this knife came to kill and skin the bear, the bear's Innua, her spirit, desperately offered to become the man's helper. It even said it would make him immortal. But the man did not believe the Innua, and he killed the bear with his knife. Since then the knife has carried the bear's Innua, and always it seeks for revenge upon men. It is said to have killed at least five already.'

'How did Jonis get the knife?'

'He bought it, I think. To make himself seem a dangerous man.'

'Did he believe the stories about it?'

'If not, why pay ten times what it was worth? But it cost him more than money, and as for the Innua, she is still hungry.'

For a moment Larsen did not understand, then he looked sharply at Maataq. 'You mean he was killed with this blade?'

'Yes. Jonis was the sixth.'

'Are you sure?'

'There is no doubt.' The hunter stared at the knife with something that looked like fear. Or regret. 'The wound was an unusual shape, just like this knife. He was killed with his own knife.'

'Thank you,' said Larsen. 'I am very grateful. How much do I owe you?'

Maataq stepped back.

'I do not do things for money,' he said, his voice thick with anger. 'If I agree to help a man, I help him. I hunt for my own family. When I need something I cannot catch myself, I exchange goods for it. I do not use money. I do not take money for what I do.'

He left without another word.

It occurred to Larsen that the day before Maataq had been willing enough to be paid. It also seemed strange that the best suspect for Jonis's murder should suddenly find the murder weapon ten days later. Especially as a rare hunting knife like this would be far more likely to appeal to Maataq himself than to Jonis. Larsen bound up the knife in some rags, and slipped it into his pocket. Something might eventually be found out from the weapon, though in a land where gloves were necessities of life it seemed unlikely.

161

After checking his gun, Larsen went out. As he limped down the steep hill, hot and cold flushes began to swallow his foot, accompanied by fresh sensations of crawling and soreness. There were at least twenty people waiting at the helicopter pad, even though there would probably only be room for eight. To Larsen's surprise Marian Krinsky was not there.

Sitting on one of the great rocks that had been moved to flatten out the landing space was Mitti's father-in-law, an island of calm in the surging, anxious crowd. There was a bag at his feet.

'Good morning, sir,' said Larsen, pushing his way over.

'Who is that speaking?' The old man turned his open eyes on Larsen with the disturbing gesture of a man who could still see.

'Sergeant Larsen.'

'I hope you are well.'

'Yes, thank you. May I ask where you are going, sir?'

'I am not sure. Mitti told me that we must go on a journey, and so I am here. I am very obedient, as you see. But it was not so when I was younger and could see what mischief the women about me got up to. Perhaps I am luckier now.' The old man's face darkened, and his voice changed. 'Is Mitti running away, sergeant?'

'What do you think, sir?'

'I think so. She is a very affectionate girl, warm and loving, but when those feelings are not returned, they lead her astray. I do what I can, but I am too old to be listened to.'

'I need to see her. Do you know where she is?'

'I think she is still packing.'

Mitti's cluttered hall looked exactly as it had done the last time he visited, so did the dark, cramped kitchen, with a pile of dirty washing-up in the sink. The large television still stood close by the old man's tall, high-backed chair, and there was a half-full pot of coffee on a side table. The house had no aura of desertion, it felt as if its owners had only gone out for a few minutes. It still smelt of people, of life.

Larsen walked up the rickety wooden staircase, which creaked protestingly with every step he took. At the top were two rooms, the ceiling of each sloping with the sharply angled roof.

Mitti's crumpled dirty clothes were strewn over the unmade double bed, and on the floor among the shoes. Doubts that she could really be his daughter returned. Even as a child Larsen had always carefully put everything away when he finished with it. His neat little two-room apartment, in one of the multi-coloured concrete apartment blocks that reared up over the Hernhutdalen, could not have been more of a contrast with this chaos.

On one wall hung a large photograph of Mitti and Jonis's wedding.

Mitti looked scarcely sixteen, though she must have been over twenty. She was dressed in white, like any European bride, with white lace gloves on her hands and her lively face peeping out shyly from behind a veil. Jonis, visibly into his thirties, wore a sober suit and a solemn expression, looking fixedly at the camera. He was good-looking in a plain way, blunt-featured and earthy, but also vital, and Larsen barely recognised him in the limp body he had seen packed in ice at the doctor's.

Those clothes of Mitti's that were not scattered around the room were hanging on a rail, or pushed into a cheap chest of drawers in the corner. She had a lot of clothes, but there was no sign of the jacket Frederiksen had bought her, nor of a winter coat or a good pair of winter boots. Nor any jewellery.

The curtains were drawn in the other room. Larsen pulled them back, wondering. Mitti's grandfather could still see a little in good light, so it seemed strange he should keep his curtains shut during the day. By the window were some shelves. On one were a few books, a mixture of Inuit folklore and modern American best-sellers, as well as an ancient, well-worn copy of *The Arctic Pilot*. On another shelf was the book Evat had mentioned about Alaska, together with an assortment of Inuit carvings, small sketches in bone or teeth: a polar bear looking over its shoulder; a sea eagle that must be from the west coast, as there were no eagles around Sermilik; a sledge; and several studies of huskies and hunters.

One piece, much larger than the others and carved from pure black soapstone, stood out, both physically and aesthetically. From the shiny rock a seal reared up, as if from water. Tentatively Larsen put out his hand, and seemed to feel the warmth and shiver of life in the stone. The carver had put his very soul into the form, which was so smooth and slick and alive, on the brink of movement, that the seal seemed certain to open its mouth and bark the alarm. But there was more to it than that. Then it struck Larsen what he was missing. For this was the seal a single heartbeat before the rifle bullet struck home. Suddenly, nightmarishly aware of danger, but just that fatal instant too late to save itself. Wary, poised, living every fraction of the last flashing moment of its life, which all its inbred animal caution had not been enough to save. Larsen touched its head again, with pity, and wondered who was that seal.

There was an open cupboard on the other side of the room. At one end of it were Jonis's clothes, jeans, jackets, T-shirts, the sub-American clothes of most Greenlanders under the age of forty-five. Then came the more practical and battered clothes of the old man. At the very end was a complete outfit of traditional Inuit dress – but for a woman. The narrow trousers, reaching down only to the knees, but covered with beautifully embroidered thigh-length sealskin leggings, and these in turn worn with knee boots, also elegantly patterned. The hooded jacket tight around the body with long flaps reaching down before and behind, also patterned. Larsen looked at them, then glanced up. His eyes met the eyes of a stocky, black-haired Inuit woman, smiling affectionately at him from an old photograph. She was wearing the same clothes. These had been the best clothes of Jonis's mother, carefully kept and tended by the widower, having long outlived their owner.

As he stood in thought, there was a faint creak from outside. Slowly, stealthily as a breeze, Larsen stole across the bare floorboards. He reached the doorway just as a dark figure emerged from the other room, carrying two large bags. There was a stifled yelp and the figure half leapt, half fell down the stairs. Larsen hurled himself in pursuit, scrambling down as fast as he could go, then springing the last seven or eight steps in spite of scorching pain from his foot. As the figure darted out into the hall, Larsen threw himself forward and, crashing full-length on the carpet, he reached out a hand and flicked up the escaper's foot. His quarry fell with a crash right by the door, and a pile of motor-boat spares, sledge runners, dogs' harnesses and ice-axe stocks toppled on to them.

Larsen got back to his feet, and limped over to free his captive. It was Mitti, dressed in black and panting. She was clutching the handles of a large soft bag packed so full the zip would not do up. Another bag lay on the ground. Her face gazed stoically at him.

'I did not expect to see you again,' she said.

'Where were you hiding?' he demanded.

'Under the bed. I heard you come in and I was frightened, I thought it was . . . someone else. But I must go, my father-in-law is – '

'He is waiting for you. He will not mind waiting a little longer. Now sit down and tell me what you're doing here.'

'This is my home. What right have you to come sneaking about my home, looking at my private things? Do you have a search warrant?'

She stared at him defiantly. Larsen saw a little girl challenging the whole adult world, and he felt emotion rise up and block his throat. His body was clenched.

'I do not want to arrest you for murder,' he said, almost pleading.

'Then don't,' she answered.

'Then help me.'

She said nothing.

'Give me that bag,' he said, after a moment.

She kicked it across the floor to him. Larsen opened it and looked inside, while keeping a wary eye on her. Although he had blocked up the doorway with his chair, his frost-bitten foot was sending louder and louder messages of pain. If Mitti got away, she could easily outrun him down to the helicopter pad.

At the top of the bag was a wallet containing about 5000 Danish crowns, a small roll of US currency, and two tickets to Fairbanks Alaska, via Søndre Strømfjord. The bag also contained a scattering of Mitti's best and thickest clothes, some clothes for her father-in-law, their passports, and a few small possessions: make-up, an old fountain pen, a gold watch, a cassette recorder with a few tapes, and a silver-framed photograph of a fresh-faced Inuit girl of about eighteen holding a well-swaddled baby. Larsen stared at it.

'Yes,' said Mitti. 'That is me and my mother. Can you remember her now?'

Larsen put down the photograph and looked inside a jewellery box. All the ear-rings seemed in pairs.

'You were not planning to come back, were you?' he said.

'Why should I? This town has no work, no comfort, no chance of bettering oneself, no change. The old people sit in their houses and listen to long boring stories on the radio, hoping they will send them to sleep. The young ones stare at America on the television and wish they were there. A few people have cars, but what use is a car when there is nowhere to go? A few have money, but what use is money when there is nothing to spend it on? It is a living death.

'At school they told us that after the World War America tried to buy Greenland from Denmark, but the Danes refused. That is a good reason to hate them, isn't it? In America every year there is more to buy. Here, every year the KGH shelves grow emptier. There is no sugar, soon there will not even be enough food.'

'So you were going to America.'

'Yes.'

'Why?'

'I have relations there.'

Larsen shook his head.

'You have no relations in America.'

'What do you know?' she flared back. 'You may be my father, but you know nothing of me. There are many Inuit in Alaska.'

'None of your relations. We Greenlanders have been cut off from them for many long years. And what makes you think the Alaskan Inuit are any better off than we are?'

'Half of the land is about to be handed back to them, so that they can rule themselves.'

'That is in the Canadian North-West Territories. Not Alaska.'

'Wherever it is, it is not Greenland. And what about that television show, *Furthest North*?'

Once more the ten-year-old girl broke through the skin of a woman. Larsen felt a sad, sympathetic father's desire to stroke her head, and explain to her gently that the world was not what she thought.

'It is filmed in Montana, as far from Arctic Alaska as we are from New York. Most of the Inuit are played by Chinese and American Indian actors. There is no answer for you in Alaska, Mitti.'

'At least you are not there,' she answered sullenly. 'And they have skidoos, jobs and money from the oil. They do not live in Sermilik.'

Larsen picked up the second bag. It was full of clothes, but at the very bottom, carefully folded, was a man's high-collared, black leather trench coat. Larsen pulled it out and let it run heavily through his fingers. It was very fine leather, soft and superbly cut. He glanced at the label. Claude Montana. There was only one man in Sermilik who could afford such a coat, the man who had been wearing it on Tuesday evening. But Larsen felt no satisfaction at having found the evidence he had been looking for.

'Where did you get this?' he said, holding it up.

'Otto gave it to me.'

'It is a man's coat.'

She shrugged.

'Did he give you all this money as well?'

'No. I saved it.'

'Mitti, I am not a fool and my ears are tired of your lies. It seems that my warnings have meant nothing to you, so I no longer have any choice.'

'What do you mean?' She stared at him. 'You will not send me to prison?'

He said nothing.

'But my father-in-law – '

'He will be looked after by the social services.'

'The social services,' she spat. 'Half this town is looked after by the social services. A couple of worried women hurry into your house, give you coupons for a few days' food, and then you do not see them again for a month. That old man has waited three years for the operation to his eyes. Three months ago they told him it could not be for at least another year. It may already be too late, it will certainly be too late in another year. They know that, but all they do is smile and apologise and give us extra milk coupons.'

'I am sorry, but – '

'This is a good way to treat your daughter, Tomas Larsen.'

166

Larsen knew she was using their kin as an emotional weapon against him, to bend him to her will. But that did not stop it hurting. Nor did it stop him realising how unjust he was being. Mitti and Marian Krinsky were equally likely to have been involved in Frederiksen's murder. He had evidence against both, proof against neither. The American was allowed to go because she was white and might be rich and powerful. The Inuit could be bullied mercilessly, even thrown in prison. And this by her own father. Perhaps that even sharpened his treatment of her: if he could prove she was a liar, a thief, a killer, then he could lock her up and forget all about her, safe in the knowledge that she was not worthy of the love he had never given her.

'Where did you get the money?'

She did not answer. Certain that she knew something crucial about the mysteries that webbed him round, Larsen stared at her and pushed his ragged fingernails into the palm of his hand.

'On the night Frederiksen died, when you said you were here, you were with him, weren't you?'

'If you are so sure, why bother me?'

'Because so far as I know, you were the last person to see Otto Frederiksen alive. And if that is true, then you murdered him.'

'No.'

'Yes. It is a bad murder too. To kill a man in a fit of passion is one thing. To kill him when he is helpless, strung up like a tethered puppy, is much worse. Cold-blooded and calculated.'

He paused momentarily, then ground on remorselessly.

'You probably think being sent to prison will not be too bad, Mitti. You have been told that prisoners are only kept in at night, and can do what they like during the day, even have a job. Perhaps you do not know about our new prison. It is the first prison in the country for long-term prisoners, people who have committed especially savage crimes and who will not be let out, day or night, for many years. That is where you will be sent, Mitti. And you will not be young any more when you come out. Your father-in-law may be dead – '

'Bastard!' she hissed.

She was right. To make Mitti tell the truth he was beating her. Not slapping her round the face or kicking her in the stomach, but beating her just the same. Slapping and kicking her mind. And the damage he inflicted, however legal it was, went deeper and scarred longer than physical attack. It sickened him, and he could do nothing else.

'Ten years if you are lucky,' he said, lashing out at her again. 'Judges do not like people who tie up their victims then strangle them. Probably fifteen years – '

167

'I did not kill him,' she pleaded.

'No one will believe you. No one does believe you. I do not believe you.' And then the switch to throw her off balance. 'When were you given that coat?'

She looked up, wide-eyed.

'I'm not sure. A few days ago.'

'I saw Frederiksen wearing it the day before he died. It will not be difficult to prove that you murdered him.'

'I didn't.'

'Then who did?' His voice struck with the crack of a dog-whip.

'I cannot tell you. He will kill me.'

'I do not believe you. You have lied to me again and again. There was no other man. You did it alone, didn't you? Strangled him when he was helpless.'

'No. No.' The desperation in her voice stung his ears like drops of acid.

'Why did you kill him, Mitti?'

'I didn't. I didn't. I never knew, never guessed – '

'Never told the truth.'

And without warning she broke.

'All right. All right. I'll tell you the stupid, filthy story. And then perhaps you will leave me alone.'

15

ANOTHER MAN

Mitti lay back in the chair and closed her eyes. Her body was limp, slumped loose in an attitude of complete surrender. Larsen leant forward, a dog on the trail, hunting, watchful. She was an actress, untrained but natural, and she had made a fool of him before. He wanted, wildly, obsessively, to believe her this time. But another part of him, perhaps the greater part, was ready for her to lie again.

'I am listening,' he said.

Mitti's voice was soft and slow, so that at times he could only just catch her words.

'There was a man who knew of Otto Frederiksen and his room of mirrors.'

'Who?' asked Larsen.

She went on as if he had not spoken.

'Two days ago he came to me and said he wanted to come and watch that night. I suppose he prefers watching sex to having it, and perhaps he is right. There are no diseases you can catch from watching, no unwanted children, no fights, no anger. But I refused him.'

This is my daughter, thought Larsen, she is part of me. But just then the feeling did not touch him.

'He insisted. He said I must say yes. He was so angry, a fire burnt in his eyes and in his head, and I was frightened. So at last I said yes. But I never went to Otto's unless I was invited. The man told me I must go anyway, and I even agreed to that. Anything was better than his hands tight on my shoulders and his eyes nailed into mine. And I hoped Otto would tell me to go away.

'It was late. Otto had lent me a front-door key so I could lock the door after I left him in the middle of the night. Otto did not like me to sleep in his house, and he liked doors locked. So I used the key to get in. Margrethe was busy with Olssen and the man came in with me and hid in the office. I almost ran away, but it seemed easier to go on.

'Then I realised Otto had another woman with him, so I told the man nothing could happen that night. He took me by the throat and told me it must. Just then the door upstairs opened and someone came out and went into one of the bedrooms. I guessed it was the American woman. The man told me to go up, and to make sure Otto could not

169

move or see or make a sound, so he could creep into the room and hide himself to watch what happened.'

Her voice was totally flat, lacking all expression. But from one eye ran a single, thick tear.

'I went upstairs. Otto was still in the room of mirrors. He was curled up on the bed, and I saw that the other woman had been very rough with him. I was never like that. He looked up at me and did not seem surprised. He just gave a tired smile and shook his head. But I was afraid of the man waiting downstairs. So I made Otto get up and have sex. As we did that I tied him and gagged and blindfolded him, as I had sometimes done before. He used to like it, feeling me round him but unable to move or see or speak. Once he did the same to me, but I was frightened and he did not do it again. He could be a caring man.'

She stopped again, and looked down at her hands. Then went on.

'Suddenly I heard something and turned to find the man behind me. He made signs to me to come over to the door. First he gave me the money you asked about, and the plane tickets. Then he whispered that I must get away from Sermilik at once, before you arrested me. I was terrified and I did what he told me.'

The story ended without warning.

'What about the coat?'

'When I got down the stairs, I suddenly thought someone might see me, recognise me. I don't know. The coat was by the door, I put it on, pulled up the collar to hide my face, and ran away. That is all I know.'

'Except, of course, you also knew the coat was worth a lot of money. Thousands of dollars.'

She shook her head.

'I just snatched it up. I was going to give it back to Otto, I swear.'

'But then you heard about Frederiksen's death, and decided to keep it?'

'Yes. Why not? Who else should it belong to? I did more to keep him happy than anyone else. It is not so big a thing.'

'Big enough to put you in prison for life. You are telling me this man murdered Frederiksen, then got away out of a back window?'

'I'm just telling you what happened to me.'

'Who is the man?'

She said nothing.

'Why did he murder Otto Frederiksen?'

'I do not know.' She opened her eyes wide. 'I cannot believe he did it. That's why I am frightened.'

Larsen watched her thoughtfully.

'There is no proof of the existence of this man, except your word.

But I do have evidence that you were with Frederiksen the night that he was murdered, and that you have lied about it.'

He expected her to cry, to throw herself on the ground, to violently protest her innocence and honesty. But she did not move and her voice was still stripped clean of emotion.

'I do not like it, but it is the truth.'

'The man gave you the tickets to Alaska?'

'Yes.'

'Didn't you realise that by running away you would tell everyone it was you who killed Frederiksen? That this man, if he exists, wanted you to run away so we would chase you and he could go unnoticed?'

Mitti let out her breath slowly and thoroughly.

'Do you know anything about the killing of Kalaasi?' asked Larsen.

'No.'

'What about that of Jonis?'

'I have told you before, nothing.'

'You have told me many lies, Mitti.'

'And maybe you have told me some. The death of Kalaasi means nothing to me. As for Jonis, I think he met someone when he was out hunting and they had an argument. Usually Jonis seemed a quiet, ordinary man, but his temper could be hot, and he had an unpleasant way with words. I was not surprised someone killed him.'

'What do you mean?'

'Just that. A few weeks ago he had an argument with Robert Maataq . . .'

'About you?' asked Larsen.

'I do not know. But Jonis laughed at Maataq because his eldest son has bad sight. If he had not been held back by other men, I think Maataq might have killed him then.'

'Why should that anger Robert Maataq so much?'

'Because it means his son can never be a hunter, of course. There was another time last winter. One of Olssen's cousins had gone to bed with Jonis. Her younger sister met Jonis in the hotel bar. She was drunk and she began to insult him. He told her to keep her big nose out of his affairs, and she burst into tears and ran away. He had never spoken to the girl before, yet the thing she was most sensitive about was her nose. That was typical of Jonis, in thirty seconds he sensed a person's weakness, and he would use it. It is a dangerous talent, and I think he was killed because of it.'

'Who by?'

'Anyone. I told you, he said things that people did not like to hear.'

'You and Robert Maataq have had a love affair, haven't you?'

'Love?' She gave a fractured laugh. 'It could have been anyone. Anyone.'

Larsen felt in his pocket and produced the knife Maataq had given him.

'Do you recognise this?'

She looked at it in surprise, but also distaste.

'Of course. It was Jonis's.'

'It is the knife he was killed with. Some say it is a woman's murder, to use a man's own knife to stab him in the back.'

'What else would a woman use?' she snapped back. 'We have no weapons of our own.'

He said nothing. Once again she was incriminating herself.

'How long have you had that knife?' she asked.

'It was found where Jonis was murdered.'

'When?'

'Yesterday.'

'That is not possible.'

'Why not?'

'I went to Lake Tugdlik two days after he died, and spent all afternoon searching for Jonis's money. I found nothing. The knife was not there.'

'Are you sure?'

'You always ask me that. Of course I am sure, or I would not have said it.'

'What about your friend without a name? Perhaps he also murdered your husband?'

'No. I keep telling you, Jonis met some man out on the snow, they argued then fought. Perhaps Jonis tried to draw his knife, and as they struggled it ended up in his own back. That is how it must have been.'

'And you will not tell me who the man in Frederiksen's room was?'

She shook her head. Could Larsen really see terror in her face? The more he spoke to her, the less he knew when to believe her. Perhaps it was their very shared blood that made it so difficult to judge her. Unless she had lied about that too.

'Would you testify against this man in court?' he asked.

'If you catch him and hold him so that he cannot escape, then I might tell what I know, yes.'

'The easiest way for me to catch him is for you to tell me who he is.'

Again she shook her head.

'You will take him in and question him, and then you will say, "Mitti was lying and this man did not do it." Or else you will say, "Yes, I think this man did it. But I cannot prove it, so I will have to let him go." Either way he will be free, and he will know who told you about him. And he will come for me. Not straight away perhaps, for he is patient, but one day he will come. And I will die.'

'He might kill you anyway – after all, you are very dangerous to him.'

'That is why I must get away from here.'

Larsen grimaced.

'It seems you will have to wait for me to catch him by myself.'

'What do you mean?'

'What I say.' He picked up Mitti's bag and removed the air tickets, the money and the passports. 'You are a material witness to a murder and you are not to leave this town.'

She gazed at him pleadingly.

'Don't do this.'

'Tell me who he is.'

She hid her face in her hands.

'I should not have told you anything. I should have kept my mouth shut.'

Larsen picked up an empty plastic bag that lay by the door, pushed Frederiksen's coat into it, and then turned to go. There was a sob behind him. He had a fierce desire to turn back and take Mitti in his arms, as a father should hug his daughter. But he did not.

Thirty or forty yards down the hill a mud-spattered estate car came to a stop beside him.

'Want a lift?' came the booming voice of Dr Sven.

Larsen got in. The doctor looked at him disapprovingly.

'From the way you're walking, you haven't been doing that foot of yours any good. I told you to rest.'

'I didn't say I would,' replied Larsen.

'No. You didn't. Where are you going?'

Larsen did not answer.

'Well, if you don't tell me, you'll just have to go where I'm going,' growled the doctor, starting the car.

'Where's that?'

'To see Margrethe, the girl who was Mr Frederiksen's servant. She's gone back to her parents and she's not well.'

'What's the matter with her?'

'The usual mixture of things caused by poor housing and primitive hygiene and sanitation – otitis and a simultaneous gastro-intestinal infection.'

'Actually I'd like to go down to the helicopter pad.'

'Not the way I was going at all. And if you were planning on catching the chopper, you're too late. See.'

He pointed outside.

There was a steady, repeated beating of rotor blades. Larsen suddenly realised there were people everywhere, clumps and knots of them, on the road, outside their houses, down by the harbour and up on the hill crests. The whole of Sermilik was outside. There was no cheering or waving, scarcely a word was spoken, but everyone watched as the red and white helicopter swept away down the fjord towards Cap Gad, and the town's lifeline to the rest of the world was reconnected.

A shrinking crowd was morosely taking the dusty road back up to the town. Among them Larsen saw the two English campers, weighed down under huge rucksacks, talking quickly, agitatedly, gesticulating. There was no sign of Marian Krinsky, no doubt her money had made sure she was on the flight.

The old man was still sitting alone, his stick unmoving in his wrinkled bony hands. Larsen went over to him.

'Mitti will not be coming, sir.'

'Is that Sergeant Larsen?'

'Yes. She cannot come. Shall I help you to return home?'

The old man sighed.

'Perhaps a little way, if you would not mind.' He smiled, an old smile that broke up his face into range after range of eroded mountains. 'Just to the main road. It is a long time since I had any reason to come down here. Once we reach the football field I know my way about.'

He took Larsen's arm unselfconsciously and the two of them walked up the steep hill. The old man held himself stiffly upright, full of dignity as he used his stick delicately to tap the ground in front of him. His eyes were screwed up to extract what little sight could filter through their near-opaque lenses.

'Will you tell me what Mitti has done?'

'I am not yet sure,' said Larsen cautiously. 'Perhaps nothing. But I think she needs . . . looking after.'

'I try my best, but she is a wild girl. She needed a father's hand.' The old man smiled affectionately. 'When I was young I believed I should try everything once. I think she believes that also, but not once only.'

'Do you know who her father is?'

'No. If he has no place for her in his life, then ignorance is best. I love her as if she were my daughter, perhaps even more. She is a good girl at heart, but not to be restrained. Young people today are undisciplined little children who say, "I want it. Now." They even think they have rights. Rights to money, to comfort, to health, to pleasure, to happiness. To what they want when they want it. But you and I know there are no rights in life, sergeant. There never have been. Many, many duties, but no rights. That is God's world.'

174

Larsen glanced up and saw Mitti thirty metres away, staring grimly at them. She came down the road and took her father-in-law's skinny arm.

'Hello, Mitti,' said the old man, though she had not yet spoken. 'I hear we are not leaving Sermilik after all.'

'The sergeant says we are not to,' she replied. 'Let's go home.'

'Home,' he repeated, and his voice was sad.

The two of them slowly went on up the road. Larsen sucked in his cheeks. As ever Mitti seemed veiled from him. He returned to the police station, put away the money, passports and tickets, tossed the coat down on a table, then went out again. The saturnine seed bank worker, Saqaq, was strolling towards the KGH store. He raised his hand to Larsen.

'You have heard the news? Kalaasi is back.'

'What?'

'He is at the hotel.'

Larsen scarcely noticed his protesting feet as he ran up the hill.

Kalaasi was in the breakfast room, sipping a coffee. Beside him was Secretary Bronlund. Several other people were standing close by, watching. Larsen pushed impatiently past them.

'Ah, sergeant,' said Bronlund, looking up. 'It seems you were mistaken after all.'

Larsen ignored him.

'Kalaasi,' he said. 'What happened? Where have you been?'

The policeman turned and looked at him. There was a grimy bandage around his head, and one of his arms was in a sling.

'Hello, sergeant.' He gave an unsteady smile. 'I had an accident, I think.'

'I thought you had been killed. What happened, for Christ's sake?'

Kalaasi stared at him blankly.

'We went out together to Lake Tugdlik,' he said. 'Didn't we?'

'Yes. Yes, of course.'

'I must have fallen or something. The mist came down. I don't really remember anything clearly, except walking and falling and walking some more, until the sun came out and I found myself near the Gultop Glacier.' That was at least fifteen kilometres from the lake, in the direction of the inland ice. 'It took me a long time to get back, then I went to my brother's. I didn't feel well. This morning he told me everyone was saying I was dead, and I should go and explain. So here I am.'

'You don't remember being shot at?'

'No. I am sorry, sergeant.'

'It was probably a careless hunter, who hadn't seen you,' said Bronlund pleasantly. 'Nothing to worry about. Or it might even have been the ice-melt – that can create many strange sounds.'

Before Larsen could reply, the doctor came bustling in.

'I've just heard,' he said. 'Good to see you back, Kalaasi. Let's have a look at what you've done to yourself.' He deftly raised the bandage and peered underneath, then shook his head.

'Not good. You'd better come with me, my lad.'

Two of the watchers helped Kalaasi get to his feet, and escorted him out, to the doctor's car.

'Wait!' Larsen hurried after them. 'I must ask him some questions.'

'Impossible,' said the doctor, as he carefully sat Kalaasi down in the passenger seat, then got in himself. 'He shouldn't be up at all, that's an ugly gash on his head, and it'll need careful treatment. He may even have a fractured skull.'

He started the engine. Larsen put his head in the open window.

'But – '

'No.'

The doctor threw the car into gear, and Larsen only just pulled back in time as it bounced off down the road.

Not that it really mattered. Things had already fallen into place in his mind. Kalaasi must be pretending to suffer from amnesia. Out on the Tugdlik ridge he hadn't been stalking the gunman at all, probably he hadn't even seen him, he was simply trying to get away. And, despite the wound, he had got away, had probably hidden himself in his twin brother's home at Ikateq ever since, not even daring to tell his parents where he was. But no one could prove it. No one could prove he didn't have amnesia.

Back at the helicopter pad a Greenlandair worker was lounging about, a cigarette in his mouth. He wore a personal stereo.

'When is the helicopter for the seed bank leaving?' called Larsen.

The man did not answer. Larsen raised his voice and shouted. The man reluctantly pulled off the headphones. High-pitched music issued out: 'Your town is dragging me down, dragging me down-down-down'.

'Well?' said the man, with the sullenness of someone woken from a pleasant dream.

'When is the helicopter to the seed bank leaving?' repeated Larsen again.

'Usual time,' the man answered, relighting the cigarette with a match sheltered from the wind by a hard hand.

'That was "Your Town" by the Beautiful South,' squeaked the stereo in thick American. 'After these messages it's the Boss, Bruce Springsteen . . .'

'When is that?'

'Twenty minutes or so.'

The personal stereo was clapped back in place. A piece of prestige hardware to cut off the assault of real life.

Larsen sat down on the rock vacated by Mitti's father-in-law and waited. He felt tired. There was no joy in him at Kalaasi's extraordinary return from death, only weary relief. And Mitti's story weighed down on his heart, wearing away his energy and will. His body ached. His mind ached worse. He might, at last, be coming close to unravelling events in Sermilik, but the events were just symptoms.

Symptoms of a corrupted town, unable to support its people, that herded them towards darkness of the mind. He glanced up at Sermilik on its three steep hills, and his thoughts were grim. One cannot touch filth and stay clean, and filth lay thick in Sermilik – casual violence, disease, drunkenness, greed, sloth, lechery. A grip of sin that was all the stronger because no one would admit it.

The previous Sunday Larsen had visited the church for Jonis's funeral. The battered little building was packed full. Seeing the formidably bearded minister, Larsen waited for a fierce denunciation, a hell-fire and damnation sermon, a thundering condemnation of the lives of the congregation. What he heard were trite regrets over the loss of a beloved brother, together with some pathetically grateful tributes to the enthusiasm with which people still attended church in these difficult times.

Gradually the roar of the approaching helicopter wore itself into his preoccupied mind. Larsen got up as it landed.

'Hi, sergeant,' shouted Bob, the American pilot, tipping back the inevitable baseball cap. 'You want to come?'

'If that's OK.'

'No problem. I'm only collecting Olssen.'

The small, sly Olssen had slipped up without being noticed. He smiled warily at Larsen, and they got in, ducking low under the whirring rotors, then taking their seats behind the pilot.

'I hear Kalaasi is back,' said Olssen, his small eyes peering at Larsen. 'But that he can't remember anything.'

'Yes.'

'We live in a strange land. A land of illusions, mirrors . . .'

'What do you mean?' demanded Larsen sharply.

'You know, mirages, northern lights, white-outs, false dawns, false suns. Nature plays many tricks on us. I have heard what sounds like a battle, and seen nothing. I have seen a complete dog sledge upside down above my head, and the sky grow red as heart-blood.'

'I have seen men who cannot explain where they found enough money to visit Nûk,' said Larsen.

Olssen looked away.

The helicopter ran low, between the shoulders of the mountains, then skimmed above the surface of Lake Tugdlik and its tributary lakes. The area of ice had shrunk appreciably in the past two days, and snow-melt had at least doubled the flow of water, which foamed fiercely down the valley. Larsen looked down over the peninsula where Jonis had been murdered. Suddenly he was aware of Olssen close beside him.

'If it was worth my while, I might be able to tell you something about Jonis's death,' said Olssen softly, his voice scarcely audible above the roar of the engine.

'What?' demanded Larsen cynically.

Olssen gave an unconvincing smile.

'I am a poor Greenlander,' he said.

Larsen turned away in disgust.

On landing, Olssen and Bob headed straight inside.

'Aren't you joining us, sergeant?' shouted Bob.

'There is something I must do first.'

'You won't get far, limping like that.'

'I can walk it off.'

Larsen set off as if to return to the lake but, once out of sight of the windows, he ducked behind a spine of rocky ridge and, stooping to make sure he could not be seen, followed it. Curving back towards the seed bank, the ridge led him round by the far end of the living quarters, towards an iron fire door. Larsen nodded to himself. There had had to be a way in and out of the seed bank that was not under the gaze of the television room windows.

He hurried across a short stretch of open ground, then pressed up against the double door and listened. After a moment he put his strong fingers into the break between the two doors and levered them easily open. He glanced down and saw the hinges had been freshly oiled.

Close by him the generator hummed, and in the distance he could hear talking and laughter and the mumble of the television. Cautiously Larsen closed the fire door, then began opening other doors. After a couple of fuel and food storerooms, Larsen discovered the clothing store. Inside was an enormous array of protective and winter clothing, waterproofs, heavy fur parkas, insulated winter boots, padded overalls, two complete fire-fighting suits, cold-water diving equipment, anything that might be necessary to deal with Greenland's innate hostility.

After a moment's thought he put on an extra pair of winter trousers and a thick oiled woollen sweater. Emerging, he peered up and down the corridor, then slipped along, tense to dart into shelter. No one appeared, though through one quarter-open door he glimpsed a back bent over a computer screen. The outer entrance to the seed store was open and he slipped inside, glancing at the first of the massive airlock doors opposite.

The only place to hide was in the cupboard that contained the protective suits. He squeezed to the back of the far corner, and squatted down among a chaos of discarded gloves and boots. Now he must simply hope that his guess was right. He looked at his watch: 4 p.m. The private plane into Cap Gad was expected in thirteen hours, so if anything was to happen, it must be soon. He made himself as comfortable as he could, and settled down to wait. Soon he found himself yawning. He felt warm and lazy. Time crawled by. Larsen closed his eyes and tried not to think, there was too much that stabbed at him, especially Mitti. And Kamik. After a little his eyes slid shut.

The nightmare he fell into was one he had had, in one form or another, many times before. It was his first night in Denmark, and he was sharing a small room with Solomon Rosing. Solomon, as usual, was talking.

'You see, Tomas, the important thing with women is not to try to understand them. Just to accept them. If they tell you their problems, then listen, sure, but you don't have to pay any real attention, all they care is that you seem to be interested. You don't really have to be. You think that Danish women are different, but . . .'

His voice swam away, even though Larsen struggled to hold on to it, because he knew what followed.

Ann-Marie was standing above him, thin-faced, curly pale hair cut a little above her shoulders. On her face was the smile. The faint patronising smile that he had never been able to bear, and which had so often sat on her face at rest. It was always a fresh astonishment that he could have married a woman who so clearly thought herself better than him.

'You were right, Tomas,' she said, her voice as soft with the promise of love as her expression denied it.

'Was I?' he asked, forcing out sluggish words.

'Yes. I didn't kill myself. You see, I couldn't decide what to wear.'

'I told you so,' whispered Solomon.

'But you didn't help.' Ann-Marie was suddenly angry. 'You sat back, quiet and controlled and self-sufficient, and did nothing.'

'He doesn't dare to compete, in case he loses.' Solomon was laughing.

179

'But you compete, don't you?' said Ann-Marie.

'Oh yes, I compete. Poor Tomas.'

'Poor Tomas.'

Then the inevitable denouement as Solomon and Ann-Marie fell into each other's arms and made love, while in the background Solomon's voice commentated to the watching millions. Larsen writhed and woke suddenly, feeling hot and dirty and stupid.

As he blinked, there came a sound of footsteps outside. Larsen shrank down into his lair. A moment later the cupboard door opened, and someone groped among the suits, and the carefully shelved face masks and air filters. Eventually a suit with its attendant accessories were pulled out, and the cupboard closed again. There was a rustling outside, then the sound of the airlock door being opened, then hissing heavily shut. It was half-past five. Larsen wriggled forward and poised himself.

Twenty minutes later the cupboard opened again, and Larsen lunged out.

16

THIEF

'Jesus Christ!' exclaimed Mitti, staggering back. 'You almost scared me to death. What were you doing in there?'

'I guessed you must be mixed up in it,' said Larsen, trying to ignore the hopeless anger in his chest.

'Mixed up in what?' she asked, her eyes wide.

'You know well enough. The seed business.'

'What seed business?'

Larsen's temper snapped. His hands tightened on her shoulders and he shook her viciously, his face thrust centimetres from hers.

'No more, Mitti. I'm sick to death of your innocent looks, your fantasies, your never-ending lies.'

'But I don't know what you're talking about,' she pleaded.

Trembling with the force of his rage, he released his hold on her and stepped back. He took several long breaths to regain his calm.

'What are you doing here?' he asked at last.

'Looking for the money.'

'What money?'

'The money Jonis had when he was murdered. I told you about it. 10,000 crowns. I thought Jonis might perhaps have left it here. He has a locker, but I don't know where the key is. I was about to look for it in his cold suit when you jumped out at me like a jack-in-the-box.'

'Were you in this room twenty minutes ago?'

'No. I've only just got here.'

'How did you get here?'

'By walking. How did you think?' She stared him straight in the face.

Her clothes supported her story – a thick dark blue woollen jumper, heavy-duty trousers stained with fresh mud, thick long socks, and tough walking boots.

'Do you ever get tired of asking questions?' she enquired.

'Only when people don't answer them.'

'It's no way to live your life.' She leant back against the wall. 'Are you married?'

Again she had thrown him on the back foot, using his own weapon of the disconnected question against him.

'Not now, but . . .'

'I'm not surprised. I suppose you inflicted a mixture of long silences and rapid questions on the poor woman. I wouldn't put up with it for three months. Any children – besides me, of course?'

'Yes, a daughter. But I don't see her . . .'

'No. You wouldn't.'

'Mitti, this is not the time. If you haven't been in here, then someone else has. And they must still be inside the seed store.'

'And here they are,' said Mitti calmly.

With a clank and a hiss the airlock door slid open, and there was a wave of bitter cold. A silver-clad figure, unsettlingly inhuman in mask and hood, entered carrying three well-insulated seed boxes. There was a tall stack of other boxes just by the door. Suddenly the newcomer saw Mitti and Larsen and checked. Larsen had drawn his gun.

'Stop!' he rapped out. 'Put those down.'

Reluctantly the figure obeyed.

'Mitti, take that mask off him.'

With a quick glance at Larsen Mitti went over and pulled back the concealing mask and hood.

'Gudrun!' exclaimed Larsen.

'Who did you expect?' demanded the Danish biologist hoarsely.

'What is in those boxes?'

'I suppose you think they're drugs. Policemen are always obsessed with drugs.'

'No. I think they are seeds. Very valuable seeds. The seeds that Frederiksen lost. Where were you going to take them?'

Pale-faced, Gudrun said nothing. Mitti leant back against the wall, watching and listening.

'Perhaps we should consider your situation, Miss Eistrup,' resumed Larsen. 'I think you are in very serious trouble.'

'Of course I am in trouble,' she said in a distant martyr's tone. 'Anyone who tries to save humanity from destruction is in trouble. Anyone who – '

'Take off your suit.'

Gudrun tightened her lips and obeyed. While pulling off one of her boots, she slipped and fell awkwardly, with a grunt of pain. No one moved, or said anything. Slowly she picked herself up again, then winced with pain as she finished removing the suit. After tossing it into the cupboard, she slumped down on to the floor.

'What now?'

'When are you planning to leave Sermilik?'

'I have told you before. In about a month.'

'You haven't booked a ticket.'

'I wanted to leave quietly,' Gudrun pulled back her sock and gingerly investigated her ankle. It was red and slightly swollen. 'I don't like long departures, with everyone saying goodbye five or six times, and wasting money on parties and drink . . .'

'I'm sure leaving quietly is just what you did intend,' said Larsen. 'But not in a month's time. Get up.'

'I can't. I've twisted my ankle.'

'Mitti, will you help her, please?'

The two women looked at each other doubtfully. Then Mitti laughed.

'Come on,' she said. 'We all need someone to lean on, and you can lean on me.'

'That's the Rolling Stones,' said Larsen, momentarily deflected. 'The music of your father's generation.'

'It takes a long time for some songs to reach Sermilik,' said Mitti.

Her eyes rested on him without their customary hostility, and Larsen felt an unexpected rush of warmth within him.

Gudrun staggered back to her feet, put one arm over Mitti's broad shoulders, then limped painfully out along the corridor. Larsen followed them, watching minutely, prey to many suspicions. His gun was still levelled.

'Where're we going?' asked Mitti.

'To the communications room. To send a message.'

'Then again, perhaps not,' remarked Mitti, a few moments later.

The radio was a wreck. Every electrical connection had been cut, the panels were broken, and the internal equipment had been ripped out like spilled entrails, hacked and torn. Larsen swore, then turned on Gudrun.

'You did that, didn't you?'

She shook her head.

'Then who did?'

'I don't know.'

A quick search found nothing else, although Larsen briefly thought that he heard a faint scuffling noise in one of the storerooms. Outside the helicopter had gone. At last they returned to the empty, silent living-room. Mitti and Gudrun sat down on the sofa, while Larsen stayed by the door.

'Olssen came with me on the helicopter only about three hours ago,' he said. 'Where is he now?'

Gudrun shrugged, and massaged her ankle.

'Probably out hunting. He often slips away for a few hours.'

'You mean he's gone hunting like Jonis? And perhaps the same thing has happened to him. You don't have an alibi around lunchtime on the day Jonis was murdered, do you? You said you were working, but no one saw you then.'

'But Jonis was killed in the afternoon, sometime after the helicopter left . . .'

'When everyone saw you. Yes. I thought so, but Dr Sven says it is more likely he died around two, if not earlier. If that's right, then you could have done it.'

'She never killed anyone,' broke in Mitti contemptuously. 'She hasn't the nerve.'

'If Jonis found out about the plan to steal the seeds, then Miss Eistrup had plenty of motive,' said Larsen.

Gudrun glanced at Mitti, who had lain back and put her arms behind her neck.

'Jonis died by accident,' she said.

'Of course.' Larsen's tone was weighed down with sarcasm. 'His back was split open by a knife, but it was an accident. Next you will tell me that the seeds in those boxes are worthless.'

'Of course they are valuable, like every single seed in the seed bank.'

Larsen laughed.

'Most of the seeds in there are not worth $30 million . . .' Mitti started and gaped. 'But you don't care about that, do you?'

'No.'

Something in the flat certainty of the monosyllable almost convinced Larsen.

Gudrun's pale blue eyes were still fixed on him.

'It's the times, isn't it?' she said. 'No one will do anything, except for money. But if that's the only way you judge people, then you only understand the fools.' She smiled drily, then suddenly nodded. 'Of course. I've been trying to think how you could have been waiting for me. But it's simple logic. You knew the seeds hadn't left Sermilik because of the strike, so there was only one place where they would be guaranteed the right conditions – where they had been taken from. The seed bank. With the strike over, you figured someone would collect them as soon as possible. And I fell straight into your trap.'

Larsen should have been feeling pleased with himself. He had cast his net and caught his fish. But not the one he had expected, and his certainties were withering. He found it hard to believe that Mitti was involved in smuggling out the seeds. Or that Gudrun had stabbed Jonis, strangled Otto Frederiksen, and tried to shoot him and Kalaasi.

'Where's Kamik?' he asked suddenly.

'Kamik?'

184

'The little boy who lives up the hill from you.'

'The not so little brat,' growled Mitti. 'He's always sneaking around my house, causing trouble.'

'He's disappeared,' said Larsen.

Mitti frowned.

'I don't know who you're talking about,' said Gudrun with finality. She lay back and stared at the low, white ceiling.

'It seems we just wait for the next helicopter then,' said Larsen.

Time passed, marked only by the soft tick of an electric clock on the wall. It was warm, and the chairs were soft and comfortable. Mitti yawned and closed her eyes. Fiercely Larsen resisted the drowsiness that threatened to overtake him, but he was very short of sleep, and three times he found himself dozing off, waking a moment later with a great start, clutching his gun. Each time Gudrun had not moved, but was still sitting, staring into nowhere. The fourth time Gudrun too was asleep. The fifth time, in spite of his burning foot, Larsen slept.

'Take another step and I'll shoot,' shouted a familiar voice, catapulting him back into wakefulness.

Gudrun was only a couple of metres away, but her eyes were to his right. Slowly she retreated to the sofa.

'It's a good thing I was here,' Kamik said, handing Larsen his gun back. 'She was about to jump you.'

Mitti whistled, and slowly let go of the chair arm she had been clutching.

'What are you doing here?' asked Larsen, recovering himself, and checking the gun's safety catch was down.

Kamik grinned.

'I thought about the people you were interested in, and most of them worked here. So I guessed that whatever you needed to know must have something to do with this place. Bob is a friend of mine, he's been teaching me about helicopters, and he flew me out yesterday afternoon. I've been here ever since, hiding in the storerooms.'

'So it was you I heard earlier. Why didn't you come out?'

'I was in a big box of baked bean tins, I couldn't see who it was. Or anything.'

Larsen laughed.

'You should have told your grandmother where you were going.'

'You don't know my nan. Tell her anything and she'll tell everyone in Sermilik inside an hour.'

'And then tell them again and again and again,' commented Mitti.

'She's been worried about you.'

'Then she'll be pleased to see me back.'

185

'I wouldn't bet on it,' said Mitti drily.

'Aren't you interested in what I heard?' Kamik's face was glowing with pride.

'All right. Tell us.'

'I wrote it down.' The boy pulled out his battered notebook, and carefully consulted it. 'Here it is.' He pointed at Gudrun. 'She was talking to Olssen a while ago. She said, "It's all right. You can go, Olssen. I'm happy to look after the place myself." And he said, "Oh no, Miss Eistrup, I mustn't do that." So she gave him something, money I suppose, and said, "Perhaps that will help."'

'Did it?' asked Larsen.

'He made a long speech. He said, "Miss Eistrup, I am a poor Greenlander. I have no money, but I have pride in my work. If anyone found out I had been away, the shame I felt would be worse even than losing the job. I would like to help you, Miss Eistrup, but you remember what happened last time." So she said –'

'All right, all right,' growled Gudrun, pushing a hand through her short hair. 'I gave Olssen more money and he left.'

'Is that what happened, Kamik?' asked Larsen.

'Yes, Sergeant Larsen. And after he left, she smashed up the radio,' said the boy delightedly.

'The case against you is building fast, Miss Eistrup. Theft, the destruction of government property, refusal to assist the police, perhaps conspiracy. And I think most juries would suspect your involvement in at least one of the murders.'

'I have tried to save people, not kill them.'

'Why did you warn me this morning?'

Her expression was guarded.

'I like you, I felt sorry for you.'

'That is not what I meant. Do you think I am in danger?'

She shrugged.

Larsen sensed she might talk if he found the words to unlock her. But Kamik had lost interest.

'I'm hungry,' he remarked, to no one in particular.

'So am I,' put in Mitti.

Larsen realised he was too. And food might help drive back the cloud of weariness at the back of his mind.

'All right,' he said.

As Larsen stood at the door, his gun in his hand, Mitti cut slices of whitish cheese and laid them on pumpernickel bread, while warming up a huge pot of baked beans, while Kamik eagerly opened several tins of American peaches. Beside them Gudrun made a large pot of coffee.

Unexpectedly she turned to Mitti.

'Do you think It's better to trust an idea, or a person?' she asked.

Mitti looked at her with little enthusiasm.

'I'd say it's best not to trust.'

Gudrun didn't seem to have heard her answer.

'Just before I went to university, my mother had a long talk with me. Most of it I forgot straight away, but I remember she said it was better to trust a person than an idea. Maybe she was right. Once you know people well, you can usually guess how they'll behave. Ideas are different. They can lead you into places you don't recognise, or even change into something completely different. Something that doesn't have anything in common with what you thought you believed.'

Mitti considered.

'You mean things look straightforward when you plan them, but real life trips you up, and chucks you in the shit.'

'I don't know,' said Gudrun quietly. 'Perhaps that's what I mean.'

She poured out three mugs of coffee, and comforted herself with the thought that there was still a good chance everything would go off as planned.

Back in the sitting-room, as they ate, Larsen returned to his questions.

'If it wasn't for money, why did you steal the seeds?'

'Steal,' repeated Gudrun. 'What about the greatest thieves of all? What about the governments and companies that take everything from the people, and give back only enough to ensure their own obscene profits, their own perpetuation of power? Every election manifesto in every country, every advertisement for every multinational corporation, shares one thing. They tell us they are doing it for us. But they do nothing for us unless they are made to. They take, take, take. They swear to impartiality and justice and friendship, they promise the earth, and destroy it – '

'Everyone seeks profit,' interrupted Larsen impatiently. 'That's the way of the world.'

'It will not be the way of the world much longer.'

'Are you going to change human nature, then?'

Kamik and Mitti were still hungrily shovelling food into themselves, but Gudrun had forgotten what was in front of her.

'The idea that everyone seeks profit at any cost is another lie they want us all to believe. But would you sacrifice the future of your friends, of your children, just for more money now?' Larsen glanced across at Mitti, and said nothing. Gudrun was still talking.

'This seed bank is only necessary because of the destruction unleashed by the greed of businessmen and politicians. It is a pathetic

187

gesture to our descendants, a hint of the riches we have burnt, torn up, chopped down, poisoned. What percentage of plants can we gather in seed banks? Five per cent? Ten if we're very lucky. But species people never knew existed, irreplaceable species, are being destroyed every day.'

'At least some effort is being made,' replied Larsen.

'You think so?' she sneered. 'But most of the money and specimens for this seed bank are provided by the very companies that are cutting down the forests. If the seeds are safely frozen and filed, it's fine to destroy the real ecosystem. Seed banks have become a justification for continuing to rape the earth. But they won't work.'

'Why not?'

'You can save the seeds of an orchid in here, but once it's extinct in the wild, then so will be the hawk-moth that relied on it, and that fertilised it. So that orchid can never again be grown anywhere, except perhaps in a laboratory.'

'Perhaps you're right, I don't know. But it is no justification for theft.'

'Isn't it? Let me tell you what will happen to the seeds after the seed bank has been sold. The ones no money can be made from will be dumped. The rest will be ruthlessly exploited for profit, making more easy profits for the very people who are doing the damage, and who already own far more than they could ever need.'

'Shall we forget principles for a moment, and talk about the practical details,' said Larsen. 'How did you find out what Frederiksen had been doing?'

Gudrun shrugged.

'One day I was inside the seed store doing a routine maintenance check. I happened to see someone, and I was curious so I followed them. It was Frederiksen, going to check on his secret hoard. He didn't see me, and after he'd gone, I went and had a look. And realised how important those seeds were.'

'So you stole them to stop whatever company buys the seed bank getting them?'

'Yes. They belong to the world, not a few rich men.'

'If your motives are so pure, why did you steal exactly those seeds that might be worth millions?'

'With the most commercially valuable seeds gone, companies won't bother to buy the seed bank. Governments are no more to be trusted than companies, but it's better for the seeds to stay in the hands of a government which has no concept of their value, rather than be handed over to a profit-making machine that will soon guess.'

Bored, Kamik returned to the kitchen, collected more bread and cheese, and went outside to eat it, watching the sun sink among the needle peaks of the coastal mountains. The excitement of helping a policeman had faded away into the usual endless adult talk. He sat on a rock and considered what he would be when he grew up. It was always the same contest. On one side a helicopter pilot like Bob, wearing a baseball cap, casually taking the machine through its paces to the astonishment of his passengers. The alternative was a hunter like Robert Maataq, prowling the snowy wastes, no sound but the hiss of the sledge runners on fresh snow, the gentle breath of the dogs, the occasional crack of his whip . . .

'Is all this so important?' Mitti asked, finishing off a piece of cold sausage.

'It is the most important thing in the world,' Gudrun replied, her eyes blazing. 'Plants are the heart of life. Losing species at the rate we are losing them now will soon make this world little better than a desert. Increasing lack of variation will encourage those pests and diseases that prey on the plant species that are left. Research will concentrate more and more on killing those pests. But just as antibiotics are growing less effective, and resistant bacteria ever commoner, so pesticides and herbicides will become less effective. That means they'll have to be more toxic, and the poisoning of our food will continue and worsen, with terrible long-term effects on human health, and a continued crash in fertility rates. Meanwhile famines will grow more frequent, first in the Third World then spreading everywhere, and so will the wars that come from famine. Humanity is on the very brink of destroying itself, and much of the planet with it.'

'Oh.' Mitti looked unconvinced.

Larsen contemplated the grim prophecy and wondered how Gudrun could keep her sanity if she really believed such a nightmare vision.

'It would be worth a few lives to prevent that,' he remarked.

'I know what you are saying,' said Gudrun. 'Yes, it is worth lives, many lives, to save our planet and its bio-diversity. But I have not killed anyone.'

'Someone has.'

'Are you sure? One of Frederiksen's sex games may have gone wrong. Such things have happened. And you were wrong about Kalaasi.'

'We were shot at.'

'Perhaps Kalaasi had a gun hidden somewhere and fired off a few shots to make you think that was what was happening.'

The comment rocked him, for it had been a dim suspicion at the back of his own mind. He had never had a clear sight of more than one person at a time. And the shots had always seemed to have come from the same direction as Kalaasi.

'Why should he do such a thing?'

'Our own motives are hard enough to work out, let alone other people's. Perhaps he's going crazy, or he wanted to scare you, or get some attention for himself – '

'Kalaasi doesn't think like that,' put in Mitti. 'He doesn't think much at all.'

'So what do you think has been happening then, Mitti?' asked Larsen.

Mitti flicked back her thick black hair and considered.

'I don't know,' she said, after a moment. 'But if these seeds are worth so much money, then someone will be after them.'

Gudrun shook her head.

'I knew you couldn't understand.'

Suddenly, viciously, Mitti turned on her.

'Don't speak to me that way. I know you were sleeping with Jonis – and I know why.'

'What are you talking about?'

'You're older than me, and hundreds of thousands of crowns have been spent on you, to look after you, keep you healthy, and educate you until you are so clever that you can understand almost anything. Well, I may have left school without being able to do much more than read, add a few numbers, and write a letter, but I know people better than you ever will. You slept with my husband because he was an Inuit and you wanted to show how brave and unracist and liberated you were. And also because he was married to me, and all Sermilik knew what I did with Otto Frederiksen, so you didn't have to feel guilty. There is nothing worse than guilt, is there?'

Gudrun's face was scarlet with fury.

'At least I'm not a whore!'

'That is what you would say,' spat Mitti. 'But Jonis slept with other women. He always did, from the first weeks, and he never troubled to hide it. I didn't complain, but why should I not sleep with other men? And where does this put you, who fucked my husband to make yourself feel a better person?'

The door slammed behind her.

'Poisonous bitch,' hissed Gudrun, beneath her breath.

'Tell me about Jonis?' Larsen said, after a moment.

'Do you want to analyse my sex life too?'

'No,' said Larsen patiently. 'I want to know how he died.'

'I told you. It was an accident.'

190

'How do you know?'

Gudrun hesitated, recovering her breath and composure. Larsen saw that she was phrasing ideas, deciding how much to tell him, and his readiness to believe her lessened sharply.

'Jonis was always listening to things that were none of his business, and somehow he found out about the hidden seeds,' she said at length. 'He told me that he was going to inform Frederiksen. I gave him some money, and promised more, but I was frightened he would double-cross me, sell the information to Frederiksen as well, or even steal the seeds himself. So when I had the chance, I persuaded him to come for a walk with me.'

'How?' asked Larsen.

'We had been lovers during the winter. Anyway, he always thought women wanted to be alone with him.'

'This was the Tuesday before last?'

She nodded.

'What time?'

'Maybe eleven.'

'Olssen was in the seed bank as well that morning. What did he think about you and Jonis going off together?'

'I paid him to go off hunting. Like I did today.'

Larsen nodded. That explained where Olssen had got the money for his trip to Godthab.

'Go on.'

'I told Jonis there was something very important I had to show him, and I led him to Lake Tugdlik. He was too greedy and excited and full of masculine pride to suspect a thing, until I came up behind him, and hit him on the head with a stone. I tied him up and left him there, then came back here to move the seeds out of Frederiksen's hiding-place. After finishing, I went straight back to the lake.'

'You chose the place to leave him very carefully,' said Larsen.

'Yes. I couldn't risk anyone finding him by accident.'

'What if he'd brought charges against you for assault?'

'He would never have admitted he'd been knocked down and tied up by a woman.'

That, at least, rang true.

'Go on,' repeated Larsen, non-committally.

'When I saw him, I thought he was still unconscious, then I thought he was asleep, then I thought he'd frozen to death, although it wasn't very cold.' As she relived the moment, her obvious distress swung Larsen back towards belief. 'But then I saw the knife in his back and the blood on the snow.'

'So someone else murdered him?'

'No, it was an accident. When he came round, he must have managed to get out his knife – I never knew he had one on him – and wedge it between two stones. I'd tied his hands behind his back, and while trying to cut them free, he slipped and fell on it. It was a very sharp knife.' She hesitated, then made herself continue. 'I cut him free, threw the knife away, and cleared most of the bloodstained snow. Then I remembered the helicopter would come soon, so I panicked and ran back here as fast as I could.'

'Bob and Olssen both saw Jonis setting off by himself at about three. Bob even spoke to him.'

'That was me,' admitted Gudrun. 'I dressed myself in Jonis's spare clothes, went out and waved to Bob, then hurried off. Once out of sight I doubled back, crept in by the fire door, and returned to my work. I thought that would prove I couldn't have had anything to do with his death.'

'It also made it likely that whoever found Jonis would be accused of the killing.'

She said nothing.

'Do you have any proof of all this?' pressed Larsen.

'No. But – '

Kamik burst in.

'A helicopter is coming.'

Larsen frowned.

'There isn't one due till six o'clock tomorrow morning.'

'Listen,' said Kamik.

They could all hear the beat of the rotors. Larsen went over to the window and stared out. An unfamiliar helicopter was landing gently on the pad. As he waited to see who would emerge, his legs were suddenly taken away from under him and he fell sprawling to the ground. The gun spun from his hand. As he grabbed for it, Gudrun's foot slammed crushingly down on his wrist. A moment later she snatched the gun up.

'Run, Kamik,' gasped Larsen between clenched teeth. 'Run!'

17

CLOSED DOORS

'Wait, Kamik,' called Gudrun. 'There's nothing to be scared of.'

Footsteps scuttled away. Gudrun turned on Larsen.

'What did you do that for? Frightening the child. I won't hurt him.'

'How do I know that?'

'Get up!' She held the gun tightly in her fist.

Larsen tried to steal a glance out of the window, but she did not give him the chance.

'Let's go. And keep your hands up, or I'll shoot. Don't believe I won't.'

Such was the ringing tension in her voice that Larsen believed her implicitly. Hands high, he walked out of the living-room and down the corridor.

'Stop,' said Gudrun. 'Go in there.'

The door crashed shut behind him and a key rattled in the lock. He was imprisoned in a bare metal room, windowless for it was on the inner side of the building, and with only a single, long-life light bulb hanging from the ceiling. Most of the space was taken up with a disconnected emergency generator.

Larsen flopped on the floor and cursed his own foolishness. Mitti had told him that the letter threatening Frederiksen came from Gudrun, and he had ignored the warning. Even after catching her with the seeds, he had never really believed Gudrun would do anything to him. Not until she had his gun, and he heard the frenzied edge to her voice. Lulled by the grave humanity of her manner, and their sex together, he had utterly failed to recognise the fanatic in her character.

If only people were more cynical, he thought glumly, then they would be less likely to try to rip up the world no matter what the cost. Or were those just the thoughts of a defeated man, old and tired before his time? They were certainly light-years from his own youthful beliefs. Yet Larsen knew he was still not a cynic. Cynicism provided its followers with a convenient escape clause, a justification for doing nothing and blaming everyone else: the certainty that individuals could change nothing. Larsen did not believe it. No policeman could. But neither did Gudrun.

In the light of her chilling conviction that what she was doing was worth a few deaths, his future looked bleak. But although his life had been something of a disappointment, he had no intention of letting it slip away. And he still had one card left in his hand.

Slowly he drew out Jonis's knife. With its wicked razor edge reflecting the light bulb back into his dazzled eyes, it became easy to believe in the bear's vengeful spirit, and its long history of victims. It was lucky for him that Robert Maataq had changed his mind about keeping it – if that was what had happened. Or maybe it was lucky for Maataq. He slipped the weapon back into hiding.

A mumble of conversation from outside echoed faintly in the steel of the door, and he realised that the bottom did not quite fit flush. He bent down and words seeped through to him.

'Is everything set?' The words were in English, but it was surely Gudrun speaking.

'Sure,' came a distant reply. 'The helicopter'll take us to Cap Gad, and the Keflavik plane will be there at five. From Iceland there's no problem in reaching the cold stores within fifteen hours. That gives us around forty-eight hours' leeway.'

Leeway for what? Then Larsen remembered that seeds could only be kept in their boxes for seventy-two hours before they began to defrost and rot.

'Are you absolutely sure your cold stores are good enough? If the temperature varies by more than a couple of degrees either way – '

'We've been through this a hundred times,' interrupted a man's voice, speaking Danish.

It was hard to hear clearly when even the slightest move reverberated in the metal door. Larsen lost the next sentence, then their voices dropped and he could hear nothing but a buzz, dotted with random words. He pressed himself hard against the crack. Footsteps clattered closer, and the voices came back.

'. . . I've told you. He can't get out.'

'How much does he know?'

There was a pause.

'I don't know,' said Gudrun.

'I can't find that woman anywhere.'

'She's probably run off back to the town. Don't worry. She's got no idea what's going on, and isn't interested anyway.'

'What about the boy?'

'Who would believe him?'

'OK. But the policeman is something else. If he gets free before we reach Iceland, we'll be in big trouble.'

'He's not to be killed,' came Gudrun's voice. 'I still think of Jonis, even though it was an accident. I will not have another man on my conscience. Especially one who is innocent.'

'No policeman is innocent. And what we're doing is more important than any single life.'

Helpless, Larsen was listening to his judges.

'But they'd find his body tomorrow morning, then launch a massive search. It wouldn't take more than an hour or two to trace our plane . . .'

'What about an accident?'

'There have been too many accidents already.'

'Gudrun's right,' came the third voice.

'But – '

'She's right.'

'If you say so. But we can't afford to have the police after us, so how do we make sure he's securely held?'

'What about the airlock? He couldn't get out of there.'

'I suppose not. But – '

'Right. Gudrun, go and make sure the helicopter hold is ready for the seed boxes. There mustn't be any damage during the flight. We'll begin loading up, and deal with the policeman.'

'What do you mean, deal with?'

'Don't worry.' There was a faint laugh. 'I don't want a murder charge hanging over my head.'

'But you suggested killing him. I couldn't believe it when you said that.'

'Just panic. Forget it.'

'He is only going to be shut in the airlock, isn't he?'

'Yes, yes. Of course. Let's get ready. The sooner we leave the better.'

There was a sound of feet scuffling away along the corridor. Silence crept back outside. Larsen got to his feet. At least Mitti and Kamik had got away.

His hand closed on the concealed knife handle, even though there was little chance of surprising anyone who came in, certainly not someone wary and armed with a gun, for the generator room door opened outwards. Perhaps he should gamble everything on surprise, a single reckless charge, knife in hand. But it is hard to resolve cold-bloodedly to throw away your life in a moment. Easier by far to hope that they were not going to kill him, to wait for the better opportunity, that may never come. So Larsen sat and waited.

The film of his life did not flicker past, even though he made a half-hearted attempt to start it up. He suspected it was because he had left behind so few shadows of his life. Except for one, no, two daughters, neither of whom he had really known. And now past and future decayed into a tiny, paralysed fraction of present, trembling on the edge of extinction.

At last the door swung slowly open. Larsen's hand hovered momentarily near the knife. Then his hopes crumbled into emptiness.

Two people waited outside, both clothed from head to foot in protective clothing, both holding guns. They motioned him down the corridor towards the airlock. And Larsen went meekly.

Inside the airlock, one of the figures stopped by the outer door.

'Did you remember the alarm system?'

'It's disconnected.'

'OK, then take him in.'

'He's got to go right in. Where no one'll find him for days. If at all.' Those muffled, almost indistinguishable voices were talking about his death. They were talking as if he was dead already. Larsen felt removed, as if he had already given up hope.

'Do what you want. I'll check on Gudrun.'

'Wait. I think perhaps you should take him in.'

'Why?'

'You're the only one who knows where the seeds are to go. You might be tempted to close the doors on him and me at the same time . . .'

'That's crazy. But if you're scared, it's all the same to me.'

Larsen's feeling of detachment faded. A few fragments of hope still smouldered within him after all. One of the silver figures left the airlock, closing the door. The second watched Larsen with visored eyes.

'I know who you are,' said Larsen softly.

The figure did not move.

'You're Marian Krinsky. And you won't kill me, Marian.'

'Shut up.' The gun was pointed at his head.

'You're not a murderer,' said Larsen. 'You don't want to be a murderer. You won't kill me.'

She said nothing, but suddenly Larsen's certainty shivered and cracked. For the sight of that empty masked face had brought back part of his police training, a course on riot control. They had been divided into two groups – rioters with stones, and police with shields, gas-masks and tear gas rounds. Larsen had a vivid memory of the total lack of empathy between the two sides. As a rioter, his eyes burning, his throat screaming for air, he saw the masked police as loathsome aliens, and he hurled his stones with all the savagery he could. If they had given him a petrol bomb, he might have thrown that, even though he would have been trying to set light to his companions and partners.

In sharp contrast had been his emotions safe inside his gas-mask, as he watched the 'rioters' choking and gasping and finally turning and running. He had had a sense of absolute invulnerability, of super-human control. And with it came an instinct that those who were not equipped and protected as he was were somehow inferior, sub-human scum who deserved everything they got. After the course there had been discussions, and everyone had confessed to that same feeling behind the mask, which made brutality so much easier. The feeling Marian Krinsky must now be experiencing. Somehow he had to establish a relationship with her.

'Marian, don't do this,' he said. 'You won't forget – '

'Open the inner door,' she ordered, and he had no idea from her muffled voice if he was making any impact at all.

'Marian, think about it – '

'Open the door.'

Direct defiance would be dangerous. Larsen reached for the wheel and slowly turned it to open the inner door.

'Marian, we have talked a lot together. We – '

'Get out there.'

And Larsen realised that by mentioning their talk, he had made another mistake. A fatal mistake. His talk with Marian Krinsky had been about what she did with Otto Frederiksen. She had used him to purge her guilt, but reminding her what he knew had given her another reason for murder. If he was dead, she might hope that her guilt would die with him.

Rather than undermining her will to kill him, he had strengthened it.

Larsen got out of the airlock and she began to follow him. Slowing, he allowed her almost to catch him up, then suddenly darted aside, swung round, and flung himself at her. He was almost too quick for her. Almost.

The gun went off with a tremendous explosion, and fire and burn and smoke engulfed his face. Something, which for that moment did not hurt, spun him round and sent him crashing to the ground. By the time he staggered back to his feet, to feel blood pouring from his shoulder and pain and cold cutting at him, the airlock was closing on a fleeting flash of silver. He rushed forward, but it was too late. As he reached it, the door shut with a definitive final click. The sound of a coffin lid nailed down.

18

THE OTHER SIDE

Mitti stood precariously on the toilet bowl and edged open the tiny, frosted-glass window, until she could just see out of the crack. The helicopter, which she recognised as the seed bank standby machine, was still on the pad. There were two figures beside it. One was Gudrun, for she could just see the clipped blonde hair. The other, dressed in bulky clothes and with black hair, might have been almost anyone. Mitti watched as they spoke together for a few moments, then climbed inside the helicopter. Minutes trickled past.

It was midnight and the sun had dropped out of the white-clouded sky and slipped behind the mountains. There were no flowers in sight, no birds, no trees. Blue shadows and silence lay heavy over the snow and rock. On the mountainside above, melting snow sent a trickle of water toppling headlong over the cliff-edge in a thin waterfall, to spatter on the rocks below.

Abruptly there came a sound from within the seed bank of slamming doors and running feet. A moment later Marian Krinsky, hair awry, a silver low-temperature suit flapping around her, a gun in her hand, came running towards the helicopter.

She sprang inside, and the door slammed shut. Mitti waited for the explosion of sound as the engine started, but it did not come. There was only a faint choking sound, repeated several times, then nothing. After a couple of minutes the helicopter door swung open again, and someone got out and went to investigate the engine. Even from where she was, Mitti could hear the explosive curse. A moment later Gudrun and Krinsky got out, and joined their companion. All three of them spoke together for a few moments, then the two women came walking back towards the seed bank. Mitti ducked down.

'I still think we should walk back to Sermilik,' came Gudrun's voice. 'It'd only take about three hours.'

'And how would we carry all those boxes?'

'Then we'd better call the whole thing off,' said Gudrun. 'I could easily hide the seeds in the seed bank again, and – '

'What about the policeman?' interrupted Krinsky.

There was a brittle silence.

'I'm not calling the whole thing off,' the American went on. 'Not when we've got so far. And don't forget what that Secretary guy said, two more policemen are expected any day.'

'Well then,' said Gudrun, 'I've got another idea. Our plane isn't due at Cap Gad till five, and it's sure to wait at least a couple of hours. The relief helicopter will be here at six. We could use that, forge a requisition form for the seeds – '

'You know that won't work,' snapped Krinsky. 'The policeman put out an order to Cap Gad that all baggage is to be searched, and anything which might contain seeds should be impounded.'

'Then there's no choice but to call everything off.' Mitti could hear the relief in Gudrun's voice. 'I'll talk to Larsen. He's a reasonable man. I'm sure we can sort something out – '

'It's much too late for that now. We've got to stick with what we agreed.'

'But you heard what he said. It's not easy to put on a patch, and if it comes apart while we're in the air, that could be the end of all three of us – and the seeds.'

'It's a gamble we have to take.' Krinsky's voice was iron. 'I'm going inside to get some shut-eye. I advise you to do the same.'

Outside the remaining person had produced an arc of tools, and was bent head-down over the helicopter engine.

Half an hour later the door to the toilets opened with a soft creak, and Mitti emerged. She looked swiftly up and down the corridor, then tiptoed towards the lounge and peered through the three-quarters shut door. Marian Krinsky was slumped, boneless, eyes shut, breathing heavily through her open mouth. On the table in front of her were a bottle and an empty glass. Gudrun was sitting at the window with a typescript in front of her, marking it up with a biro, and occasionally glancing blearily outside.

Mitti crept past, then hurried to the airlock door and opened it. There was no one there. She stepped inside, then swung round.

Evat stood behind her, a cigarette in his mouth, his sun-glasses hiding his eyes.

'Hello, Mitti,' he said, reaching out to close the outer door behind him.

'You!' She stared at him for a long moment. Then shook her head. 'You wrung poor Otto's neck, you bastard. Why did you have to do that?'

Evat smiled mildly.

'I don't know what you're talking about.'

'There's no need to lie any more. You made a fool of me about Otto, didn't you? I really believed your story about wanting to watch, and you used it to murder him, and to make it look as if I'd done it. You've fooled that Danski girl too, because she wants to believe in you. But I know you, Evat Jonsson. You can spout theories and principles and morality until the glaciers melt, but I know you're only out for yourself. Gudrun stole those seeds for the good of mankind, and you're going to sell them for your own profit, aren't you? To that American woman, who has the hard face of success which doesn't care where it comes from.'

Evat reached for the inner door.

'I've always thought you were cleverer than you seem,' he said. 'But stupid too. Stupid enough to be a policeman's daughter.'

'Where is Larsen?'

'Your dear father. Let's get him.'

'When Gudrun Eistrup realises you're throwing your principles into the shit for money, there'll be trouble,' needled Mitti.

Evat's smile rotted into a scowl.

'It's easy for the Danes,' he snarled. 'They are so used to having money that they think they don't care about it. We are only just learning what money is, what it can do, how much there is slopping about, so we can't regard it with the carefully assumed contempt they do. The contempt of possession. Why shouldn't I get some of the millions those seeds are worth? They're as much mine as anyone's, and if I don't take them, they'll just stay here until our government sells them off to someone else, or throws them out.'

Only then did Mitti see the gun in Evat's hand. And found terror, like a black smoke, rising up to choke her.

'What are you doing?'

'It's only to stop the policeman from jumping me.'

'No, it isn't. I don't want to go in there. Please.'

The inner door swung open with a blast of cold air.

'Get out.'

'I haven't told anyone it was you, Evat. I swear. I didn't tell Larsen. You can trust me, I won't tell anyone. Please, Evat. I haven't done anything. Please.' There were tears in her eyes.

'I'm counting to five. One, two . . .'

Mitti stumbled backwards, and opened her mouth to beg again.

It was already too late. The great door swung ponderously shut with a faint hiss. The lock clicked and Mitti was alone. Surrounded by bitter cold, in the ground, in the air, all-enveloping.

Beside her was a dark stain on the ground. Like blood. She rubbed her eyes, looked at it more closely, then touched it, but the stain was frozen hard.

She found Larsen ten minutes later, unmoving, curled up in a tiny ball. Mitti crouched down beside him and shook his shoulder, but he did not respond. His skin seemed thick and congealed, but when she shook him again, harder, he grunted and steam crept from the side of his mouth.

'Larsen, Tomas Larsen, wake up,' she shouted. 'Wake up!'

He sat up groggily. His left shoulder was encrusted with dried blood.

'What?' he muttered. 'What is it?'

'It's me, Mitti.'

'Have you come to kill me?' he whispered, and his eyelids sagged shut.

'No, stupid.' She slapped his face. 'Wake up. Wake up. I've been locked in here with you. We must get out.'

'We can't,' he said. But he rubbed his eyes and shivered, life seeping back over his face like the rising tide covering a sand bank. 'The doors are locked and the alarms have been disconnected. It's my fault, isn't it? I didn't think Gudrun would help to murder me. Isn't that stupid?'

'You wanted her,' said Mitti. 'That's why you couldn't see what she was.'

He looked up at her for a moment, then shut his eyes and lay down again. It was like a blow to her belly. Exerting all her strength, she seized his limp cold arms, and dragged him back up.

'Get up. If you stay here any longer, you'll die.'

'I don't want to get up. What's the point of getting up? We can't get out, and no one knows we are here except those who shut us in. I'm going to lie down and stop caring and go to sleep. Everyone dies. What's the problem?'

'Get up,' she insisted. 'We only need to hang on for a few hours and then the next shift will come in and find us. Don't worry.'

'You sound like one of those stupid TV films, where the hero keeps promising that it'll be all right. He's read the script and he knows he's right. But I never watch them to the end. I know what would happen in real life, and I switch them off, so it never is all right. They all die.'

'Let me see your shoulder.' She probed the blood-caked mess, and Larsen gave a yelp of pain.

'Careful.'

'Why should I be if you're just going to give up and die? What happened?'

'I tried to jump the American woman, and she shot me.'

'It doesn't seem bad.'

Mitti felt adrenalin pumping through her veins. She was confident, ready for the fight, even eager for it, primed like an athlete at her peak about to face the ultimate challenge. She sensed her strongly built body holding the cold away from her, and felt sure she could go on for as long as it would take. She did not doubt she would escape, though she had no idea how.

'Come on, get up,' she rapped out.

He did not answer. She took his cold, flaking, stubbled cheeks in her hands and pushed her face into his.

'Evat put me in here with you. Well, I'm not dying for him, or you, or anyone. Now, move!'

'Move where?' asked Larsen. But he slowly got to his feet.

'It doesn't matter. Walk.'

She pushed him, and they began to walk. Up and down, up and down the tunnels. First the Oriental and Australasian, then Ethiopian and Neotropical, and finally Nearctic and Palearctic. They walked mainly in silence, for talk sent cold air racing down their throats, spreading ice into the inner walls of their chests, and they needed all their strength to keep their heavy, cooling blood circulating. But occasionally their frozen hands would reach out and touch each other.

At first Mitti needed to drive Larsen almost every step, but gradually, and despite, or perhaps because of, the pain in his shoulder, he recovered himself. Together they walked through that dead place, which was packed with untold potential for life. Mitti briefly remembered an old song she had heard on the radio, 'There's Always the Sun'. It had been wrong. These tunnels would never see the light of the sun, or feel the touch of its warmth. The very air felt thin and moribund, as if they were on an alien planet.

Except for the signs, every dismal tunnel looked the same, every side gallery, every passage and chamber. They walked on into the Eastern Palearctic, and signs flickered past, promises of a lost world neither of them would ever see: Altai Mountains, Kazakhstan; Tien Shan 1, Kazakhstan; Tien Shan 2, Uzbekistan; Kyzl Kum, Uzbekistan; Pamirs 1–4 . . . Suddenly the lights stopped, but the tunnel kept going, plunging on into the rock beneath a slanting roof, a shrinking, black hole.

Mitti turned back, but Larsen stopped.

'I wonder where that goes,' he hissed, keeping his lips almost closed, as the white vapour of his breath poured out and scattered ice crystals on his hair.

Mitti rested her hand on his shoulder.

'The old mining face, I suppose.'

'Let's see.'

'We can't see,' pointed out Mitti.

Larsen held out his hand for his daughter, then strode into the darkness. Reluctantly Mitti followed.

Bandaging his leading hand with a handkerchief, as protection against the icy cavern walls, Larsen patted his way along, ducking as the roof slanted down upon them. Soon Mitti also had to stoop.

'What're we doing?' she whispered.

'We are trying,' came Larsen's voice, chittering round the rock that hemmed them in.

'It's colder.' Mitti was speaking more to retain contact than because she had anything to say.

'We are walking slower,' said Larsen, relentlessly pulling her on.

The ground underfoot grew rougher and both of them stumbled several times. Their bent necks ached, Larsen's shoulder and foot threw long needles of pain into him, but still he went on. The insipid yellow gleam of the seed bank lights behind shrank to a dot, then vanished as the path turned downhill and away to the right.

The blackness was solid, pushing Mitti back, closing over her face and mouth and mind. Every second she expected to strike her bowed head against something hard and sharp and impassable. But above them the roof had levelled out.

'We're blind,' she said.

'Like your father-in-law,' replied Larsen.

Briefly she felt a fresh return of courage and determination. If she did not return, the old man would be alone in the world.

They passed another opening, but it was smaller than the tunnel they were following, so they ignored it and pressed on. Their way swung in slow curves until they lost all sense of direction, and on either side the walls imperceptibly closed in until the tunnel was only a metre wide, and the air felt stale and old. Still they burrowed, mole-like, into the deep, forgotten shafts of the mine. At last they came to a fork where two narrow corridors separated out from each other. They ran their hands over the openings, but could find no difference between them, nor decide which to take.

'I want to go back,' said Mitti suddenly.

'What's the point?' came Larsen's voice.

'It is better to die in the light.'

'When we die, we go into the dark, why not get used to it?'

'I don't want to be buried alive.'

'You are.'

'You want to die,' she accused him.

'I expect to die. It's not the same. But first I want to learn just one more thing.'

'What?'

'What is at the end of this tunnel?'

'A blank wall. The mining face where they stopped work.'

'No doubt. And maybe they left a drill or a pick-axe behind.'

'But – '

'Where did Evat catch you?' he asked suddenly.

'In the airlock.'

'You came back for me, didn't you? To try to get me out.'

Uselessly she nodded. Tears pricked her icy eyes.

'Yes,' she whispered.

'Why?'

'It is hard to live with no parents.'

'You saved my life and you stopped me giving up. Now it is my turn.'

'I won't do it. You think because you are my father you can make me do this,' she cried out. 'But I won't.'

Larsen did not reply, only held out his arms and enfolded her. Momentarily she resisted, then gave way and buried her face in his chest. For a long time they did not move. Then, as if making their farewells, they separated and Larsen led her into the right-hand tunnel, which closed over them like a mouth. Bent almost double they staggered along.

'It was Evat who murdered Frederiksen,' said Mitti. Although it hurt her to talk, the confining blackness was sapping her will to resist, and she must do something to loosen its hold. 'It must have been him who shot at you and Kalaasi too.'

'I think I had guessed that.'

'All three of them, Evat, Krinsky and Gudrun, are still here.'

'Why?'

'Their helicopter broke down. Evat is trying to repair it.'

A thought came to Larsen, but he ignored it. That was far away, in the living world, nothing to do with this black borehole.

'If they are still here, then there is no point in waiting for rescue from the morning shift. The last reason to go back is gone.'

'Not the last. There is still one – to see each other's faces.'

Larsen stopped, and a moment later Mitti felt his frost-cracked lips brush her icy forehead.

'Feeling is more important than seeing,' he said. 'It has taken me a long time to learn that. Perhaps you taught me, my daughter.' It was the first time he had called her that. 'And now we must crawl.'

'No.' She was almost crying. 'Please don't make me do that.'

Waves of uncontrollable claustrophobia came sweeping up to overwhelm her, blackness piled upon blackness, swelling in her brain, but this new dark carried breathless panic.

'Hold my foot and crawl behind me,' said Larsen.

'Why? Why must I?'

'Because I can hear something. That's why I took this tunnel.'

'What can you hear?'

'Listen.'

All she could hear was the same distant steady white noise that she had listened to for an eternity. A meaningless interference that never changed, never altered in pitch or tone, a noise that said nothing.

'It is only blood in our ears.'

'People have died looking for more stupid things. Crawl.'

And because her fear of being deserted was the greater, she closed her eyes – as if that might quieten the quivering nerves of her frozen body – and got down upon her knees. With one hand she gripped Larsen's ankle, with the other she groped in front of her face, feeling her way along.

On and on, crawling in the nothingness, the walls slowly but inexorably closing in to entomb them. She might have lain down and given up, but her terrors would not let her. And her father's ankle in front of her kept dragging her forward, and the panting of Larsen's breath a few feet away was an engine that would not let her rest.

Soon there was only just room for them to keep going. The tunnel was scarcely wider than a badger's lair, the rough rock rubbing against them on each side, above and below, threatening to snap suddenly shut, crushing them into two-dimensional fossils to be unearthed in millions of years, the look of terror still perfectly preserved in the rock. If they wanted to go back, they must crawl backwards, for there was no longer any room to turn. The only way left was forward, along the tunnel that must surely lead to a dead wall and their own extinction. The roof crept down further, and Mitti found she was no longer crawling, but wriggling like a snake, stretched out flat, clutching Larsen's ankle, loose stones scratching her numb, grovelling face.

Now the rock was like a second skin, clinging to Mitti's broad hips, clawing her shoulders. The tunnel would not end after all, just go on and on, an inescapable, body-hugging, infinitely shrinking trap for all life. Mitti's face was turned to her left to gasp what air she could, for it was impossible even to hold her head upright. Then suddenly she found herself pressed up hard against solid rock. It was over. She could never travel backwards over the agonising way she had come. The nightmare of utter surrender closed in around her.

Only gradually did she realise that she still held Larsen's ankle in a vice grip, and that it was kicking weakly. How could it be? Where was Larsen if she was at the end of the tunnel? Of course, it must bend sharply. The torture of struggle was not over yet.

Mitti tucked in her head as tight as she could, jack-knifed round the hairpin, and felt herself slipping down. As she did her heels locked against the roof. She was stuck.

Desperately she tried to push her legs forward then back, but they did not move. Panic seized her, blotting out her mind, and her shrieking body wildly writhed the few millimetres the merciless rock walls would permit. As a little sanity slowly returned, leaving terror like a choking bubble still poised in her throat, she found she had edged herself round on to her back. She wriggled more carefully, tiny twitching movements. Her head slipped a little, her knee bent sharper, and abruptly she was free but lying on her back, with uncountable tons of rock pressing down a few hairbreadths from her panting mouth. Again her body shook convulsively as the terror rose up and clutched at her brain afresh, but Larsen's ankle dragged her on and she kicked and twined and squirmed.

And in her straining, freezing ears the meaningless sound grew slowly louder.

Unbelievably the floor and roof began to slip away from each other a little, and Mitti was able to flip herself back on to her front. A few minutes later she could actually crawl on her arms and knees again. The tunnel was almost back to the size of the one she had refused to enter, but now it seemed like some wonderful release, and the first faint sparks of hope glimmered before her blind eyes. Perhaps the tunnel would keep getting larger, until at last it emerged into the open. She hurried on so fast that when Larsen suddenly stopped, she would have sprawled on top of him, if there had been a little more room.

'This is it,' he said breathlessly.

'What?' She had to shout, so loud had the sound become. And the air seemed colder, but also moving. It had not moved for an unknown limbo of time.

'The end of the tunnel.'

So it had all been for nothing. But she could not go back. Could not.

'There is a drop at the end,' came Larsen's voice. 'And at the bottom is a river. It is what we have been hearing. An underground river.'

He wriggled a few inches forward, then stopped.

'I am on the edge of the drop.'

'How far down do you think it is?'

'It sounds deep.'

He scrabbled for a stone, then let it fall. But he could hear nothing over the roar of the waters.

'Is there room to turn round?' Mitti asked, not letting go of his ankle. Her heart was vibrating as if to split her breast.

'I don't think so. Nor can we cross it. We'll have to go back.'

'I cannot go back,' said Mitti.

'There was another tunnel to try.'

'No. I only just escaped from being trapped at that corner. I dare not face it again.'

'Do not give up.'

'I am not giving up,' grilled Mitti, stretched out along the tunnel like an eel in a mud-hole. 'But I am not going back.'

'I cannot stay on this ledge,' said Larsen. 'And that means you must start crawling back. You have to.'

She heard the fear in his voice, and felt stronger.

'We are going to jump into the stream,' she said.

'No.'

'I do not have the strength to go back, and even if I had, I am sure the other tunnel would at best only bring us back to this stream. I want to jump.'

'What about dying in the light?' he asked.

'There is no light,' she answered. 'And if there is, then maybe the stream will take us out into it.'

'Why should it take us out?' Larsen's voice was taut, on the edge of breaking. 'More likely it will just plunge down further into the ground, down to . . .' For a fleeting moment he had a ludicrous thought of a Jules Verne-like lake full of dinosaurs, deep in the heart of the earth. Then fear overwhelmed him afresh.

'There's nothing else we can do,' said Mitti.

'No.' Larsen was almost screaming. 'Get out of my way. I must go back. Get out of my way.'

'I can't.'

He kicked blindly back at her, catching her in the face. Mitti cringed away and began crying, aching dry sobs wrenched up from deep inside her.

'I will not go back,' she wept. 'I will not.'

'We must.'

'No.' Her cheek was cold with tears. 'I would rather drown than be buried. I would rather lie down and die here, where I can move a little and there is a breeze on my face, than go back. Rather go to sleep with you here than go back.'

Weeping overcame her.

'I will not give up,' came his voice from the dark.

'Then we jump,' she said. 'Hold hands and jump.'

'Jumping is another way of giving up. I do not want to drown or be dashed to pieces.' Larsen thought longingly of the seed bank. That underground maze of cold tunnels, with its signs and its dull yellow lights, seemed a sort of lost paradise, a beautiful rich place of light and life and joy. 'We must go back.' His voice allowed no argument.

'No,' she whimpered.

He pushed his feet back at her again. And suddenly rage ignited in Mitti. She braced her feet against an unevenness on either wall, bent her knees, then hurled her body as far forward as she could, clutching his waist as she did.

Larsen was caught utterly unawares as the force of her lunge propelled him over the invisible cliff. For a moment Mitti's arms held him head down, dangling, then his weight dragged both of them forward and down.

A scream rent the air, even above the blaring, crashing of the waters. But neither of them knew if it was themselves or their companion or both of them at once who had screamed.

As they struck the water, Mitti's hold on Larsen was ripped apart, and she felt herself spinning away, choking, gasping, freezing. The bitter cold constricted her lungs to bursting. The river swept her to oblivion.

19

HUNTERS

Kamik was over half the way back to Sermilik when he saw a man crossing the thick ice at the head of the fjord. After hesitating for a moment, then shading his eyes, he headed towards the distant figure. By the time the boy reached the sheer, black basalt cliffs that blocked any further progress along the shoreline, the man was just coming off the sea-ice. It was Robert Maataq, his rifle slung over one shoulder, a large leather bag on the other.

'What are you doing out here at this time of night?' said the hunter.

'I am looking for help.'

'You are going the wrong way for the town.'

'I saw you and came to ask you. The help is needed up at the seed bank.'

Maataq scowled.

'Nothing but bad luck ever came out of that place. Before the mining, I could be sure to get at least a fox up there, but not now. I used to enjoy a dinner of agdlek eggs, but now Lake Tugdlik is all but deserted by wildfowl, and who can blame them? Would you rest where helicopters crash overhead four times every day?'

Kamik shifted nervously from one foot to the other.

'What is it, boy?' demanded Maataq. 'Make it quick. Those are snow clouds, and there is a storm in the air.'

'But it's the first of July.'

Maataq smiled grimly.

'In April was the seal pup born, the snow came in September. "Now such a fearful storm as this," says he, "I can't remember." If you had lived as long as I have, then you would know that there have been many snowstorms in July, and any other month you care to mention.' He shifted his pack, and ran his thumb up and down the worn strap of his rifle. 'What are you going to tell me about the seed bank?'

'Sergeant Larsen . . .'

'The man who calls me a murderer, and thinks I am for sale. What of him?'

'I do not think he calls you a murderer now, sir. He has been locked up, but I cut the fuel feed on their helicopter. Bob showed it to me a few weeks ago and I remembered where it was and I cut it. So they cannot get away.'

'Tell me more clearly, boy.'

The words gushed breathlessly from Kamik.

'. . . I am afraid they will kill him,' he finished. 'Please help me.'

Maataq shook his head.

'This is not my business. You and I will go back to Sermilik and give the warning. That is enough.'

'By then it will be too late.'

'It is too late now.'

'Mitti Hendrik was there as well, and . . .'

'Mitti?' Maataq looked at him sharply. 'What was she doing there?'

'I'm not sure. But they've probably caught her too.'

'Very well, I will go to the seed bank. You return to Sermilik.'

'What shall I do there?' asked the boy eagerly.

'Nothing. No one will believe you if you arrive by yourself with such a tale. I am not sure I should.' He glanced restlessly up at the sky again. 'Anyway the snow will probably be upon us within two hours, long before they can send any help. I may not make it in time myself. Go home to your grandmother.'

Maataq turned on his heel and set off up the river valley towards the lake and the seed bank beyond. After he had gone a few strides, he stopped.

'I told you to go home, boy.'

'Sergeant Larsen owes me something for my help,' said Kamik determinedly. 'I want to make sure he will pay.'

'Is that all?' asked Maataq.

'No,' admitted Kamik. 'He is my friend.'

'You will slow me down and get in my way.'

'I won't. I promise.'

'You promise what you do not know. The weather is worsening as we speak, and those cold gusts are outriders of the storm. Go back to town.'

'No.'

The hunter looked at the boy with calm calculation.

'Can I stop you?'

'No, sir.'

'What if I beat you?'

'I would wait until you were on your way, then come after you again. But you will not beat me.'

'Come then, but you must do what I say.'

'Thank you, sir.'

'You may not thank me soon.'

They made their way up the river valley. Maataq's walk was deceptively fast, his short bandy legs covering the ground easily, and Kamik trotted after him. The boy had covered many kilometres already, but to be with the greatest hunter in East Greenland, the man who always travelled alone, was something that cleaned away tiredness, something every boy in Sermilik would envy.

At length they reached the waterfall, where the lake waters tumbled over the outflung ridge. Maataq stopped.

'Get on my back,' he said shortly.

Kamik did as he was told, clinging on tight, and under Maataq's thick clothes, he could feel lean, wiry muscles and powerful shoulders.

The hunter paused for a moment, swaying from foot to foot, getting the feel of his new weight and balance, then strode to the very top of the fall. Suddenly he sprang out. In four long, carefully paced steps he was across the river, never having gone in over the top of his knee boots.

'I thought the river was deeper than that at this time of year,' said Kamik, as he scrambled down on to the spray-worn rock on the far side.

'It is. I knew where to step.'

'How?'

'I have done it many times. Do not waste breath.'

They pushed on along the east side of the lake. The shore sloped steeply down from the mountains, and their way was constantly interrupted by scree slopes or fast-flowing streams that came crashing down the hillsides, fed by the melting snows above. Kamik's legs were beginning to ache, but Maataq was steadily, imperceptibly, accelerating.

Kamik bit his lip and concentrated on keeping up. Several times, in spite of all he could do, he fell behind, but then Maataq would stop to look up at the sky, or around him, and the boy would have a chance to catch up.

Above them yellowish-grey clouds were pouring forward, appearing around the mountains in an ever-increasing stream. The wind had almost died away, but every now and then bitter gusts whipped among the stones. A snow bunting fluttered away from under a rock like a preliminary snowflake. Still the clouds came on, hanging lower and lower, great heavy clouds that sprawled just above the peaks, mimicking their frost-shattered shapes. By the time Kamik and Maataq reached the cliffs at the head of Lake Tugdlik, the first thin snow was curling idly down and the light was worsening.

Some distance short of the usual pass through to the seed bank, they came to a huge scree slope of frost-shattered slivers and shreds of rock.

Maataq skirted part of it, then began to climb. It was steep and slippery with crumbling stones and melting snowfields. Scattered here and there were the rosettes of Arctic saxifrage, the occasional budding glacier buttercup flushed with pink, and untrustworthy branches of crawling dwarf willow. Kamik tried to use exactly the same hand and foot-holds that Maataq did, and found that about thirty metres up it suddenly became easier. Soon they were making their way into a dry gully, lined with large boulders.

Almost entirely hidden from above, the gully sloped upwards, carving into the sheer flank of the mountain. A high road towards the seed bank.

Unexpectedly Maataq stopped and looked back the way they had come.

'What is it?' asked the boy.

'Ssh.'

He stood stock still for a moment, then began to retrace his steps. Kamik obediently followed, but the hunter was moving fast, and by the time the boy reached the top of the scree, Maataq was already at the bottom, wading into the lake. After a moment he dragged something large and heavy out of the water, and put it down on the shore, close by a second shape. Kamik flung himself down the slope, using giant strides to ride the tumbling frost debris and pebbles.

Two bodies lay on the ground. The hunter was thumping the chest of one. The other moved feebly, then groaned as Kamik ran up.

'Sergeant, sergeant, it's me. Kamik. Are you all right?'

Larsen was soaked to the skin. His face and hands were dead white, but he opened his lips and croaked something.

'What did you say, sergeant?'

'Mitti,' he gasped.

As Kamik came over, Maataq gave a great blow, and there was a weak cough, then another. A moment later the second body jerked up and was abruptly and violently sick, before collapsing back on the grey-sanded shoreline. Water fell from her clothes, her hair, her sodden body, but she was visibly breathing. Maataq gently pushed her upright, holding her or she would have fallen forward like a doll, unable to help herself.

'Go back to the man,' he told Kamik sternly. 'If you think he will be sick, make him lean forward.'

The policeman had already sat up, resting against a rock and shivering.

'How is she?' he asked.

'She has been sick.'

'Is she all right?'

Kamik shrugged, unsure what he should say. Larsen struggled to his feet and, brushing aside Kamik, he tottered over to where Maataq was supporting Mitti.

'Is she all right?' he repeated hoarsely.

'Neither of you will be well if you do not take these wet clothes off,' said the hunter.

'You want us to run around naked?'

'It can be better,' said Maataq, without a trace of humour. 'But things are not yet that bad. We must get you straight back to the town.'

Larsen bent down and put his arms round Mitti.

'How are you?' he asked tenderly.

'Cold,' said Mitti, through chattering teeth. Then she lifted a hand and patted him on the face. 'I was right, wasn't I?'

He nodded.

They hugged each other for a minute or two longer, then Larsen got up and turned to Maataq.

'Have any helicopters passed over?' he asked.

'Not for many hours.'

'Then they must still be at the seed bank.'

'Little Kamik did things to their helicopter.'

Larsen glanced at the grinning boy, then looked up at the sky.

'What time is it?'

'You have a watch.'

'It's broken.'

'Three hours after sunrise.'

That made it four in the morning. The relief helicopter would arrive in two hours.

'Do you have some dry clothes?' he asked.

'Of course.'

'Could you lend them to me?'

Maataq opened his pack and brought out three dead ptarmigan, then a parcel tightly wrapped in waterproofed cloth, and began to unfold it.

'What about me?' demanded Mitti. 'I need dry clothes too.' She flapped her arms weakly about herself and coughed.

'You must get back to the town as quickly as you can, with Kamik and Maataq.'

'And where will you go?' asked Maataq drily.

'Back to the seed bank.'

'If you go hunting on your own, you will fail.'

'I am not going hunting. I am going to – '

'I will come with you. There is no difference between hunting seal or ptarmigan or man.'

213

'Thank you,' said Larsen, with sudden relief.

Maataq said nothing. Larsen turned back to Mitti.

'You must alert people in Sermilik.'

'No,' objected Mitti. 'I want to – '

'Listen. Someone must take Kamik back to his grandmother. She has not heard from him for two days. For another thing, you heard, there are only enough dry clothes for one. And finally a warning must be sent to Cap Gad, Keflavik, and Søndre Strømfjord.'

'Perhaps I was lucky not to have had a father,' Mitti said sullenly. 'The moment anything dangerous happens, you start beating your chests and flexing your muscles, sending the women and children off to safety with a smug expression on your hairy faces. The satisfaction, and relief, of discovering at last what you are for.'

'I have told you the reasons,' said Larsen, with a flash of anger. 'Now hurry. None of us have time to waste.'

He turned away and finished stripping off. Mitti had a glimpse of solid buttocks, a broad, powerful naked back, and a ragged, blood-smeared hole in his left shoulder, where the bullet had come out. Then Larsen swiftly pulled on the clothes Maataq produced from his pack.

'You are wounded,' said Maataq.

'It's nothing much,' replied Larsen, putting his own wet clothes into a small pack, slinging it on his back, then transferring Jonis's knife to a pocket of Maataq's jacket.

'That should be mine,' objected Mitti.

'Do you want it?'

'No.' She put out a hand for Kamik. 'Let's go. The men have work to do.'

'But it was me that stopped them getting away,' objected Kamik. 'By cutting the fuel feed. If it wasn't for me – '

'If it wasn't for you,' said Mitti, 'Evat and the others would have left, and I could have got Tomas out of the seed store without any trouble. After that it would have been easy to get back to Sermilik in time to send out a warning, and catch them at Cap Gad.'

The boy's face fell, and disappointment spread over him like a cloak.

'I thought I was helping . . .'

Mitti looked at him for a moment, then her face changed. She put her arm round him.

'You were helping,' she said more gently. 'Don't take any notice of me. I was talking nonsense. If you hadn't damaged the helicopter, they would certainly have got away, and probably killed us too.'

'Really?' he asked, brightening.

'Really. It was a brilliant idea.'

Her arm still round him, Mitti and the slightly reluctant boy walked

214

off along the shore of the lake. Larsen watched them go over his shoulder, and wished she had said goodbye.

'I would be proud of such a daughter,' remarked Maataq.

'Why?' asked Larsen, startled.

'She knows what she is. It is a rare thing.'

'I suppose so.'

'Still, what you did was right. There is no place for women and children where guns may fire.'

'They took my gun,' said Larsen.

'Do you want my rifle?'

'No. I'm sure you are the better shot. And I've never killed a man. You have, haven't you?'

'That is the question of a policeman.'

'What is wrong with this town that policemen are so hated?' muttered Larsen.

'I do not hate policemen. I do not often see them. Are you strong enough for this?'

'Yes. Let us go.'

On the shore of the lake, Kamik looked back and saw Larsen and Maataq vanish up the side of the cliff.

'Shall we follow them?' he said suddenly.

Mitti did not reply. The boy saw that her face was leached of all colour and she was shaking.

'Come,' he said, taking her cold, damp hand. 'Let's get back to Sermilik.'

With an effort she smiled at him.

Larsen felt warmth steadily flowing back into his cold wet body.

'These are good clothes,' he said.

Maataq nodded.

'My wife made them. If anything happens to your ordinary clothes, then you should have better ones to change into. That sealskin jacket and trousers are the best I have. You had best wear these mittens too, hands take long to warm up again after wetting. And chew this.'

'What is it?' asked Larsen, looking doubtfully at the deep blueberry-red strip of meat.

'Mattak. Narwhal skin. The first of the summer.'

Reluctantly Larsen accepted it. To his surprise it had a pleasant, salty taste, not at all fatty and with no hint of fish.

Maataq led the way up the gully towards the seed bank. He still did not ask what had happened to Larsen and Mitti, simply accepted the situation and reacted to it.

After they had covered two or three kilometres, Maataq stopped.

'It is not far now,' he said. 'But you have not told me what to do. There is a place near which provides good cover and an excellent view. We could watch for them there.'

For a moment Larsen did not understand what Maataq meant. Then it struck home.

'You mean you could just pick them off?'

'It would probably not be hard.'

Larsen thanked his stars that it had been Evat shooting at him last Monday, not Maataq.

'No, no,' he said hastily. 'We cannot kill them as if they were ducks.'

'Anything else will be much more difficult.'

'Our job is to make sure they do not get away and, if possible, arrest them. We only use guns when our own lives are in danger.'

'As you wish,' said Maataq.

They continued up the gully, which was growing steadily shallower. Although there was still only the occasional snowflake curling down, the light was very poor. Suddenly a heavy beating sound broke the silence, then faded away equally quickly. Larsen looked anxiously up, but the thick-clouded sky was empty.

At the end of the gully was a shallow basin, hemmed by rocks. Larsen crouched behind one and looked out. The disabled helicopter was still on the landing pad, and as he watched its rotors began to go round again, then stopped. A figure got out and vanished inside.

'Follow me,' said Larsen.

He put his head down and sprinted towards the landing pad. There were no shots, no shouts, and he dived into cover behind a low ridge, not far from the helicopter. After a moment to regain his breath, Larsen ran again, darted through the helicopter's open door, leapt over the passenger bench, and threw himself flat in the back.

Robert Maataq was still irritated that the policeman had opted for such a foolish way of dealing with these people – following a polar bear into its snow-den rather than sitting outside and picking it off when it reappeared. Nevertheless he was about to follow Larsen across the open ground when a hint of movement in the furthest reaches of his eye made him pause. Three thickly clad figures appeared and walked over to the helicopter. They checked the baggage compartments along its sides, then climbed in.

The engine started. Larsen had told him they were not to get away, so Maataq emerged from cover and ran towards the helicopter, rifle poised.

'Stop!' he shouted.

There was a flash of silver and three shots rang out. The hunter fired his rifle once, then fell to the ground as there was an explosion of shattered glass. Three more shots echoed in the cliffs, and the fallen body twitched and lay limp. The helicopter door, its window broken by Maataq's shot, slammed shut and the engine roared afresh.

'Who the bloody hell was that?' blurted out Marian Krinsky.

'I don't know,' said Evat. His tone was tight, staccato.

'You killed him,' accused Gudrun. 'God in hell, you just shot him down.'

'He had a rifle. He shot at us. We couldn't have stayed and talked to him.'

'You murdered him in cold blood. You – '

There was a sharp, savage slap, then a whimper.

'Shouldn't we go back and hide the body?' said Krinsky.

'No,' said Evat shortly.

'But – '

The helicopter gathered itself with a roar of power, rose slowly, jerkily, into the air, hovered a moment over the empty pad, then lunged away down the valley.

'Landing and taking off put pressure on the engine, and that patch on the fuel line could go any moment. I don't trust the weather either. The snow's getting thicker, and the wind's strengthening all the time.'

'Can't we fly above the snow?'

'No. Clouds like those are two or three thousand metres high, and the air currents inside them would drag us around like a mosquito. Also I wouldn't be able to see where to come down at Cap Gad.'

They flew on. Larsen lay where he was, unmoving, unnerved, crushed by what had happened.

'It was you who tried to kill Kalaasi and Larsen, wasn't it?' came Gudrun's voice unexpectedly.

'I don't know what was the matter with me that day,' replied Evat, distractedly. 'I missed one easy shot after another. I even thought I'd got Kalaasi when I only nicked him.'

'Perhaps you didn't really want to kill them,' said Gudrun.

Gradually the helicopter was bucking around more and more, swinging to one side then the other, rising then dropping savagely, shuddering, bumping, while the engine growled and hiccuped in strain.

'It's no good,' said Evat at last. 'We can't go on in this.'

'We must,' replied Krinsky.

'We can't. I can scarcely keep us level, if the wind gets any stronger it could flip us over. The patch is much more likely to go in these conditions, and with snow this heavy, I can scarcely see a thing. I'm going to land, and let the worst blow over.'

'But – '

'I'm not throwing my life away when we're carrying millions of dollars' worth of seeds.'

'The plane'll go without us.'

'No. This storm is certain to ground it at Cap Gad.'

'What about the relief team arriving at the seed bank?' burst out Gudrun. 'They'll see that dead man. Then – '

'Bob won't take the helicopter out in this,' interrupted Evat. 'And the snow may cover the body. We only need to find a good landing spot, and another few minutes will take us to the thick sea-ice by the mouth of the fjord.'

As he finished, the tone of the engine changed, and Larsen felt a lurch that seemed to leave his stomach plastered all over the ceiling, then another. Evat swore.

'What is it?' asked Krinsky and Gudrun together.

'Can't you smell it? Petrol. The patch is going. We must land.'

'But – '

'If fuel starts spraying over the engine, we'll go up like a torch. We've got to get down now.'

Cowering in the hull, Larsen could feel the helicopter being tossed from side to side. The smell of petrol was growing stronger and stronger. Evat's breath whistled in and out of his teeth, and every time the helicopter shuddered or jolted, Gudrun let out a shriek until Evat told her to shut up.

'Look for the ground. Tell me the moment you see something . . . I knew I should have stopped before this, curse it.'

The helicopter dropped lower and lower, then suddenly swirled up into the air.

'That wasn't sea-ice,' said Krinsky in strangled tones.

'No. But the engine could go any second, and to the right of that hillside was a flat area. I'm going to try for there.'

The helicopter started to descend again. Battered by winds and backdraughts, it dropped lower and lower. Just as Larsen was sure they were down there came another sickening lurch upwards, and from where he lay, he caught a fleeting glimpse of a black mountain-side, barely visible through the thick snow that was whipping horizontally across the landscape, whistling in through the broken window.

'What now?' Krinsky's voice was bow-string tight.

'We try again.'

Evat's touch on the controls had to vary between featherlight and a full-scale wrestling match with the wind, but he held the helicopter nearly level and stopped it from dropping too far too fast. Down, down, then suddenly the engine choked and stopped. The helicopter reeled, slid sideways, and fell like a stone. A moment later the engine roared again, but it was too late. There was a scream, a shudder through the whole machine, then a hard snapping thud, followed instantly by a great cracking sound.

'Quick!' yelled Evat. 'Get out and unload the seed boxes.'

'What – ?'

'We're on ice and it's breaking.'

Cold air laced with snow sliced into the heart of the helicopter, where Larsen crouched. A few inches away, through the inner skin of the machine, he felt knocking and thudding as Gudrun, Evat and Krinsky opened the storage compartments and flung out the seed boxes. At the same time there were more cracking sounds, not as loud as before, but a steady volley of them, infinitely threatening.

Abruptly the helicopter plunged downwards again. One of the landing skis must have broken through the ice, for the whole machine was lying askew. A minute later there was another loud crack, another sudden drop, and then more cracking together with an ominous feeling of movement. The ice was giving.

With exaggerated care Larsen got up and peered out of the windscreen, but he could see nothing through the encrusted snow. He hesitated a moment, then pulled up the hood of Maataq's jacket and took a step forward. The helicopter rocked fiercely from side to side. Trying to ignore the renewed creaking and cracking of the ice, he made his way to the open door and looked outside. Water was welling up all around, spreading swiftly over the breaking sheets of ice.

Larsen took a deep breath and jumped. The ice splintered and one of his legs plunged into the black water. Desperately he clutched at the door, and it swung further open, carrying him away from the side of the helicopter, which tipped towards him, dragged by his weight. For a moment he hung there helplessly, his hurt shoulder screaming with pain, then he kicked out and managed to plant his feet on to a plate of more solid ice. He closed his eyes and let go. The ice slipped and for a moment he teetered on the edge of falling, then recovered his balance. As he did the helicopter slumped down a little further, waves scuttered through the rotten ice about it, and Larsen almost toppled into a pool of water that gaped open in front of him.

As quickly as he dared he staggered away from the doomed helicopter. Abruptly he found himself exposed to the full lash of the storm; the wind, driving savagely across the ice, flung refrozen snowflakes into his face, to lash him like a million tiny whips.

Bent almost double he hurried on. From behind him a rending tearing crack cut through the wail of the wind like a knife through thin silk. Larsen stopped in spite of himself. Huge black cracks were opening up around the helicopter, snaking out with the speed and unpredictability of living creatures, flashing this way and that across the pure, snow-swept whiteness of the ice. As the cracks lanced out, the helicopter's front pitched down through the ice. Water flooded into the open doors, and within a minute the whole machine had plunged head-first into the water and vanished. There was a huge upswelling of bubbles, a confusion of sounds, and another outburst of snaking cracks making a lethal patchwork over the surface of the lake.

As Larsen retreated, he heard another sound, smaller, seemingly insignificant compared with the thunder of splitting ice, but just as dangerous. A dry distant cough, then another. Larsen glanced over his shoulder, and saw through the rippling curtain of snow a pile of boxes and three figures. He turned and leapt away across the ice.

Two minutes later the roughness of the snow beneath his feet told him he had reached the shore. The strengthening blizzard had blotted out everything more than a few metres away. Larsen ignored the continual burning of his shoulder. He knew that they dare not let him get away, so they must surely follow the lake edge, expecting to find either him or his tracks. Scarcely had the thought come to him, than he heard something whine, and saw figures emerging from the snow.

Larsen turned and ran as fast as he could go. For a little way he ran well and fast, but his frost-bitten foot began to beat out a rhythm of pain, and the accumulated exhaustion he carried slowed him down. There was no sign of pursuit, but he did not doubt there soon would be and he looked around desperately for a hiding-place. Ahead a sculpted snowdrift, like a tiny arete, linked two rocks at the foot of a tor. He gathered himself and with a great effort sprang clean over the drift, landing in deep snow on the far side. Far deeper than he had expected, for he vanished into it completely. Snow filled his face and he thrashed around like a man caught in liquid mud, until he realised his feet were on rock, and the hole he had made as he fell was only a few centimetres above the top of his head. Recovering himself, he patted out a space around his face, like a deep-sea diver's air helmet, then stood still where he was. Out of the wind, the snow buoyed him up, lying comfortably all around him, and Maataq's jacket and trousers kept him warm.

Fragmented voices came to him, gradually assembling into sentences as they grew closer.

'The snow is covering his tracks. I can't see them any more. Perhaps he used that patch of bare rock to give us the slip.'

'Wait. What about Gudrun? Her nerve's gone.'

'That's why I left her to watch the seed boxes. She won't go anywhere. We'll deal with him, then go back for her.'

'Did you see who it was?'

'No. But whoever it was, we've got to find them. The problem is that if we leave the lake shore in snow like this, we're certain to get lost. Listen, you stay here while I cast around for tracks. I won't go far. If I'm not back in ten minutes, start shouting.'

Larsen pulled out Jonis's knife and began to dig into the snow. The drift was old and firm, and he was able to hack out a narrow tunnel just over a metre long, slanting down towards the ground. At the end was a faint glow that spoke of light. Realising he was close to penetrating the drift, Larsen lay down and listened, but heard only the wind.

With ever greater caution he pulled away a small plug of snow, and found himself looking at the lake. The blizzard had lessened a little, and he could see cracks in the ice and the open water where the helicopter had sunk. He widened his hole, then froze. Less than a metre from him was a leg. Sudden rage struck through Larsen. That leg represented the chance of revenge for Robert Maataq, perhaps even revenge for himself. He poised himself and listened again. Still nothing but the wind. Snow came down more heavily, and the lake disappeared behind a fresh curtain.

Amid an explosion of ice, Larsen launched himself from the drift, thrusting out his knife as he did so and slashing into the leg. There was a scream and a pale, snow-suited figure crumpled. Larsen stumbled headlong, lost his balance, tripped over a rock and fell to the ground. As he jack-knifed up on to his knees and twisted round, the blizzard blew straight in his face, slashing at his eyes. He found himself facing a sprawled featureless shape wearing snow goggles, but in the shape's gloved hand was a gun. For a moment he was helpless. Then came a shocked gasp.

'You. But – '

Larsen threw himself to one side, ignoring the screech of agony from his wounded shoulder, then lunged forward. Jonis's hungry knife caught his enemy neatly in the chest, and the figure collapsed back. Larsen bent down to scrabble where the gun had fallen, when a second figure loomed out of the snow, levelling a gun. Instinctively, even before red flame ripped open the white of the blizzard, he flung himself aside and hurled himself back into the tunnel. He shot through it in two wriggles, then scrambled half over, half through, the snowdrift to a ragged ridge of rocks on the far side. To the right was a narrow cleft and he darted into it, emerging in a small walled-in basin. For a moment of horror he thought he was trapped, but then he saw one of the rock walls was climbable and began to claw his way up it. With a desperate spurt he emerged at the top, and almost lost his hold as the storm struck him with renewed force. Recovering, Larsen flipped himself over the ridge, and slid down the other side. To his left more heights rose up, but on the right the ground fell away, a barren open tableland, scattered with erratic boulders left by the glacier that had once filled the valley. Larsen glanced around.

It was not only the pursuer he must fear, for Larsen had no idea where he was. If he fled blindly, he could easily find himself penetrating deeper and deeper into the mountain ranges that rimmed the inland ice, a wilderness of glaciers, high peaks, ravines, and treacherous weather where a storm might linger around a single mountain for days, and he would not be found for months. If at all.

Larsen began to creep up the heights. As he stopped and looked down, he saw a vague figure flitting among the boulders on the barrens. He was briefly tempted to retrace his steps and try to shadow his enemy, but he knew his limitations. Robert Maataq might have been able to do it, not Tomas Larsen.

Ducking out of sight, he worked his way around the shore of the lake until the heights of his cover faded away, running up the side of the valley. As he hesitated, a rattle of stones behind made him start. Instantly he slid down from the rock where he sat and found shelter along a ledge which curved to the right above the lake, shielding him from anyone at his back. Here he waited, straining to hear further sounds of movement. Wind still filled his ears, but the snow appeared to be lessening. Eventually he pushed his head above the rampart and peered out. Nothing. A little further. Still nothing. His eyes flickered back and forth, then, making up his mind, he swung himself down from the ledge and set off along the open lake shore, his head down against the snow that was once again blowing almost full in his face.

After five or ten minutes, he saw the pile of seed boxes straight ahead. He had walked right round the lake. At almost the same moment he glimpsed two figures crouched on the bluff above the seed boxes. An ambush, waiting for him. Instantly he dropped to the ground and lay there, unmoving. Completely out-thought, Larsen had fallen into the trap and walked into the very gun-mouth. If he had not seen his enemy first, he would have had no chance at all.

It was only Maataq's sealskin suit that stood between him and death. The pale, spotted camouflage that had protected generations of fjord seals from predators, human and animal, now served to protect one human from another. Larsen lay motionless on the snow, face down, and waited for a flurry of snow to give him a chance to get away. It seemed an eternity, knowing that at any moment his enemies might see him and pick him off where he lay. But the dead seal which covered him won this last battle, and at last the snow thickened enough for Larsen to flee back to the shelter of the rocks.

Unable to advance, unwilling to head off into the wilderness, Larsen retired to a rocky eyrie above the valley floor, from where he could see anyone approaching, while watching largely unseen and with several possible escape routes. A slight overhang gave him some protection against the lashing snow which was closing in again, shrinking his world to a tiny hemisphere. His foot and shoulder beating with pain, his mind heavy with fatigue and guilt, knife in mittened hand, eyes raking the snowstorm, Tomas Larsen prepared to wait his enemy out.

20

BACK IN TOWN

The snowstorm struck Mitti and Kamik just as they reached the side of the fjord, but they knew their way back and hurried along as fast as they could. Mitti's cold, wet clothes lay heavy about her, a freezing mantle. Kamik's face was drawn and shadowed from weariness. When they reached Sermilik, Mitti took Kamik straight back to his grandmother's, in spite of his vehement protests. The old woman was asleep, but when she emerged, rubbing her bloodshot eyes, she shrieked her joy, hugged Mitti, hugged Kamik, then dragged the boy inside, raining furious recriminations down on him.

Mitti's father-in-law was already awake, if he had ever been asleep, sitting downstairs in his usual chair. He smiled as she came in, recognising her footstep.

'You have been a long time, Mitti. Did you find what you were looking for?'

She went up to him, kissed him on the forehead, then hugged him tight.

'I have found out what happened to Jonis,' she said at last. 'It was an accident. Caused by the Danish woman, Gudrun Eistrup.'

'An accident,' he said, and sighed. 'But the worst accident was that he thought he could get something for nothing. However much I told him, he always believed somewhere there was a treasure he could just pick up and walk away with, and never worry again. That is what led to his death.'

'I think I thought the same,' said Mitti.

'But not now?'

'No.' She paused. 'I have been with my father.'

'The policeman?'

'You knew? I did not realise . . .'

'Did you go looking for him?'

'I don't know. Perhaps.'

'It would be best to forgive him,' said the old man.

'Why?' she demanded, with sudden ferocity.

'You do not need me to tell you.'

She closed her eyes.

'Because you think hatred costs more than forgiveness?'

'Not in a short time. But over the years, yes.'

'I am not thinking over the years.'

She ran every scrap of hot water into the battered old bath, then went to sleep in it. Woken by the water cooling round her, she got out, put on her warmest clothes, drank three blisteringly hot cups of black coffee, made her father-in-law his unvarying breakfast of thin fish soup, then dragged herself out into the driving snow to see the commune Secretary.

It was still only seven in the morning, but Mitti hammered on the door until Bronlund's nervy round-faced wife opened it.

'I must speak to the Secretary,' insisted Mitti.

'He is asleep – '

'Well, he shouldn't be. This is important, the most important thing he will do in the next ten years, I should think.' Mitti pushed her way into the warm little hall, thawing snow dripping from her coat. 'Mr Secretary,' she called.

'Ssh. Ssh. I will get him.' The woman hurried submissively upstairs.

It was at least ten minutes before she came back down again. Ten minutes during which Mitti had to curb a rising desire to go up and pull the man out of his bed.

'He will not be a moment,' said the woman, a cowed smile on her unusually freckled face.

Ten more minutes passed before the Secretary came down, his face set in lines of benevolent complacency. He ushered Mitti into the sitting-room as his wife scuttled away, to return shortly with coffee. There was a bowl of sugar on the tray.

Almost before the Secretary sat down, the story burst from Mitti. It was like a dam breaking, it swept out of her unordered, raw, violent, pinning Bronlund to his chair. He sat, not missing a word, sipping his coffee, yet the half-smile never left his puffy face, and he gave not the slightest sign of surprise.

When she finished, he took it on from her with a sharpness that showed how rapidly he had sifted out the facts that mattered from the chaos of her recitation.

'So Robert Maataq and Sergeant Larsen have gone to the seed bank to stop these people seizing the seeds and getting away?'

'Yes.'

'I will arrange for the airstrip at Cap Gad to be informed immediately, though . . .' He looked at the hard lashing snow outside his window. 'No planes or helicopters will be moving just now. The moment the storm lessens, I will also send men to the seed bank.' He paused. 'Can you think of anything else that should be done, Mrs Hendrik?'

Mitti detected a trace of irony in his words.

'They are armed, and dangerous,' she said.

'Armed and dangerous,' mused the Secretary, the half-smile still firmly in place. 'Like an American film. But all men here have hunting rifles, as you know.' He sighed. 'I had hoped that the arrival of a big American company would help revive this area, but it seems not. Anyway, Mrs Hendrik, I think you need to sleep. You do not look well.'

'You will radio Cap Gad – '

'And Keflavik and Søndre Strømfjord as well. Nothing else can be done until the snow lets up. Go home. I will let you know if there is any news.'

It was good advice and Mitti knew it. Parallel with the uncertainty, fear and suspicion that dominated her mind, her body ached from head to foot, and she could barely stifle her yawns. She left Bronlund's house and battled back through the blizzard. Her father-in-law was listening to the radio, where a man from Pond Inlet on Baffin Island was being interviewed.

'Don't you feel that banning beer, and closing down one of the local television channels, is a rather backward step, councillor?'

'On the contrary. To protect our Inuit culture, it is necessary to . . .'

Mitti went into the kitchen, made her father-in-law a cup of coffee, then turned off the radio and sat down opposite him.

'Do you want to hear what has happened to me?' she asked.

'When you want to tell me,' he replied.

She went upstairs, lay on her bed and fell asleep, still in her clothes. She did not stir all day, except when she woke briefly in the late afternoon, pulled the bedcover over herself, and slept again, the dreamless, colourless, fathoms-deep sleep of utter exhaustion.

She was roused by a hand over her mouth and a hissed whisper.

'Get up.'

Her heart sprang into her throat. The cold barrel of a gun was pushed under her ear. Slowly the hand was withdrawn. A grey uncertain light came through the curtains and Mitti guessed it was early morning.

'Where is Larsen?' she asked.

'Dead.' The word struck her like a fist, and her courage crumbled.

'How the two of you got out of the seed store I do not understand. Not that it matters. He is dead, and so will you be, unless you do what I tell you. Exactly what I tell you, without making me even slightly nervous.'

The words were insane, coming from a man whose every word and breath exposed the fear that dominated him. She said nothing. Evat slowly moved round to watch her face.

'I want the tickets,' he said.

'What tickets?'

'Don't pretend to be a fool. The ones to Alaska. I want them back.'

'They are out of date. Useless.'

'Oh no. Greenlandair has extended all tickets because of the strike, so they are perfectly valid. Get them.'

'I cannot.'

The gun was back under her ear.

'Cannot?'

'Larsen took them.'

'If you're lying to me – '

'I'm not.'

Evat thought for a moment.

'He must have left them at the police house. Come and help me find them.'

Mitti could hear her father-in-law snoring faintly in the other room, but she dared not wake him, in case the gun should be turned on him also. They crept downstairs and outside.

A few stray flakes of snow were still falling from the slowly lifting skies, and Sermilik was blanketed in white, which made the town seem cleaner, more pleasant, more natural. There was no one out, except for a couple of figures down by the harbour, preparing to take their boats out. Even the huskies all seemed to be asleep.

Mitti walked steadily with Evat at her back. She knew that once he'd got what he wanted, the only way he could guarantee his own safety was to kill her.

'Kalaasi may be at the police station,' she said, clutching at straws.

'Kalaasi!' Evat laughed. 'Dr Sven sent him back home to Ikateq. And he'll be as much use there as he would have been here.'

Half-way down the road Gudrun appeared from behind a house, limping slightly.

'What's happened?' she demanded. 'What are you doing? Where – ?'

'Larsen took the tickets,' interrupted Evat. 'She's going to help us find them.'

The police station was unlocked, and the three of them slipped inside. Evat leant back against the wall, gun in hand. Gudrun hovered uncertainly beside him.

'Start looking,' said Evat.

'Where?' asked Mitti.

'Anywhere. Everywhere. Look.'

Mitti began opening drawers and pulling out their contents at random, gradually spreading a wave of paperwork over the floor.

'You know he's going to sell those seeds,' she remarked suddenly.

'What?' said Gudrun.

'Frederiksen asked $30 million for them,' continued Mitti. 'It was to get that money that Evat killed Frederiksen . . .'

Evat's hand was tightening on the trigger, then he caught Gudrun's gaze on him.

'She's lying,' he said dismissively. 'Trying to confuse you.'

'You see, Frederiksen could have ruined the deal.' Despite the fear that stalked her, Mitti went on. To separate the two of them was her only chance. 'If he had informed the police about the stolen seeds, no big company would risk buying them. So Evat made me tie him up, then strangled him. He didn't tell you that, did he?'

'I don't believe you,' said Gudrun.

'Of course not,' said Evat. 'Everyone knows Mitti Hendrik tells lies. No doubt it was her who murdered Frederiksen, for his money.'

'Evat's going to sell the seeds to that American woman,' said Mitti, pulling down files from one of the shelves.

A thick silence sank over the room. Gudrun went over to one of the files and began to flick through it.

'You don't know anything,' she said at last. 'Marian Krinsky was a committed environmentalist. She helped us for nothing.'

'That's what Evat told you,' said Mitti.

'Shut up and look for the tickets,' flashed Evat, menacingly.

But Gudrun found her mind was leaping along pathways she had previously ignored. It was Evat who had made contact with the 'green terrorist', as he laughingly called her. He said she was part of an extreme US conservation group, and that she worked at a Midwestern university and had access to a seed storage system. He had also suggested that the woman masquerade as a would-be purchaser, to make sure that Frederiksen did not sell the seeds elsewhere before he and Gudrun could remove them.

When Krinsky arrived, Gudrun had found the very perfection of her performance unsettling. Several years ago she had met a real terrorist, a woman linked to the Red Army Faction during the 1970s. She had had unevenly cut hair, and a habit of biting off her sentences before she quite finished them. She waved her hands around, smoked heavily, made sweeping generalisations, never smiled, and seemed neither clever nor dangerous. But whenever a door opened, she started and looked jaggedly round. When Krinsky was in a room and a door opened, she ignored it.

Ever since the death of Jonis, Gudrun had sensed matters gradually spinning out of control, sliding into a new savage guise. Now Mitti's words made many things come together in her mind. She looked across at Evat, and found she did not recognise him. Over the past two years the two of them had argued and bickered and shared many long talks late into the night when their feelings started at opposite ends of the spectrum and struggled, kicking, scratching, closer to each other. Like the quarrels and fights of brother and sister. Such things could not be faked, yet now he seemed infected with something stronger, more assertive, coarser. A new aggressive arrogance that she had never seen before, and which did not stem only from the gun in his hand.

'Is she right?' said Gudrun suddenly.

'Of course not.'

'I don't believe you. I think Krinsky was just who she pretended to be, an agro-chemical boss.'

'Don't be a fool,' retorted Evat. 'Mitti's only spouting this nonsense to try to save her own skin.'

'I don't think so.'

Evat looked at her, and recognised that he had lost her. His face changed.

'All right then. It's true.' He spat out his words as if they were bullets. 'So what? Krinsky's company would create resistant crop strains that can save millions of lives in the Third World. You may care for nature rather than people dying of starvation, but we Inuit are yellow-skinned, colonially ruled, our sympathies are for our brothers in Asia and Africa and South America, not for you and your national parks and animal protection. Trash your own environments, then force others to look after theirs, that is your idea of ecology.'

'You believe Krinsky's company cares for the Third World?' demanded Gudrun.

'Of course not. But they will go where the money is, and that is in supplying improved seeds.'

'You mean the money for you lies in selling your principles,' snapped Gudrun viciously.

'What do you know of principles? They are toys to you rich people, things you pick up and drop at the passing of a fashion. But to us, who know what suffering is, they are matters of life and death.'

'How have you suffered? You know no more about starvation, disease and war than I do.'

'Yes. I am just like you! Look at my wretched home, then tell me about your flat in Roskilde, about the well-paid job you will get with your doctorate.'

'I am not saying we are not richer than you –' began Gudrun, thrown on the defensive.

'Yes. You are richer than I. Much, much richer. There is barely an Inuit in the world who has all the possessions considered "necessities of life" by any middle-class European. But you *ukissut* can never see through the veil that hides our thoughts. We are a people beyond your comprehension, and deep down every one of us carries a secret untouchable pride. Pride that our forefathers drove out your barbarian Viking ancestors, and killed those who stayed. And the time is coming when we will do the same to you.'

'You are talking shit!'

'It is not shit. It is –'

'It is worse than shit. Every living Inuit has abandoned the ways of their forefathers. Even those who still live by hunting depend on telescopic-sighted rifles, skidoos, radios, motor boats. Western technology. Put you in a kayak and you would overturn it inside five minutes. Send you out with two bone harpoons against an old male sperm whale or an angry walrus and you wouldn't last half that long. You've never even shot a seal, and when you ate raw blubber you were nearly sick on the spot –'

'Because your people have destroyed our culture is no reason to think there is no other way to live. No. Say nothing else.' The gun was suddenly swinging ambiguously between Mitti and Gudrun. 'This argument can wait. First I must have the tickets.'

'You cannot get away,' said Mitti. 'The Secretary has warned Cap Gad about you.'

'Bronlund has not been Secretary of Sermilik Commune for ten years by doing anything,' sneered Evat. 'And we will have those tickets.'

'You only need one,' said Gudrun firmly. 'I am not coming with you.'

Evat levelled his gun at her.

'What do I care?' he rasped. 'I'll kill you too, if I have to. Now get upstairs and look for those tickets.'

Gudrun did not move. Suddenly he lashed out with the gun and caught her full across the face. She reeled back and almost fell. Blood started from her nose, and ran down her chin.

'Get upstairs,' he repeated, threatening her again.

Cowed, she obeyed. Evat turned venomously on Mitti.

'And you, go through those drawers.'

Shuffling through piles of paper, eyes down, Mitti could feel the gun and the dark staring eyes at her back, like a solid pressure on her shrinking shoulders. Gudrun could not save her now. Her only hope lay in throwing herself aside and praying Evat missed when he shot.

But what then? Even if she could jump him before he fired again, he was stronger than her. And, not for the first time, she cursed the physical differences between the sexes.

'What's in that bag?' growled Evat. He was in total command now.

Mitti pushed it towards him, and he pulled out Frederiksen's coat.

'Very nice. I'll have that.' Evat began to put it on. 'Hurry up, we don't have long.'

'I'm trying.'

'Try harder.'

Mitti felt a passport under hand. It was hers. Underneath was another, her father-in-law's. And the deadly tickets.

'What have you got there?' demanded Evat.

As she reluctantly began to bring them out, there was a knock on the door.

'Do not answer,' hissed Evat.

There was no sound from upstairs.

Obediently Mitti stayed where she was, but hope, unlooked for, had blossomed within her, and her mind was a ferment. This must be the moment to try to escape, while someone else stood just a few metres away. While Evat's attention was elsewhere. But her back was to him, so she did not know whether he was looking at her, or even exactly where he was standing.

There was another sharp rap on the door.

'They must have heard us,' whispered Mitti.

'If they knock again, go and answer,' said Evat. 'I will be behind the door. If you say anything I do not like, I will kill you and your visitor.' His voice was quivering. Mitti guessed that his finger was already very tight upon the trigger.

A third knock.

Taking Mitti's shoulder, Evat pushed her towards the door. He was so close that any idea of hurrying ahead and hurling herself out of the door was impossible. But this interruption must offer hope.

As she came to the door, Evat, with Frederiksen's coat still draped over one shoulder, stepped swiftly round her. He poised himself in the hall where he would be shielded by the opening door, but could still see Mitti. The gun in his free hand, small, black, unanswerable, was pointed at her stomach.

There was a fourth knock, and Evat gestured with his gun. She opened the door, then stared blankly at the empty landscape, across which the chill wind blew a dusting of new-fallen snow. She closed the door again.

'There's no one there.'

'You are making a fool of me.'

'No.'

At that moment there was another knock on the door, a loud authoritative rap that echoed through the whole house. Evat fell back again.

'It must be kids playing a game. Send them away.' His long, wide-pupilled eyes were riveted to her face.

Again Mitti opened the door.

As she did so, Gudrun gave a piercing scream from the top of the stairs.

'Now! Now!'

Evat looked up, and in one lightning movement Mitti swung the door violently in at him, and dived headlong outside. The gun fired and there was the splintering crack of a bullet ripping into wood. Mitti scrambled to her feet.

As she did, Evat burst out of the house, half tripped on a trailing arm of the coat, then recovered his balance. He raised his gun to kill. Then something smashed into his head. There was the crack of another shot, and the bullet whined harmlessly into the air as Evat staggered. There was a thud as he was hit again, and the gun spun from his hand.

Mitti darted after it and snatched it up. When she whipped round, she found Evat on his knees, groaning and clutching his head, while over him stood Kamik, wielding a sledge runner.

He gave her a grin of sheer triumph.

'Shall I hit him again?'

'I don't think it's necessary,' said Mitti breathlessly.

Gudrun came tumbling downstairs, and took in the scene.

'Thank God!' she muttered.

Kamik brandished his sledge runner at her, eyes gleaming.

The gun clenched in her fist, Mitti seized Evat's pony tail and dragged his head back so she could look him in the eyes.

'Get up,' she said. 'Get up and walk in front of us. If you try anything, I'll be only too happy to kill you where you stand.'

The shots had brought a growing stream of astonished people out of the neighbouring houses. Kamik waved jauntily at the watchers as Evat began to trudge unsteadily towards the Secretary's house.

21

CLEARING UP

'What is this?' demanded Secretary Bronlund, clutching a bright green dressing-gown around him, as Mitti, closely followed by Gudrun and Kamik, drove the groggy Evat into his kitchen. Outside the Secretary's front door, a large crowd gathered, and the steady buzz of intent conversation grew gradually louder.

'Evat Jonsson has just tried to murder me,' began Mitti. 'He, Gudrun Eistrup and Marian Krinsky – '

'Krinsky is dead,' broke in Gudrun. 'Sergeant Larsen too.'

Mitti swung round on her.

'What happened to Larsen?' she demanded hoarsely.

'He tried to creep up on us, but the lake ice broke and he fell in. He drowned.'

'You're sure?'

Gudrun nodded. Blood was still running down her face and dripping on to her white jumper. Her pale eyes, one of them bruised and swelling, were wet with tears. She rubbed them, then stretched out her hands to Mitti, in appeal.

'I'm sorry. It is all my fault. But I never meant such things to happen. I was trying to help.'

Mitti could find nothing to say to her.

'I'm sorry,' repeated Gudrun, and hid her face and wept.

And Mitti, to her own astonishment, looked at the bowed Danish woman with pity.

When Evat and Gudrun were under lock and key in the police station, and some of Bronlund's assistants had shooed away most of the curious crowd, the Secretary turned to Mitti.

'What is this boy doing with you?'

'Yes,' said Mitti. 'What were you doing sneaking around outside the police station at six in the morning, Kamik?'

'I had been watching,' explained Kamik. 'When I saw Evat and Gudrun and you walking down the hill, I followed, then crept up and listened through the door while I tried to think what to do. It was the right thing, wasn't it?'

'It was,' said Mitti. 'You probably saved my life.'

'I know.'

Ignoring the sadness within her, Mitti ruffled his hair then bent down to give him a kiss, which Kamik deftly dodged.

The men Secretary Bronlund sent out to look for Larsen came back mid-afternoon. Mitti saw them coming down the hill and ran to meet them. Fear was a hollow in her stomach.

'Couldn't you find him?'

Larsen was hobbling along at the back, being supported by two men. Mitti let out a squeal of delight and relief, sprang forward, and knocked all three of them clean over. The rest of the team burst into loud guffaws, doubling up, slapping their thighs and rocking with laughter.

Larsen picked himself up ruefully.

'I thought you were dead,' said Mitti. 'They said you'd been drowned.'

'It was what I wanted them to think.'

'What happened? What happened?' she demanded impatiently, walking beside him and putting her arm round his waist.

'I was hiding in the snow when I thought of the wet clothes I was still carrying. I tied them up with a large stone, and threw them into the lake. There was a crash as the stone went through the ice, then my jacket, which I had left free, floated up to the surface. Evat and Gudrun were sure I'd fallen through the ice and set off back to town. That was where my plan fell apart. I'd intended to follow them and get help to make an arrest, but my foot was so bad I couldn't keep up.'

'He'll be lucky if Dr Sven leaves him two toes.' One of the rescue party grinned. And several of them laughed again.

'Was Robert Maataq dead?' asked Larsen quietly.

She nodded.

'The relief shift called from the seed bank this morning. I am sorry.'

The others had fallen silent.

'He was a great hunter,' said one of the Greenlanders at last. 'We will look after his wife and children.'

'If I hadn't asked him to come with me – ' began Larsen.

'No,' interrupted Mitti, almost fiercely. 'He was killed by whoever pulled the trigger. You must not blame yourself.' She stopped, looked him in the face, and put her hands on his shoulders, but he winced and turned away.

'Maataq died for me. I will not forget that.'

'I did not say forget it. I said do not blame yourself.'

He gave a small, unconvincing smile, and limped on towards the surgery. She watched him go sadly, then returned home. Her father-in-law was in his chair, and she went over and put her hand on his cheek. The old man smiled, and patted her hand gently.

'Why did you not stay with your father?' he asked.

'You are my father, and all my family,' she replied.
'I am old.'
'You will live for ever,' she said, with utter certainty.

Two and a half days later, as he waited for the helicopter which would take him to Cap Gad for his delayed flight back to Godthab, Larsen saw Mitti coming down the road towards him. He dropped his bags and went over to her.

'I hoped you would come.'

'I thought I should say goodbye.'

'Thank you.'

She gave a characteristic, self-effacing shrug.

'I suppose that's all, really.' His heart fell, but Mitti had not finished. 'You know that Gudrun helped me, at the end. Evat even shot at her, tried to kill her.'

'You've already told me that,' said Larsen gently.

'I know. But I don't think she should be blamed. It was Frederiksen who stole the seeds in the first place, and Jonis's death was an accident. She was just naïve. That's all. Her motives were good ones.'

'Yes.'

'What do you think will happen to her?'

'She's agreed to give evidence. I'm sure things will be taken into account, and she does not need to worry too much.'

'Mm.' Mitti looked up at him. 'What happened to the seeds?'

'Evat and Gudrun had a few in their packs, the rest they hid in a cairn. I suppose they planned to come back and get them. They've all been returned to the seed bank, and now their value is known, the Greenland government has changed its mind over privatisation, and intends to install special locks and security procedures.'

'Was Jonis's money ever found?'

He shook his head.

'Probably Frederiksen never gave it to him. But . . .'

'Yes. I know. Even if it had been found, you wouldn't have let me keep it because it was the profits of blackmail. Yet it might have bought the old man his sight back.'

'If he knew where it came from, would he accept it?'

'Maybe not.'

'I'm sorry,' said Larsen.

'What about Jonis's knife?'

'It is an evil weapon. It must be kept for the court case, but after that I hope it will be thrown away. Destroyed.'

'It is not weapons that are evil. Only people.'

Larsen shook his head.

'Many things are evil, and may make people so.' Momentarily he glanced up at the sprawling extent of Sermilik on the hills above them.

The sound of the helicopter was approaching fast.

Suddenly Larsen bent down, burrowed into his bag, then pulled out something and pushed it into her hands.

'Here.'

She looked in wonder at Frederiksen's Claude Montana coat.

'Why are you giving me this?'

'It's not needed as evidence. You told me Frederiksen gave it to you, and I cannot prove he didn't.'

'It's worth a lot of money.'

'Yes. Perhaps enough to pay for a trip to Denmark for a cataract operation.'

'Thank you.' She looked at him, then frowned. 'Evat was such a clever, serious man. What happened to him?'

'You know him better than I do. But I'd guess he had become obsessed with money. Money to get away from Sermilik.'

'As you are doing.'

He nodded.

As the helicopter landed, bouncing on its skis, the wind of its arrival swept over them, blowing Mitti's hair up into a wild black wave. Larsen picked up his bags.

Suddenly Kalaasi came running down towards them.

'Sergeant Larsen,' he shouted. 'Chief Thorold has just telephoned.'

'What did he want?' asked Larsen wearily.

'I'm not sure. He said something about not forgetting a report that you are supposed to be writing. And have you finished it yet?'

'I haven't even started it.'

'But – '

'I must go,' interrupted Larsen.

'Goodbye,' said Mitti.

'We'll see each other at the trial.'

'I suppose so.'

'Aren't you pleased?' he asked.

'I don't think I'll like the trial,' she said softly. 'Oh I've just remembered a message for you. Kamik says he hasn't forgotten about the big reward you promised.'

'What should I get him?' said Larsen helplessly.

'Don't worry. I'm sure he knows. I'll see that he writes to you. Goodbye.'

The helicopter door was open. The other passengers had already climbed in, and Larsen followed them, putting his bags into the back.

'Hurry up,' said the pilot. 'Sit down and strap In. We're running late.'

'Whose fault is that?' demanded the policeman sharply.

The helicopter radio was on. It was a World Cup football qualifier in Copenhagen, with Solomon Rosing commentating:

'And Schmeichel comes to claim that high ball with an easy confidence. Yet again he's reinforcing his claim to be the world's best goalkeeper. The score remains at nil–nil, with just twenty-seven minutes left . . .'

'Goodbye,' called Mitti again, and turned to go.

'Wait,' said Larsen to the pilot, who was gunning the engine. He jumped down, ran over to Mitti, and took her in his arms.

'I'll see you again,' he said. 'Soon.'

He kissed her on the cheek, hugged her again, then ran back to the helicopter. As they took off, he watched Mitti walking back up the hill. She looked fragile and alone. Then a small figure dashed down to join her. Mitti turned and pointed up at the helicopter. Larsen smiled and waved out of the window as Kamik jumped up and down, throwing his arms around. Mitti stood behind him, still, patient, waiting.

Six weeks later a letter arrived for Mitti. As she opened it, her hands shook a little, but she did not know why. It was written in a thin, spidery hand. Not at all what she had expected.

Dear Mitti,

You will not need to come for the trial. Gudrun's testimony meant Evat had to plead guilty to the murder of Robert Maataq. Jonis was ruled to have died in a hunting accident, and Dr Sven agreed to testify that Frederiksen had a heart attack. Gudrun has been put in my charge, to stay with me until things are finally sorted out. She sends her best wishes. As for Marian Krinsky, the government didn't want to upset the US, so her relatives were told that she died in a helicopter crash. Apparently the American television and newspapers gave the accident a lot of coverage, and said she had done a great deal to further the cause of women in business. I have ordered the book about helicopters Kamik wanted, and will talk to Greenlandair about arranging a flight for him. My shoulder is recovered, but unfortunately the surgeon had to amputate one of my toes because of frost-bite, so now I can only count to nineteen. Still the government has not decided what to do about Sermilik.

I am writing this while I drink a coffee at the Kristinemut restaurant, on my way in to work. It is a beautiful day, and Godthab (I should say Nûk) is looking its best. I enclose two air tickets for you and your father-in-law to come and see me here. I have been promoted, which means I can afford a bigger flat. I know that you cannot have what you haven't paid for, and I have never given you a father's love, but please come. Perhaps it is not too late. Best wishes. Tomas Larsen.

Mitti read the letter three times, then found herself crying.

Half an hour later she was on the telephone.

'Hello, who is it?' came Larsen's cautious voice.

'It's Mitti, father. We'll be with you in a week.'

At the other end of the telephone, across seven hundred kilometres of ice-cap, she heard him laugh.